Praise for *Queenie*

'Sexy, kick-ass and of the moment, it's a wry look at dating and independence for black women' — *Observer*

'Funny and perceptive' — Malorie Blackman

'Sharp, relatable, and incredibly evocative' — Jenny Colgan

'*Queenie* has all the things you want in a debut novel - a startlingly fresh voice, characters you fall in love with from the very first page, and a joyous turn of phrase that makes this book almost impossible to put down. In turns hilariously funny and quietly devastating, *Queenie* is an important, timely story' — Louise O'Neill

'Candice Carty-Williams is a fantastic new writer who has written a deliciously funny, characterful, topical and thrilling novel for our times' — Bernardine Evaristo

'Brilliant, timely, funny, heartbreaking' — Jojo Moyes

'Funny, wise and of the moment, this book and this writer are the ones to watch' — Kit de Waal

'*Queenie* is the sort of novel you just can't stop talking about and want everyone you know to read. Snort your tea out funny one moment and utterly heart-breaking the next . . . I absolutely loved it' — AJ Pearce

'Hilarious and off the wall and tender' — Nikesh Shukla

Candice Carty-Williams is a marketer, author and journalist based in London. Born in 1989, the result of an affair between a Jamaican cab driver and a Jamaican-Indian dyslexic receptionist, Candice worked in the media before moving into publishing aged 23. In 2016, Candice created and launched the *Guardian* and 4th Estate BAME Short Story Prize, is a Penguin Books WriteNow mentor, and she also contributes regularly to *Refinery29*, *BEAT Magazine*, *Guardian* and *i-D*. *Queenie* is her first novel. She can be found on Twitter at @CandiceC_W.

QUEENIE

Candice Carty-Williams

TRAPEZE

First published in Great Britain in 2019 by Trapeze,
an imprint of The Orion Publishing Group Ltd
Carmelite House, 50 Victoria Embankment,
London EC4Y 0DZ

An Hachette UK company

7 9 10 8

A CIP catalogue record for this book is
available from the British Library.

ISBN (Hardback) 978 1 4091 8005 0
ISBN (Export Trade Paperback) 978 1 4091 8006 7

Typeset by Born Group

Printed and bound in Great Britain by Clays Ltd, Elcograf S.p.A.

MIX
Paper from
responsible sources
FSC® C104740

www.orionbooks.co.uk

To all the Queenies out there – you are enough. Trust me.

In loving memory of Dan O'Lone and Anton Garneys

Chapter One

I locked my phone and carried on looking at the ceiling before unlocking it and sending a follow-up 'xx'. That would prove to Tom that I wasn't as emotionally detached as he accuses me of being.

'Can you just bring your bottom riiight to the edge of the exam table?' the doctor asked as I inched myself down closer to her face. Honestly, I've no idea how they do it.

'Deep breath, please!'

She said this a bit too cheerfully, and with no further warning inserted what felt like the world's least ergonomic dildo into me and moved it around like a joystick. She placed a cold hand onto my stomach, pressing down every few seconds and pursing her lips every time I squealed. To divert my attention away from this manipulation of my insides, I checked my phone. No reply.

'So what do you do . . . Queenie?' the doctor asked, glancing at my chart.

Wasn't it enough that she could see literally inside me? Did she *need* to know about my day job?

'I work at a newspaper,' I said, lifting my head up to make eye contact, as it seemed like the polite thing to do.

'That's a fancy career!' She pressed on, plunging her way back in. 'What do you do at the newspaper?'

'I work at *The Daily Read*. The – ouch – culture section. Listings and reviews and – '

' – in the technology department? That makes sense,' she said.

I hoisted myself up on my elbows to correct her but stopped when I saw how concerned she looked. I glanced at the nurse behind her who looked *just* as concerned, and then back at the doctor. She still looked concerned. I couldn't see my own face but guessed that my expression mirrored both of theirs.

'Hold on a tick, we're just going to – Ash, could you get Dr Smith in here?' The nurse bustled out.

Many uncomfortable minutes passed until the nurse came back in with another doctor, a man who looked as standard as his surname would suggest.

'Let's get a closer look . . .' Dr Smith said, bending down and peering between my legs.

'What's wrong? Can you not find it?' I asked, worried that the coil had maybe been absorbed into my womb, the way I still worried that every tampon I'd ever inserted was still knocking about inside me.

'What do you think, Ray?' the first doctor asked her colleague.

'We might need to get Dr Ellison in here, you know,' Dr Smith replied, standing back up and putting his hands on his hips.

'I saw a cleaner mopping up some sick in the hallway, why don't you get him in here to have a look as well?' I asked all three hospital staff as they stared at the ultrasound image.

'Aha! Look, the coil is there!' the original doctor said, pointing at a speck on my onscreen uterus with the excitement of someone who'd just discovered a new planet. Relieved, I lay back on the examination table. 'But could you pop your clothes back on and have a seat in the waiting room? We just need to have a quick word, and then we'll call you back in.'

'Never, ever trust a Gemini man.'

I plonked myself down on a chair next to Aunt Maggie.

'Here,' she said, holding out a bottle of antibacterial hand gel. She squeezed some into my palm and as soon as I had rubbed it in, she grabbed my hand to consolidate her point. I thought that Maggie coming with me would be a calming and firm adult presence, but instead she was just transferring her germ OCD onto me.

I tried to focus on the peeling Gynaecology Unit sign on the wall to stop myself from pulling my hand out of her grip.

'You know I don't believe in astrology, Maggie.'

She squeezed my hand tighter, I suppose by way of punishment. I slithered my hand out of hers and crossed my arms, tucking my hands into my armpits so she couldn't grab at them again.

'Your generation don't believe in anything,' my aunt told me. 'But listen to what I'm telling you, it's for your own good. Gemini men, they are takers. They will take every single thing from you, and they will drain you. They will never give to you, ever, because it's not about you, it's always about them. And they will leave you broken, in a heap, on the floor. I've seen it happen a million times, Queenie.'

The woman opposite raised a palm to the ceiling and 'Mm-hmm'ed in agreement.

'As you know, I steer clear of *all* men, apart from our Lord and Father, because I haven't had time for them since 1981, but believe you me, it's the Gemini ones you need to watch yourself with. Get yourself involved with a man born in June, and there'll be trouble.'

I chanced an interjection – 'But Tom is born in June!' – and instantly regretted it.

'Oh! Exactly! This is what I'm saying!' Maggie exclaimed. 'And where is he, please?' She looked at me quizzically. 'You're here at the hospital and he's nowhere to be seen!'

I opened my mouth to make the point that not all men born at a certain time of year were variations of Lucifer walking the earth but, always wanting to fully explore any subject, Maggie had more to say. In the increasingly busy waiting room, she continued to use her best outside voice to lecture me (and everyone sitting around us), and though I was too anxious about the goings-on of my womb to take any of it in, the woman opposite us was nodding along aggressively and staring at Maggie's auburn wig as though it could fall off at any minute. 'Wasn't Prince a Gemini?' I asked. 'I'm pretty sure he was born in June.'

'Prince – God rest his soul – was Prince,' Maggie said, looking me dead in the eye. 'Astrology did not, and does not, apply to Prince . . . if you get involved with a Gemini man, you'll regret it. They like the chase, trust me. The pursuit of a woman makes them feel strong, it makes them feel good and it makes them think they have a purpose in life. And we all know that unless men have a purpose, they feel aimless. But Gemini men are a whole different story,' Maggie continued with awe-inspiring enthusiasm. 'When they do finally get the woman, they'll drop her. Drop her like they didn't even *know* her. Gemini men don't mind who they hurt, who they have to use, who they have to step over, they don't even bloody notice.'

'. . . are you sure you don't mean white men, Maggie?' I asked, narrowing my eyes. Her line of fire sounded a little too specific.

'You can take it how you want to,' she said, folding her arms and pursing her lips. 'You're the one who thought she found her white saviour. And now look!'

Maggie is a big woman. In all ways. She has a new and even more surprising wig made every week, she doesn't like to wear the colour black because it's too depressing and she has to wear more than one pattern at any given time, even when she's pottering around the house, because 'Jesus wants life to be about colour'. The obsession with colour is a nod to her fleeting career as an artist; a career in which she never created anything but hype around herself. Maggie is also intensely religious, but the less ever said about that, the better. My aunt and grandmother always use religion as a stick to beat everyone with, and to even dwell on it for more than one second would be to entertain something I had no time for.

I sat on the edge of my seat to prevent the hospital staff from screaming my full name out this time around.

'What's to stop them from looking me up when I've gone?' I asked Maggie, trying to derail her rant. 'What are the rules?'

'Who's looking you up?' she asked me.

'Anyone in the waiting room?' I answered quietly.

'You're not a celebrity, Queenie,' Maggie said. 'Don't be so paranoid.'

'Queenie Jenkins?' the nurse from before bellowed. I patted Maggie on the knee to signify that I was about to go in and jumped up; she didn't stop talking.

The nurse didn't smile back at me, instead she placed a hand gently on my shoulder and trotted me down the clinical corridor and led me back into the room that smelt like someone had spilled a bucket of bleach.

I glanced nervously at the ultrasound machine as it hummed in the corner.

'You can put your things back down there,' she said, pointing to the chair by the door. For the second time, maybe more so this time, I wished it had been *Tom* there in that chair, but I didn't have time to lament because the nurse was staring at me, so I threw my bag on it.

'Can you remove your tights and your underwear and put your legs back in the stirrups, and I'll go and get the doctor.'

'Again?' I asked, throwing my head back like a surly teenager.

'Mmm. Yes please.' She left the room.

I should have worn tracksuit bottoms for this, both because I would live in them if I could and because tights are a complete faff. Putting them on requires half dance, half contortion, and should only be done once in a day, in a private sphere. I got my phone out to text my best friend, who was probably doing something less horrifying with her afternoon.

Queenie:

Darcy. They're asking to examine me for the second time! I'll have had this machine in me more times than Tom in the last few weeks

The doctor, a brisk woman with kind eyes that had clearly seen a lot of women's fear, swept back into the room. She spoke very slowly, explaining that she was going to have one more check of something. I sat up.

'What are you looking for?' I asked. 'You said the coil was there.'

She responded by snapping on a pair of latex gloves, so I lay back down.

'Okay,' she uttered, after a pause and a prod. 'I've asked another doctor for a second opinion. And having had another look, it's just that – well, is there any chance you were pregnant, Queenie?'

I sat up again; my stomach muscles would be shocked into thinking that I was exercising at this rate.

'I'm sorry, what do you mean?'

'Well,' the doctor said, peering at the ultrasound, 'it looks like you've had a miscarriage.'

I lifted my hand to my mouth, forgetting that I was holding anything. My phone slipped out of my grip and onto the floor. The doctor paid no attention to my reaction and continued looking at the screen.

'Why?' I asked, desperate for her to look at me, to acknowledge that this news might have affected me in some way.

'It can happen with most forms of contraception,' she told me clinically, her eyes that I'd previously thought were kind still fixed on the screen. 'Most women just don't know about it. At least it's done the job.'

I lay back on the examination table long after she'd left the room.

*

'Oh, you two will have beautiful children,' Tom's grandmother said, staring at us from across the table. Joyce had cataracts, but she could still see the future, it seemed.

'Your lovely soft brown skin, Queenie, but lighter. Like a lovely milky coffee. Not too dark! And Tom's green eyes. Your big hair, Queenie, those dark eyelashes, but Tom's nice straight nose.' I looked around to see if anyone else at the table was shocked by what she said, but apparently it was acceptable.

'I don't think you can pick and choose like an e-fit, Joyce,' I said, fiddling with the pepper grinder.

'True,' Joyce said. 'It's a shame, that.'

Later on when we were in bed, I turned to Tom and put my book down. 'What's wrong with *my* nose?'

'What do you mean?' Tom asked, concentrating on whatever tech article he was reading on his phone.

'Your grandma. At dinner she said that our future baby should have your "nice straight nose." '

'Ignore her. She's just being old, isn't she?' Tom said, putting his phone down on the bedside table. 'Your nose is nice and squishy. It might be my favourite thing about your face.'

'Oh. Thanks, I guess,' I said, picking my book back up. 'Well, let's hope that our children don't get any of my squashed features.'

'I said squishy, not squashed. And I'd rather our kids looked more like you than me – your face is more interesting than mine. And I *love* your nose, almost as much as I love you,' Tom said, booping me on the appendage in question with a finger.

He moved so that I could nuzzle into him and although I wasn't a person who ever felt particularly safe, I did, but just for a second.

'So you've thought about it?' I asked, looking up at him.

'Your nose? Sure, I think you've got a lovely nose.' He rested his chin on my forehead.

'No, our children. Future babies.'

'Yeah, I've got it planned out. In six years when we've got a house and I've forced you down the aisle, we'll have children,' Tom said, smiling. 'Three is the right amount.'

'Three?'

'One is selfish, two means they'll always be competing, but when you have three they can start looking after each other as soon as the eldest is eight.'

'Okay, okay. Three coffee-coloured babies. But, milky, right? Just like grandma ordered.'

*

Queenie:
Tom, hello

Queenie:
Are you seeing my messages?

Queenie:
I'll call when I'm on my way home

Queenie:
Got to go to the chemist and get some pills

Queenie:
Let me know if you need me to bring anything home

I sat in the corridor staring at my phone's smashed screen, waiting for Tom to reply. A few minutes passed and eventually I walked back towards the waiting room. I could hear Maggie talking as I made my way towards her.

'One day, years ago now, my ex-husband told me was popping

out for petrol, and do you know what? He was gone fifteen hours! When he got back, I said, "Terrence, where did you get the petrol, Scotland?"' She paused for effect. 'I told him to get out after that. I had a baby to look after, I had my bills to pay, I couldn't deal with any man's nonsense.' Maggie paused to adjust her bosom. 'The day after he left I went to the doctor and I said, "*Listen*, tie my tubes in a knot, I'm not having any more!" I'm telling you. The one I've got is fifteen now, all she gives me is trouble. It's all about make-up and boys and fake eyelashes and making videos for YouTube. This isn't what my mum came over from Jamaica for, for her granddaughter to be throwing away her education.' Maggie folded and unfolded her arms. 'I go to church and I pray, I pray for myself, I pray for my daughter, for my niece. I just have to hope He's listening, Marina.'

How were my aunt and this stranger already on first-name terms? I hadn't been gone that long. I threw myself down next to my aunt. Marina, sat opposite, was nodding vigorously, although Maggie had finished speaking.

'What did they say?' Maggie asked, pulling out the hand gel again.

I swerved the question. 'Nothing, really! Just women's problems, you know.'

'What women's problems?' Maggie is a first-generation Jamaican and therefore a woman entitled to information about others.

'Just women's problems!' I said, forcing what I hoped was a convincing smile.

Maggie and I stood at the bus stop outside the hospital. She spoke about something I couldn't quite pay attention to as I looked up at the three gigantic tower blocks looming opposite, so high up that dark clouds almost hid their tops. I kept my head tilted back, hoping that if I held it there long enough, the tears that were brimming in my eyes wouldn't fall out.

'Queenie, what did the doctor say?' My aunt narrowed her eyes at me. 'I don't buy this "women's problems" rubbish. Do I have to prise it out of you?'

Why did I think I'd got her off the topic earlier?

'She wanted to look at my cervix, Maggie,' I said, hoping that would get her off my case. 'Something about it being narrow?'

She looked at me, annoyance and then shock contorting her face. 'Pardon? Must you embarrass me?' she said through gritted teeth, looking around. 'We do *not* talk about our *vees* in public.'

'But I didn't say vagina, I said cervix,' I replied.

Her lips tightened.

'Anyway, the bus is here!'

The 136 crawled down Lewisham High Street, Maggie speaking a hundred words for each yard we moved.

'You know, back in the day, when Mum came over, they used to put implants and coils in black women without us knowing, to stop us getting pregnant.' She cocked her head. 'To stop us procreating. That is true, you know!' She raised her eyebrows. 'Mum's friend Glynda, the one who eats Mum out of house and home when she visits? Well, *she* couldn't get pregnant for years and she had no idea why. So you shouldn't even have had that *thing* put in in the first place, politically as *well* as physically. You don't know what it's doing to you.'

She was talking so frantically that her gigantic plastic earrings were providing a soundtrack to her chat.

'Black women's bodies don't work well with this sort of thing. Have you read up on it? Chemical imbalances, the absorption to our melanin – *that* affects the pineal and pituitary glands. *Swelling*, also.'

Maggie stopped talking to call Diana, so I tried to call Tom. The first three times it had rung out, but now it was going to voicemail. It was gone six; he'd be out of work by now.

'Is he still not answering?' Maggie asked.

'Huh?' I looked out of the window. 'Who, Tom? Yeah, he sent me a text to say that he'd see me at home.'

She knew I was lying, but my stop was coming up so she couldn't interrogate me about it.

'Are you sure you don't want to come to church with me on Sunday? All are welcome. Even you, with that *coil*.' She looked at me out of the sides of her eyes. 'God will save even the most wanton . . .' I rolled my eyes and stood up.

'I'll call you tomorrow,' I said, before I pinballed my way down the bus, careful not to touch anything or anyone with my hands, and stepped off.

I stood waving at my aunt as the doors closed and the bus pulled away. It's a family thing. It is an annoying and time-wasting thing.

When I got home, the flat was cold. I ran a bath and wriggled out of my clothes. I crinkled my nose at the goo from the ultrasound that had stuck itself to the gusset of my knickers and chucked them into the wash basket. I doubled over and sat on the edge of the bath. The bleeding had stopped, but the cramps hadn't.

I wrapped my hair in my headscarf and stepped into the bath. I sat in the water and prodded at my stomach, wincing as I hit tender spots. Why had this happened? I was twenty-five,

I wasn't going to have a baby. Obviously. But it would have been nice to have had the choice. Having a contraceptive placed in my body wholly suggests that I was not wanting to have a baby, so yes, my choice would be to not actually carry a child to term and then raise it, but that isn't the point.

'Would I have been ready?' I asked myself aloud, stroking my stomach. My mum was twenty-five when she got pregnant with me. I guess that says everything about how unprepared I'd be. I lay back, numbness cloaking my body as the hot water swathed my cold skin.

Midnight, and Tom still wasn't home. I couldn't sleep because my womb felt like it was trying to make its way out of my body, so I assembled some boxes and started to wrap up and pack my half of our separated belongings in the living room so it at least looked like I was going somewhere soon. A snow globe from Paris, mine and Tom's first holiday together; a comically ugly porcelain donkey from Spain, our second holiday together; and a Turkish eye ornament from our third. I wrapped all of these memories of our relationship with care, swaddling them in layers of newspaper and sealing them with tape. I moved on to the plates, then the mugs, before I stopped to get the donkey back out of the box. I unwrapped it and put it back on the mantelpiece. If I was going to leave a reminder of our relationship, it was going to be the thing I didn't want in my new place. I carried on wrapping until I got into a frenzy of paper and tape, only pausing when I reached for two mugs on the drying rack. One embossed with a T, the other with a Q.

*

'Why have you got so much *stuff*?' Tom asked, leaning on a cardboard box marked 'Miscellaneous 7' and wiping sweat from his forehead. 'I've only got a few hoodies and two pairs of socks.'

'I don't know, maybe I've become a hoarder without noticing?' I said, cupping his face in my hands. 'But you wanted to live with me, so you're going to have to live with it all.'

'Fine, I regret nothing,' Tom said, kissing me on the forehead. 'Queenie, you have a very dry forehead for someone who is meant to be lifting boxes.'

'Yes, maybe so, but I am organising, as opposed to lifting,' I told him. 'And making sure that the boxes marked "kitchen" are in the kitchen.'

'Well, if you're going to be in the kitchen could you at least make some tea?'

'Yes, now that you mention it, your clever girlfriend has just found the box with the kettle and bought milk and teabags on the way here,' I said. 'But I don't know where the mugs are.'

'Look in my rucksack, my mum bought us mugs. Moving-in present, she said.'

I found Tom's rucksack in the hallway and when I opened it, there were two gift boxes containing a white mug each. I washed them out and made us tea, plucking the hot teabags out with my fingers in the absence of a spoon.

'How do your fingers not burn?' Tom asked, walking into the kitchen, a box under his arm.

'They do, I just don't talk about it,' I said, handing him a hot mug. 'These are fancy, where did she get these from?'

'No idea,' Tom said, taking a sip.

'Oh, hold on, you've got the Q mug,' I realised, reaching out for it.

'This one's going to be mine,' he said, lifting it out of my reach. 'Like *you're* mine,' Tom added, putting an arm around me.

'Do you know,' I said, 'whatever tone you'd said that in, it would have sounded creepy and possessive.'

'Creepy and possessive.' Tom took a sip of tea and laughed. 'Were they the qualities that initially drew you to me?'

*

I packed until I was exhausted, falling asleep on the sofa boxed in by years of accumulatively unimportant stuff that I probably didn't need to continue carting through life. When I woke up the next morning, my alarm chirping obnoxiously from the bedroom, Tom still wasn't back. I sat on the tube to work, doubling over when pain ripped through my stomach. A woman handed me a plastic bag, saying, 'If you're going to be sick can you at least do it in here? Nobody wants to see a splattering so early in the morning.'

I snuck in late, turned my computer on and fake-smiled my way through the morning. The television listings got confused with the club listings, and I asked Leigh to fix it before our boss Gina noticed. One day, he's going to tell me to do my work myself, but as long as I listen to him talking about his boyfriend Don's faltering DJ career in great detail, he lets me get away with a lot.

At midday, I walked over to Darcy's desk, a grey metallic dock in the quiet corner of the office that she shares with Silent Jean, the world's oldest and *The Daily Read*'s longest-employed subeditor. She was a ghostly-pale waif of a woman who didn't fit with the aesthetic of a flashy news institution, and one who seemed to hate me without ever having spoken to me. Or to anyone, actually.

'Good afternoon, Jean,' I said, bowing. She tutted, nodding swiftly before putting her surprisingly snazzy earphones in. I placed both hands on Darcy's head and began to plait her thick, heavy brown hair, an activity that, thankfully, she found as satisfying as I did, so no HR summons for me.

'*Please* keep doing that. It is *literally* the most soothing thing,' she said. I looked at her screen and began to read aloud the email she was composing.

'Simon, you just can't expect me to reconfigure my wants and my needs to suit you. Knowing that I'm at a different point of my life to you, instead of understanding it, you almost use it as a weapon –'

Silent Jean looked at us and sighed unexpectedly loudly for someone who rarely exercised her vocal cords.

'Queenie! Privacy, please!' Darcy snapped, turning to look at me. Her bright blue eyes looked straight through my dark brown ones.

'Uh-oh. What's wrong?' she asked.

'Lots,' I groaned, banging my head down on her partition so loudly that Silent Jean jumped in her seat.

'Right, let's go, come on!' she chirped, looking apologetically at Jean and sweeping me up and away. Though Darcy has known me the shortest amount of time, she is the most intuitive of my best friends. We've worked together and spent every weekday talking to each other for the last three and a half years, and this means that we know each other better than we know ourselves.

She's very beautiful, with a complexion as rosy as her outlook, and looks like one of those wartime girls whose pictures their army husbands would kiss at night. You might think that that aesthetic didn't really have a place in the present day, but she made it work.

Darcy bundled me into the lift, forcing me to step on the foot of a man I hadn't seen before. He was dressed in a tweed jacket with glasses too big for a face that I would have thought was handsome if my entire brain wasn't concentrated on heartbreak. He looked at me and opened his mouth to complain, but instead stared, until he looked down at his phone.

'It'll be all right, Queenie,' Darcy whispered, putting her arm around my shoulder.

'You don't even know what's wrong,' I whispered back at her, 'so you can't say that.' The lift zoomed to the ground floor and we bundled out, words of sadness and betrayal and abandonment firing out of my mouth at a hundred miles per hour.

'I just don't know what to do! Things have been so bad for such a long time, Darcy. It's relentless,' I told her, my pace quickening the more irritated I got with my stupid situation. 'We argue every single day, about absolutely everything, so much that he's started going back home to stay with his parents at the weekends, and when it's *really* bad, he stays there in the week and commutes! From Peterborough! Then this weekend, when we really got into it, he told me that he needed a break, and that he thought I should move out.'

'Yeesh,' Darcy winced. 'Did he mean it? Or was he just angry?'

'Darcy, I have no fucking idea. We stayed up all night talking and bickering about it and I agreed to move out for three months, after which point we could revisit things.'

'Why are you the one moving out when he can go and stay with his parents? It's not like you have that option.' Darcy linked her arm through mine.

'He said he can afford to stay on in the flat because my entry level wage is *nothing* in comparison to his big-boy fucking web developer salary.'

'Is that a direct quote?' Darcy asked, horrified.

'He's always been like that about money, so I shouldn't be surprised that he's using it against me.' Darcy squeezed my arm tighter to her. 'I just don't understand why he isn't better. He knows I love him,' I huffed. 'Why doesn't he fucking see that?'

My expletives weren't suitable for a public dining space, so Darcy herded me away from the canteen and towards the tiny park near our office. I guess it can be called a park even though it is really only patches of damp earth and bare branches surrounding what is mainly concrete, but it's nice to have something resembling greenery in central London. We warded off the sharp October air by huddling together on a wooden bench that wobbled dangerously, especially when my gesticulating really tested it.

'He knows that I have *stuff*, he's *always* known about my stuff, so why can't he be understanding?' I looked at Darcy for a response but carried on talking before she could say anything. 'It could all be fine. We have a break, I move out for a bit, sort my head out, then in a few months, all fine, I move back in and we're happy forever.'

'Like an interracial Ross and Rachel?' Darcy offered.

'*Friends* is the only reference you could think of?' I asked her. 'There weren't really even any black people in *Friends*.'

'I think you just need to give him a bit of time, and a bit of space. Once you get out of there he'll realise how hard it is not having you around,' Darcy said. She is very solutions-driven, a welcome counter to my impulsiveness and inability to think things through. 'Have you been sleeping together?'

'No, not that I haven't been trying.' I sighed. 'He thinks it's a bad idea. It's been a month since we had sex.'

Darcy winced.

'It's killing me. I just wish it could all be fine,' I said, resting my head on Darcy's shoulder. 'What if this is the end?'

'It's not the end!' Darcy assured me. 'Tom loves you, he's just hurting. You're both in pain, don't forget that. His pride will be in pieces because of this whole break thing. Men don't like to admit that they've failed at anything, let alone relation-ships. I once suggested a break to Simon and in response, he booked a triple session with his therapist and then got his eyebrow pierced. Things will get better.' Darcy rested her head on mine. 'Oh! What did they say at the hospital yesterday, by the way? You know, the scan thing?'

'Oh, all fine.' There was no point in telling her. 'It's just stress, or something.'

'Tom went with you though, right?'

'No, he went back to Peterborough on Sunday evening. Haven't seen or heard from him since.'

'Are you kidding?' Darcy squawked. 'Do you need to come and stay with me and Simon for a couple of nights? Are you still having those stomach pains? We can look after you.'

'No, I'm all right,' I said.

I wasn't hurting anymore, but in the place of the pain was something else, something sitting heavy that I couldn't quite identify.

Wanting to kill some time before I got home to reminders of my disintegrating relationship, I went to Brixton for some Jamaican bun on the way home, hoping that I could kick-start my appetite with my favourite comfort food. I climbed the steps out of the underground and stood catching my breath once I got to the top.

The smell of incense from the street sellers made me sneeze as I turned into the market. I hopped over a suspicious puddle and carried on weaving through what always felt like thousands of people. I made it into Brixton Village and followed a route to the Caribbean bakery that was etched in my memories of Saturday shopping trips with my grandmother. I turned a corner and went to walk straight into the bakery, but was instead faced with a trendy burger bar full of young couples. The men were all wearing colourful, oversized shirts and their female companions were all wearing colourful, overpriced coats.

I frowned and retraced my steps, turning various corners in my search and convincing myself that I'd dreamt the bakery's existence, before going back to the burger shop. I stood for a minute, trying to recall some memory of going there.

*

'Hullo, hullo, how you keeping, Susie?' My grandmother smiled at the plump Jamaican woman behind the counter. The whole bakery smelt so sweet. And not sickly-sweet, it smelt sugary and warm and familiar. I stood on tiptoe and looked over, seeing how her pristine white apron strained over her soft, round stomach.

'I'm good, tank you darlin', you good?' the woman replied, flashing a gold tooth at me. 'And the little one, she getting big!'

'Too big!' My grandmother cackled her reply.

I looked up at her and scowled.

'Why you fixin' up your face like that? She's just saying you're growin' up,' an older Jamaican man stepped out of the back room and reassured me.

'This one is *too* sensitive, Peter.' My grandmother dismissed me with one hand. 'Anyway, let me get a bun – not that one, the big one. No, no, the *biggest* one. That's it – and two hard-dough bread, one bulla and a likkle pound cake for my husband, put a smile on him sour face.'

The woman handed a giant brown bag of baked goods over to me, with a smile. 'Haffi help Grandma, she won't be around forever.'

'Why Susie haffi be so morbid?' my grandmother asked me in a tight-lipped whisper as we walked out. 'Sometimes Jamaicans are *too* overfamiliar.'

*

With the memory confirming that I was right, I walked with renewed purpose over to the fish stall opposite.

'Excuse me?' I said to a fishmonger as he slopped some octopuses that were on display into a basin. 'Was there a bakery opposite here?' I pointed to the burger bar, its neon lighting shining on other shops and stalls. I noticed many of them had SHUT DOWN and RELOCATED signs across their shutters.

The fishmonger said nothing.

'It had a dark green front, bread in the windows? I can't remember the name,' I continued, trying not to look at the octopus activities while talking about food I actually liked eating.

'Gone,' the fishmonger finally said, throwing the basin down and wiping his hands on his apron. 'Couldn't afford the rent,' he continued in broken English. 'Then these people came.' He gestured to the burger bar.

'What?' I yelped. 'How much is the rent?' How could it have been raised so much that people who were forced to come specifically to Brixton, make lives here and create a community here be pushed out to make room for corporate-friendly burgers bars?

He shrugged and walked away, his waterproof boots squeaking on the wet floor with each step.

*

Queenie:
Tom, are you home tonight?
Let me know

I stood at the bus stop, the pains in my stomach starting up again. I bent over and took a deep breath and when I straightened up, a black BMW stopped in front of me, the bass pumping from it hitting me with each beat. The passenger window rolled down and fragrant smoke seeped out and towards me. I took a step back.

'Eh, big batty,' a familiar voice laughed.

It was my old neighbour, Adi, a very compact and handsome Pakistani man with facial hair so precise it looked like it had been styled with a laser. 'How's that big bum since you left the ends? Ready for me yet?' He laughed again.

'Adi! Stop!' I said, embarrassed, stepping towards the car. 'People can hear you!'

The minute I moved into my dad's house, Adi had been on my case relentlessly, both before and after his lavish Desi wedding to his girlfriend of eight years. Whenever I bumped into him he'd talk very matter-of-factly, and at excessive length, about black women being forbidden fruit to Muslim men, but mainly he gave me lots of chat about big black bottoms.

'Let me give you a lift, innit.' He smiled. 'But not if you're gonna be sick. I saw you bending over.'

22

'I'm fine, thanks,' I said, giving him a thumbs up.

'Then get in the car, there's a bus coming up behind me.' He leaned over and opened the passenger door from his seat.

I opened my mouth to say no again, but a pain like no other made my legs feel weak. I climbed into the BMW.

'Watch the leather!' he said, his voice higher than I'd ever heard it. 'These are custom seats.'

As soon as I closed the door, Adi sped off so quickly that I felt like I was in a g-force simulator.

'Let me just do my seatbelt,' I said, reaching clumsily behind the seat for it.

'You're safe with me, innit.' He smiled again and put his hand on my thigh. His thick silver wedding ring flashed at me.

'Adi,' I said, removing it. 'Both hands on the wheel.'

'So as I was *saying*,' he started, 'is that big bum ready for me? It's looking bigger, you know.'

'It's exactly the same size, Adi.'

Why did I get into the car? It would have been better if I'd just collapsed at the bus stop.

My phone buzzed in my pocket. I took it out and read the message from Tom on the screen, feeling my stomach drop.

Tom:

Just saw your text. Not back
tonight.

'I can change your life, you know, Queenie.' Adi put his hand back on my thigh. 'Girl like you, man like me? I can guarantee you've never had sex so good.'

I let it stay there.

*

When Adi had dropped me home and screeched away, I stood outside the front door with the key in my hand, hoping that Tom had changed his mind and would be on the other side. He wasn't.

The flat was cold, again. I got into bed and tried to cry in an attempt at catharsis, but it was useless. Nothing. Kyazike called. I cancelled it. Maggie called, and I knew that she'd just tell me that Jesus was the answer so I cancelled that too. My grandmother called, and you don't cancel her calls, so I answered.

'Hello, Grandma,' I croaked.

'What's wrong?' She always knew when something was wrong.

'Nothing.'

'You know I always know when something is wrong, Queenie,' she growled, so I told her that I had a headache. 'No, you don't. We don't get headaches. It's that white boy, isn't it?'

'You can't say that!'

'Is he white or not? Look – if you are sad, you have to try not to be. If I had let myself be sad when I got pregnant with Maggie at fourteen, then where would that have left me?' All of my grandmother's responses come with a Caribbean frame of reference that forces me to accept that my problems are trivial.

'I know, but it was different back then.'

'Yuh tink suffering discriminate against time?' The patois always comes out when she's feeling self-righteous.

I fell asleep on the sofa again, this time with a hot-water bottle pressed against my stomach, and woke up to the sound of running water. I heaved myself up and stumbled towards the bathroom, flicking lights on as I moved through the dark flat.

Tom was sitting on the edge of the bath facing away from me, his hand testing the water. He turned the cold tap off and stood up, his big frame tensing slightly when he saw me.

'I didn't know you were up,' he said quietly. 'Scared me.'

'Sorry. I thought you weren't coming back tonight?'

'I worked too late and missed the last train back home.' Tom squeezed past me. 'It needs another minute or so of hot water.'

'But this is home,' I said to him.

He didn't reply.

I started to step out of my clothes as Tom leaned against the doorframe. My turtleneck got stuck on my head so he was presented with my once-white, now mostly discoloured, bra and wriggling torso.

'You sure you want to take a break from all of this?' I forced a laugh, my voice muffled by fabric. I got free in time to see him roll his eyes and turn away.

'So you're packed, then.' I heard an unmistakable tremor of emotion in Tom's voice. 'When are you leaving?' He cleared his throat.

'Can you give me until next week?' I asked, stepping into the bath and turning off the hot tap. 'That way we can have a few more days together.'

Tom shook his head. 'I don't think that's a good idea, Queenie.' He put the toilet lid down and took a seat, facing away from me. 'I'll head back to my mum and dad's tomorrow.'

'And when will we speak?' I asked, my voice so small.

'I don't know, Queenie,' he said, placing his head in his hands.

I smacked the water. 'God, I don't know why you're being like this!'

'Why I'm being like this?' he said, his voice finally cracking. 'These last few months have been awful. I'm still trying to forgive you for that shit you pulled at my mum's birthday, for a start. But Queenie, this *whole* relationship, you've refused to talk to me.'

My breath caught in my throat. I didn't know he'd felt like this, and I certainly hadn't expected him to vocalise it.

'You never tell me what's wrong,' he continued. 'Ever! And you'd close off, you'd cry and you'd lock yourself in the bathroom while I sat on the floor outside telling you I was there if you wanted to talk, but you never did. You've pushed me away for so much of this relationship.'

'It's my stuff!'

'We've all got stuff, Queenie!' Tom shouted. 'And I've tried with yours, I really have.'

'Tom,' I said, quietly. 'However shit I've been, you've always forgiven me.'

'Yeah, I have.' He looked at his feet. 'But I don't know if I can do it anymore.'

That night, we fell asleep in the same bed, me nestled into Tom's back. When I woke up at dawn, he was gone. There was a mug of cold tea next to me on the bedside, the Q looking back at me cruelly.

Chapter Two

Instead of helping with the move, I watched Leigh from work and Eardley, family friend and the world's smallest removal man, carry what looked like hundreds of boxes and IKEA bags full of books, trinkets and clothes into my new house.

My new lodgings weren't ideal. At £750 a month, it was the cheapest room I could find in Brixton, in a house built in the Victorian era and clearly never taken care of since then. When I arrived for the viewing, it was crumbling from the outside in, with weeds and ivy creeping across the door and filling the front garden. I didn't and still don't know if some dead thing is dwelling in there, but there was definitely a smell emanating from some unknown and unseen object.

When I'd stepped into the house, there was another smell that hit me, and, unsurprisingly, not a good one. Although brown, beige and outdated in design, apart from the damp patches the kitchen seems perfectly fine, though I don't imagine I'll cook in it. And I know I can't see myself sitting on the mustard-yellow velvet sofas in the living room.

'Only this to go,' Eardley said, in a strong Yorkshire accent that seemed incongruous to his dark brown skin and gold teeth, as he thumped my mum's old dressing table along. The chipped, stained antique was the most awkward piece of furniture I'd ever owned and made moving house a bother, but I still lugged it around with me everywhere I went. I used to watch my mum getting ready in its mirror for hours. I'd sit on the bed behind her and stare as she took rollers out of her hair and pinned them up expertly with small, delicate hands, and I'd move even closer to watch as she applied various lotions and potions that I was too young to understand, and still don't really understand now.

Eardley's bald head glistened with sweat as he put his hands on his hips and stretched from side to side. He wiped his forehead on the sleeve of his blue overalls.

'Just need a second, my back feels like it's going to go!' Eardley was always so cheerful despite the extreme circumstances and short notices I threw at him, but small parts of me died every time I watched him bang that dressing table on all of the floor and wall surfaces he possibly could.

'Can we just get this bit over and done with, *please*?' Leigh said, running his hands through his dyed blond hair. He looked up to the sky, extending his neck to catch the passing breeze. The sun made his green eyes glisten. 'My skin is the perfect colour for my foundation and if I stay out in the sun I'll get darker. It won't match, Eardley.'

'Okay, let's get back to it,' Eardley said, stretching his wiry frame from side to side. 'I'm sure my back'll be fine.'

I left Eardley and Leigh to get on with the whole bother of carrying things into the house and made my way up to the bedroom. It was darker, dimmer and smaller than I'd remembered. Patches of mould lurked in all four corners, the garden-facing window was small and dirty, the carpets were cheap and beige, much like the rest of the house, and the yellow walls were stained and cracked.

Three seconds later, Leigh came into my new bedroom while I was observing one of the many damp patches. Had they grown since I first came here?

'Are you going to that party tomorrow?' Leigh asked, reclining on a pile of boxes.

'Oh god, which party?' I was now standing on a box to get closer to the damp patch. I couldn't retain any plans, recently.

'James,' Leigh said. I stared down at him. 'Fran's boyfriend? Darcy's friend Fran from school? Invited us last week?'

'Oh, I hate those parties.'

When Darcy first started inviting me to these parties, I thought it was for a social experiment or hidden camera show, like 'put a black person in *Made in Chelsea* and see what happens', but ultimately these gatherings really are as simple as 'posh people and me'.

'Nobody goes to parties because they *like* them,' Leigh said. 'We go because we want to either show everyone else there that we're better than them, or because we want to distract ourselves.'

'And which one are you?'

'The former. But you, dear heart, are the latter, and you need to take your mind off Tom and this break-up – sorry, "break", whatever you're calling it.'

'Fair,' I said, immediately rummaging through bags to find something to wear. 'You'll be there, though, right?' I cringed at my neediness. I'd only been away from Tom a day.

'I'll see if I can pop in after Don's gig. I'm making no promises, though, I'll probably be off my face,' Leigh said, standing up and winking at his reflection in the smudged window.

I was as surprised as the next person that I'd moved into a house with strangers from the internet. The prospect itself filled me with dread, with fear and a healthy amount of disgust, but £21k a year wasn't going to get me anything bigger than someone's garage space.

The housemates themselves didn't seem awful, but I felt very nervous at the prospect of living with white people, because I know that my standards of inherited Caribbean cleanliness are bordering on clinical OCD levels.

I grew up watching my grandmother wash bottles, cartons, everything, before they were allowed to go into the fridge, and she'd clothesline you if you walked your shoes through the house.

Living with Tom didn't count because I'd trained him up and we'd had some clean-house trial runs when we'd stay at his family holiday home in Turkey that almost, but didn't quite, break us.

I had been shown around my new house by my then-prospective housemates: Rupert, twenty-nine, a little bit shorter than me and markedly angry about it, didn't make eye contact; in essence, little more than a posh boy with a beard and those deck shoes and no socks. Even at the end of September.

The girl, or woman, Nell, is thirty-five, works in a deli and wears her short blonde hair in high bunches. She is the nicer of the two, and has already admitted that she has a drinking problem, demonstrated when she opened the door to me with an XL glass of white wine in her hand at 11.30 a.m.

As bad as that was, it was the best of some very, very bad housing situations. *How* do seven people live together and share only two bathrooms, was my first question when I saw room number one in Stockwell, on the top floor of a narrow four-storey house. All four storeys were a mess, which I suppose is unavoidable when seven are squashed into a five-bedroom property that is shoddily converted. In at least one case, a sheet divided one large room in two.

I had to step over a minimum of ten bikes on the way in, and the kitchen was so cluttered that I could have sworn that whoever lived there was playing crockery Jenga.

The bedroom, a steal at £800 a month, was absolutely tiny. I'd barely be able to fit my bed in there, let alone the books I'm determined to carry through life with me. When the tiny Withnail wannabe in a dirty trench coat and flip-flops who showed me round let me out and told me he'd be in touch, we both knew that it wasn't going to happen.

The second place I went to see was a studio in Camberwell. Completely out of my price range, but I'd watched a YouTube tutorial on haggling that I was going to put into practice. I had to use CityMapper to find my way to it, so obviously I was sent on an urban scenic route all around the houses.

The area was looking very grey, but as expected the app sent me the wrong way so I cut back through the not-so-Camberwell-Green-in-winter park with its little playground in the centre.

I was running late, so when I eventually turned onto the road that the flat was on, passing a fleet of Nigerian men sitting and chatting in fancy cars, I was sweating from every pore. I walked towards number twenty-three, looking up and down at my phone map so much that I was like one of those nodding bobblehead dogs you get on car dashboards.

'Hello, lovely girl, are you my five o'clock?' a man with a strong Polish accent had asked as he stepped out of the car that he'd parked next to me at speed, bringing the stench of stale cigarettes out with him. His suit was cheap, his hair thinning.

'Queenie. Sorry, yes, I got lost.' I took off my coat and put it through the strap of my rucksack.

'Okay, don't worry, I have someone else coming in five minutes, so quick, quick!' He smiled in a way that suggested he thought I would be charmed.

Why did they *do* this, this organising of forty viewings at a time so that everyone panics and throws money at these overpriced and under-kempt boxes masquerading as flats?

When we'd made it in, me having to contort myself so that we didn't merge into one person in the three-inches-square hallway, I stood in the flat trying to calculate how I'd fit any of my furniture into an area so small. The estate agent shocked my socks off and out the door by telling me the price of a month's rent.

'One thousand, two hundred?' I shrieked, holding a hand to my mouth in a move usually deployed to express faux shock. This was real shock.

'Well, you know, that's the cost of living in London, lovely girl.'

'My name is Queenie,' I reminded him. 'The cost of living in London? There's not even a washing machine.'

'Launderette is close, no problem. You put it all in a bag, carry it down the road, five pounds, easy.'

'There's no actual oven.'

'There's room for a microwave, yes? And look, a hob.' He opened one of three cupboards to show me a two-ring plug-in hob that looked back at me as though it knew it would never be enough.

'But it's one room! The kitchen is the bedroom! I could cook my Bolognese from my bed!'

The estate agent told me that everything in the flat was state-of-the-art, new, refurbished, and that even though I wouldn't have access to the garden, I had a garden view. When I looked out of the window at the patch of grass and four concrete slabs below and asked where the rest of it was, he tried to distract me by showing me the bathroom. He opened a door in the corner of the room and beckoned me over. I left the pull of the garden view and went in, ducking through the low doorframe as I felt for the lightbulb cord.

'Oh, the light is here.' He crossed the room and stood by three switches next to the front door. 'These two control the main room,' he flicked each switch up and down, bright spotlights beaming white, artificial light down onto the kitchen surface and then the middle of the room, 'and this one is for the bathroom.' He flicked the final switch down and the light went on above my head.

'Why is there no window in the bathroom?' I asked, turning round once to look around the room, my bag hitting every area in there: the shower, the bathroom cabinet, the sink.

'No window, but extractor fan . . .' He opened the small cupboard underneath the light switches and pressed a button.

A whirring began above my head.

'You see? The bathroom, everything new. Power shower, newly fitted toilet, sink.' The estate agent slid past me, his face too close to mine, and lifted a handle to turn the sink tap on. Nothing came out. He pushed it down again. 'It will all be working once you move in.'

'I don't think it's for me, but thank you for taking the time to show me,' I said, making my way two steps to the front door.

'Don't go so soon,' the estate agent said, stepping close to me. 'There is a way that it could be a bit cheaper.'

I stepped back.

'You know, I do you a favour, you do me a favour?' He placed a hand on my shoulder and moved it down, the moisture on his palm making it stick to my cotton jumper as he moved it down to my chest.

I stepped further back, falling into the kitchen counter.

'What's wrong? You don't want us to help each other out?' He smirked as I reached for the handle and backed out of the front door. 'My people, we like your people. We're all outsiders. First Brexit, then Blaxit,' he chuckled.

Disgust and anger had propelled me out of the flat, and to another viewing at a tiny cottage in Mitcham that smelt of lavender. When I arrived, I wasn't shown around, but was instead sat on a sofa and interviewed by two women who introduced themselves as Lizzie and Sarah without differentiating who was who. They were in their late thirties, possibly a couple, and visibly realised that they should have specified a higher age bracket when advertising the room as I walked in the door with my hair falling out of its bun, my coat hanging off my shoulders and my open rucksack spilling various sanitary products onto their beautiful wooden floor.

'Are you clean?' was the first question one of them asked. 'It's very important that you're clean.'

'Do you make a lot of noise?' the other asked. 'Sarah and I don't like a lot of sounds.'

'Do you have a lot of guests?' The one who I'd now deduced was Lizzie informed me. 'We don't like visitors.'

'Do you cook a lot?' Sarah asked me. 'We don't like a lot of . . . fragrant foods. The smell hangs in the fabrics.'

'Do you keep yourself to yourself?' Lizzie folded her arms. 'Sarah and I very much keep ourselves to ourselves.'

'Do you shave?' Sarah asked. 'It's just that we have a very delicate drainage system that can't really cope with thick hairs.' That question felt *pretty* personal.

'I just need a room because me and my boyfriend are on a break and I'm sorry to be dramatic, but if I have to look at another house I'll honestly *kill* myself!' I exploded, and they both jumped in their seats.

'Oh no, sorry to hear that,' Lizzie said quietly.

'How did you . . . meet?' Sarah asked out of politeness, desperate to move the conversation away from me potentially living with them.

*

'I've read that.'

'Huh?' I looked up at the stranger who had sat right next to me on Clapham Common, despite the unlimited grass that surrounded us. I was trying out this whole 'being outside in the summer' thing that people seemed to like so much, and it was mainly fine apart from the insects. I should have known that someone would come along and spoil it.

'*The Lost World.*' With one hand, the stranger covered his eyes to shield them from the sun, and pointed at my book with the other. Even though they were partly hidden, I could see how green they were. 'I like it, as far as sequels go. Didn't like the film, though.'

'It's one of my favourite films,' I said, lifting my sunglasses and letting them rest in my hair.

'Ha, sorry. I'm Tom,' the boy said, holding out his hand.

'I don't like touching strangers. Don't take it personally, though. I don't really like touching anyone.' I put my book down on the grass. 'I'm Queenie.'

'Is that a nickname? Or your actual name?'

'Yes. Is Tom *yours*?' I smiled at him.

35

'Yeah, fair point.' He laughed nervously. 'Do you live around here?'

'No. But I like the Common. I grew up not far from here.'

'Oh, cool. Were you born here?'

Why was he asking so many questions? Was he an immigration officer?

'. . . in the UK? Yes. I know that I'm black but I wasn't born in "nebulous Africa".'

'You're a funny one, aren't you?' He laughed again.

'Funny weird or funny ha-ha?'

'Both. Not that being funny weird is a bad thing.'

'No, I know. I think it's my personal brand.' I smiled at the floor, fiddling with the corner of my book. He was the first man I'd met who seemed not to want to immediately push any weirdness out of me.

'I like your hair. It's really long,' Tom said.

I wasn't used to being approached by men who wanted to say nice things to me. It was very weird and unfamiliar. But it was nice.

'Thanks. I bought it myself.' I flicked it over my shoulder and it whipped him in the face accidentally. He ducked and laughed again. He had a nice laugh, I noticed. There was nothing about it that made me think he was laughing at me.

'Do you live around here?' I asked, panicking a bit as I felt myself soften.

'No, I work just over there.' He pointed into the distance. 'I'm a web developer. Started a few months ago, but I've been working on this killer project for days.' He lay back on the grass. 'I've had too much coffee and my eyes were going a bit funny. My colleague told me to get some fresh air.'

'Web development, huh? Fancy,' I said, impressed. 'Can I ask you a question?'

'Sure, go for it.'

'Is that your job because you see the world in code, like in *The Matrix*?' I asked sincerely.

'Ha, good question.' He laughed his nice laugh again. 'No. Almost. I guess I like it because it's very logical. I like logic, I like rules.'

'Oh god, I don't.'

'Ah, a rule-breaker.' He raised his eyebrows. Like his laugh, they were nice, too. 'So what do you do, Queenie?'

'Nothing, yet.'

'What are you going to do?'

'I'm going to change the world,' I said. 'The world of reporting, anyway. I graduated last year and have been doing absolutely nothing with my degree ever since. I had an interview this morning at a newspaper, though. *The Daily Read*. Can you believe that they interview people for an *internship*? All I'll be getting is lunch money and they asked me to give *five* examples of culture websites and what makes them so successful. I had to do a PowerPoint and everything.' I was talking so much.

'Ah, welcome to the world of free labour,' he said, standing up and taking his phone out of his pocket. 'Shit, I need to get back. They've found some sort of bug.' His leaving unexpectedly took me by surprise.

'Bye, then,' I said defensively.

'Can I, er, have your number?' Tom asked, his voice breaking slightly. 'It'd be nice to talk to you again.'

I raised an eyebrow. 'That's very forward of you.'

'Like I said, I'm very logical. No point talking to a pretty girl if you aren't going to ask for her number.'

'Who, me?'

'I'll text you,' he said, handing the phone to me. I put my number in. 'Hope you get the internship! They'd be mad not to hire you.'

I watched him walk away, bouncing lightly with each step he took.

*

'Anyway, that's basically how we met,' I said, taking a deep breath after giving them a potted version of mine and Tom's meet cute.

'We'll let you know tomorrow,' they'd said in unison.

On the way back to the flat, I'd bought a twenty-pack of cigarettes, sat on the doorstep and smoked half of them before stepping back through the front door. The next day, Lizzie and Sarah had rejected me. They thought they 'were going to go in a different, older direction'.

Chapter Three

I stared in the mirror after getting ready for the party, trying to summon the courage just to leave the house. My new housemates weren't in, so it wasn't as though I could flake and use getting to know them as an excuse. I was wearing a tight, black dress, the first thing I could find at the top of the pile of unpacked clothes. I turned sideways in the mirror and looked at my stomach. The bloating and cramps were gone, finally. Without thinking, I took a deep breath and pushed it out to replicate a pregnant belly. I rubbed my stomach slowly. 'What are you doing?' I asked myself, angry with the reflection I'd seen. I slammed out of my bedroom and out of the house.

When I arrived at the party I was greeted at the brushed-glass door of luxury apartments by Fran and James, who genuinely and unironically refer to themselves as 'couple goals'.

'Queenie! You look amazing! Love your hair! It looks great, what have you done to it?' Fran cooed as James clung onto her, his arms around her waist.

Had they both walked to the door like that? Surely it wasn't comfortable for either of them.

'Nothing, it's the same as normal!' I fake-smiled.

'Well, it looks great,' James echoed his girlfriend.

'No Tom with you?' Fran asked, looking behind me.

'No. We, er – ' I started, feeling my throat tighten. 'Can we not talk about it?' I handed them a bottle of wine.

After Fran and James untangled themselves from each other, one whipped my coat off and the other (hopefully unintentionally) ushered me into a corner next to Sam, the only other black person there. He looked like my mum's old partner, Roy. Stocky, short, dark-skinned and with a bald head that I think he shaves so closely with a razor so as not to let any afro hair come through, Sam goes by Sambo. He turned to look at me, and the resemblance to Roy made my stomach lurch. I nodded a hurried hello and he looked back at me blankly, as always.

When I once told him that if he wanted to stop people calling him Sambo I'd back him up, and followed that by asking if he'd seen the film *Get Out*, he firmly told me that the nickname was 'ironic'. He'd gone to boarding school with James and was adopted by white parents, which I think you can tell quite quickly by the way he publicly ridicules anything resembling black culture and carries his mute blonde girlfriend around like she's some sort of symbolic rite of whiteness.

He's been introduced to me many times, and pretends not to know me every time. It's tedious. I always want to take him by the shoulders and shout, 'Sam, we're the only two black people at these functions, just say hello, you don't need to be dismissive of me because your black family rejected you!' But it's best to keep a low profile when you always feel like you could be kicked out at any minute if someone starts feeling a little 'uncomfortable' in your presence.

I made my way to the bar that James has told me many times he installed in his not-quite-a-bachelor-pad the second he moved in. He's told me about the bar almost as much as he's told me about the roof terrace, even though my deliberately lacklustre response to these fixtures surely didn't do anything to justify their cost. When I got there, I found Darcy, who was pouring herself a glass of white wine.

'You made it!' she said, getting a glass down from the shelf for me. 'Want one?'

I nodded quickly, taking her glass and downing the contents.

'Ah, I see. Today was moving day.'

I nodded again.

'Okay, well, let's have a drink to your break, shall we?'

'I'm not toasting to heartbreak!'

'No, we aren't toasting to heartbreak,' Darcy told me, filling her glass and then mine, 'we're toasting to the fact that you're both having a little time out, after which your relationship will be better than before.'

'Okay. I'll cheers to that.' I clinked my glass to hers and downed my drink again.

'Besides, Tom wasn't great at parties anyway!' Darcy reminded me. 'He'd always just pull you into a corner and talk to you about his job. You'll have more fun without him here.'

'But at least I had an ally,' I whispered as she pulled me across the room. 'Plus, he always made me feel safe from *him*.' We walked past Sambo, who looked at me with disdain.

There was more alcohol than I'd ever seen at this party, and while making sure that I was drowning any sorrow that I might currently or have ever had, Darcy and Fran, once Darcy had filled her in on the break, thought it would be fun to rally some of their school friends around me in order to create the best OkCupid profile a team of six could construct.

'I don't want to do this,' I said as Fran took my phone from me.

'But it'll be fun!'

I was too tipsy to protest.

'Okay, so, I think that you should accentuate your features, hun?' Like, your voluptuous figure?' Fran pushed me against a white wall. 'And maybe, like, pout your lips? God babe, you're so lucky your lips are just *like* that.' She stared at my mouth in wonder.

I stood against the wall and folded my arms awkwardly. 'I'm not really good at the pouty stuff,' I said. 'How about I just smile?'

'Okay, well, why don't you just give, like, a sass face?' another girl suggested.

'Mmm, I don't think so. I reckon I'll just look pissed off, and guys don't seem to go for that angry black girl thing.'

The girls carried on pulling me this way and that. Then a boy who'd been pointed out to me as James's only single colleague came over and told me that it wasn't necessary. He introduced himself and handed me a glass of something that, after drinking it in three hungry gulps, I deduced was a lot of spirit and a little bit of mixer.

Quite a bold thing to say, and he was tall, which made me feel petite, I thought, woozily. Something that doesn't happen very often, given that I am the average height for a woman in the United Kingdom but, unlike all of my friends, a size sixteen.

'Why isn't it necessary?' I asked, looking up and blinking about a million times in an attempt to be doe-eyed because I read in a teen girl magazine when I was about fifteen that boys like that sort of thing.

'Why do you need to go on a dating app when I'm here?' he smiled. 'Do you like playing games? I don't.'

I took a swig of wine that finished me off. I was drunker than I'd ever been.

'Sorry, what did you say?' I asked him, my eyes blurring.

*

'What did you say?' I asked Tom's uncle, trying very hard to register what he'd just said. I could feel my face getting hot.

'You're not going to take that seriously, are you?' Stephen barked his reply. 'Come on, don't be so *politically correct*, you silly girl.' He twirled the Cluedo cards around in his hand before smacking them down on the table. 'We're having fun!'

I looked at Tom, who avoided my gaze and looked at his brother awkwardly.

'Tom?' I asked him sharply. 'Don't look at Adam, look at me!'

'Queenie, leave it,' Tom finally said, quietly.

'Leave it?' I asked, looking around the room, waiting for anyone to defend me. 'Did you hear what your uncle just said?'

'He was joking, Queenie, don't get worked up!' Adam scoffed. 'And the character is actually black, so – '

'Am I in some alternative universe?' I stood up. 'Your uncle just said, "Was it the nigger in the pantry?" and you've got nothing to say?' I looked back at Tom. 'I'll go, if you're going to pretend I'm not here.'

I charged out of the living room and fell straight into Viv, who was leaving the kitchen with her birthday cake, a beautifully decorated thing that she'd explained had been made by her ninety-five-year-old great-aunt 'despite the unyielding arthritis'. We both watched it slip out of her hands and fall on the floor and land at our feet with a loud splat, the iced '60' still intact.

'Look what you've done!' Tom said, appearing behind me.

'What's going on?' Viv asked, confused and agitated. She looked at Tom and me, then to the mess on the floor.

43

'Ask your son!' I said, stepping over the cake and walking towards the front door.

'Don't fucking walk *out*,' Tom groaned. 'Why have you always got to take this stuff so seriously?'

I looked at Tom, saying nothing as I pulled my trainers on.

'The silent treatment has started already? Fucking hell, Queenie.'

I stepped out of the door and slammed it behind me, walked down the front path and onto the silent suburban street. I looked behind to see if Tom had followed me, but the front door stayed closed. I carried on walking until I eventually got to a smelly bus shelter and perched cautiously on the bench inside, making sure not to sit on the wet patch at one end or the brown patch at the other. I didn't have my phone and I'd given up smoking ages ago, so had no way to occupy my hands. I was forced to sit with my own thoughts until I calmed down. Why would Tom never stand up for me? What would happen in ten years' time when his uncle was saying that word, making racist jokes to our children? Would he defend *them*, or would they have to grow up being attacked by their own family? I wish there was some sort of interracial dating handbook to consult when these things happened.

I stayed sitting in the shelter until it got dark and I got frightened. I'm not used to this provincial silence; I need sirens and noise from passing cars to make me feel safe.

'I should have handled it better,' I ended up telling myself.

'His uncle is an idiot and a bigot, but he didn't mean it,' I repeated over and over.

Maybe it was better for me to suffer these things in silence. Buses came and went, passengers and passers-by alike looking at me more cautiously the closer to night-time it got. I stood up to walk back to the house, the late-autumn air making me shiver.

'Queenie.'

I peered into the darkness. Tom.

'This is where you are. It smells awful in here,' he said, before taking a deep breath. 'Sorry I got angry before.'

I kept my mouth shut.

'But you can't keep doing this, Queenie.' His tone was disappointed. 'I know that in your family everyone is loud and you solve problems by shouting about them, but my family is different!'

He looked at me as if searching for an apology, before continuing.

'This keeps happening, and I don't know what to do. I can't protect you when it's my family you think you need protecting from.'

Tom ran his hands through his hair dramatically and I rolled my eyes. 'You know what my uncle is like, he's from a generation where they said the n-word *quite* a lot.'

I looked at him and blinked slowly. By now he knew that this meant, 'If you think I'll agree with you, you're wrong.'

'Not that I'm excusing it,' he said quickly, 'but come on, you can't ruin my mum's birthday because of it.'

There was a silence.

'Here you go,' he conceded eventually, handing me my coat and rucksack. 'All your stuff is in there.'

'Thanks.' I felt myself soften at this act of kindness. Plus, easy to forgive someone who is bringing you a coat when you're freezing cold. 'You didn't need to do that,' I said quietly, reaching out for my things. I put my coat on and moved into Tom.

'No,' he said, stepping back.

'What's wrong? Let's forget it. I needed a bit of space, but I've calmed down now. I should apologise to your mum. I feel so bad, that cake was so nice, and the sentimental valu – '

'You should go home,' Tom said firmly, cutting me off mid-ramble. 'You ruined my mum's birthday, Queenie. She's been wiping bits of cream off the walls since you slammed out. I don't want any more drama.'

I felt the anger that had dissipated in the bus shelter rise again.

'Me? Drama? Me?' I spluttered.

'You can get the bus from here to the station, the next train is in an hour,' Tom said, looking over my head. 'I'm going to stay with my family for a few more days.'

'So I'm just meant to go back to the flat alone? You know I can't sleep anywhere by myself!'

'It's constant, with you. It's too much.' Tom said, his voice deepening. 'You're too much, Queenie.'

I opened my mouth to speak but closed it again.

'Hope you get home okay,' he said, turning to walk away.

'Do you know what?' I shouted behind him.

He stopped walking.

'I hope your next girlfriend is white, Tom. That way she won't be too fucking much for you.'

He stood still for a second before continuing on again, disappearing into the darkness.

*

'I'm just going to go to the bathroom,' I said, slipping away from Rich and into James's bedroom, where I sat on the bed to have a minute for myself.

46

I was about to leave when I heard footsteps outside the door. I went to it, opened it slightly and saw Fran at the end of the corridor, trying with clumsy hands to open the front door. James ran past and stopped next to her.

'Fran, for fuck's sake, stop running off!' he hissed.

Were my drunk ears and eyes deceiving me? What could 'couple goals' be arguing about?

'It's okay, you go back in there and carry on chatting to her,' Fran shot back, her unnaturally high-pitched voice piercing the air. 'Why did you invite her? Who invites their ex, the ex they *know* is still in love with them, to the fucking party they throw *with* their girlfriend?'

I knelt on the floor by the door and leaned against a pile of wax jackets to get comfortable. It's not often that you see the perfect pair disintegrate before your eyes.

'Oh, come on, she's got a boyfriend, Fran,' I could hear James plead.

'Does she? Nobody has met him, *James*. And she can't take her eyes off you. And – and I know that you've been checking her Facebook even *though* you hang out with her once every two weeks!' Somehow her voice was getting even higher.

'Just calm down.'

'Don't tell me to calm down! I can't keep doing this, James. It's not just you and Evie. It's me working a full-time job and coming here to iron your shirts and cook your dinner and then you coming home late or not at all! Yet you still won't let me move in! It's the lads' nights taking precedent over *our* nights, or your nights with Evie that you think I don't know about. How could I not? She Instagrams every aspect of her day, and trust me, you get the most flattering filters! Three years we've been together, no sign of marriage, all the signs of you wanting to have me around but not commit. I can't do this.'

I thought she might take off at this point; she was doing a good job of sounding like she'd inhaled helium at the very least.

'Oh Fran, come on,' James snorted. 'I think you've had a bit too much to drink.'

I locked eyes with Fran as she suddenly came towards James's room and pushed the bedroom door open.

'Sorry, I was just looking for my – ' I stuttered.

Fran stepped over me and I got up off my knees.

'I'm going home,' Fran squeaked. ''Night, Queenie. Sorry about Tom, by the way.' She grabbed her bag from James's desk and breezed past me, then James, and slammed out of the front door. I slipped past James as I walked back into the living room.

'It'll be all right, mate,' I said, patting him on the arm.

I tried to get back into the party but could think about nothing but Tom. We'd hurt each other, but that's what couples did, right, they wound each other up. Look at Fran and James! I got my phone out of my pocket and tried to call Tom. No answer. I called again, nothing. Twice more. Nothing. I sat on the sofa as everyone chatted and danced around me. The phone buzzed in my hand.

Tom:

Clean break, Queenie.

I read Tom's text through blurring eyes. I missed him so much that my chest started to ache. Did he not miss me? How could he just ignore my calls? I snuck away and stood outside the house, about to order an Uber. The cold air sobered me.

'Shall we?'

An arm wrapped around my waist as Rich slotted himself against me presumptuously. I didn't want to go back to my new house alone, but as I looked into the unkind eyes of Rich and remembered how I felt when I first locked eyes with Tom, I knew that I didn't want to go home with *him*.

I got my phone out to call Tom again. He still wouldn't pick up.

What would make me feel better? I thought.

Nothing.

What would make me feel happy? I asked myself.

Tom was the answer. But if Tom wasn't answering, what would distract me until he did?

Queenie:

Adi, can you meet me outside some luxury apartments in Fulham? We can go for that drive you're always on about

I tried my luck. It was two in the morning. I'd give him five minutes and then I'd get an Uber.

Adi:

You serious?

He replied before I could put my phone in my coat pocket.

Queenie:

Sure. Why not?

49

Adi:
For real? You're not tricking man?

Queenie:
I'm about to change my mind, I'm cold

Adi:
Okay okay, what about your white boy, is he there? He can watch me at work innit, man will show him how it's done

Queenie:
We're on a break

Adi:
For real?

Adi:
Lol

Adi:
No such thing as a break

Queenie:
Are you coming or not?

Adi:

Queenie, if I'm gonna hit it, man needs to come into the yard. A bum like yours needs room for manoeuvre, you get me? No space in a car for you, TRUST me

Queenie:

Just moved house, everything is in boxes. No bed. Also so much of that is offensive

Adi:

Alrite, alrite, don't start. I'll come get you. Text me the address

Twenty minutes later I was back in the passenger seat of Adi's flash black BMW, the seat reclined completely backwards because 'These ends are hot and I don't want anyone to see that I'm driving some girl who isn't my missus.'

I lay back, the nasality of Drake's voice making me vibrate on my makeshift bed.

'Where are we going?' I asked, in the absence of being able to see for myself. The adrenaline that was flooding my system had cancelled out any trace of alcohol.

'Don't worry, innit, just relax,' Adi said, digging a hand into my thigh and flashing me a smile that was, genuinely, somewhere on the way to charming. I dissociated by thinking about how his teeth are so white. He must put a lot of money into keeping them that way; I know how much he smokes.

As Adi drove, unease started to rise in me. What was I about to do? Was sex okay, given the whole gynaecological situation? I wished the doctor had given me just a little more information. The car slowed down.

'Can I sit up now?' I asked, sitting up anyway. 'I'm starting to feel queasy.'

I looked around as Adi parked up. When he turned the headlights off and my eyes had adjusted to the dark, I saw that we were in some sort of warehouse car park.

'Do you come here often?' I asked, to no response. Clearly Adi didn't think I was very funny.

'I want you to take your thong off, innit,' he said, wasting no time.

I pulled my dress up and put my thumbs in the sides of my knickers, ready to pull them down.

'Why are you wearing full knickers? I like my girls in thongs.'

'You can just drive me back home if you want,' I suggested, pulling my dress back down.

'Nah, don't be so hasty! Man was just saying, innit.'

I pulled my knickers off and, in trying to be sexy, got them tangled at my ankles before I put them in the glovebox.

'All right, so now I want you to just turn round and face the back,' Adi told me.

'What, like get in the back of the car?' I asked.

'Nah, just turn in the passenger seat and pull your dress up so I can look at your bottom.'

'What? Why?' I still wasn't getting what he was asking.

'Cause I love black girls' *bums,* innit, Queenie. *Das* why. My wife, yeah, she's got a pretty face but she's skinny. No bum.'

He manoeuvred me into the position he wanted and I did as I was told because, frankly, it was easier to just do, than to think.

If I thought about what I was doing, I'd have to think about why I was doing it, and I wasn't prepared for that at this moment.

'Can you turn the heating up?' I asked. 'It's a bit chilly.'

'Shhh,' Adi whispered, smacking my bottom once.

I winced as I stared out of the back window, trying to direct my attention to something completely removed from the car. I focused on a streetlight in the distance.

He smacked my bottom again. 'You like that, yeah?'

I glanced at Adi and he flashed the charming smile again. I looked at the streetlight.

'Yep,' I said.

'Nice, nice.' He smacked me again and this time kissed the area. It stung as his facial hair grazed the skin.

'Do you want to see my tings? I'm hard.' Adi gestured to his crotch.

'Your . . .?'

'My tings, my dick, innit.' He smiled.

'No, I know what you mean when you say "your tings", but why are you asking? I assumed that at some point in the evening I would see everything, you don't need to ask.' I laughed.

'You've always got to make man feel dumb, innit? I didn't go uni and I don't talk all posh like you but I'm not a idiot,' Adi grumbled.

'No, no, I'm not, sorry, go on. I didn't mean to. Please, Adi. Let me see your "tings".'

'All right.' He smiled, his angry pride retreating. 'That's more like it.'

His hands shook as he unzipped his jeans and pulled them down, along with his long johns. It was cold, but not cold enough for so many layers. When he got himself naked from the waist down, he very proudly presented me with his 'tings'.

Circumcised. Along with having sex with men in cars, another first for me.

'What do you think?' Adi asked, flashing a nervous grin.

'Of your penis?' I asked, politely.

'Yeah, of my tings, innit.' He shrugged.

'Nice?' I ventured. What was the right answer here?

'Is it *big,* though?' Adi questioned, almost agitated that I wasn't showering his manhood with praise.

'Why does that matter? That shouldn't matter.'

'So what you saying, that it's small?!'

My eyes must spend at least fifty per cent of any given day rolled to the back of my head.

'No, Adi. It's huge. The hugest I have ever *seen* in my little life. How will it fit?' I said flatly.

'Yeah, *that's* it, that's what I'm talking about.' Adi bounced in his seat excitedly. 'Do you want to touch it?'

I placed my hand around it and, as I started to move my hand rhythmically, was struck by how odd a dick feels when it's exactly that: an anatomical penis from a science book, and not the familiar and less hostile penis of the person that you love.

*

'Queenie, wake up!'

'I'm up!' I said, 'I'm up. What's going on? Where am I?'

Light from Tom's lamp filled the room.

'You're okay. We're at mine,' Tom said, stroking my arm. 'I think you were having a nightmare.'

'Oh god, I'm so sorry.' I groaned and turned away from him, embarrassed.

'I thought the house was being robbed – you landed a punch right on my jaw and started shouting at me.'

'What was I saying?' I asked quickly, looking at him.

'Nothing I could work out,' Tom said, touching his jaw tenderly. Relief filled me.

'I'm so sorry,' I said, rubbing my eyes. 'I meant to warn you, but we must have fallen straight to sleep.'

'*You* fell straight to sleep, you were hammered,' Tom said, handing me a glass of water.

I sat up and downed it. 'I should have warned you I was a cheap date, too.'

'Two glasses of wine. *Two*.'

'I hadn't eaten!' I handed the empty glass back.

'Are you sure you're all right?' Tom asked, wrapping his arms around me and covering us with the duvet in one move.

'Are *you*? Sorry for the punch.' I wriggled around so that we faced each other.

'Nothing I don't deserve.'

'I can't guarantee that it won't happen again,' I said quietly. 'It's a "thing".'

'That's all right. Everyone's got a thing,' Tom said, kissing my forehead.

'Yeah, but my thing could have knocked you out.'

'I think you're overestimating your strength, Queenie.' He laughed again.

'Maybe I can kiss it better?' I kissed Tom softly on the jaw. 'That feels better.'

'Okay, I'll stop,' I said, closing my eyes.

'No, no, it's actually really hurting again, I think you need to keep doing that,' Tom said, sticking his jaw out.

I went to kiss his jaw again and he moved so that our

mouths connected. As we kissed he moved again so that he was on top of me.

'Hold on, Tom, you're leaning on my hair,' I said, trying to pull my head free.

'Shit, sorry!' Tom said, lifting his arm up. 'Are you okay?'

I nodded and smiled up at him. We kissed again, me enjoying his weight on top of me. I felt safe underneath him.

'How easily do these things come out?' Tom stopped to ask, lifting a handful of my twists from the pillow.

'They're not going to fall out!' I laughed. 'But I don't know how wet I'm going to get with a headache.'

'Okay. Maybe you should tie it up.'

Tom lay back and watched as I stood up and ran over to my rucksack. I reached inside for a hairband and ran back over to the bed, climbing under the covers.

'Could you not just stare at me like that, please? This is the first time you've seen me naked and I'm going to worry that you're looking at all of my bad bits,' I said, turning away from him.

'What? You don't have any bad bits,' Tom said, sitting up and kissing my shoulder.

'I am made up of bad bits, actually,' I told him as I wrapped my hair in a bun and tied it on top of my head. 'I'm actually one whole bad bit.'

'Nonsense,' he laughed, pulling me on top of him. I could feel his erection through his boxers. 'I've been observing closely. There's nothing bad about you.'

'Oh! Who's this?' I asked, moving my hand down.

'I could make a joke about naming my penis, but now isn't really the time, is it?'

'Tom,' I said. 'There is honestly never a time for that.'

*

'I call him "The Destroyer",' Adi said, confidently. 'And The Destroyer wants to be inside that mouth.' He winked.

'Sorry, no,' I smiled back.

I'm *very* particular about that sort of thing. Interestingly, my gag reflex is fine, it's more the sexual power play that I think about.

'Ah, come on, I beg you, suck it,' Adi said, frowning.

'It's not going to happen, I'm afraid.'

'Will you kiss it, then?'

'Will I kiss your penis? No, I won't.'

I only wanted a bit of sex to tide me over, not all of this back and forth.

'Just a peck, I beg you,' Adi pouted.

'. . . I don't know what to tell you, sorry.'

'Just lick it one time.'

'Nope.'

'All right, spit on it then.'

'I just feel like, the more you ask me these things, the more you're going to get annoyed. So I would stop there.'

'All right, all right, jeez. You black girls are so up yourselves, innit.' Adi sighed. 'If I'm not getting my dick sucked, shall we move to the back?'

Is that the automotive alternative to moving to the bedroom? Wanting to get things over and done with, I squeezed myself between the driver and passenger seats with no grace and pulled my dress over my head.

Adi joined me and beckoned me onto his lap. He grunted with satisfaction as I lowered myself onto him and pressed my chest onto his, resting my chin on his shoulder.

I didn't want to kiss him. That would be too intimate. I moved up and down rhythmically, slowly, measured, listening to Adi's moans. I kept the streetlight in my sights the whole time. I'm not sure that I blinked once.

*

'Have you ever had sex in a car before?' I stuck my head out of the door of the neon-lit staff kitchen before I said anything else.

'What?' Darcy asked.

I rinsed my *Daily Read*-branded mug under the boiling water tap and threw a teabag into it.

'A car,' I repeated, opening the high-tech chrome fridge and taking the milk out.

'No. Have you?' Darcy took the milk from me and poured it into her mug, directly onto the teabag. As always, I turned my nose up at her technique.

'After the party,' I said, shame flooding my body.

'With the Uber driver?' Darcy asked, slamming her mug onto the counter. 'Queenie!'

'What?' I snorted. 'No? Obviously not?'

We finished making our tea and scuttled into the meeting room next door. All of the rooms in the building had glass walls, so we laid out some pens and papers and a rogue iPad so it looked like we were talking about work.

'Not with my Uber driver, with Adi,' I told her, watching people moving around in the street below.

'Are you serious? That sleazy guy who's always asking about the size of your bum?' Darcy asked, mouth agape.

'I know, but I was just feeling so lonely and shit after that party, so I sent him a text not really thinking that he'd respond, but he did, and now I feel so bad.'

'Because of Tom? Well, you are on a break, so what you do in this period doesn't matter.'

'Partly because of that, but mainly because it's not me! I don't do this sort of thing!' I yelped.

'Well, look. You're going through something confusing, so you're allowed to do some out-of-character stuff,' Darcy reassured me. 'And you know I would never judge you, but I hope you were at least careful?'

'We were careful,' I lied. I opened my mouth to speak again, knowing that I should probably tell her about the miscarriage. 'No sleazy babies on the way.'

A day of very minimal work passed, and I stayed late to avoid going back to the house I still wasn't anywhere near settled in. On the bus home, dodging waves of guilt after my car encounter, I stared at mine and Tom's message chain, willing him to reply. Nothing since his clean break reinforcement on Saturday night. My phone buzzed in my hand, but after checking my texts and WhatsApp and email, I couldn't figure out why. I scrolled across screens and saw an app with a heart icon, a red notification dot in the right-hand corner. It was the OkCupid app that the party girls had installed on my phone. I took a deep breath and opened it up cautiously, having no idea what it would contain.

> Nice pics. How big would your tits be in my hands? **From This_ Guy_Fucks**

Is this how it's going to go? I am a young woman, with a good job and fairly nice pictures and the first message is about my breasts?

> I like the one of you laughing.
> What else does that mouth do?

And the second message is about my mouth, fantastic.

> Chocolate girl ;)

Oh and some classic fetishing. This was a really, really good start.

> Nice curves, I like bigger girls.
> Some of my favourite porn is
> BBW

Do women respond to that positively, I wonder?

> I want to go out with you,
> chocolate girl. How about it

Another chocolate reference, this time from 'Sexy69', whose age range of preference was a very discerning 18 to 99.

*

When I got back to the house, I skimmed the OkCupid messages again. Is this what my life without Tom could be? Men in their droves calling me confectionery? Even with his neuroses and his love of logic and his racist family, at least with him I knew where I was with him. At least he cared about me, and at least with him I didn't have to delete all of this thinly veiled sexual harassment. What could I do to get Tom to love me again? Was time really all we needed? With a big heavy groan, I got ready for bed. I had to go to the hospital in the morning to make sure everything had 'passed smoothly'. I wish I could tell someone about it, but, as with other parts of my life I'd rather bury, better to just keep it moving.

*

The hospital was fine. Apparently all of the 'foetal tissue has gone, lovely', but because some of the pain had come back after having sex with Adi I needed antibiotics to ward off potential infection. The sex wasn't even worth it. Should I tell Tom about any of this? *Not* the stuff about Adi. I guess he should know about the miscarriage, because it's part of him? Is that too romantic a thought? Anyway, surely clean break rules don't apply when you add a miscarriage to the equation. I sent him a text on the way back to the office.

> **Queenie:**
> Hello, Tom. Could you give me a call? It's kind of urgent.

I went back to work clutching the new round of antibiotics and for the rest of the day was a mix of fifty per cent public smiling and fifty per cent talking to myself, listing reasons why Tom should know that I'd had a miscarriage. Tweed Glasses saw me pacing in the smoking area and walked past, paused in front of me as if to say something, but then carried on walking. Maybe he was going to have a go about me stepping on his shoes a few of weeks ago; they *did* look really fancy.

I put my phone in my desk drawer in an attempt to get even the simplest of tasks done, and when I got it out four hours later, no missed calls from Tom. Not even a text. That answered my question. He doesn't deserve to know about the miscarriage, I thought, angrily.

Still not able to focus on any work but feeling less shame about Adi, I checked OkCupid. I'd filled in my profile and had added some things in the 'About Me' section that might remind men that I was a person as well as someone they could have sex with. Turns out the sadness that silence from the person you love brings can be temporarily erased by the dull thrill of attention from strangers.

Good profile. How's it going? Just putting it out there but I know exactly how to handle a girl with a body like yours. I might not be black but trust me, you wouldn't know it from my dick.

. . . albeit mainly negative.

Chapter Four

I sent a text to Kyazike. The first friend I made on the first day of our secondary school when we found each other amongst a sea of white faces. We all had nametags and she blew my tiny westernised mind when she told me that her name was pronounced 'chess-keh'. She continues to blow my mind.

Queenie:
Kyazike, what are you up to?

Kyazike:
Nothing. Just chilling. U?

Queenie:
Just sitting in bed, being sad

Kyazike:
Come thru

I was on my way there when my phone started to buzz with requests. She hadn't changed since school.

Kyazike:
Can you bring me a Ribena

Kyazike:
And a packet of Thai sweet
chicken McCoys, it's cheat day

Kyazike:
A Twix

Kyazike:
NOT Ribena, changed my mind.
Any Rubicon

I walked through Kyazike's estate and arrived at her block, a high-rise within a cluster of buildings just like it, blue plastic bag in hand. When I stepped into the elevator I stood as close as I could to its stained mirror and pulled at the bags under my eyes. When had they got here? When I got to the eighteenth floor, I knocked and waited outside Kyazike's front door. Rapped it again. Nothing.

I put my hand through the iron security bars that covered the entrance and knocked three times. Kyazike wrenched the front door open so quickly a blast of food-scented air blew my hair from my face.

'Why you banging the door like police, fam?'

I rolled my eyes as she unlocked the iron grill and stepped back as she swung it open.

'What's good?' she asked, hugging me.

I think I held on a bit too long.

'Ah, fam. You struggling?'

'The struggle is very real, as my cousin Diana says.' I took my shoes off and crept into the living room. 'Have I said it right?'

I heard Kyazike laughing behind me as she closed the grill.

'Why you creeping? My mum's not here, she's on nights this week.' Kyazike carried on laughing as she followed me.

'Force of habit. How is she?' I carried on creeping into the turquoise living room and lay face down on the cream leather sofa, burying my face into similarly coloured cushions that were covered in smears of dark brown foundation.

'Tired, fam. They've got her working nights in the nursing home in Camberwell, then she has to go straight to her day job at the Maudsley.'

'And when exactly does she sleep?' I turned my head to look at Kyazike and was faced with a television that filled the whole wall across from me.

'She gets to nap, I think, when the old people are sleeping, but like, she doesn't actually *sleep* sleep, if you get me. Cause she's on call. But she's been doing this for years, so she's used to it. How's your – ' Kyazike hesitated.

'How's what?'

'Sorry. I was about to ask how your mum was.'

'I'm sure she's fine. Probably still trying to grow a spine,' I growled, my mood plummeting fast.

'Is she, er . . . she still in that hostel?' The only time Kyazike went into any conversation with trepidation was when she asked about my mum.

'I don't know,' I told her firmly, wanting to shut the conversation down. 'Last thing I heard was whisperings about a court case.'

'Mad ting. Anyway, let me tell you about this date I went on,' Kyazike said, desperate to lift the mood. 'Have you got the stuff?'

'When you say "stuff", do you mean the snacks?' I said, chucking the bag over to her. 'I'm not your dealer.'

Kyazike reached in for the crisps and started munching on them. 'Fam, let me tell you. I was at work the other day, and – oh! I beg you, do me a favour.' She jumped up and left the room.

I picked up the remote and turned on the sixty-inch TV. The brightness nearly blew my eyes out.

'New TV big enough?' I called out.

Kyazike walked back into the living room. 'It's not like we're gonna be able to buy a house in London, is it? We're in this council flat for life, fam. You think my mum can get a mortgage? And African family rules say I'm not leaving until *I've* got a mortgage, and we all know that ain't happening. Might as well spend our money on things that will make us happy.'

'Yeah, or things that will make you blind,' I said. 'It's as big as the room.'

'I beg you, take my weave out?' Kyazike handed me a razor blade. 'It's long overdue, and my hairdresser will charge me just to unpick the string.'

'Have you got any Blu Tack?' I asked, holding the blade carefully between the nails on my thumb and forefinger.

'What for?' she asked, confused.

'If I squash the blade in some Blu Tack it won't slice my fingers when I hold it,' I said, knowingly. 'I've learned from my mistakes. I'm evolving.'

Kyazike went over to a shelving unit and lifted the Ugandan flag that hid various partitions holding various things. She rummaged around.

'There you go.' She threw a packet at me and sat on the laminate floor between my legs. I got to work on the weave as Kyazike flicked through music channels and settled on MTV Base, our historic favourite.

'Right, so listen; yeah . . .' she began.

As the most beautiful person I've ever laid eyes on, and with a consumer-facing job, Kyazike got asked out on a daily basis. More frequently than daily. By the hour. Her dark skin was the richest, softest I'd ever felt; her dark, sharp eyes were framed by fake eyelashes that enhanced their shape, and the rest of her features, so well defined and delicate, made her look like she had royal ancestry.

Her relaxed hair had been short since secondary school, but these days she preferred to buy 'sixteen- eighteen- or twenty inch Brazilian weave at £350 a pop'. She, and the men who frequently slid into her DMs, described her body as 'thick'; ultimately, she was a black girl body goals. Long, delicate, slim arms and legs; a tiny waist; big, firm breasts that sat high on her chest and a firm, round bum that didn't jiggle like mine when she walked.

'It's that gym life, Queenie,' she'd say every time she caught me silently comparing my heavy limbs and soft stomach. 'You can tone up. Anyway, body ain't everything.'

'. . . So I must have been serving some *any* woman who's counting out her pennies, and I look in the queue behind her and the buffest guy *ever* is standing there waiting,' Kyazike started energetically. 'I'm trying to get this woman to hurry up in case he goes to Sandra next to me but she's taking *tiiime* so I tell her that my computer has frozen and she needs to go to the next window.'

She paused to chomp on her McCoys.

'So anyway the guy comes to my bay. He's so buff, he's light-skin, he's got these hazel eyes and his hair? Waves, fam, like the *ocean*. The eye contact is *strong* and he's biting his lip when he's chatting to me so I know he's feeling me. But *then*

I check his accounts: minus £400 in his current, six grand in debt on his credit card. Queenie, I just bid him a good day and let him pass.'

I stopped hacking at the thick string holding the weave in place. 'But this could have been "the one", Kyazike. What if you fell in love? You could have financially guided hi – '

' – financially guided who? Excuse me, Queenie, I cannot be with someone in that much debt. I have a lifestyle that needs sustaining. My Mr Right cannot have minus money.'

'All right, all right, sorry.' I carried on with my task, putting the razor blade down and trying to disentangle the string with my fingers.

'So. Behind *him* is some small guy. Looks Ghanaian. He's aight.' Kyazike shrugged. It didn't matter that I was looking at the back of her head, her body language was as expressive as her face. 'Not as buff as my man before him, but still, he's passable. Anyway I check *his* account, and my man has *p's*. I'm talking six figures, fam. *No* credit cards, no minuses in sight. So we chat, and he slips me his card, tells me to call him. I look at it, he's called Sean, I see that he works in finance, cool, but told him that *I* don't call guys, *they* call *me*. You know what I'm saying?'

I would never have the self-esteem to know what she was saying.

'I wrote my number on the back of his card and handed it to him. That night, he calls me, telling me he's going to take me out, treat me like a princess, telling me how he knows what a girl like me deserves, and how he's going to give it to me, all that. So I'm like, aight, cool – can you pass me a cushion?'

I passed Kyazike a cushion and waited as she slid it under her bum.

68

'So we arrange to go out on Sunday just gone. Are you still with me?'

'Yep. Just got to concentrate on this bit, it's a bit tricksy,' I said, peering into the maze of canerows, black string and weave.

'Don't cut my hair, you know. I don't have much after the relaxer's burned it out,' Kyazike warned me. 'Okay so, before the date, I text Sean and I ask him where we're going. He tells me it's a surprise, so I'm like okay, fine, but I need to know so that I'm properly dressed, innit. He still doesn't tell me so I think, okay, it must be a surprise. He must want to take me somewhere *fancy*. He tells me he's coming at four so I get in the bath at one, I soak myself in oils and that so I'm smelling all nice, I straighten my hair, give it a little twist at the ends with the curlers and *listen*, my make-up is *on point*, Queenie. Now remember this guy has *money*, so I slip into my black Balmain dress *and* I wear the Louboutin thigh-high boots. I'm not ramping with him, you know.'

She paused to eat some more crisps.

'So I'm sat there ready and waiting at four, where is he, please? Not here. I'm giving him *five* more minutes until I go and take my make-up off. He turns up at three minutes past. Wasting my time.' Kyazike kissed her teeth. 'He texts me to say he's in the car, waiting outside. Lemme just go wee.'

Kyazike stood up, putting all of her weight on my thighs as she did. She stretched her legs, and hobbled to the bathroom.

I splayed my fingers and winced as the joints clicked. Kyazike returned and nestled between my knees again.

'So where was I?'

She opened her Twix, elegant fingers tipped with white acrylic nails, and took a bite.

'I get downstairs, and when I open the door and spot his BMW I just stand for a couple minutes so he can take in how *amazing* I'm looking.'

She paused for me to really take in how amazing she might have looked.

'Sean gets out the car and *I* clock that he's just in a T-shirt, jeans and trainers. From *then* I'm *vex*. He opens the door for me, and I slide in. When he gets in the driver side I cross my left leg to make sure he can see the red sole. He sees. He tells me I look "nice", and he starts driving. Remember I told you he wouldn't tell me where this date was? Well. When he gets to the turning, I'm expecting he's going to buss a left, towards West End. So let me know why this man is going right, please?' Kyazike asked, her head turning to ask an imaginary audience.

'But look, I don't say anything, I just bite my lip and I keep quiet. I thought, okay, maybe he has a surprise for me, and I don't want to spoil it. *Queenie*, the next thing I knew, we were parking up in Crystal Palace, fam! And no offence to Crystal Palace, but is my outfit a Crystal Palace outfit? *No*. So he gets out and starts walking, and from then I'm not saying anything to him, I'm vex. We get to some Thai restaurant and he stops and I just stand there and look at him because I can't believe this is where he's taken me.

'Listen, Queenie. I'm not saying that I'm too good for Thai, but this is where you come on a Friday night when you've been in a relationship for two-plus *years*, not where you take someone on a first date. But I just thought to myself, let's see what this guy is about. So we walk in. The lady comes over and asks if we've made a reservation. Hear Sean, "Table for two under the name Kyazike, please." *I'm sorry?* Is that even legal? How can *you* be booking to take *me* on a date and you're telling the people *my* government name?' She rolled her eyes. 'Anyway, I take a deep breath and I just think, it's calm, keep going. We walk through the restaurant and *everyone* is looking at me in my outfit, wondering what I'm doing there. We sit down at the table and start talking. Queenie. I feel a draught and look up next to me – why is there a hole in the wall being half-filled by a piece of wood? Is this guy *mad*? Is this really where he's bringing me?'

By this point I had to put the razor blade down because I was laughing so much that I was scared I'd do one of us damage.

'Oh, but he can't help it! And maybe the food was really nice?' I offered weakly.

'Queenie, I ask him if we can move tables. He calls the waitress over and *this time* they take us to a table on the other side of the restaurant by some stairs to the basement. They put Sean in a seat that's about one centimetre away from the top step and he asks *me* if he can swap seats. In *my* heels he wants me to sit at the top of the stairs so *I'm* the one who can fall and break my neck? I tell him to stay where he is.'

I was lying on the sofa by then, shaking with laughter, even though I'd sworn I wouldn't be able to smile again.

'It's not funny, fam, this is my life!' Kyazike shouted. 'So listen, it's not over yet. We eat dinner, the food is average. He manages not to fall down the stairs, even though it might have been better if he had. The waitress comes over to ask if we want dessert and he says no, because he has a special surprise for me. Do you know what his surprise is, Queenie?'

'What is it?' I asked cautiously. 'Do I want to know?'

'He wants to take me to a golfing range.'

She turns around to face me.

'In. This. Dress. In. These. Heels.' Kyazike claps her hands with each word.

'Queenie, when I tell him that I'm not stepping onto a golf course in five-point-five inch Louboutins, do you know what he says?'

I was laughing so much that trying to breathe was futile, so I mouthed, 'What?'

'He says he'll take me to Tesco Express to get some trainers. Fam, *which* branch of Tesco Express sells trainers? I told him to express me home.'

Though Kyazike's date wasn't especially aspirational, it certainly is inspirational. Without using the term 'putting myself out there', if I go on some actual dates of my own in this stopgap between mine and Tom's reunion, maybe I'll stop thinking about how heartbreak might actually kill me. That night before bed, I checked OkCupid yet again.

'So don't forget to wash your sheets . . . And your penis'

Hold on, this one is quoting *Spaced*, which means that he's actually taken a full three seconds to read what my favourite TV shows are. I replied, and after swiftly arranging to go for a drink the next day, I went to sleep clutching a T-shirt of Tom's that I'd stolen from the wash basket, breathing in the scent that I was determined to smell again on him.

Chapter Five

In the pub, people spoke excitedly and glasses clattered noisily.

'My last girlfriend was black.'

I looked at my date and blinked, sure I'd misheard him.

'Sorry?' I asked, leaning across the table.

'My last girlfriend was black,' he repeated, not a trace of irony in his voice.

'That's nice. Was she a nice person?' I asked, taking a very large gulp of my wine. I was still on antibiotics and this red was not going down well.

'She was crazy,' he said, shaking his round head as alarm bells and red flags popped into mine. My date was almost as wide as he was tall, with a huge big belly straining under his T-shirt. Blond curls framed his big, rosy cheeks. In essence, he was a giant cherub. He didn't look like a giant cherub in any of his OkCupid photos, obviously.

I made eye contact with a girl across the room who also appeared to be on a first date. We smiled at each other in solidarity.

'Maybe we should go to the smoking area?' I suggested. 'Get some air?'

'Or we could go back to mine?' he shrugged. 'I'm up for it.'

It just didn't *feel* like courtship to me. Maybe I was too old-fashioned in my thinking? I feigned illness and got the bus home. I must have jinxed myself because on the way back I did start to feel ill. My head felt heavy and my stomach churned. I went to text

Tom but stopped myself. If a clean break was what he needed to remind him that he loved me, it's what I should give him. Instead, I began to type a message to the group chat I'd formed with absolutely no permission from the people I'd put in it. Darcy, Kyazike and Cassandra, three long-time friends who knew most of my secrets. I had no business throwing them all together in this digital pen, but it saved me having to copy and paste my thoughts and feelings from one to the other. They'd taken to it quite well, actually.

Queenie:
I'm on my way home from the date. It was awful. He looked like a giant cherub

Queenie:
But that's not why it was bad, because big is beautiful as we know, but he didn't look like that in his pictures! The date was bad because he was awful

Darcy:
Awful how?

Queenie:
He dropped that his ex-girlfriend was black

Kyazike:
Looool

Queenie:
And 'crazy'

Cassandra:
He actually said 'crazy'? Or are you paraphrasing?

Kyazike:
Why did you even go, fam

Queenie:
Something to do while Tom has his space?

Cassandra:
I would argue that there are better diversion techniques.

Darcy:
At least it reminded you that Tom is the one for you?

QUEENIE CHANGED THE GROUP NAME TO 'THE CORGIS'

Cassandra:
What's this?

Queenie:
What do you mean?

Cassandra:
Corgis. Obviously.

Queenie:
The Queen loves her corgis

Queenie:
And they support her

Queenie:
Like you're all doing now

Cassandra:
And you're the Queen in this?

Queenie:
Of course

Cassandra:
I think we all know that the monarchy is obsolete.

Darcy:
I think it's quite sweet

Queenie:
Cassandra it's just a play on words, relax. Unless there are any objections from you, @Kyazike?

Kyazike:

Nah, it's calm. Do what you're
doin, innit

*

'Do you know what, Darcy?' I said the Monday after a Halloween party at the weekend that was mostly an emotional blur. 'I'm going to make some promises to myself, and uphold them.' I recalled my decision to avoid all men, that I'd made after my disaster date with the giant cherub a few days before.

'What you mean?' Darcy asked.

'Number one, work harder,' I said, beginning to recite the list I'd saved in my phone. 'I've let work slip so much lately, and there are serious things going on in the world that need reporting and *The Daily Read* don't seem to be doing it.'

'Like what?' Darcy asked.

'Um, like, the killings of unarmed black men and women in their droves at the hands of police, here and in the US. Mass gentrification. Modern-day slavery? *Obviously*?'

'I don't see anything about that, really.'

'Yeah, of course you don't, Darcy. I was thinking that I could start pitching ideas to Gina?'

'That's a good start.' Darcy was nodding heavily, her hair falling around her face.

'I worked really hard to get this job, really fucking hard, and I feel like I'm spunking it all away,' I said.

'It's too early to use the term "spunking",' Darcy sighed, putting her head in her hands.

'Number two, maybe slow down with OkCupid,' I said, ignoring Darcy's disdain. 'I'm getting a bit obsessed with the digital attention. About five boys I haven't met are already giving me their life stories. And when Tom has finally had his space and comes back to me, even though I won't *tell* him about dates I've been on, I don't *really* want to have spent the *whole* time sleeping with boys in cars and meeting crap men who do a good job of occupying my brain space but will ultimately diminish my self-worth.'

'You could delete the app?' Darcy offered.

'No, too far,' I said, shaking my head. 'At this point, I have to wean myself off it. Three. Spend more time with family.' I held three fingers up and waggled the third. 'Four, just forget men for a while, and use this break with Tom as a break from men. And five, don't go home with boys after parties when it turns out the drunken jokes they were whispering in your ear about spaffing on your chest is genuinely all they want to do – '

'Queenie,' Darcy cut in sternly. 'I know that we always do tea and talking on a Monday morning but recently it's getting a bit too x-rated for the time of day.'

'Fran's Halloween party really was a night of extreme variables,' I sighed slowly.

'Men like to do that to you, don't they? It must be because of those.' She pointed at my chest.

'Doesn't Simon do it?' I asked, sipping my tea.

'God no, he wouldn't. Even if he wanted to, I don't think my boobs are big enough to be sexy for that.' Darcy looked down at her own chest.

'But what *is* sexy about that? And why are they so proud of doing it?' I wondered aloud.

The kitchen door opened and Silent Jean shuffled in. She stared at both of us in turn as she made a cup of coffee slowly and silently. When she finally left the kitchen, she shot me a suspicious look as she closed the door behind her.

'Did you have fun, despite the . . .?' Darcy asked, gesturing at my chest again. 'I was looking after Simon for the half an hour we were there. He got so smashed that I had to take him home.' Darcy hoisted herself up onto the kitchen counter. 'He always gets too into his own head about being the oldest one at these things, so drinks himself into oblivion.' She crossed her legs and shook her foot agitatedly.

'Before you left, Simon found the time to take me aside in an annoyingly forty-year-old and patronising way to tell me that you were worried about me, or something,' I told Darcy, hoping that he'd been making it up.

'Well, Queenie, I am worried about you. But we can talk about it later, I need to go and pick our summer interns.' Darcy squeezed my shoulder and left the kitchen.

'*I'm* worried about me,' I said to the empty kitchen.

Later, while Gina was moaning (something about her children not wanting to go to boarding school, so acting up by bullying the nanny), my stomach started to hurt, and my vision began to blur at the edges. I excused myself and went outside for some air. A security guard found me crouching by the entrance so asked me to move along to the designated outside space, pointing towards the smoking area. I stumbled over and leaned against a wall. I felt myself sliding down it slowly but didn't have the strength to stop myself from falling to the floor. I opened my eyes when I felt someone grab onto me with both hands.

'Are you okay?' A man holding me firmly at arm's length asked me.

It took me a few seconds to realise who he was.

'Tweed Glasses,' I mumbled. 'Sorry about your shoes.'

'I beg your pardon?' he asked. I hadn't expected his voice to be so deep.

'Nothing,' I said, looking up at him as everything stopped swirling so violently. He wasn't actually wearing his glasses, and looked down at me with bright green eyes dotted with flecks of amber.

'Don't apologise.' He smiled, and his eyes crinkled.

'Okay.'

It was so nice to be physically supported by someone.

'Right, if I let you go, are you going to hit the floor?' he asked, gently.

'I think I'll be okay,' I said, the feeling coming back to my legs. He let go and stood back, his hands hovering by my sides.

He was taller than I'd realised. I went to do the doe-eyed looking up and blinking to appear more attractive, but I didn't have the energy.

'Well, at least you aren't ruining my shoes this time.' He laughed.

'God, you actually remember that?'

'Yeah, I had to go home and give them a polish.'

'Sorry, I was having a bit of a day. Boy troubles. Nasty business.' The memory of that week flooded my head and I reached for my stomach, hoping I wasn't about to hit the deck again.

'Okay, let me get you back upstairs,' he said. 'You sit in the Culture section, right?'

I nodded a yes and let him steer me through the building and back to my desk.

'Thank you,' I said to him, sincerely. 'I think I should just make a sweet tea or something, I think my blood sugar is off.'

Tweed Glasses wrote his email address down on my notepad and made me promise to email him when I was feeling better, 'So that I know if I should switch careers to be your day nurse.'

On Monday, 1 November, Jenkins, Queenie <Queenie. Jenkins@dailyread.co.uk> wrote at 16:02:

I've managed to make it through the afternoon without falling on any of my colleagues. Thank you again for earlier!

On Monday, 1 November, Noman, Ted <Ted.Noman@ dailyread.co.uk> wrote at 16:10:

The pleasure was all mine. It's been a long time since a pretty girl fell for me. I could get used to it.

On Monday, 1 November, Jenkins, Queenie <Queenie. Jenkins@dailyread.co.uk> wrote at 16:17:

Woah. Very corny response, Ted. I take it back.

What was going on here, then? Was this flirting? Why would he want to flirt with someone who looked half-dead and had acted as such by quite literally falling to the floor?

On Monday, 1 November, Noman, Ted <Ted.Noman@ dailyread.co.uk> wrote at 16:25:

You can't blame a man for trying, Queenie. I finally get to talk to the girl I've been tracking around the building for weeks and I lose my cool . . . Forgive me.

On Monday, 1 November, Noman, Ted <Ted.Noman@ dailyread.co.uk> wrote at 16:30:

Nice name, by the way. Suits you . . .

I recalled promises one and four that I'd made to myself that morning. Focus on work, and no men. I took a sip of sweet tea and worked on some pitch ideas for Gina. I'd wanted this job so that I could be a force for change and for representation, but so far all I'd done was file listings and check copy.

*

A few days later, no more fainting, but I'd exhausted myself by arranging for my best friend tier to go to a firework display. The thinking behind it was that friend activities might make me feel a bit more myself, but so far I was feeling more social secretary and mediator than anything. Darcy, Cassandra and Kyazike have all individually surpassed themselves when it comes to support recently, mainly just by allowing me to text and text and text, though I was beginning to worry that it was all a bit of a Queenie show at the moment. I don't want my friends to think they exist purely to listen to me talk about how much of a joke my life is.

THE CORGIS

Kyazike:
Is it gonna b cold

Cassandra:
Well it's November, so
probably.

Kyazike:
Kmt you know what I mean. Is it gonna b cold for November

Cassandra:
Shall I rework what I said? Probably, yes.

Darcy:
It's going to be 4 degrees! So we should all wrap up! I've got a spare pair of gloves if you need them, Kyazike

Kyazike:
Lol you're all right

Cassandra:
Well there's no point in refusing something you need.

Kyazike:
I don't need them, I'm asking if it's gonna b cold

Darcy:
Either way, they're there if you want them!

Queenie:
Gloves and weather aside, this is going to be a nice evening, I hope you're all excited. Meet at 6 outside Crystal Palace station?

Kyazike:
Can't do 6

Cassandra:
There's a surprise. When can you do?

Kyazike:
Queenie, beg you tell your girl to relax pls

Queenie:
She doesn't mean anything by it, Kyazike

Darcy:
Shall we say 6.30?

Kyazike:
6.30 I can do but I'll meet you lot outside the park, I'm not walking down that big piece of hill to the station just to walk back up to the park again

Needing a break from the most stressful group chat I'd ever been in, I ambled over to the kitchen to make a cup of tea.

On the way back, I saw Ted striding across my floor, a vision in tweed, and glasses on this time. My heart did a little leap when I remembered how strong his hands felt when he was holding me up. I sat back at my desk, opened up a new email window and began to type.

'Tea?'

I turned around at the same time as trying to minimise the email window. Darcy leaned over me and peered at my screen.

'Who are you emailing, "Well don't be a stranger" to?' she asked.

'Nobody!' I spluttered. 'I mean, no, somebody. The freelancer who used to come in on Tuesdays! I was going to see if she wanted to come in and do a few more shifts.' I turned the screen off. 'Energy-saving.'

'Careful. Bit of an inappropriate thing to say to a colleague,' Darcy said. 'Anyway, I thought I'd come over to tell you in person that I'll have to stay here a bit late, since you've stopped replying to the corgis. Gina needs me to sort something. It's amazing, these bosses call *all* the shots but are flummoxed by the smallest technological advances.' She ran a hand through her hair agitatedly and walked away.

On Friday, 5 November, Noman, Ted <Ted.Noman@ dailyread.co.uk> wrote at 14:04:

Here she is. What are you doing after work? Fancy a quick one? . . . A drink.

I felt a pop of excitement in my stomach and typed out a reply that showed as much before deleting it and replacing it with something a bit less keen.

On Friday, 5 November, Jenkins, Queenie <Queenie. Jenkins@dailyread.co.uk> wrote at 14:10:

Yeah, I got that thanks. Good to see that your need to be corny hasn't subsided.

On Friday, 5 November, Noman, Ted <Ted.Noman@ dailyread.co.uk> wrote at 14:15:

Ouch. Okay, must try harder. But that drink?

On Friday, 5 November, Jenkins, Queenie <Queenie. Jenkins@dailyread.co.uk> wrote at 14:25:

Only if it's very quick. I'll have to sneak out at five, and can stay forty-five minutes max. I've spent weeks convincing my friends to go to a fireworks display and can't be the one to cancel, you see.

On Friday, 5 November, Noman, Ted <Ted.Noman@ dailyread.co.uk> wrote at 14:30:

Fine by me, I've got a dinner to go to. See you at the pub next to the church?

At half four, I ran around the office asking different colleagues for various make-up products. Being the only black girl in the office, I had to make do with liquid eyeliner from Zainab in

Digital, some mascara from Josey, the antisocial Iranian girl in the music department, and had to ask Darcy for blusher, although I knew it would be imperceptible even when seven layers were applied to my cheeks.

'Why do you need blusher? It's going to be dark in the park.' Darcy's solutions-driven way of thinking wasn't always welcome.

'I just need it, I want to look nice,' I said. 'Boosting my self-confidence and all that.'

'You already do look nice. Where are you going?'

'I feel like you're being suspicious?' I said to her.

Darcy looked back at me and raised her eyebrows.

'Fine. That guy from Sports, the one in all the tweed and the glasses, he emailed saying that he wants to go for a very quick drink.'

'Like, a flirty drink?' Darcy asked. 'What about all of your promises?'

'Well, yes, you're right, but I think it's fine to go for a drink with a colleague?' I said unconvincingly.

'Okay. Well. Be careful. You don't want to dip your nib in the office ink,' she said, handing me the blusher. 'And don't forget about fireworks!'

'I wouldn't, not after all the work I've put into getting you all in one place at one time.' I rolled my eyes and applied more blusher. 'If Gina asks where I am, say I had a small family emergency.'

'Queenie. You know what you're doing, don't you?' Darcy asked me solemnly. 'I don't want to be all Jonathan Jobsworth, but if you get fired, they can replace you with a hundred other girls like us.'

'Oh, so I'm dispensable?' I snorted, to cover how hard I'd been hit by the truth in her words. 'It's only half an hour.'

'Yeah but it's also been the last couple of weeks.'

'Darcy. I'm good at my job, and I *like* my job, and I want to be better at my job, and I will be. This is just a welcome distraction.' I maintained my smile, not wanting to fall out with my best friend at the worst point possible. 'Are you keeping track of me?'

'Not keeping track of you, but trying to remind you what else you can lose.'

'I haven't lost anything, and I'm not going to lose anything,' I reassured Darcy as I walked away.

When I got to the pub, I tried to find a seat outside that was both dry and somewhere discreet, as about ten of the senior men from my office were already dotted around and giving me eyebrows whenever I squeezed past them to look for a table. I met none of my desired criteria, and when Ted got to the pub and we bought our drinks, we ended up standing next to a wet table. We chatted for ages, at first tentatively, and then quickly, excitedly, with his hand inching across the table closer to mine.

'So, how do you like the building?' I could feel myself doing the doe-eyed thing.

'Yeah, I like it. There are a lot of secret rooms, too. Have you explored?' His little finger brushed mine.

'Huh?' I asked, heat rushing through my body. 'What?'

'I said, the building, have you explored?' Ted repeated, his voice dropping to a sultry rumble.

Tom flashed into my head and I drew my hand back.

'No, I haven't! How's your commute, though?'

'Right, yeah, good commute,' Ted said, visibly confused by my derailing of the conversation from the track it had been on. 'When I do nights I've got to get the bus from Hackney. But I'm hard, so, I can handle it.'

'Oh, am I meant to laugh at that?' I smirked, feeling my face cool down.

He truly wasn't very funny but:

1. Apart from Kyazike who is ten times as funny as me, I don't find anyone as funny as me, even in this, the darkest period of my life.
2. Actually, no man is as funny as me or any woman I've ever met.
3. Does funny matter when over the course of the evening, I'd been able to stop thinking about Tom for more than three minutes?
3a. AND been reminded what it was like for a very attractive man to speak to me like I was more than an orifice or someone hugely inferior?

'Oh, I'm sure you're very hard, Ted,' I purred.

What was I doing? I thought of another boring and practical question to ask. 'And who do you live with, Ted?'

'I live with – hold on a sec, you've got something in your hair,' he said, moving towards me, his hand reaching for my hair, getting so close that there was about a millimetre of space between us.

I looked up at him and my mouth parted as he leaned down.

'What time is it?' I asked.

He laughed. 'Oh, come on!'

'Seriously, what time is it?' I repeated, panic taking over.

'Five past six,' he said, showing me his watch.

'I have to go, sorry, late, fireworks!'

I ran out of the pub and continued running until I made the Overground train to Crystal Palace. I didn't catch my breath until I met Cassandra, who was shivering outside the station.

'Ready for the hill?' she asked, blowing warm air into her bony hands. Cassandra was the first Jewish person I'd ever met. This was probably because I grew up in south London and only ever ventured north to see our other side of the family. I'd put my stuff next to Cassandra in an English Language seminar and as soon as I sat down, she leaned over to me and said that as the two minorities on the course, we should stick together.

The first thing I'd noticed about Cassandra, after her pushiness, was her hair. It was long, dark brown, but shone gold when it caught even a glimpse of light. Like her hair, her eyes were brown but specked with shards of gold. Other classmates avoided her, I'm guessing because her leading personality trait is 'spiky', but I didn't mind it. I still liked her. Not in spite of the spikiness, either. After introducing herself in that seminar, she told me that I should let her cook me dinner that evening, and has told me how to live my life at every given opportunity since.

'Is anybody ever ready for this hill?' I said, looking up the almost vertical incline. 'We need to wait for Darcy, though, she got held up in the office.' I checked my phone. 'And we're meeting Kyazike at the park gates.'

'Oh, before I forget . . .' Cassandra said, pulling an envelope out of her pocket. '£150, right?' She seemed to dangle the envelope in front of me.

'Yes, thanks. Sorry, I know it's annoying, but I can't really borrow any money from Tom anymore . . .'

'It's not annoying, but I don't understand it,' Cassandra said. 'When you run out of money, why don't you just use your other money?'

'What?' I laughed. 'What other money?'

'You know, savings, an ISA, that sort of thing.'

I looked back at her blankly.

'Don't worry about it. We'll start a tab.' She handed the envelope to me.

We continued to stand in the cold waiting for Darcy, Cassandra telling me that every man she met fell in love with her but it had been so long since she'd actually met a man she could actually have a *connection* with.

'. . . and Derek was such a *bore*, Queenie. He didn't ask me *any* questions about myself in the four months we were dating. I had to drive all conversation. I decided, one evening when we went for dinner, that I wouldn't ask him anything about himself. Guess what? We didn't exchange a word after the hellos.'

By the time Darcy got to the station, we were frozen solid. My nose had almost fallen off, and Cassandra's teeth were chattering comically.

'Sorry I'm late! Sorry! Hello again, Queenie! How was the drink?'

'A lot. Too much,' I said, as she hugged me quickly.

'Well, I did tell you,' she said, raising an eyebrow at me.

'Nice to see you again, Darcy. Should we all get moving?' Cassandra said flatly, wrapping her scarf tighter around her neck.

We all began to walk up the steepest hill in south London, my knees practically hitting my chest with each step. The girls strode up, chatting. I was too out of breath to get involved, instead listening along and either nodding in agreement or shaking my head.

'So, how are things with you and your boyfriend, Darcy? Are you still together? Sorry to play catch-up, I just haven't seen you for a while. I hear bits and bobs through Queenie, though. What's his name again?' Cassandra interrogated, the click of her heels echoing around us as we walked.

'Simon? Yes, he's good! We moved in together a few months ago and it seems to be going well! There are some issues, some troubles, but – '

' – like what?' Cassandra asked, almost greedily.

'Well, you know he's fifteen years older than me? He's ready for a life that I didn't think I'd have to even start thinking about for years! Children and mortgages and . . .' It all came tumbling out.

'Why do you never talk to me about this?' I puffed.

'It all seems a bit trivial, given what you're going through.' Darcy smiled. 'It's okay, it's nothing I can't handle.'

'How long were you together? You know, before you moved in with each other? Do you think you did it too soon?' Cassandra pressed on.

'Um, I think six years?' Darcy said.

I nodded.

'Six years?' Cassandra repeated. 'That's a good amount of time to be moving in together, isn't it, Queenie?'

I was facing ahead, concentrating on the top of the hill, but with my peripheral vision I could see Cassandra looked at me pointedly. I nodded again, swerving her dig, and I tried to breathe in through my nose and out through my mouth.

'Well, you know, it's always a tricky thing, and some couples just aren't cut out for it. But it's no bad thing if they aren't!' Darcy said, putting an arm around my shoulders, as if getting up the hill wasn't hard enough.

I nodded, switching to mouth-breathing.

'I'm not being mean, I'm just thinking out loud,' Cassandra snipped. 'Plus, along with everything else, Queenie didn't even want to move in with Tom so soon. She told him that she wasn't ready, and he basically gave her an ultimatum. That's not fair.'

I nodded in agreement.

'I don't think she should see him again,' Cassandra concluded.

'Isn't that a little bit harsh, Cassandra? They were together for three years. They're *still* together, sort of. And they love each other.' Darcy clearly didn't understand that the best way to deal with Cassandra was to let her think that she was right about everything.

'A break may as well be a break-up,' Cassandra said definitively, and Darcy was silenced by this pronouncement.

We finally got to the top of the hill, me hoping that the sweat at my temples wasn't visible, the girls unbothered by the hike. We walked towards the entrance of the park and through the clusters of crowds, I saw Kyazike leaning against the iron gates. We weaved our way over to her, me trying to touch as few people as possible.

'You lot took your time,' she said, blinking slowly. 'It's chappin' out here. And you're lucky it's not raining anymore.'

Kyazike didn't like mud, or fireworks, or the cold, but I'd convinced her to come out and meet my other best friends, given that they'd been in a group chat for the last two months and them not knowing each other irl was going to get weird soon. I may or may not have suggested that I wouldn't do her hair again unless she came out with us.

'Sorry, it's my fault! I'm Darcy, hello!' Darcy leapt towards Kyazike and hugged her tightly. 'I can't believe we're only just meeting, I've heard so much about you. And spoken to you, fellow Corgi!'

Kyazike hugged her back, surprised at the physical contact. 'You didn't tell me she was so friendly, Queenie,' she said, smiling at me over Darcy's shoulder.

'I realised earlier, you've met Cassandra. Remember?' I said, putting a hand on each of their shoulders when Darcy finally released Kyazike's. 'Last year, at my twenty-fourth?'

'How do you pronounce your name again?' Cassandra asked.

I winced. Although it's better her asking than attempting a guess and butchering the pronunciation, I'd spoken about Kyazike enough for Cassandra to have remembered. She'd have remembered if it had been a basic name like Sarah or Rachel or something.

'Chess. Keh,' Kyazike said.

'Oh okay, like Jessica without the "ic" in the middle?' Cassandra asked.

'No. Like my own name. Not some any Western name. Chess. Keh,' she repeated. I was worried that she was going to tell Cassandra about herself, but instead she looked down at Cassandra's feet.

'Nice shoes. Miu Miu?' Kyazike said, impressed.

I exhaled.

'Yes, got them in the sale, though.' Cassandra lifted a foot and twirled it daintily.

'Always good to find some common ground!' Darcy said to them both. 'Shall we go, then? Get a good space?'

She charged onwards through the park and we all followed her, me in my Dr. Martens and Cassandra and Kyazike instantly further bonded when they realised that heels at a fireworks display were an incredibly bad shout, holding onto each other to make their way through the mud.

Half an hour later, having passive-aggressively bickered about the optimal place to stand that would allow us to see the fireworks and feel like we were in a crowd while observing that two of our party were in heels, we were all standing on a bit of solid path at the edge of the park waiting for things to start. As I clutched a foam cup of tepid chocolate in my hand, my motley crew of friends swigged from a bottle of Prosecco.

'So you went on a date with your colleague?' Kyazike asked. 'Who told you *that* was a good idea?'

'No, it just was a drink,' I said, burying my face into the cup. 'Just a nice drink with a colleague.'

'Is he single?' Cassandra asked. 'If he's single and thinks that you're single, it was a date.'

'He didn't do the girlfriend drop, so I'm guessing he's single?' I shrugged. 'Not that your theory is right.'

'What's the girlfriend drop?'

Darcy always needed to be clued in on these things.

'It's when a guy, even if he's the one who approached you to, say, ask what the time is, needs you to know that he's attached,' Cassandra explained, rolling her eyes. 'Like last week, I was in a café, and there was a guy at the table next to mine who had a smear of ketchup on his face. I was so distracted by it that I kept looking over and staring, wondering how acceptable it was to go and wipe it off. He eventually turned to me and said, "Cool laptop. My girlfriend has the same one". It's their way of telling themselves that a) they're irresistible to women, and b) they're in control of all of their interactions.'

'Do you think Tom has stopped doing the girlfriend drop?' I asked.

'Have you even heard from him?' Kyazike asked.

'Huh?' I said, lifting the cup to my mouth. 'No.'

I swallowed down my drink and my sadness. 'All fine, though,' I said, 'good to maintain the space from each other.'

'He should be begging you to come back by now, fam,' Kyazike said, shaking her head.

I looked up at the sky even though the fireworks hadn't started, willing the tears that were brimming to go back in my eyes.

'Are you sure you don't want some, Queenie?'

I was suddenly wrenched out of my own thoughts, that were switching between wondering what Tom was doing to guilt for going for what ended up being a non-colleague drink with Ted and feeling a bit like I wanted to throw myself at him and let him do whatever he wanted to my body.

'No thanks, Cassandra, I've had wine. Plus I've already got heartburn,' I said, refusing the Prosecco. Kyazike took it from Cassandra, wiping the mouth of the bottle with her sleeve before she put it to her lips.

'Is this champers? Don't taste like it,' she said after taking two big gulps.

'It's Prosecco, champagne's Italian cousin!' Darcy said. 'Could I have one last sip?'

'Ha. Thanks for the education. You can have more than one sip, there's loads.' Kyazike handed the bottle over to Darcy.

The fireworks started, and we watched in silence. I looked at my three friends, the lights exploding in the sky and illuminating their beautiful faces. They all represented a different part of my life, had all come to me at different times; why they'd stuck with me I was constantly trying to work out.

'Queenie, I can see you staring at us and smiling. Stop being a creep,' Cassandra whispered.

Chapter Six

I scrolled Tumblr for articles about the most recent protest in America, reading long-form pieces from eyewitnesses, their words broken up by pictures of black men and women being surrounded by police in riot gear or having milk poured on their faces to numb the sting of tear gas. The next article showed a video of a young black man called Rashan Charles being choked in an east London shop by an undercover police officer. I attached two articles to a pitch I'd painstakingly composed for Gina titled, 'Racial tension: US or us?' From the corner of my eye, I saw someone coming over and minimised the browser. When I looked up from my screen, Darcy was staring at me with a grin so wide that her face was split in two.

'What? What could possibly be making you smile so much on a Monday morning?' I asked her. My eyes were barely open.

'*Wait* until you see the new intern,' Darcy whispered. 'He's American.'

'Why is that a plus point? Are you saying that like it's a good thing? They're all bonkers. Do we know if he voted for Trump?' I asked as the new intern strode past in a confident, American way. He was very tall, and his hair was brown. There wasn't much to note beyond that.

'You see? Don't you think he's classically handsome?' Darcy said, smiling again.

'He's fine?' I said, turning back to my screen.

'He's called Chuck. I picked him because I thought he'd be a good, healthy distraction. He's almost too young for you to fancy him, but not too young for you to look at,' Darcy whispered. 'And *just* look at. Remember what I said about Ted and dipping your nib in the office ink.'

I spun my chair to face her.

'Isn't that illegal?' I asked. Surely this broke some sort of duty-of-care best practice.

'No, and besides, it's not like we're hiring him for a proper job. Plus, he's twenty-two. Legal.'

Is this what it has come to?

'Tea?' Darcy held up her empty mug.

'I'll meet you in the kitchen, I'm just sending Gina an email,' I said.

'Oh, finally back in the swing of work? Good to see,' Darcy said, and turned to walk away.

'Another black man died in America today,' I said to Darcy as I walked into the kitchen, blinking as my eyes adjusted to the bright light. 'Police killed him.'

'Oh no, what was he doing?' She asked absent-mindedly.

'What do you mean, "what was he doing"? He wasn't doing *anything*, he was driving.' The words burst from me. 'And even if he was doing something, doesn't mean he should be killed for it.'

'All right, calm down.' Darcy said, holding her hands up. 'Sorry, my mind was elsewhere. And I'm on your side here, I was just asking!'

'You asked a stupid question,' I snapped. 'That sort of attitude is the problem.'

'Woah, Queenie. It's me you're talking to.' Darcy frowned at me. 'Remember? Darcy? Best friend? Annoyingly liberal?'

'I'm not calling you racist, I'm saying that if the thinking is that someone should be killed for doing something wrong, that thinking is dangerous,' I said.

Why was I taking it out on her?

'I'm going for a cigarette.' I left the kitchen before I said something I'd regret. I knew Darcy hadn't meant it, and she is only guilty of it this one time, but I wished that well-meaning white liberals would think before they said things that they thought were perfectly innocent.

I went down, and put a cigarette in my mouth, patting my pockets for a lighter. I looked across the smoking area to see who I could bother for one, and locked eyes with Ted. Excitement and guilt crept back in. Must summon nice memories of Tom when tempted by Ted.

He dropped the end of his cigarette to the floor and walked over.

'You ran off the other day. Left me all alone.'

He lit another cigarette with a lighter then, flame still burning, held it out for me.

'I can do it,' I said to him, reminding myself how stupid it would be to get sucked into something while I had a relationship to go back to.

I took the lighter from him, lit my cigarette and inhaled too quickly, and defiantly choked as too much smoke hit the back of my throat.

'All right, Ted?' A burly man in clothes that were all too tight nodded a hello at Ted as he walked past.

'All good, thanks, Gordon!' Ted waved, turning to stand next to me. He waited until the man was out of sight and moved closer to me so that our arms were touching.

'Sorry, that's my desk mate,' Ted asked, running the hand that wasn't next to mine through his thick hair. 'How were the fireworks?'

'I think I lost my scarf, but otherwise, they were nice, thanks,' I replied, purposefully avoiding eye contact. That's where these men get me.

'The tartan one you have?' he asked.

'Yeah. No sentimental value, so it's all good.'

'You know, I was going for dinner with my friends that night, but I wish I'd stayed with you,' he said, looking around and moving so that he was in front of me.

'Ah, that's nice of you. I bet you had a nice time anyway.'

He moved closer to me.

'Not as nice a time as we could have had.'

'Got to go!' I said, breaking away.

Do not get sucked in, Queenie.

I got back upstairs to an email from Ted.

On Monday, 9 November, Noman, Ted <Ted.Noman@ dailyread.co.uk> wrote at 11:04:

That was an abrupt ending. I like that shirt, by the way.

I flushed with what I tried to pretend wasn't arousal, but my pretence wasn't clever enough to fool my body because guilt soon followed. I sent a text to Tom.

Queenie:
How are you?

**On Monday, 9 November, Jenkins, Queenie <Queenie.
Jenkins@dailyread.co.uk> wrote 11:26:**

I'm probably making a fool of myself by saying this, because
you're probably only being a friendly colleague, but if you
aren't, it's probably a bad idea to get involved with someone
at work, don't you think? We had a nice drink, and we should
probably leave it at that.

I went to make a mint tea to calm myself down and came back to:

**On Monday, 9 November, Noman, Ted <Ted.Noman@
dailyread.co.uk> wrote 11:30:**

But I don't want to leave it at that. Besides, I'm not one of
those guys who wouldn't respect you enough not to behave
properly if things didn't work out.

I decided to wait and see if Tom replied. If he didn't reply by
this evening, then maybe, just maybe, I could go for another
drink with Ted.

**On Monday, 9 November, Noman, Ted <Ted.Noman@
dailyread.co.uk> wrote at 11:31:**

I'm here if you want me

**On Monday, 9 November, Noman, Ted <Ted.Noman@
dailyread.co.uk> wrote at 11:35:**

When you want me

On Monday, 9 November, Jenkins, Queenie <Queenie. Jenkins@dailyread.co.uk> wrote at 18:03:

Darcy, I have a new promise to replace promise number four, which was: 'Just forget men for a while, and use this break with Tom as a break from men.' The new promise is: 'Forget men who you might want to get into something long-term with, but casual encounters are acceptable for as long as Tom isn't replying'

On Monday, 9 November, Betts, Darcy <Darcy.Betts@ dailyread.co.uk> wrote at 18:10:

Hi Dua Lipa, nice to hear from you. Why do you need caveats, why can't you just stay away from men altogether?

On Monday, 9 November, Jenkins, Queenie <Queenie. Jenkins@dailyread.co.uk> wrote at 18:15:

1. Dua Lipa's song is called 'New Rules' not 'New Promises', Darcy, come on
2. Until you've experienced heartache and uncertainty at this level, you aren't allowed to judge me
3. You know that I need attention and some excitement, and while I am waiting for my is-he-is-he-not boyfriend to text me back and tell me that he wants to make things work, this is the least-complicated way of getting it
4. And actually, as per point 2, you haven't been single since you were about eleven, so less of the 'why can't you just stay away from men altogether?'
5. I am telling you these things so that you can basically tell me when I need to hear it that I am doing the right thing. Maybe you

could just create a specific email bounce-back for me that says, 'What you're doing is fine'?

On Monday, 9 November, Betts, Darcy <Darcy.Betts@ dailyread.co.uk> wrote at 18:20:

Oh, I beg your pardon. Do you want to write this bounce-back yourself, or would you like me to draft something for your approval?

*

I went to my grandparents after work because I needed to bathe somewhere that saw regular bleachings and could offer more than five seconds of hot water. I crunched up the gravel driveway and paused outside the gate, taking a few breaths before I faced my grandmother.

This was the second house my grandparents had owned; my grandad had put all he had into buying the first house in the sixties, and my grandmother had put all she had into cleaning it until she'd had enough and forced my grandad to downsize when I was a teenager. This sat high on a quiet hill where a lot of other old people lived. There were never any fast cars or parties, only elderly women pulling shopping trolleys down the road and old men slowly tending to their front gardens.

'How's your past friend?' my grandmother asked, flipping fish fingers over in the frying pan.

'My "past friend"?' I asked her, confused. 'What does that mean, who is that?'

'You know, the white boy.'

'Do you mean Tom? My boyfriend of three years that you spent quite a lot of time with?'

'Mmm,' she confirmed.

'Can I have a bath?' I changed the subject. I did also want a bath.

My grandmother tapped her nose and walked over to the boiler, flipping various switches. 'A quick one. You know what he's like.' She gestured to the garden and I saw my grandad pottering around with his walking stick. 'You'll have to wait for the hot water, it's like you've got to beg the boiler to heat it up these days.'

I laid my head on the kitchen table. 'Why does life have to be so hard?' I groaned, deciding that I wanted to change the subject back to my heartache.

My grandmother came over and put a plate of fish fingers, baked beans and fried plantain in front of me.

'I'm not hungry,' I said, and was met with tightened lips and raised eyebrows.

I picked up a fork.

'You'll feel better,' she said, wiping her hands on her apron. I ate in silence, absent-mindedly reading the American gossip magazines that were on the table in front of me.

'Go upstairs now and run the bath, while he's in the shed,' my grandmother hissed, taking my plate away.

'I wasn't finished!' I said, a bit of plantain falling off my fork.

'You said you weren't hungry. Go!'

I ran upstairs – 'be careful on the stairs' – and into the bathroom. I turned the hot tap on and the water tank rumbled with a tell-tale growl.

'The water rates, Queenie.'

My grandad appeared behind me.

'Wilfred, leave her *alone!*' my grandmother shouted from the kitchen, forcing my grandad to shuffle back down the stairs. My grandparents might be getting older, but their hearing only seems to be improving.

I lay on the floor of the spare room as I waited for water to fill the tub. I heard the familiar voice of John Holt start playing through the floor. He was my grandmother's favourite reggae singer, and her preferred song of his was all about his broken heart.

'If I've got to be strong, don't you know I need your help to fight when you're gone?' he sang.

'CAN YOU TURN THAT OFF, GRANDMA?' I shouted down. 'YOU KNOW I AM STRUGGLING.'

There was a long pause.

'Who yuh tink yuh talking to?' my grandmother shouted back. 'Yuh tink say you can be DJ inna *my* house cause of a man?'

I undressed and climbed into the tub. I lay back and moved a hand across my stomach the way I'd done when I'd last had a bath. Tom wasn't here this time, though. I didn't know *where* he was. I stared at the ceiling and felt my chest tighten. The bathroom door opened and my grandmother burst in. I covered myself with the flannel.

'Let me wash your back,' she said, grabbing the flannel and lathering it up with a bar of Imperial Leather that she must have bought reserves of in the sixties.

'No, no, I'm fine, I'm not a baby,' I said, covering myself with my hands.

'I washed your back when you were a baby and I'll wash it now,' she said, tipping me forwards until my forehead rested on my knees. I closed my eyes and let her scrub my skin.

'I'm no stranger to heartache, you know,' she told me. 'You need to get over it, Queenie. Life goes on.'

'You've been with Grandad since you were fourteen,' I said. 'If there's anyone who has never known heartbreak, it's you.'

She kissed her teeth. 'You must think you know everything. *Your* grandad got me pregnant when I was fourteen. Not even

Diana's age! Then he disappeared, and I was left in Jamaica with Maggie, living with Gran-Gran.'

My grandmother paused.

'I fell in love with a man. He was very kind to me. Always met me at the end of the lane and helped me to carry the sugar cane up to the house. Albert, his name was.'

She put the wet flannel on her lap and watched as the water seeped into her apron. She started to wring her hands, her fingers settling on her wedding ring.

'Albert loved Maggie as much as he loved me. It was a secret, of course. He looked after us, for two years. I couldn't tell Gran-Gran about him.' My grandmother laughed. 'She almost killed me when I got pregnant and I couldn't shame her twice by bringing another man into the house. But Albert, he was everything. He was funny, he was generous, used to listen to me.'

She paused to sigh heavily.

'He gave me this necklace one day. He'd saved up for the gold, and he'd made it himself. A 'V', for Veronica. He was so proud to give it to me. Every day he waited at the end of the lane for me.'

'Well, what happened to him? And to the necklace? Also have you seen *Titanic*? This sounds a lot li – '

'Your grandad came back. Turns out he'd been over here finding work, squatting in a bedsit in Mitcham and saving some money. He came to Gran-Gran's house one night, told me that he was taking me and Maggie to London, and two days later we were on the plane. A year later I was pregnant again with your mother.'

'And what happened to Albert?'

'I don't know. I couldn't ask anybody about him, because nobody knew about us. So, you see. We all know heartbreak. We just have to learn to live with it.'

She lifted the flannel and carried on scrubbing my back, her movements softer than before.

I woke up in the middle of the night. I was half-asleep and I could see a man standing in the corner. I tried to shout, but nothing would come out. He was moving closer. I tried to shout again.

'NO!' I finally screamed, falling out of the bed.

'Queenie?' My grandmother flew into the room, her nightie billowing behind her like a cape. 'What is it? Wh'appen?'

'Sorry, it's nothing. Nothing.'

I climbed back into bed and put a hand to my chest. My heart was pounding.

'The nightmares,' she said knowingly. 'Tek water.' She gestured to the glass by my bed and shuffled back into her room.

I couldn't sleep, so checked my phone. Two texts from Darcy.

Darcy:

Nosy man on floor hovering around your desk. Quite fit. Big glasses. Tweed jacket.

Darcy:

Hold on is he Tweed Glasses??

I went to work the next day, physically cleaner than I'd ever been. Brain still tired from eschewing thoughts of Ted, heart still sore every time I thought about Tom. How much more time did he need? How much time did *I* need?

*

Later that week, when I made it to my desk by way of the canteen and the smoking area and before I could sit down, Gina came over to tell me that she'd been watching me and Darcy 'gasbagging' from her office.

I apologised and vowed (truthfully) to spend more time at my desk during working hours and less time literally everywhere else, pulled my chair out to sit down and disrupted an ASOS parcel that fell on the floor.

I picked it up and opened it, pulling out a tartan scarf. I put it on and started to walk over to Darcy's desk. Gina was coming towards me.

'No. Queenie. Back to your desk. *Do* something, *please*. You haven't filed the weekend's listings yet and it's Friday, come *on*.' She turned me around by the shoulders and gently pushed me back to my section of the floor. 'You can talk to her at lunchtime.'

I dragged myself through the morning and at 11.59 a.m., went over to Darcy.

'God, Gina is all over the place recently,' I bitched, feeling bad and obscenely hypocritical given I was even more all over the place. 'One day she's nice, the next she ignores me, today she's having a go at me. I can't keep up. Was it always this bad?'

'No,' Darcy confirmed. 'I think she's having some proble – '

'Oh!' I interrupted, fanning the scarf out around me and spinning round in a mock twirl. 'Thank you for this!'

'For what?' Darcy asked.

'The scarf,' I said.

'It's nice. Looks almost exactly like the old one. But it's not from me,' she said, standing up and rummaging around in her pockets.

'You were with me when I lost it, at the fireworks.' My arms fell to my sides. Knowing I couldn't afford to replace it myself, she probably didn't want to make a big thing out of it.

'I know, but I didn't buy you a new one. Should I have?' she asked, holding up her purse. 'Lunch?'

I couldn't bear to go home, so left the office well after dark. As I walked to the bus stop, Ted fell in line with me.

'Hey you,' he said, softly. 'How's it going?'

'Fine, thanks.'

I carried on walking, still trying to avoid getting myself in a sticky situation. I'd already found myself in some very compromising positions of late.

'Fancy a drink?' he asked. 'I'm on lates, popped out for a smoke. We could head across the road for a swift one?'

I wanted to go, but I also knew that going would make me want to kiss him. 'No, I've got to get home!'

'Nice scarf, by the way. I knew it would suit you.'

I stopped walking.

'This was you? Why did you – oh, thanks for that, I guess?' I said, surprised.

'Why are you so shocked?' Ted laughed.

'Just that nobody ever buys me anything, is all. And you . . . don't know me well enough?'

'Not for want of trying,' Ted said.

'If you're on lates, you should get back to work. I have to go! My bus!' I said, before I sprinted to the bus stop, holding my breasts down under my arm and panting aggressively after about fifteen metres. I should not, under any circumstances, get involved with this. I should not, under any circumstances, try to run again.

I spent Saturday morning in bed, my stomach growling. At lunchtime Rupert knocked on my door and asked if I wanted to have lunch with everyone.

'No thanks!' I said, before adding, 'I'd sooner die' in a whisper.

'What was that last bit?' he asked.

'I said I'm going for pie.' I smiled and pulled the covers over my head, burrowing into my pillows and looking through mine and Tom's message thread. I noted how many arguments we'd had. Most of them started by me. Top three were:

Number 1:

Tom:

What do you want for your birthday?

Queenie:
Oh.

Tom:
What?

Queenie:
So you're not going to put any effort into it? You're literally going to just ask me like that

Tom:
Well for your last two birthdays and Christmas just gone, you've been disappointed by what I've

got you, so it's perfectly logical to ask, surely?

Queenie:
Tom, do you want ME? Or do you want someone you can MOULD into the girl you want for yourself?

Tom:
Oh god

Queenie:
Oh god indeed. Just get me VOUCHERS, Tom, if disappointing ME is killing you

Number 2:

Queenie:
I've been thinking

Tom:
Oh dear. Go on

Queenie:
I don't understand why you don't want to introduce me to your colleagues

Tom:
What? I didn't know you wanted

to meet them. They're not particularly interesting

Queenie:
Well I DO, because I'm your GIRLFRIEND, I'm meant to be a huge part of your life, and I feel totally hidden away from what you do every day, and the people you do it with

Queenie:
Are you ashamed of me?

Queenie:
Do your colleagues know I'm black?

Tom:
What? Why should they?

Queenie:
I see

Queenie:
It's fine

Queenie:
I've decided I don't want to meet them. Don't want to give them a shock

Number 3:

Queenie:
I feel like you need to think more about my orgasms

Tom:
Oh trust me, I do

Queenie:
DO you?

Tom:
You're always satisfied, aren't you?

Queenie:
Well yeah, but how much are you THINKING about them? But not just thinking, I mean feeling. Like SOMETIMES it feels like it's a chore for you

Tom:
Well it's not

Queenie:
I don't know, I feel like you're concentrating so much on ME that I can't just let go. Sometimes I feel like I'm having an orgasm FOR you

Tom:

I don't understand what your
argument is here

Queenie:

Forget it

Tom:

Okay

Queenie:

What do you mean 'okay'? Don't
you want to communicate about
this?

Tom:

I'm in a meeting

Queenie:

So am I, Tom, but it's important
that we talk about these things

When I woke up, it was dusk and my phone was still in my hand. I checked my phone and saw two texts from Darcy.

Darcy:

See you later, Simon's party
starts at nine. It's at that bar
in Dalston, the one where he
smashed his tooth xxx

Darcy:

Should have said, you'll be late
and will definitely miss the
surprise element at nine, but
can you at least get here before
eleven? The venue is kicking us
out by one

I couldn't bear to eat anything so watched *Insecure* and then *Atlanta* in bed, pulled some clothes on and threw a bit of glitter on my face. I got to the party at ten to eleven, thank you very much, and found Darcy. She was sitting with Simon and although it kills me to spend any time with couples, these two weren't happy so it didn't really count. Simon's age was showing more and more these days; it looked like Darcy was sitting with an uncle. Not a very *old* uncle, more like her dad's youngest brother or something.

After again drinking more than I'm used to, and on an empty stomach, then forcing all of Darcy's friends to form a circle around me while I danced very sloppily to 'LMK' by Kelela, I stumbled off to the bar to get some water. On the way there I tripped over my own foot and reached out to steady myself, but instead of grabbing onto something solid like a table or the back of a chair, I grabbed onto a thigh. I looked up at its owner, mouth wide open, and locked eyes with the most beautiful boy I'd ever seen.

He pulled me back up, mainly so that I would take my weight off his leg.

'Come on, let's get me some water,' I said, grabbing his arm. I wasn't sure I could make it to the bar alone.

'Er, sure? Yeah, okay,' he said, in the strongest Welsh accent I'd ever heard and definitely wasn't expecting. Unlike the Irish, who have a long-standing bond with us since, 'No Irish, No Blacks, No Dogs', I'm not sure how the Welsh feel about black people, but I decided to go with it. I led the boy over to the bar, not entirely sure where this surge of confidence was coming from. Probably the alcohol.

'I like your, uh, hair. All this,' he said, awkwardly patting the bun on my head. 'Don't touch it!' I ducked out of his grasp, losing my footing and falling again, this time against the bar.

He picked me up.

'Sorry, you aren't meant to touch a black girl's hair, are you?' He put his hands in his pockets as if to restrain himself.

'If you could try not to,' I smiled, captivated by his nice face.

Approximately three minutes later, we were kissing against the bar, with the Welshman pausing to tell me that he'd worked in Cameroon for a year so had a thing for black girls. I wasn't sure if his background meant that I was being fetishised or actually I was just his type but I pushed it all to the back of my mind because he was a good kisser.

Suddenly remembering that I wasn't in the privacy of my own home, I pulled away from him and looked across the bar. Many, many people were looking. The Welshman looked around, too.

'Maybe I should come back to yours?' he asked, pressing his hand into my lower back.

'So. What do you do?' the Welshman asked as he slid down next to me in the Uber.

'Does it matter?' I replied, looking out of the window as the driver moved off. Why was I doing this? Was I so attention-deficit that I needed this? I knew that I should probably push him very gently out of the car when it stopped at a traffic light, but that meant going home alone. It meant going home alone, getting into a cold, empty bed and falling asleep wrapped in Tom's T-shirt. And I really didn't want to do that, not again. Maybe tonight would be good, as long as there were boundaries. No personal details necessary, this was nothing but a fling, I told myself. He put a hand on my thigh and moved it higher, digging his nails into my skin. That'll be a pair of tights gone.

He turned my head to face him, and instead of kissing me on the mouth, bit me hard on the cheek. At least it sobered me up a bit. He moved his lips to my mouth and grabbed the back of my head, forcing our faces together. I couldn't breathe.

I punched him on the leg in an attempt to make him stop.

'Ow! Jesus, you're strong. What's wrong?' he asked. 'You don't like it?'

'It's not that I don't like it, just more that I can't breathe,' I told him. 'Just ease off about thirty per cent.'

When we got back to my house, the door was double-locked. Rupert and Nell were out, so after showing Welshman around the house, he suggested that we had sex in the living room. This was met with a firm 'no' and a nod to the horrible sofas.

As I led him up to the bedroom, he smacked my bottom the hardest it has ever been hit. Now, I am no stranger to pain. I had my hair relaxed every two months from the age of eleven to twenty-three, and the feeling of your scalp burning away so that it weeps and scabs over the next day has set me up to deal with any injury you can throw at me. Sexual or otherwise.

Tom wasn't so adventurous, but in the last few weeks, I've learned a lot about my preferences and my pain barriers. Spanking, I like it. Hair-pulling, I'm not mad for it, but I'll take it if you let go of the ponytail if you think it might come off in your hand. Biting, I've really learned to love. Choking is dependent on the choker, and how long their nails are. So on and so forth. When Welshman pushed me onto the bed, face down, and hit my bottom with the back of his hand as hard as he could, I realised that there *was* a pain that I couldn't take. I gritted my teeth and said nothing.

'Take your clothes off,' he sneered, removing his shirt and then his trousers. 'Hurry up, come on, I haven't got all day.'

I lifted myself onto my knees and, still facing the pillow, pulled my dress off, wondering if it had been my encounter with Adi that had turned me into some sort of male-voice-command-activated sex-bot.

'Turn around, face me,' he commanded. His tone had changed.

I turned slowly and sat, cross-legged.

'I hope that glitter doesn't go all over me,' he said, and I went to respond that it would only improve his look but he grabbed me gently by the jaw and shoved his tongue in my mouth. He climbed onto the bed and pushed me onto my back. He spread my legs and pulled my knickers to the side, penetrating me with jabbing fingers and sharp nails.

I made no sound as he leaned down and bit my neck, then my shoulder, leaving what I knew would be deep, red impressions on my skin. I was in pain, but still I didn't cry out, didn't ask him to stop. I didn't want him to.

This is what you get when you push love away. This is what you're left with, I thought.

'Get onto your knees and take your hair down,' Welshman said.

I did as I was told.

He knelt behind me and smacked me hard on my thighs.

I gritted my teeth in shock.

He did it again.

I had to bite into the pillow. I let out a cry of pain, turning to face him.

'Stop your noise, girl,' he growled, digging his nails into each of my buttocks and parting the cheeks roughly, burying his face between them.

I could add rimming to another of my sexual firsts, along with sex in cars, uncircumcised boys and questionable emails with colleagues. Temporarily, the pain was numbed by the shock. I squirmed with discomfort, but instead of taking a second to step out of his own pleasure and see that I didn't like what was going on, he reared up and pushed himself into me from behind.

'Do you like that, Queenie?' Welshman asked, inserting a finger into a place that he was dead set on *fully* exploring before he was finished with me. Another first.

I didn't say anything.

'I said, do you like that?' He pulled my hair so that my head was whipped back next to his mouth. I should either wrap it up or take my twists out because recently my hair was getting used as a control for my head, which was not what I had in mind when I bought bundles from the hair shop.

'Yeah, yeah, I like it, I like it, fine,' I lied, convincing him, and myself. Maybe I did like it? Maybe this is what I'd been missing with Tom.

'Yes!' Welshman shouted as he came and immediately withdrew, putting his full weight on my shoulder blades to push himself away from me. He lay next to me on his back, panting. I turned to look at him and went to put a hand on his chest.

'I don't really like people touching me,' he said, moving away and rolling onto his side to face the wall.

I apologised and went to the bathroom. I sat on the toilet and inspected the raised marks on the outsides of my thighs.

When I went back into the bedroom, he was asleep. I got under the covers, fighting for my fair share of the duvet and failing as Welshman's weight trapped the majority of it. I fell asleep, somehow.

'Hey.'

Someone was shaking me awake.

'Huh? What?' I croaked. 'What's going on?'

'You were just kicking me!'

I turned my lamp on and looked over at who the voice belonged to.

'That really hurt, that did,' the Welshman said, blinking the light out of his eyes with his thick lashes.

'Sorry, I was asleep.'

'Yeah, I figured. You were shouting, "Don't touch me!" over and over, I thought you were possessed,' Welshman said angrily.

'I should have warned you, that happens sometimes,' I explained, sitting up. 'I didn't mean to hurt you. Sorry.'

I reached over to my bedside table and turned my phone over. It was 6:12 a.m. I had a text from Darcy doing her best Mrs Bennet impression.

Darcy:

Who did you leave with?
Someone said you left with
Welsh Guy, Fran's friend from
Oxford? He's very handsome
isn't he? Good prospects, too.

Does any person who didn't go to Oxbridge care about anyone going there?

'It's all right, you can make it up to me,' the Welshman said, taking my phone out of my hand. I lay back and let him part my legs even though I was so disorientated that I couldn't yet register how much pain I was in from our earlier activities.

If I could have fallen asleep as he rutted into me I would have, but he kept lifting one leg up and throwing it over his shoulder, then putting that leg down and the other would go over. At one point it was both; I didn't know where he'd put which one next, but before I could worry about it, as if by magic, he came, rolled over and said, 'Try not to attack me again, eh?'

I lay there, still, until he started breathing deeply.

'Hello?' I whispered.

No reply. He was asleep.

I shuffled over to him and tucked myself into his back, my heart soaring at the close human contact that I'd been yearning for for so long.

'Can you get off me?' he said, his accent more pronounced by the annoyance in his voice.

Chapter Seven

'So then we woke up properly and we had sex *again*. Four times in total, three times more than Tom could ever manage. But the third time, anal. Can you believe it? It was so hot,' I said to Darcy as she added sugar to her mug. 'And he used to play rugby, so has these amazing, strong shoulders.' If I pretended the night had been amazing, maybe I could rewrite the memory of Guy in my head so that I felt like slightly less of a sex aid to him.

'Do you think the anal thing is because he plays rugby?' she asked.

'What do you mean?' I had no idea what the correlation could be.

'You know! All of that testosterone, and the scrum, and they're always doing that thing where they're bent over waiting for the ball to be passed between the legs? Their eyes are literally always on bottoms,' Darcy said, putting the milk in the fridge.

'I think that's American football, isn't it? With the bending and the ball between the legs?' I corrected her despite knowing nothing about any sport. 'Anyway, that's not the point, the point is that I had *actual* anal sex. For the first time ever,' I said smugly, hiding a wince as I leaned on my bruised thighs.

'Did you never do it with Tom?'

'What, with Mr Logic, the man who used to only want to have sex in two positions? No. Do you ever do it with Simon?'

'Only on Valentine's Day. It's my annual gift to him.' Darcy said as we walked to the meeting room and sat at the table. 'Did you like it?'

'I think so. Anyway, he left at about midday, and then came back an hour later, when I was trying to sleep off my hangover, to ask for my number. And despite not wanting to betray Tom by having any sort of long-term thing, I gave it to him. Tom still isn't replying, you know,' I said, my tone switching from matter-of-fact to plain sad.

'Do you think you'll see Guy again?' Darcy asked, losing her face in her mug as she took a gigantic gulp of tea.

'Yes, tell us, do you think you'll see him again?' Gina asked, taking a seat at the table. 'Or do you think you'll actually do some work, the work that we're paying you to do? *Again* you haven't filed your listings.'

'Sorry, Gina,' I said, mortified. 'I'll go and do it now, I was just waiting for someone to check – '

'No, no, you stay,' Gina said, putting a hand on my arm as I got up to leave. Darcy took the opportunity to slip away, sneaking me an apologetic smile.

'What's going on?' Gina asked irritably, running a hand through her short blonde hair.

'What do you mean?' I asked, knowing exactly what was coming. I was surprised this telling-off had taken so long to arrive.

'I mean, what's wrong with you? You're being odd. Your behaviour,' Gina said.

'Nothing, Gina, I'm fine,' I lied, getting up from the table.

'No no, sit down,' Gina said.

I did as I was told.

'Don't lie to me, not when I've taken the time to talk to you about this properly rather than giving you a written warning.'

My heart lurched.

'You aren't fine. You've been late, you keep getting things wrong and I know that Leigh keeps covering for you. Last Wednesday you just didn't come in?'

I felt the pride in myself and my job that I'd worked so hard to cultivate slip away. There was no point in lying.

'I'm sorry, Gina,' I said to my boss and looked at the floor. 'It's relationship stuff, but that's no excuse.' Embarrassment coated my words. 'It's not like anyone has died,' I said. 'I'm sorry again. It won't keep happening.'

I tried to look up and into Gina's cat-like eyes, but instantly looked down at the table. How could I have let this happen, despite promising myself that it wouldn't? Even if, worst-case scenario, I got fired and had to re-build the tiny career I'd had, I didn't have Tom's financial help anymore; how would I pay my rent? My stomach dropped further than I thought it could.

'It isn't fine. I've been there, I know what it's like, and I know that you have a habit of minimising things.'

Gina was being nice today, it seemed.

'You mustn't. Look, Queenie, some advice for you. Whenever I've had a huge upheaval, my mother has always said, "Keep one foot on the ground when two are in the air." At least you've got your job, and you've got a place to live, so try to keep your focus on those things.'

'So, like, I have three feet in this? Like a tripod?' I asked her.

'You know what I mean.' Gina waved my question away with a flick of the wrist. 'Why don't you take a couple of days off? Go away for the weekend, give yourself some proper thinking space.'

'I'm okay, really I am. It's better for me to come to work,' I said, knowing that I could never afford to just go anywhere for the weekend. 'I'm not good at sitting home with nothing to focus on. It's when the demons come knocking.'

'The offer always stands. Whenever you need it. I'm sorry to say it, but you will need to face up to those demons at some point.'

She stood up and patted me on the shoulder. 'Now if you are going to be here, can you get back to work? Thank you in advance.'

I went back to my desk and sat down ever so gently, vowing that today would genuinely be the day I stopped fucking about and got on with my job. I breathed out slowly as my bum touched the seat. Everything from the waist down was so tender. I worked solidly through to lunch, padding over to Darcy's desk as soon as the clock struck one.

'Can you do me a favour? It involves following me some-where,' I said, trying to sound persuasive.

'Depends,' she said, not looking away from her screen.

'The sexual health clinic,' I said, knowing that I was really testing her dedication.

'We'll be waiting for hours.' She turned to face me. 'And I do care about your sexual health, but we *cannot* just disappear for hours.'

'Darcy, *do* you care about my sexual health?' I asked her. 'I've been having more . . . indoor activity than usual recently, and it occurred to me that I should check that things aren't going to start falling off.'

Darcy rolled her eyes. 'You sent me an email about ninety minutes ago telling me that this was the day you got your act together. Just go at the weekend?'

My hangover sunday had allowed for some dark thoughts and fears to creep in. Those dark thoughts and fears were mainly that before Guy had obliterated me sexually, I'd been tearing through men at a rate that I hadn't ever thought myself capable of. If I let myself think about it too much, I felt quite unwell, and also convinced myself that I'd contracted some untreatable disease.

'Honestly, it won't take long,' I pleaded. 'And Gina's calendar says she's out of the office this afternoon. I just want company, please, please.'

Two hours later we were sitting in the waiting room of the sexual health clinic round the corner. When we walked in and were on speaking terms, we'd agreed that it was the most depressing room either of us had ever been in, before we'd even sat down. The only colour came from the dozens of posters that covered every wall. Darcy was refreshing her work emails next to me, and had stopped talking to me out of anger an hour ago.

'I *said* it would take hours.'

She put her phone in her pocket and turned to me.

'Only two and a half. It's a busy time of year, Darcy, I couldn't predict this,' I protested.

'What, November?'

'It's close to Christmas, everyone is getting jolly!'

'*I* predicted this, didn't I? I'm going to go back to work.'

Just as she jumped up to leave, a male nurse came through the doors and, as expected, screamed my name through the waiting room.

'Coming, coming.'

I got up and the nurse smiled at me and walked through the double doors to the assessment rooms.

I followed him in, my legs beginning to feel wobbly when I was taken into a room a little too similar to lewisham Hospital scanning room. I sat in a squeaky plastic chair next to an old brown desk. The nurse tapped some things into his computer.

'Now, it says on the form that it's your first time here?'

'Yes.'

'At this clinic, or any sexual health clinic?'

'Any,' I told him.

'Right, so you've never been tested before?'

'Never.'

The nurse smiled at me flatly, his grey eyes peering out from behind his narrow glasses. He took another look at the form I'd filled in. 'So, no symptoms, just a check-up?'

'Exactly.'

Why wasn't I able to say more than one word? Fear, probably.

'Okay, so I have a few questions,' he said. 'It shouldn't take too long.'

I wanted to turn and run back out into the waiting room. It was times like this I realised that I was desperately lacking some sort of maternal figure in my life. Though there's no way that Maggie would have followed me here. Ever since I said 'cervix' after the gynaecology unit she'd kept her distance.

'So, Queenie. Your last sexual partner. When was that?' The nurse probed without looking at me.

'Um. Two days ago.'

'And was it a casual partner, or a long-term partner?'

'Casual,' I said.

'Right, okay. And was the sex protected or unprotected?'

'Unprotected.' I crossed and uncrossed my legs.

'And this partner, where were they from? Were they from Africa?' the nurse asked.

'Were they from . . . Africa?'

'Higher risk of HIV,' the nurse told me.

'Maybe you should explain that. But no. He was Welsh,' I told him, Guy's accent popping into my head. He didn't say he'd slept with anyone when he'd worked in Cameroon.

'And was this oral, vaginal or anal sex?'

'Um. The latter two. And all three for him. But you probably don't need to know that. You know what I mean. Sorry.'

'Don't worry, it's good to know as much as possible.' The nurse smiled and typed some things into the computer.

'And the partner before that. When was that?' he asked, turning back to me.

'Um. Three days before that,' I said quickly.

'And is that a casual partner or a long-term partner?'

'That partner was also casual.'

'Okay, great,' The nurse said.

I suspected that he did not think it was great.

'Protected or unprotected?'

'Unprotected.'

'Okay. And was *he* from Africa?'

More tapping into the computer. I could swear it was getting faster.

'From the nebulous Africa? No. He was just . . . white? Sorry, is white offensive to you? Should I say . . . Caucasian?'

'White is fine. And before that?'

I counted on my fingers. 'A week and a half before that?'

'Was the partner – '

'Casual!' I responded.

'Okay, thank you. And was the sex – '

' – unprotected. Not African.' I nodded.

'And before – '

'One week before that, casual, unprotected, vaginal.'

'Okay, I think I get the picture.' The nurse scratched his head and began to type.

'. . . so I'm going to test you for HIV, gonorrhoea, chlamydia . . .'

'Please could I have a pregnancy test?' I asked the nurse, looking at the floor as I did.

'It says here that you have a coil fitted?'

'I am, but, I've been, uh.' I couldn't get the words out. 'I've, uh – ' I could feel something in my throat.

'You've been pregnant?'

The nurse said what I couldn't.

I nodded.

'I think I'm just from a very fertile family! Ha.' A nervous shot of laughter escaped from my mouth.

'Okay, well, we can do the pregnancy test afterwards. Would you pop your jogging bottoms off and jump on the exam table?'

I'd come prepared this time.

The nurse steered me towards the table, told me that he was going to get a female nurse to 'chaperone' and drew a curtain around me. I wasn't sure why he was trying to spare me any dignity when he was about to be poking around inside me.

The chaperone came in; a young mixed-raced girl with loose curls that reminded me of my mum's and the sort of cheekbones that could cut you. Again, chair, stirrups, edging my bottom to the end of the table until my vagina was almost touching the nurse's nose.

I gritted my teeth as he touched me.

He inhaled sharply.

'So, Queenie. As well as the marks on your thighs, I'm also seeing some internal bruising . . .' He went further in and I bit down on my phone to stop myself from crying out.

'There's also some tearing. Do you know how you might have sustained these injuries?' The nurse leaned back and lifted his glasses so that they rested in his hair.

I looked at the chaperone, whose face was one of abject horror, as though she'd just witnessed a car crash or a drive-by.

'Um, just some rough sex, I guess?' I offered.

'This is *very* severe bruising.' The nurse removed his latex gloves. 'You can pop your legs down, now. It'll be far too painful for me to insert a speculum. My colleague and I are going to step out. You pop your bits back on, and I'll come back in for a chat. Don't go anywhere.'

The nurse returned as I was staring at the clear plastic drawer full of pregnancy tests and weighing up the pros and cons of being caught stealing a handful.

'Do you have anyone here with you?' he asked, pulling some pamphlets out of his desk.

'Er, my work best friend came with me, but she's gone back to the office.'

'And what about your mother, is she around?'

'No, she's no – ' I began. 'Do *you* talk to your mum about your sex life?'

'I see your point, but I need to check. This work best friend, are they somebody that you can confide in?'

'Yeah, I guess so. Why? That's quite dramatic.' I laughed nervously again.

'Well, I have concerns about those injuries, Queenie. They are largely consistent with sexual violence.'

The nurse put the pamphlets on his desk and although they were upside down, I read the words 'victim support'.

'Oh god, no, I'm not trying to cover up for some abusive boyfriend, honestly,' I said.

'You know, this is a confidential space, and we can absolutely steer you towards the right support – '

' – I'm fine, really. Trust me, I would say.' I looked the nurse in the eye very sincerely. 'I don't have an abusive boyfriend. I can't even get anyone to take me on a date,' I joked uncomfortably.

'I'll take your word for it, but I'm going to need you to come back in a couple of weeks. In the meantime, I think you ought to refrain from any sort of sexual activity. Now, let's get you a pregnancy test before you leave.'

*

The pregnancy test was negative, so we can thank goodness for small mercies. Not entirely sure whose it would even be at this point, but it certainly wouldn't be Tom's. As I walked back to the office I opened our message thread again. He hadn't said anything to me in forever. How had so many weeks passed without a word?

I rushed back to the office to try and do an hour's work, thinking about how (im?)possible it would be to refrain from sex for a fortnight. What was happening to me? I was meant to be taking this time to get better and to work on being a nice girlfriend so that when Tom and I reunited I'd be normal, but instead I was just having sex with everyone. And I wasn't willing to think about why. This break isn't going the way I thought it would. I wonder if Tom is suffering as much as I am? I really hope so.

I made my way to the smoking area before going back into the office and facing the wrath of Darcy, but saw Ted lurking in the corner so went to sneak into the office. He must have sensed my presence as he looked up and came over. I put a cigarette to my lips.

'You've been avoiding me, Queenie.'

I lit it and looked at him.

'I haven't been avoiding you, Ted,' I exhaled.

'Oh but you have . . . You can't lie to me.'

I turned away from him and took another drag on my cigarette. I was having too many feelings that I couldn't keep a hold of, and another man and what he wanted from me was the last thing I needed.

'Hey, talk to me?' Ted said, standing directly in front of me and putting both hands on my arms the way he had when we first spoke. It was the very worst timing, bumping into him after a trip to the sexual health clinic that had left me feeling so vulnerable. My bottom lip trembled.

'Let's go for a walk, get some proper air,' Ted said, taking my hand.

We walked in silence until we got to the park, stopping by the precarious bench. I hoped that he didn't want us to sit on it. If it had collapsed, that would really be the end of my entire bottom half.

'Tell me what's wrong?' Ted asked, lighting a cigarette. Smoking was going to kill either one or both of us.

'It's just all a big mess,' I said, feeling him reach for my hand.

I pulled it away.

'Ah. Those boy problems you mentioned. Ongoing?' he asked gently.

'You're not the person I should be talking to about all of this,' I said, playing with my hair.

'You can trust me,' he said. 'I promise to stay objective.'

'Ha, sure.' I snorted in Ted's face and watched it crumple the way that Tom's would when I inevitably and deliberately said something to push him away.

'We're meant to be on a break,' I said to Ted, and took a deep breath. 'When I stepped on your foot, the day I first saw you in the lift, I was about to move out of the flat I shared with my boyfriend. And I haven't spoken to him since, because he wants us not to speak for a while, but obviously I still feel so guilty every time I email you or see you because even though I don't know you, you make me feel excited, which is probably really intense, but also I know it's because there's some rebound energy in me even though it's not a proper break-up, and I don't know *when* he's going to call me and tell me that he's ready to go back to how things were, but I know deep down that he *is*. So.'

I took a breath.

'I'm trying not to get involved in anything that could be serious, because that would feel like I was cheating on someone that I worked so hard to let in after a childhood of negative reinforcement from the men around me.' I looked at Ted, expecting him to turn on the heels of his polished brogues and run away. 'I told you. It's all a mess.'

'I don't mind a bit of mess,' Ted said, weaving his fingers through mine.

I tried to pull my hand away but he held on.

'That's not so bad, is it?' he said.

I looked at him and shook my head. It had been so long since somebody had touched me gently. He flicked his cigarette away and put his other hand on the back of my head.

'Don't touch my hair,' I whispered, priorities always in place.

133

He kissed me softly, running his free hand down to my neck, then my back. As he kissed my neck and moved his hands around mine, a wave of guilt threw me from him.

'Sorry, that's too intimate,' I said to him.

'What?'

'It doesn't feel right,' I said, stepping away. 'I think it's best that you stay away from me. I don't want to drag you into stuff.'

'You can't just decide that, Queenie,' Ted scoffed. 'See it from my point of view. I meet this beautiful girl who works in my building and within about three seconds realise that she's brilliant, that she's someone I want to spend all my time with, and touch, and kiss, and . . .'

He leaned down and kissed me again, pulling me into him.

I'm always worrying about my lips compared to the lips of the person I'm going to kiss because, as it stands, mine have always been the bigger lips, and kissing someone with no lips or small lips is just so sad. But even though Ted's lips weren't very big, they were very good. But it wasn't just how his lips felt, it was how he made *me* feel. I felt how I did when someone actually cared about me, and that really fucking frightened me. I pulled away again and looked at him.

'Please listen to what I've said! I can't do this.'

I let go of his hand and walked away.

Chapter Eight

I went back to the sexual health clinic after two vaginally restorative weeks of no sex. Darcy refused to come with me this time, something about 'needing to work harder', 'job security' and 'deadlines'. She didn't need to be worrying so close to Christmas, the office was half-empty. I sat in an observation room alone, reading a pamphlet on chlamydia, until a health adviser came in for a chat.

This last fortnight, pretending that I'm okay has been the performance of a lifetime. I haven't been fired yet, I've only been late when Gina isn't in, I haven't made any visible mistakes (mainly because Chuck is now begrudgingly covering for me, in the place of Leigh), and I've been working late most evenings.

One positive to the no sex is that I've been taking proper care of my hair. Shea butter, coconut oil and rose water blend to condition, and spritzing it every other day to keep it moisturised. I have so much discipline when I'm not worrying about men, I thought to myself as my phone pinged.

Unknown:
We had fun the other night, didn't we?

I always spoke too soon when it came to these things.

Queenie:
Could you be a bit more
specific?

Unknown:
I came to yours and fucked you
senseless?

Queenie:
Which day?

Unknown:
Saturday

Queenie:
Which Saturday? Could you
remind me of the date?

Unknown:
Christ alive, girl, how many boys
have you had in your bed? It's
Guy.

Queenie:
Oh! Guy! Sorry yes, we did have
fun, sure.

Guy:
I'm hankering after your arse
again. There's a lot I wanted to
do to you

Queenie:
Oh well that's sweet. How's work and everything?

Guy:
If I wanted to talk about work I would have sent a text to my mum. When are you free?

Queenie:
For?

Guy:
I want to come round, obviously. Give you a second dose

'Hello, Queenie, sorry to have kept you waiting. I'm Elspeth, a health adviser here at the clinic. How are you?' A slim, pale woman with almost white-blue eyes and grey hair chopped into a harsh bowlcut sat opposite me.

I put my phone away as she started tapping into the computer on her desk. I didn't want this woman to advise me; she looked like she was going to tell me off, like she'd heard it all in the sixties and was tired of it.

'Um. I'm fine?' I seemed to ask her. 'They told me to come back?'

Elspeth's lips tightened. 'It doesn't look like you're fine.'

What was on that computer?

'I'm reading over your notes.' She clicked the mouse a few times and leaned in to the screen. 'The last time you came in here you had vaginal bruising, some anal tearing and bruises on your bottom and thighs, which meant that you weren't able to have a full examination.'

'Ah, but at least I had my pride,' I said, looking down at my shoes.

'I also see here that you haven't been using protection, and have been sleeping with multiple partners?' she asked, still looking at the screen. 'Is there a bit more to the story, here?'

'Nope.'

'You know, we don't offer counselling here, but we can refer you to the right service.'

Tapping again. Why wouldn't she look at me?

'If you're in an abusive relationship, if somebody is forcing you to sell your body for sex, then – '

'Your colleague implied this two weeks ago and I found it very offensive,' I said, finally finding my voice. 'This is ridiculous. I had some sex with a guy who just got a bit carried away, that's all.'

'Was the sex consensual?'

'Yes, it was! My god, listen to me! If I were in danger I would say!' I squawked angrily. 'You're all so judgemental.'

'Well, I've got to do my job, Queenie,' Elspeth clucked at me. 'Besides, your ethnic group puts you in a higher risk of being in an abusive relationship. No need to be so shrill. I'll update the system.'

Tap tap tap.

'And a word of warning,' Elspeth said. 'Being on the coil actually makes you more likely to contract a sexually transmitted infection. Use protection if you're going to have such varied and frequent sex.'

'Is *any* of that science?' I asked her, putting on my coat.

'Yes. Go down the corridor to room three. A nurse is waiting to examine you.'

The test was okay, but still, suitably uncomfortable. I made my way to lunch with Cassandra afterwards. I was fine; I don't know why all of these nurses were so worried, and so *rude*. Elspeth could try to be a little more approachable, maybe that way she wouldn't need to basically waterboard information out of me.

I squeezed my way into the crowded café, pirouetting clumsily through prams and trying not to sweep babycinos off tables with my coat. I spotted Cassandra in the corner.

'Hello, sorry I'm late!' I said, trying to remove my scarf as it got tangled in my twists. Eventually, having made it worse, I gave up and sat opposite her, half of my face covered by fabric.

'What's new?' she said, pouring me a glass of water. 'Still making your way through all of the men on OkCupid?'

'What?' I spluttered.

'I'm only teasing, don't take it personally!' Cassandra laughed. 'Casual sex is a perfectly normal coping mechanism.'

'. . . everything is fine,' I said, forcing a smile.

'So. I think I've met someone?' she said, smirking as she took a delicate sip of her coffee. It was these almost imperceptible actions of hers; the smirking, the faux coyness, that made me cringe and also question our friendship. But, if I was anything, I was loyal. And she couldn't help but be low-key the worst, I reminded myself regularly.

'Who?' I said, taking a giant gulp of water.

It's never great, losing a fellow single friend to a relationship, but given that Cassandra spends most of the time we're together either judging or psychoanalysing me, her locking herself away with a boyfriend was no bad thing. I fiddled with my scarf as she told me about this *amazing* new boy that she'd met at the Design Museum.

'As I was looking at this installation on coloured wool he sidled up next to me. I thought I was in the way so moved aside, but he moved closer, and told me that I was more interesting than anything he'd seen that day.'

Joy shone out of her and a pang of jealousy spiked through me.

'So we just left the museum, went for a coffee and spoke so much that coffee turned into dinner, then dinner turned into him walking me home.'

I was wide-eyed with wonder. I thought that being walked home only happened in films.

'But we didn't have sex,' Cassandra continued. 'I've decided that I'm not having penetrative sex with someone until I'm sure that I'm into them. He didn't mind that, though.' She put a hand to her chest. 'We spoke about it and he said that it was admirable, in this age of instant sex. We fell asleep hugging, Queenie. Properly wrapped around each other, with my head on his chest and his hands stroking my hair and face. It was so nice.'

'And have you seen him again?' I asked, when given a second to speak.

'We've seen each other every day for the last two weeks!' She raised an eyebrow smugly.

'No wonder I haven't heard from you!' I said, jealousy now flooding every bit of space in my body.

'He comes to meet me after work and we walk back to mine, or dinner, cinema, you know, just nice date things.'

Just nice date things. What were those?

'I think the sex will happen soon, though,' Cassandra said coyly.

'Well, I'm really happy for you, Cassandra.' I smiled. 'Let's see what he looks like?'

I pulled out my phone and tapped the Facebook icon.

'He's like me, he doesn't have any social media, so no stalking, I'm afraid,' Cassandra said, turning my phone over. 'But rest assured, he's very good-looking. Anyway. Should we eat? I'm starving.'

She opened her menu.

'I'm not hungry, actually. Lost my appetite,' I said, taking another sip of water. My head felt cloudy and my stomach didn't feel much better.

'It just goes to show, doesn't it? All that worry I had about me not connecting with someone, and look!' Cassandra squealed.

'It's so great, really!' I said quietly. 'When are we going to meet him?'

'Soon.' She seemed to hesitate for a second. 'I'm going to do things the other way round, get him to meet the family first, I think, then friends. How's work, by the way?'

'It's fine.' I shrugged. 'It's frustrating, sometimes. You know, I really *care* about things, and when I pitch them to her, Gina always tells me they're not good enough.'

'What things specifically?' Cassandra asked.

'Black Lives Matter things,' I told her.

'What is it you said to me when you were going for your interview? "Even if they don't pay me, it doesn't matter, because my presence in the room will be enough," 'she recalled.

I nodded, remembering why I put up with Cassandra's cons. There were clearly a few pros.

'Well, if you care, you've got to keep pushing it. It's important, and it's why you took this job in the first place. How *are* you for money, by the way?'

'Ah,' I said, embarrassed by what I was gearing myself up to ask. 'I'm so, so sorry to ask, but could you transfer me just a tiny bit to take me over to payday? I get paid earlier because of Christmas so I can pay you back soon.' I was ashamed but also relieved that she asked before I could beg her.

'Don't worry about that, just add it to the tab. What would you do without me?' Cassandra smirked, flipping her golden-brown hair almost violently.

On the way home, I texted Guy. He came round that night, had sex with my body twice and left. We didn't use protection *again*. I need to take this seriously and not self-sabotage. The last thing I needed adding to my unclear relationship situation was an STI. What was wrong with me? I wished at this point I cared about myself enough to try and answer the question.

*

'Bruv, this club is *dead*.' Kyazike shouted in my ear. 'Shit music, the drinks cost nuff, everyone is looking at us like we're aliens.'

She gestured around the venue at the trendy boys and girls who would briefly stop gurning away in their own worlds to glance at us, the only people of colour in the club, with suspicion. I looked around the dingy room, lit by fuzzy red lighting that bothered my eyes, its close black walls making it feel smaller than it was. It smelt tangy and Kyazike and I slid across the wet floor whenever we tried to move. I'd only come out because Kyazike told me that our best years were almost behind us and that *I especially* needed to have some fun.

'This is what happens when white people come into an area and make it tame,' Kyazike shouted above the music.

I nodded, sadly. 'Gentrification.'

'What?' Kyazike asked before downing the remaining half of a glass of champagne.

I leaned over and repeated what I'd said in her ear, my voice straining over the buzzing EDM. Kyazike gestured that we go outside, so we got up and walked to the smoking area and stood huddled under a heater.

She kissed her teeth. 'Rah. Gen-trif-i-cation, yeah?' She sounded the word out. 'So *gentrification* is the reason I've wasted my make-up?' She looked at me. 'And I wore my best shoes.'

'I didn't want to come here, you're the one who chose it!' I protested.

Kyazike gently moved my head away from the heater so that my hair didn't catch fire.

'Yeah, but you're the one who lives in Brixton, you should have warned me, innit,' Kyazike said, pursing her lips.

'I can't keep up with all of Brixton's changes,' I laughed.

'Queenie. You're Caribbean. Brixton is *you lot's* domain. You should know what's going on in your area. The same way that I'm African, and Peckham is *my lot's* domain. *I* know what's happening in Peckham,' Kyazike informed me.

'So why didn't you choose somewhere in *your domain*?'

'I need to broaden my horizons, break out of the ends. My search for Mr Right continues, and I ain't finding him in Peckham,' she said, reading a message on her phone. 'But true say this club is too dead for me. My cousins are at a rave on Old Kent Road, you want to come?'

We went to slide our way inside and were stopped by a drunk girl with short pink hair who reached out and ran her hands through my twists like they weren't attached to my scalp.

'OhmygodIlovethemsomuuuch!' she gasped, mesmerised.

'What the fuck do you think you're doing?' Kyazike said, grabbing the girl by the wrist and pushing her hand away. 'You can't do that!'

'Oh my god,' the girl whimpered, clutching her wrist as if Kyazike had snapped it.

'Don't fucking touch people like they're your property!' Kyazike shouted at the girl. 'You dickhead!'

The girl's friend hurried around her and cooed over her drunkenly as Kyazike and I started to walk away, me tucking my hair into my scarf so that we didn't have a repeat performance.

'What's going on here?'

A bouncer with dyed red hair that matched a tight T-shirt straining over his muscles appeared suddenly from the darkness and put each of his giant hands on mine and Kyazike's shoulders.

'Eh, take your hands off me.' Kyazike stepped away from him. 'Ask *her* what's going on.'

She gestured at my handler.

'I was only being nice,' the blonde girl said, looking with big blinking eyes at the bouncer.

'Right, you two, you'll have to leave.' The bouncer put his hand back on Kyazike's shoulder and pushed us towards the door.

'We're leaving your shit club anyway,' Kyazike told him. 'But if you like your clientele reaching out to touch black people like we're animals in a petting zoo, then fair play, innit.'

Kyazike went off to Old Kent Road while I sat on the bus home, absolutely astonished and yet still not entirely shocked by what had happened in the club. It was unfair, whichever way you looked at it, and was pretty indisputable evidence that even in

Brixton, where we were meant to be the majority, we weren't. Another reminder that we, and our needs, didn't matter. Before I got off the bus, I made an internal list of people who could touch my hair.

1. Me
2. A hairdresser
3. That's it, that's the whole list.

Chapter Nine

The day was dragging. Darcy was on a pre-Christmas break with her family and I was too exhausted by life to try and talk to anybody else in my office, so my only interaction was with Chuck, the intern. He kept asking me to join him for coffee and I kept finding more inventive ways of saying no. He, more than anyone, needs to learn that you can't have everything you want.

Why wasn't I this much of a beacon for men when I was a teenager? It would have undone years of damage caused by being the funny friend in a group of desirable blondes, brunettes and redheads. I was about to go and make my millionth cup of tea for *something* to do when I got an email from Ted.

On Tuesday, 14 December, Noman, Ted <Ted.Noman@ dailyread.co.uk> wrote at 16:21:

Can I talk to you?

I eschewed the pull of him and carried on with a new pitch to Gina, since none of the others had been good enough. When I felt ready, I printed my pitch and made my way to Gina's office. I walked in quietly and closed the door behind me.

'What have you got for me?' Gina asked without looking away from her screen.

I took a deep breath to steel myself before I started.

'It's called "Trigger Thumbs".'

'What?' Gina asked, turning to face me.

'It's a piece about liberals who tweet traumatic content.'

'And what's the content of the piece, once we get beyond your wordplay?'

'Well, basically, it's how people post all of these horrifying stories of rape, sexual abuse, kidnapping, bombings, school shootings – basically everything bad that has happened, without thinking about how it will affect anyone who sees.'

'Who are these people who are posting?' Gina asked, going back to her screen.

'Well, mainly all of these liberal white journalists who can afford to work in journalism because their ric –'

'Careful.'

'Okay, well, how about – ' I tried to change tack.

' – you need more of a hook, either way.'

'Right. Well, what if the hook is the Me Too movement? Loads of people were posting their stories of sexual assault without thinking about how women who didn't feel like they could spe – '

' – *way* too long ago now.'

'Um, okay,' I floundered. 'How about – '

'How *about*, for the blog, you look back at, say, ten of the best black dresses Me Too supporters have worn at awards ceremonies?'

'Seriously?' I asked.

'Yes,' Gina said. 'It's Christmas season, and people need chic party dresses. Good to attach some moral standing to it.'

'But I – ' I started, before trailing off. What was the point?

'By Friday morning, please.'

*

After work I headed to my grandparents' house to meet my little cousin Diana for babysitting duties, despite telling Aunt Maggie that Diana was mature enough to look after me.

I only agreed to it because Maggie needed someone to watch her while she went on her first date since the divorce five hundred years ago, and I felt like I should support that in any way I could, even if it meant spending an entire evening being berated by a teenager I was a bit scared of.

When I got there, the front door was open and Diana was sitting on the stairs while Maggie held a finger a millimetre away from her face and spoke to her through gritted teeth.

'*Di*ana.' My aunt placed emphasis on the first syllable of my cousin's name as she always did when Diana was in trouble. 'You need to pay attention to things, and not just think about how to answer *back*. I've spoken to your teachers about it, and even *they* tell me that all you do is sit on your phone. You think that's why I bought it for you, so you can spend all day at school looking at people doing make-up? You have to *learn*.'

'I *am* learning!' Diana said. 'I watch make-up tutorials, and now I know how to do make-up looks? I did your make-up for your date, Mum.' Diana rolled her eyes.

'That's not what I mean!' Maggie turned to face me.

She looked nice, don't get me wrong, but she didn't look like *her*. That's what five layers of foundation and two sets of fake eyelashes will do.

'Queenie, Mum has a headache so you can't stay here.' Maggie walked to the door and pushed her feet into a pair of leopard-print boots with heels at least six inches high.

'Can you walk in those?' I asked.

'I'm going to have to try.' She winked as she opened the door. 'Behave for your cousin. Don't spend all your time on your phone,

and don't have chicken and chips from Morley's for dinner *again*.'
Maggie directed this at her daughter. 'Bye, both, wish me luck.'

'What would our Lord and Father say about you going on dates, Maggie?' I asked.

'Don't be so blasphemous!' Maggie said as she shut the door behind her. 'Besides, he's a pastor.'

I turned to look at Diana and shouted into the ether, 'Grandma is it okay if me and Diana stay he – '

'No!' Our grandmother shouted back from the kitchen.

We left, and as we walked down the road, I asked Diana if she wanted to walk or get the bus. She stopped and looked at me with tightened lips, a face I hadn't realised every woman in my family could master, and from such a young age. We got the bus.

'And are you hungry?' I asked, taking my duties seriously.

'No, I had Morley's earlier, some sweets on the way to Grandma's and four Crunchies.'

'That's not dinner, though, is it? You'll need something more filling than sugar. I don't have anything at home so we'll have to go to the supermarket. I'll get you an oven pizza or something?' I suggested, not sure how to talk to her.

'I'll be fine,' Diana replied, unlocking her phone. She sucked in her cheeks and took a selfie.

'I really think we should get you something. You can't just live off sweets. You'll turn into one,' I said, realising how *old* I sounded.

'What? Why are you talking to me like I'm some baby? Hello? I'm fifteen, Queenie. Anyway, I don't eat things like pizza. It's just too much of one thing. Can't you cook proper food?' she asked, not taking her eyes off her reflection on the phone's screen.

*

The next few hours were filled with Diana picking up and putting down every single thing in my room. Mainly snickering, but also taking pictures of things to show her friends on Snapchat with the caption, 'LOOOOL'. Diana tried out my small range of make-up and told me that it wasn't good enough to create a 'look'. She went through my wardrobe and informed me that all of my clothes were too "granny" for me. She knocked over my jewellery stand and sent rings, necklaces and earrings flying everywhere, then knocked my lamp off my bedside table, smashing the bulb.

'What is this?' Diana said, picking up a film camera of our grandad's that I'd found in his shed and had used for a bit when I was in my photographer phase. 'Because this can't be a camera, I can't even see what I'm looking at.'

'That's because you're not looking in the viewfinder,' I huffed.

'What's that, though?'

'The viewfinder,' I said, pointing at it. 'Look, here, look in that. Wait, don't take a pic – '

Click.

'Don't worry, I guess I needed to finish that film anyway,' I said. Is this what being a parent is like? I wondered briefly, a thought of mine and Tom's once-upon-a-baby creeping in.

'Where's the picture?' Diana stared at me.

'I'll give it to you when I get the film developed,' I said reassuringly, taking the camera away.

'The what?' I'd never seen her look more confused.

'Look, do you want to watch something on my laptop?' I said, opening it up and putting it in front of her.

She pretended to be watching *Fresh Prince*, but actually tweeted, 'Queenie is SO boring that spending time with her feels like this', accompanied by a picture of a skeleton, from the official *Daily Read* Twitter account, which was the final straw. I took the laptop away and password-protected it when she was in the toilet.

In an attempt to get her to stay still and not touch anything or critique me any further, I cooked her a pizza. As predicted, she finished it all. When it got to nine, I called Maggie, but her phone was off. I tried again at nine thirty, still nothing. I gave Diana one of my favourite books to read, promising her that she'd love it, then arguing about why *Angus, Thongs and Full-Frontal Snogging* was worth reading despite the confusing title. She started reading it while I stared at her, smiling encouragingly, and, satisfied when she started laughing, checked my work email.

On Tuesday, 14 December, Noman, Ted <Ted.Noman@ dailyread.co.uk> wrote at 21:40:

I think you need to let yourself be happy. You're waiting for some guy who should respect you enough to at least contact you. But look, I'm here telling you how I feel.

On Tuesday, 14 December, Jenkins, Queenie <Queenie. Jenkins@dailyread.co.uk> wrote at 21:42:

Ted. I'm not quite sure what your motives are here. I've said before, we don't really know each other. And as for 'some guy', my boyfriend will get in touch soon. Can you not see how this in itself is more drama than either of us needs?

On Tuesday, 14 December, Noman, Ted <Ted.Noman@ dailyread.co.uk> wrote at 21:43:

I wouldn't keep you waiting.

I looked over at Diana. She'd fallen asleep with the book on her face. I should have realised from the silence. I tried Maggie one more time but when she didn't answer, I moved Diana so that she was under the quilt. This woke her, because when I turned the light off and got in next to her, she turned to me.

'Queenie. I need a headscarf,' she whispered. 'I won't be able to sleep properly without one.'

'Oh. Sorry for waking you up,' I said, reaching into my bedside table for my spare headscarf. 'Here you go.'

I heard her tie it in the dark, then she was silent. I closed my eyes.

'What happened to your boyfriend?' Diana's words cut through the darkness.

I thought that if I stayed quiet she'd think I'd fallen asleep.

'The white boy,' she pressed on. 'The one who wasn't, like, handsome, but kinda cute in, like, a white bae kind of way.'

'Tom?' I yielded.

'Yeah. Where's he gone?'

'We're on a break,' I said firmly.

'So you've broken up?'

'Nope. A break, like, some time out,' I corrected her. 'It's what adults do.'

'Well, have some *you* time, I guess. Anyway, it's like my mum says. Men will just drain you.' I was worried she'd recite Maggie's speech from the hospital. 'You need to be ready before you let them come into your life. Maybe you weren't ready.'

Was she old enough to be talking like this?

Queenie:
Tom this is shit. I miss you. It's been almost three months. Have you had enough time yet?

He replied the next afternoon.

Tom:
I'm sorry

After work, I met Ted in the park.

Chapter Ten

On Thursday, 16 December, Noman, Ted <Ted.Noman@
dailyread.co.uk> wrote at 17:21:

My mind is racing x

On Thursday, 16 December, Jenkins, Queenie Queenie.
Jenkins@dailyread.co.uk> wrote at 17.29:

Why? Calm down

On Thursday, 16 December, Noman, Ted <Ted.Noman@
dailyread.co.uk> wrote at 17:36:

I'm being paranoid about everything x

On Thursday, 16 December, Jenkins, Queenie <Queenie.
Jenkins@dailyread.co.uk> wrote at 17:40:

Like what? Nobody saw us.

On Thursday, 16 December, Noman, Ted <Ted.Noman@
dailyread.co.uk> wrote at 17:41:

What if they saw my hands up your skirt?? What if I'm put on
some sort of register?

On Thursday, 16 December, Noman, Ted <Ted.Noman@ dailyread.co.uk> wrote at 17:43:

Sorry I'm just being stupid. I just can't believe it happened, after everything. X

On Thursday, 16 December, Jenkins, Queenie <Queenie. Jenkins@dailyread.co.uk> wrote at 17:50:

Don't worry about it. We couldn't have been more covert.

He was annoying me now. I had loads of stuff to finish.

On Thursday, 16 December, Noman, Ted <Ted.Noman@ dailyread.co.uk> wrote at 17:55:

How are you feeling? x

On Thursday, 16 December, Jenkins, Queenie <Queenie. Jenkins@dailyread.co.uk> wrote at 18:03:

Busy. Guilty.

Various stranger sex, fine. Catching feelings, not fine.

On the way back from work, I battled my way through Oxford Street and bought a present for Tom. Partly out of guilt, but mainly out of ritual. There were certain things I wouldn't let slide, break or not. I was trying to gear myself up to spending the 'happy holidays' without him and his family for the first time in three years. At least I don't have to choose his presents for his parents anymore. Or put up with casual family racism.

*

It was my second Christmas with Tom's family. The novelty of a proper Christmas meal had worn off after last year, but I was still surprised by how many trimmings there were and that pork wasn't just allowed in the house, but was wrapped in another form of pork and eaten in one bite-sized go.

'Now, here's what we should do,' Tom's aunt said. 'We're going to play a game. Found it in the attic.'

She blew dust off a board game and placed it on the coffee table in the middle of the room.

'Oh, I love a Christmas game!' Tom's mum said. 'Let me go and get some pens and paper. You can take score, can't you, Stephen?' she said to her brother.

'Yes indeed,' he replied, inching forwards in his seat and hitching his trousers up at the knee. 'We'll need to get into teams, though.' He looked around the room.

I glanced over at Tom to signal that we'd be teammates but he was deep in conversation with his brother.

'How will we split this? I think . . .' Stephen said, slowly, '. . . that we should do *dark* shirts versus *light* shirts. What does everyone think?'

My heartbeat started to quicken.

'Great!' Tom's dad said, looking down at his white shirt. 'That's easy enough!'

I looked down at my white dress. 'I'll be with you, then,' I said, getting up to sit next to him.

'Mmm, not so fast, Queenie!' Stephen said.

I felt my cheeks flush with heat.

'Maybe you should keep score,' he laughed.

'I'm wearing a white dress,' I said, my voice very small.

'But technically there's a bit more dark on you,' he laughed, looking around the room in the hope that everyone would join in.

'She'll be on my team, Stephen,' Tom's dad said, flashing me a consolatory smile.

Chapter Eleven

What is it about Christmastime and couples? It was making me completely miserable. Admittedly I was at a Hanukkah party but the Christmas sentiment still stands. Everyone in this gigantic Islington townhouse was in a pair but me. Saying that, they were all over fifty, so I guess they've had a bit more of a head start to find someone, and half of them were on their second marriages.

Cassandra's dad, the only adult man I'd ever trusted and also probably the actual main reason I endured Cassandra, asked me where Tom was every time he flitted past, tray in hand, and finally stood still long enough for me to say, 'We went on a break, Jacob. In September. But he won't speak to me. He said he needed three months, but I think he needs more time. In your experience, how long are these things meant to last?'

When Jacob looked at me in surprise, I removed the toothpick that I'd been chewing from my mouth and spiked an olive with it angrily.

'Oh, you poor, poor dear. And how are you feeling?' Jacob abandoned his serving duties and sat down next to me, putting a hand on my shoulder. All of the couples in the room turned to look at me.

'I feel lost. And confused,' I said quietly. 'I thought that after a week without me he'd be banging down my door.'

I popped the olive into my mouth and turned to Cassandra, waiting for her to weigh in. She may as well not have been in the room because her eyes darted towards the door every three seconds as she waited for this new demigod boyfriend to get here.

'It'll work itself out if it's meant to,' Jacob said softly. 'Oho! I think something is burning!' He jumped up and left the room, heading towards the kitchen.

'Hello? Cassandra?' I waved my hands in my friend's face. 'Remember me? You invited me here because we've been close for many years and coming to Hanukkah is tradition? You could actually talk to me!'

'I'm nervous, Queenie,' Cassandra said to me, folding then unfolding her arms. 'This is the first time that I've had a boyfriend long enough for him to meet the *whole* family, and you know what my family are like. All neurotic and flappy.' Cassandra stood up and smoothed the back of her dress.

'How does it look?' she asked.

'Sounds like my family. Your bum?' I asked. 'Fine? Nice, even.'

'No, Queenie, my dress. He bought it for me, and I want to check that it's okay.' I inspected the item in question, a barely describable plain black pinafore.

'Cassandra, are you losing your mind?' I asked her, pulling her back down by the arm. 'You look great, but it shouldn't matter anyway. Calm down. He'll get here and he'll love what you're wearing. Even if it is because he bought it. Which I think is weird.'

I lowered my voice before I asked my next question. 'Have you even had sex yet?'

Cassandra jumped up as though I'd thrown a bomb under her bottom. All of the adults stopped talking and turned to look at us.

'We're just going to get a drink!' she announced to the room, and pulled me into the kitchen. Jacob passed us on the way out, the tray seemingly attached to his hand now filled with steaming mini-sausage rolls.

'Pork!' he said, tutting. 'We're terrible Jews, I know.'

'Can you not talk about my relationship so crudely, Queenie?' Cassandra whispered, placing her phone face up on the marble counter. 'Things are going so well for me for the first time in ages, and it's not about sex, it's about me getting to know someone, the connection.'

'Yes, yes, the connection, I know,' I mimicked her. 'So you and this dream boyfriend, you haven't had sex yet?'

'Can you get your mind out of the gutter?' she said, eyes on her phone.

'No, but sex is important, isn't it?' I told her. 'It's the thing that stops you from just being friends with someone. Else we'd all marry our friends.'

Cassandra's phone beeped and she lunged for it, almost smashing a group of wine glasses nearby.

Her face fell. 'He's not coming.'

She slammed the phone back down on the marble counter.

'Don't break it!' I said. 'That's all right. We'll have a good time either way!'

Jacob peered into the kitchen. 'What's going on in here, girls? And where is he, then, your lovely guy? We're all waiting, Cassandra.'

'He's stuck at work, Dad. He's been asked to do another shift and he can't say no.'

'Well, the field he's in, it's no wonder at this time of year, Cassandra. We'll meet him another time, eh?' Jacob went over to Cassandra and put his arm around her. She laid her head on his shoulder.

'I'll just go back into the living room,' I whispered, walking towards the kitchen door.

'No way, come on, Queenie.' Jacob held his other arm out and pulled me into him and Cassandra.

'Jacob, I don't really like physical con – '

'Queenie, please, look beyond yourself,' Cassandra snapped, the harshness of her voice muffled by her dad's jumper.

Jacob let us go after what felt like a lifetime and went back into the living room to continue his flitting.

'I'd decided that tonight was going to be the night,' Cassandra said, smoothing down her dress again.

'For what?'

'That I was going to sleep with him, Queenie!'

'Well, you still can, just after his shift? I feel like you're making this bigger than it is,' I suggested, surprised that she was being like this. 'It's not like this is going to be your first time.'

'And I wanted him to meet everyone, I wanted this one to work.' Cassandra was starting to sound like a spoilt child.

'He *will* meet your family, and it *will* work, Cassandra!' I told her. 'And it can be just the two of us, tonight, like it has been for the past, what, seven years?'

'I don't want it to be the two of us, Queenie, I wanted him here,' Cassandra snapped.

'Okay, well, suit yourself,' I snapped back.

'Sorry, no offence.' She softened. 'Look, I know you're having a weird time of it with the Tom stuff, and it must be bringing up all sorts of mum abandonment stuff,' Cassandra dropped this in the most blasé way possible, 'and I do care, and yes, I am worried about you, but it's time to put me first.'

Her words were so cutting; why did she never think before casually deploying such on-the-nose psychoanalysis?

*

After singing 'Ma'oz Tzur', a Hanukkah song I could never quite get the rhythm of, playing with the dreidel and doing some prayer, I put my coat on to leave.

Jacob came to the front door.

'Breaks, break-ups, they're a nasty business, but you'll be okay,' he promised. 'You've lost some weight, haven't you? Try to eat what you can, keep your strength up. This won't work' – he put a finger to my temple – 'if this isn't taken care of.' He poked my stomach with the same finger.

'Thanks, Jacob. Really,' I said, enduring a hug goodbye because I felt so fucking lonely. 'This evening means a lot to me. Every year.'

'It wouldn't be the same without you, Queenie,' Jacob said, handing over a Tupperware box bursting with food.

'Bye, Cassandra!' I called up into the house, my voice bouncing around the stone floors and high ceilings.

I waited for a second.

No response.

Jacob leaned closer to me. 'I think she's taken to bed. She's a little upset. I think she's really into this one,' he whispered. 'You know, it's ages since she really connected with someone.'

I couldn't even get my dad to text me back, let alone talk to him about my connections.

Walking down Seven Sisters Road to the tube station, in a move that wouldn't be worth Freud's time to dissect, I called Guy. He didn't answer, so I sent him a text.

Queenie:
Come round?

He replied five seconds after I put my phone back in my pocket.

Guy:

You home now? Shave your legs
before I get there

When I got back, Guy was sitting on the wall outside my house.

'All right?' he said, hopping down from the wall.

I leaned in to kiss him and he stepped back.

'Steady on, I'm not your boyfriend.'

'I know you aren't my boyfriend, and I don't want you to be my boyfriend, but if you can have sex with me you can kiss me hello, surely,' I said, sorely.

'Let's not overcomplicate things.'

I rolled my eyes and changed the subject. 'Hey, what did Adam say to Eve the day before Christmas?'

I stepped into my room and Guy followed, hands on my bottom.

'What? Who are they?' he said, throwing himself into the clothes chair and pushing clean laundry onto the floor as he removed his coat.

'You know, from the Bible,' I said.

'What? I dunno,' he said, pulling his boots off.

'It's Christmas, Eve,' I smiled, proudly.

'Is that a joke?' he sneered, pulling his jumper over his head.

'Well, yeah.'

I sat on the bed and pulled my tights off, wondering at what point Guy and I had started this ritual of systematic undressing.

'That doesn't make sense. Surely he'd say "It's Christmas Eve, Eve"?' Guy mansplained, walking over to me. 'I'm too practical-minded for jokes, Queenie.' He reached down and stroked my leg from calf to thigh.

'Do you want to shave your legs now?' He nodded towards the bathroom.

'Um. Is it vital?'

'I just prefer it. I don't mind your lady garden being bushy but I don't like the scratching on my face when I throw your legs over my shoulders.'

I pulled the rest of my outfit off and wrapped my hair with Guy's eyes on me the entire time.

'You know the thing I like about black women?' he said, his eyes running from my hair to my feet. 'Even when you're big girls, it sits well. Sits nice on your hips and that. And your arse. You're lucky.'

I left him on my bed and got into the shower, dutifully running the razor up my legs. When I came out, Guy was asleep in his boxers on top of the covers, lying on his side to face me. I stared at his eyelashes, thinking about how much money I could make if I sold them as a set of fake ones.

I looked at him for a while, remembering my first Christmas with Tom.

*

I'd never had a conventional nuclear-family Christmas. When my dad lived in London, he spent Christmas with his *actual* family in his *other* house; I wasn't welcome but have always made peace with that, given that his wife is an actual living witch. Since I could remember, my mum's hostel only allowed visitors for an hour at a time, so that option was out. The week before my first Christmas with Tom, I was sitting around the table having Friday fish and chips with Tom's family, discussing how 'the little African boy' that they sponsored was doing when his mum reached across the table and put a hand on my forearm.

'You know, you're more than welcome to spend it with us here in Peterborough, Queenie.'

'Um, is she?' Tom's brother clearly wasn't up for it.

'No, don't worry, I spend it with my grandmother every year!' I said with a smile.

'Are you sure?' Tom's mum asked. 'We'd love to have you, and we've got all your presents here under the tree.'

'Well, she can open them after Christmas?'

Adam again. His voice was higher this time.

Tom locked eyes with me and nodded.

I looked over at Adam and smiled. 'I'd love to be here. Thanks, Viv.'

'Don't worry about Adam,' Viv said to me later. 'He's just jealous because you've taken his brother away.'

'I don't want to annoy anyone, especially not at Christmas!' I said. 'It's just that . . . well, your family, it's what a family *should* be. I've never had that.'

'Well, you're part of our family now, Queenie,' Viv said. 'And you always will be.'

Come Christmas Eve, Tom and I were sitting on the last train to Peterborough, Tom squashed into the window by bags of presents on the seat next to him. I sat opposite him with my feet on the suitcase full of his presents just for me. We'd been together for under a year by then, so not only had I known his parents, grandmother and Adam well enough to choose all of their gifts, but I also felt that, after never getting what I wanted and sick of being asked, I could give Tom a full list of the things that I wanted rather than just hoping for the best and getting something that I'd have to pretend to like.

'Are you excited, Tom?' I asked, leaning across and putting my hands on his cheeks.

He didn't answer.

'Tom, *please* stop faffing with your phone, it's Christmas Eve! I need attention, I am excited like a small child.'

He put his phone in his pocket.

'Yes, I'm excited too, sorry.'

'Good, you should be excited, because this is not only our first Christmas together but my first Christmas where there will be alcohol!'

'I always forget that your family don't drink.'

'Not a drop, Tom. Not since my grandad had a small sherry in 1961 and called the ambulance because he thought his heart was failing.'

I swapped seats with the bags of presents next to Tom and tucked myself under his arm.

'You make me very happy, you know. I know I'm not good at saying it, but you do,' I said, looking out of the train window, watching as the grey buildings thinned out and made way for suburban tranquillity.

He lifted a hand to my hair and stroked it. 'You make me happy too. I love you.'

'Tom, don't touch my hair.'

*

I put a T-shirt on and got onto the bed next to Guy, tucking myself into him. I sort of hated myself for doing it, and him, but of all the anonymous partners, he was the most reliable. And, reliably, he faced away from me as soon as my body touched his. I climbed under the sheets and thought of nothing but Tom as I fell asleep, Guy's snores providing a steady soundtrack to my sadness.

I woke up to a digging in my ribs.

'You're talking in your sleep.'

'Huh? What?' I sat up.

Guy was squinting at me with one eye, the other buried in the pillow. 'You're talking in your sleep,' he huffed. 'I don't know who this Tom is, but his ears must be burning.'

'Sorry,' I said, lying back down. 'Have you done all of your Christmas shopping?'

He didn't reply. Had he already gone back to sleep?

'What time is it?' I asked.

'Too early to be talking,' he said gruffly.

'But it's a week until Christmas!' I reminded him.

He took my hand and shoved it into his boxers. 'All right, I've got a present for you.'

*

'What?'

'I said I've got a present for you. Wake up, Queenie.'

I sat up, my eyes still closed. When I blinked them open, Tom was sat cross-legged at the end of the bed holding a small gift in his hands.

'Oh, Tom, what is it?'

'Well, you're meant to open it, aren't you?' he said, handing it to me and moving up the bed so that he was next to me.

I opened it slowly.

'Ha! Where did you get this?'

It was a silk headscarf.

'Happy first Christmas! Do you like it?' Tom asked, beaming from ear to ear. 'I went to one of those black hair shops in Brixton for it. I chose a green and black one because your other one is gold and all together those are the Jamaica colours, right?'

'*You* went all the way to Brixton for a headscarf?'

'Well I didn't know how to find it on the internet and I remember seeing them when we went to buy your hair that time.'

I put my arm around his shoulders and forced him into a gentle headlock. 'You're very good to me,' I said as he moved his head from my chest to my neck, kissing me behind the ear gently.

'That's because you're my Queenie,' he whispered in my ear, taking the headscarf from my hands and slipping his fingers through mine.

*

'Don't you like it?' Guy asked, disappointed that I wasn't pleased by his erection.

'Mmm, I think it's too early for that sort of present, Guy.' I removed my hand from his boxers.

'Oh come on, you said it yourself, it's Christmastime. How about a quick handjob?' he begged. 'You took so long in the shower last night that I fell asleep before I could give you a festive fuck. A handjob is the least you can do.'

'Guy. I think we should,' I said in a very small voice, '. . . maybe wrap things u – '

'Ha!' Guy cut me off. 'Come on, there's nothing to wrap up, this is never going to be more than sex, you know that!

You're a good girl, but I'm busy, I don't have time for dating and all that.'

'Guy, you know I'm a person, don't you,' I started, 'with thoughts and feelings and – '

' – and a big gob, but most of all, a big arse.' He laughed. 'Come ooon, don't get all serious, we have fun, you and me.'

He pulled his boxers down and presented his erection to me again.

'Just climb on, Santa wants to give you a ride on his sleigh.'

'I thought you were too practically minded for jokes, being a doctor?' I teased. There was no point being cross. Guy was very persuasive. He was always going to get his way.

'Junior doctor,' he corrected me. 'Anyway, we're going off topic and I'm going to lose my lob on. Come on, Queenie. Climb on board. Don't worry, I'll pull out before I give you a Christmas miracle of your own.'

Chapter Twelve

It was Christmas Eve, and I'd been staring at the phone all week having texted Tom to ask if we could see each other so I could give him his gift, dropped a present off at his office after hearing nothing back, and then sent a follow-up text asking if it would be okay for me to call his mum on Christmas Day. Still no word.

I shushed the voices in my mind that were asking what I was fighting for. In the absence of the family Christmas with Tom, I'm going to be with my grandmother, who is happy that I'm back with her after three years away. I was, I think by way of punishment, being forced to go to Midnight Mass.

We got to the church at 11.15 p.m., and Diana, Maggie, my grandad, my grandmother and me filed onto a bench near the back of the already busy church. How was it so popular? I tried to sit next to Diana but we'd been separated like naughty schoolchildren. Just before things got started, a small figure appeared next to me at the end of our bench.

'Sylvie,' my grandmother whispered to my mum as she stood awkwardly next to me. 'You're late. Sit down.'

I huffed and shuffled over to make some room for her.

'Hello, Queenie,' she whispered to me. 'I'm surprised to see you here!'

'Hi,' I whispered back, facing forwards.

'How did Mum get you here?' my mum whispered again.

'I think it's about to start,' I said, finally turning to look at her.

I don't look like my mum. She's light-skinned, some sort of genetic throwback, maybe. Though I've heard family whisperings that my grandad accused my grandmother of having an affair, after she was born. My mum's complexion glows, her hair is long and curly. Not tight, coarse curls like mine; her curls are soft, they move, they bounce, they fall around her face. Her eyes are hazel, and when she's not looking at the floor, they're searching for the niceness in people. Unlike me, my mum is tiny. Slim, fragile, the shortest person in our family.

I look like my dad. Darker than my mum, with black eyes, eyes that are either narrowing with suspicion, or rolling. I also, as my grandmother says, have 'the same figure as your dad.'

'Okay,' she said, smiling gently.

A line of choirboys and -girls walked past, singing and swinging incense. My phone buzzed.

Diana:

This stuff is gonna make me have an asthma attack

Queenie:

Can you pretend to have a coughing fit so that I can take you outside. Please

Diana:

NO, because I'd have to squeeze past the whole row and I don't want to wake grandad up

I looked down the row at my grandad, who was already fast asleep, his head as far back as it could go and his mouth wide open.

'If grandad is allowed to sleep, am I?' I whispered to my grandmother, who kissed her teeth loudly in response until she remembered that we were in a church.

'Once, in royal David's city,' the priest began to sing, his microphone-amplified voice ringing out much louder than the choir and congregation. He was ad-libbing in a way that he probably hadn't been taught in priest school.

Diana:

This guy must think he's on X Factor

Queenie:
Would you put him through?

Diana:

Not gonna lie, his voice isn't bad you know. Put a little autotune on it, he might get into the top 10

'*Di*ana. Put the phone away,' I heard Maggie hiss as I mumbled along to the hymn, my eyes grazing the words on the song sheet. To my right, my grandmother belted the words out next to me in an accent-tinged trill, most of the lyrics freestyled, while my mum sang along quietly and sweetly to my left, not missing a word or a note.

I glanced at her. She wasn't even looking at the lyrics.

'Years of Sunday school,' she broke out of song to say to me. 'I'll never forget a word.'

I ignored her and zoned out for the hour, conjuring up a frame-by-frame imagining of what Christmas would have been like with Tom this year. I looked up to the ornate church ceiling. I closed my eyes and tried out a little prayer.

'Dear Lord,' I started in my head, 'I know that I don't pray to you often, or really ever, but I just wanted to ask, please, if you do exist, could things be a bit more smooth-sailing from now on? I know that maybe I don't deserve your pity or your mercy but I am having a really bad time and I don't know what to do. Maybe I can just have some clarity?'

I squeezed my eyes tightly.

'What if you just get Tom to text me and tell me he wants to see me? That's an easy request, it's not like I'm asking for him back immediately. I understand that these things take time.' I paused to think if there was anything I should add. 'And eventually, if Tom does or doesn't love me again, can I maybe just be a bit happy? I feel like I was born miserable and never given reason to change that. Oh, and I am so sorry for all of the casual sex, so please forgive me for that also,' I prayed. 'I know that it's awful, and against everything Catholics stand for, but – ow!'

I yelped as my grandmother pinched my arm with her bony fingers.

'Don't go to sleep,' she growled. 'The priest looked right over at us.'

'I wasn't!' I whispered. 'I was deep in prayer!'

Diana:
Lol

> **Queenie:**
> How is she so strong?

> **Diana:**
> Porridge every marnin' fi 100 years

'Amen,' I said out loud in response to Diana's text, joined by the congregation as the whole ordeal came to an end.

*

Christmas with my grandparents meant nothing fun. No alcohol, no Christmas TV and definitely no pigs in blankets. Maggie was dominating the kitchen and barking orders at anyone who came near, so my grandad was hiding in his little shed, while the head of the house had left in search of custard powder.

Diana was with her dad, so instead of having the only other young person in the family to talk to, I was in the spare room under seven duvets that my grandmother put on me before she went out. I was lying down, a constant chain of Ferrero Rocher entering my mouth, and watching *Love, Actually* – a film that usually made me roar with laughter through sheer disbelief when I wasn't heartbroken.

I didn't know how I could feel any bleaker. I hadn't felt this alone in such a long time. It was fine BT (Before Tom) because I hadn't known what it was like to know closeness, to be able to share everything with one person, to have someone love you unconditionally, and to love them, despite each others -isms. AD (After our Division) was truly unbearable.

I heard the front door open and paused the film, holding my breath.

'Look who I found on the road!' my grandmother announced to the house. 'Sylvie's here!'

I strained my ears.

'Hi everyone, it's me!' I heard my mum say, very quietly.

'Go up, say hello to your daughter,' I heard my grandmother tell her. 'She's eating her way through her feelings, go and take the chocolate away.'

I heard my mum shuffle up the stairs so pretended to be asleep.

'I know you're awake, Queenie. You've been pretending to be asleep since you were little, I know the signs,' she said.

I felt her sit down on the bed and I opened my eyes.

'Hi,' I said quietly, not wanting to look at her.

'I didn't get to talk to you properly yesterday. How are you, darling?' My mum put a hand on my leg. Even though I couldn't feel her touch through all of the blankets, I moved away sharply.

'Sorry, I know that you don't like touching,' she said, pulling her hand away quickly. 'Maggie told me that you and Tom are on some sort of break. How are you doing?'

She paused for an answer she knew she wouldn't get.

'And Diana says you're living in a shared house! You must hate that. You know, if I had the room . . .'

'I'm fine, Mum.' I sighed, tired of Christmas already.

'It's okay to suffer, you know,' she said to me. 'It's okay to be in pain, and be hurting, Queenie.'

'I said I'm *fine*, Sylvie,' I repeated, rolling over to face the window so I couldn't see how much me calling her by her name hurt her.

'This isn't like you, Queenie, to be so robotic about things.'
I heard her stand up.

'Maybe I'm not me anymore.' I closed my eyes, feeling the tears that were about to come.

'Sylvie?' Maggie called my mum from the kitchen. 'Can you come and help me, please? The turkey needs a final baste and my hands are full with the macaroni cheese!'

'Well. You'll always be my Queenie,' my mum said, leaving the room and closing the door behind her.

*

After a ten-minute grace led by Maggie that my grandad drifted in and out of sleep for, we would have eaten Christmas dinner to the soundtrack of BBC News had it not been for Maggie reeling off the list of cosmetic treatments she'd been saving up for and was planning to have done in the new year.

'. . . and then my doctor, and he is a lovely doctor, Dr Elliot, what he's going to do is take some of the fat from my stomach, and then he's going to inject it into this empty part of my bosom, here.'

My grandad choked on his turkey.

'Maggie, please, we're all eating.' My grandmother put her fork down. 'Tek *water*, Wilfred!'

'I'm only saying!' Maggie said, spearing a roast potato on my mum's plate with her fork. 'You're being quiet,' she continued to my mum, shoving the stolen potato into her mouth.

'Oh, I'm okay,' my mum muttered.

'You're not eating, Sylvie,' my grandmother said. 'You get smaller every time we see you.'

'She's always been small, though. She's the lucky one,' Maggie said, nudging my mum so hard that all eight stone of her almost fell off her chair.

'Nothing lucky about being big or small. You're all beautiful. All sizes.' My grandmother looked pointedly at me and my aunt. 'But still, Maggie, I want you and Queenie to go and get your blood pressure checked. And your cholesterol.' She picked up her fork and began to eat again.

'Grandad, can we put something on the telly that isn't news?' I asked.

He finally looked away from the television and stared at me for a million years.

'As you all know, I do not like anything that is fictitious,' he announced, turning the news up and facing the screen again. 'The only thing we should be watching is what's happening in the world around us. It's a horrible state of affairs, and you, young as you are, need to stop being so ignorant.'

'Grandad, you know I work at a newspaper. I know what's going on in the world.'

'You work at the magazine, Queenie, it's all opinion pieces and clubbing, not real news,' he replied swiftly.

'Wilfred. Don't start. Nuh even *badda* start on Jesus' birt'day. Han' me the remote,' my grandmother said through tightened lips.

My grandad sighed and pushed the remote across the table to her. She passed it to me and I scanned the channels as my mum and Maggie went to sit in the front-front room, the one with plastic covers on the sofas and dust sheets on all of the best furniture. Nobody is allowed in there. I still have to clean it every time I come here, though. On my way to the kitchen to get pudding I stopped by the door to eavesdrop.

'She's fine, you know she's tough,' I heard my aunt say.

'She's not that tough, Maggie. And I appreciate you looking after her when I couldn't, really I do, but she's my daughter, not yours.' My mum was crying gently. 'And I know her! She's good at pretending. But I've let her down, I should have been better to her, that way she might have been better to herself.'

Maggie mmm-ed softly in the pauses where my mum spoke.

'I shouldn't have left her. I shouldn't have been so *controlled* by that devil man and left her all alone.'

I heard Maggie sigh quietly. 'What's the point in thinking like that, Sylv? You did it, you can't change that now. All you can do is move forward with her. Build back the relationship. You and Queenie were close, that doesn't just go away.'

'But what if it has?' my mum asked softly, fear in her voice.

'Stop worrying about Queenie, sis, and focus on yourself. Trust me, your daughter is all right. She's a brave one.'

'Being brave isn't the same as being okay.'

'You have to look after yourself, Sylvie. You need to recover. Why don't you come to church with me?' Maggie suggested.

I was surprised she hadn't offered the prospect of divine healing sooner.

'No thanks, Maggie,' my mum said.

At least we agreed on something.

'Suit yourself,' my aunt said. 'Well, look, worry about your-self. What's the latest on the court case?'

'It's killing me, Maggie. Every time I have to see Roy I have to stop myself from being sick.'

'That's why you've lost so much weight,' Maggie commented. 'Two and a half blasted years of having to go through this. You need to let me know when the hearings are, I can come along with you.'

'I don't want you to hear what we went through, Maggie. I'm so embarrassed. The lawyers, they bring it all up all the time. All of it.'

My mum sobbed and I felt tears rush to my eyes.

'They've finally found his private bank account, though, where he'd put all the money from my house, so that's something. Doesn't mean I'll get any of it back, though.'

'I hope your lawyer is pushing for something.' Maggie raised her voice slightly.

'She is, she is,' my mum said softly. 'She said it would help the case if Queenie testified, but I don't want her to relive what she saw.'

'Don't bring Queenie in,' Maggie said firmly. 'No.'

'I won't. Listen to this,' my mum spluttered. 'Remember when he slammed my face into the steering wheel when I was driving and made me crash? He told the judge I crashed because I was drinking. Lied through his teeth. He's mad, Maggie!'

'You weren't to know he'd be *this* mad, though.'

'I don't know why I couldn't see it though,' my mum said. 'I was so scared, scared of being alone after Queenie's dad upped and left me. I thought nobody would ever want me again, and when Roy came along, I thought he was a god.'

'He was a master manipulator, Sylv.'

'But I abandoned my daughter,' my mum wailed. 'I loved her so much and I abandoned her.'

I felt myself being pulled back by the shoulder. It was grandad.

'Let the big people speak, nuh?' he whispered. 'Nuttin' in there for you.'

I wouldn't feel sorry for her. She'd made her mistakes, and now we both had to live with them. I wiped my eyes quickly and went back up to the spare room and checked my phone. I had a text from Gina.

Gina

Are you not checking work email? Odd. Could you please? Need you in earlier. MC

I logged into my work account and tried to ignore everything but Gina's email. I'd made a conscious point of not checking my work inbox every single minute when I was out of the office because I read some article about how it's bad for our mental health. And yes, there are a lot of things worse than worrying about work in the holidays, but I was determined to take my not wanting to work more than I was paid for very seriously.

On Tuesday, 25 December, Row, Gina <Gina.Row@ dailyread.co.uk> wrote at 11:34:

Q. Need you in tomorrow (26th) AM. Just checked email and saw message from printer – Chuck's edits to the next issue? A mess. Need you to fix before mag goes to print. Check main drive, all there. Pages 32-60. Make changes, file new version. Can't do it myself as stuck in Suffolk. Text me when fixed. G

I went to close the browser but my eyes accidentally scanned the inbox and landed on an email from Ted sitting amongst the unopened messages.

I went to open it but stopped myself and closed the laptop.

I am not very disciplined, however, and have mainly made peace with that, so opened the laptop.

On Tuesday, 25 December, Noman, Ted <Ted.Noman@ dailyread.co.uk> wrote at 15:45:

Queenie, my head is swimming with thoughts of you. I've sat through so many dinners and family parties and I'd swap it all to be sitting with you in our park. Say we can do that as soon as we get back? Merry Christmas. X

Delete. If this was the clarity I'd asked God for, I'm never praying again.

Chapter Thirteen

Apart from Silent Jean, who I'm not sure even left the office for Christmas, I was the only person on my floor. It took me a million years to get inside because the security guard is a weird seasonal one who didn't believe that I worked for a newspaper.

When I asked why else I'd be here in the middle of the holiday break when I could be at home, his continued line was, 'because you might be a troublemaker'.

I had left my pass at home, but eventually he let me in after I forced him to get the lift up to the fifth floor and look at the poster of me that was in the canteen. I didn't *want* to take part in it, but the paper were doing a whole 'we are diverse' initiative and asked if I would be on the supporting images as I am one of four diverse members of staff who don't work in the service divisions. The poster shows me, Vishnay from the finance supplement and Josey from Music all standing awkwardly underneath the words '*The Daily Read*: News for All'. Zainab in Digital had refused to take part.

When, in my induction, the Spanish HR assistant quite literally said to me, 'You are very lucky to be working here! There are others like you, except not the same colour,' I wasn't sure that I was hearing her properly so asked her to repeat what she'd said.

'You know! There are darker ones, but they're in IT.'

I'd opened my mouth to respond (though still have no idea what I was going to say) but she jumped in with, 'Don't worry, my husband is black, so I know about you and your people.' She's gone now. Was she fired? I wouldn't be surprised.

THE CORGIS

Queenie:
Guess where I am

Kyazike:
Lol. Happy Christmas. Where are you? You're lucky you ain't in Staines, nothing to do here, fam

Darcy:
In bed. You're almost always in bed

Queenie:
I'm at the office, THANKS

Darcy:
People don't usually start with the New Year's resolutions the day after Christmas. Where has this dedication come from?

Queenie:

Gina made me come in to sort out something Chuck did. It's not bad, actually. Unlike you normal people, my family are mainly intolerable. My grandad made us watch the news while we ate dinner

Queenie:

Anyway, text company is appreciated while I'm here, thanks

Queenie:

Please. Stories, memes, pictures of what you got, anything

Silent Jean kept gliding past my desk to go and make tea. What did she achieve by staring at me? After my second hour of trying to make sense of Chuck's madness and shoving 1k miniature Snickers down my throat, I heard the lift doors open.

Thankful to have the company of somebody who wasn't Jean, I turned around to see Ted striding through the doors.

'What are you doing here?' I asked, less thankful that it was him.

'I needed to file something. Best Boxing Day Goals.'

He looked oddly proud of that headline, as though it contained any wordplay.

'Quiet down here,' Ted observed. He sat in the chair next to mine. 'What are *you* doing here?'

'Gina asked me to come in and fix something. She can't do it herself because she's "stuck in Suffolk",' I said breezily. 'Anyway, I should just get on with this.'

I turned to my screen, so thrown by Ted appearing suddenly that I couldn't remember what I needed to do. What can you do in this situation but pretend to type? What if heartbreak had made me genuinely mentally unwell?

'You're pretending to type,' Ted said.

'I'm doing very important work, here,' I assured him. 'Please leave me in peace.'

'You didn't reply to my email.'

I didn't say anything.

'Queenie.' Ted put a hand on mine. 'I've missed you.'

'Don't do this again.' I pulled my hand away and carried on looking at my screen. 'Do I need to remind you that there's CCTV in this office? And Jean is over there!'

'Can I convince you to go for a little, er, *jaunt*, with me?' Ted asked quietly.

I got up and walked towards the toilet. I could hear Ted following me, so sped up. Silent Jean looked up from her desk, scared as though I were charging towards her. I crossed the office and made it into the disabled loo. I locked myself in.

'Queenie, come on,' Ted whispered through the door.

'Come on nothing. Leave me alone, please. What you're technically doing is stalking. I could get Jean to call the police.'

'What, that woman who haunts the building? That's a bit dramatic. Come out of there, please. I need to explain.'

I unlocked the door and tried to push it open, but felt something against it. I shoved it, pushing it with my whole weight.

'Ow!' It only opened part way. I put my head around the door and saw Ted on the floor leaning against it. I remembered when Tom used to console me outside the bathroom door and shook my head to chase the memory away.

'I didn't think you'd open it, stubborn as you are,' Ted said, standing up slowly and making a big thing about stretching his legs out. 'I'm an old man, Queenie.' He forced a laugh.

'You're only six years older than me, Ted. And I'm only coming out because I need to finish my work.'

I stepped past him and walked over to my desk. He must have finally got the message because he didn't follow me. I finished correcting Chuck's numerous errors at five, filed the new version, emailed Gina and started to head out of the office. I was close to the lift when someone grabbed my hand. I snatched my whole body out of their reach.

Ted placed his hands on my waist and pulled me up and into the lift.

'Cameras!' I reminded him. 'What if someone is watching?'

He stood directly behind me and kissed my neck.

'Let them see,' he whispered into my ear.

'Fuck it,' I purred, melting into him.

We got up to Ted's floor and as soon as we stepped through the lift doors, he took a sharp right and opened the door to the disabled toilets.

'After you,' he said, my heart beginning to beat faster.

I walked in like some sort of idiot incapable of independent thought.

Ted followed and locked the door behind him. He kissed me and pushed me against the wall, unbuttoning my shirt with confident hands. I undid his coat and he shrugged it onto the floor. I tried to undo his shirt, but he took my hands and moved them down by my sides.

'No, stop, leave it. I need to keep it on.' He tore my shirt off and threw it on the floor before unhooking my bra and dropping it at my feet. He took my breasts in his hands and squeezed them roughly, staring at me as he sucked one nipple and then the other. I guess it's that thing when women are meant to maintain eye contact with a man while she sucks his dick? I've never done it, because I think it's weird. When you're on the receiving end of the stare, it's *just* as weird.

'I can't believe I'm finally seeing your tits,' Ted panted.

'And did you think it would happen in the work toilets?' I asked, using humour to give me some distance from what was happening. If I didn't want this, why was I letting it happen? Surely I wanted this?

He lifted up my skirt and pulled my tights down to my knees as he continued to stare a little too intensely into my eyes. With two fingers he began to knead at me through my knickers.

'I love that. I love feeling you. Do you like it?' he asked.

'Sure.' I nodded, undoing his belt, deciding that I wanted it to happen but also to be over quickly. I slipped my hand into his jeans and his boxers, grabbing his erection.

'You're so big!' I said, truthfully, for the second time in my life. I was shocked; I had him down as a man with a very small, very narrow penis.

'You like that?' he asked, moving my knickers to the side and inserting a finger into me.

'I want to fuck you,' he said between greedy kisses. 'Turn around, bend over.'

I shook my head.

He picked up his coat and laid it out on the floor. I lowered myself down onto it awkwardly, not an easy or glamorous move when your tights are around your knees. He unzipped his jeans, pulled out his erection and stared at me as I looked up at him from the floor.

'You're so beautiful. Look at your beautiful brown skin,' he said, and before I could say anything about his 'compliment', Ted knelt down and pulled my knickers and tights down to my ankles, giving me frog's legs as he lay on top of me and tried to enter me.

'It's probably not going to, hold on, I'm just not really warmed up and you're really big and, just wait a se – ' I tried to say.

'It's okay, why don't I just – ' Ted spat onto his hand and wiped it between my legs.

'I've only ever seen that in porn,' I joked again uneasily as he eased himself into me, his spit allowing for entry. He thrust into me once.

'Oh, fuck,' he whispered in my ear.

Three more and he was done. His entire body sagged and he lay panting as I stared up at the grey polystyrene ceiling tiles. He lifted his head up from my shoulder and kissed me on the mouth.

'Sorry, that was disappointing,' he said. 'That's not how I imagined our first time would be.' Ted stood, pulling his boxers up and buttoning up his jeans. 'I should go before anyone comes.'

He bent down and kissed me on the forehead quickly.

'The only person that came was you,' I said to his back as he ran out of the toilet.

THE CORGIS

Queenie:
I just had sex with Tweed Glasses
in the work toilets

Darcy:
Bloody hell, Queenie. Is this
because we didn't send you any
memes?

Kyazike:
You must have been REALLY
bored, fam

Queenie:
He was in the office and I tried
to get on with work but he is
so, so persuasive so we got
carried away and now I feel like
I probably, definitely should not
have done that

Kyazike:
Was it good?

Queenie:
It was fine

Kyazike:
Fine?

189

Kyazike:
What happened?

Kyazike:
He couldn't get it up, innit? Or he bussed quick? Which one??

Queenie:
The latter, BUT I think it's because of the context? Exciting, the fear of getting caught?

Darcy:
Well I'm glad you didn't get caught

Cassandra:
I'm breaking my no phone over the holidays rule to say TWO things. 1) gross. 2) do not expect to hear from him again.

Queenie:
You can psychoanalyse all you want, he's not like that, Cassandra. This might all be a bit fragmented and messy, but I think he cares

Chapter Fourteen

Why are people always complaining about the dead period between Christmas and the New Year? It's complete bliss. Rupert and Nell have gone to their respective family homes for the break so I have the house to myself.

I've been walking around in my knickers with the heating turned up, but the main joy is that I've been able to clean up after them. I don't know how two people can generate so much mess, or how the cleaner puts up with it. I've never had a cleaner before, but is she the one to dispose of Nell's used sanitary towels that she forgets to wrap up or pick up when she throws them in the bin and misses? It must be a cultural thing.

That these days all merge into one is wonderful. I've watched every good, medium and bad film on telly, I've exhausted Netflix, my sleeping pattern has reversed so severely that I haven't really seen daylight, and my appetite has returned enough for me to have been able to bake a tray of brownies and eat the whole thing with a fork (when I eventually found the baking tray under Rupert's bed). The sleep has been doing me some good, although I have been going a bit mad with so much time to do nothing but think.

Ted seems to have gone quiet. I know that our beginnings aren't exactly fairytale but what if we worked well together? His intensity and passion would be a lot to get used to, and even though the sex hasn't been great, it would *probably* be better in a bed. And what would I say to Tom when he wanted to make things work again?

I won't think about it until I hear from Ted again, then I'll know what his motives are.

As I ate pizza and watched Jools Holland and his reliable New Year's Hootenanny, I reached into my dressing table and pulled out a pink leather Moleskine that I hadn't yet managed to soil and decided to write some resolutions.

NEW YEAR'S RESOLUTIONS

1. Be kinder, and more patient with everyone. Up to and including: commuters that push onto the tube before anyone can get off, colleagues that you overhear complaining about having no money even though you know that their parents cash-bought them a house, and also housemates who continue to cook seven-course meals in a shared kitchen which stops you from being able to make basic pasta and sauce
2. Better vibes. In general, across all elements of your life and day.
3. Work harder, which should result in promotion:
    a. Get to work on time
    b. Listen to Gina's instructions
    c. Go above and beyond
    d. Less chatting with Darcy
    e. Be actively kind to the intern even though he is in a position of extreme privilege and will probably be your boss in five years
    f. No personal email, no looking on Tumblr at work, phone permanently in desk drawer when working
4. Try to sort things out with Tom. Obviously the end goal is to get back together when he is ready so continue to give him space, and in the meantime see resolution 5

5. No more men:
   a. Only speaking to men if they're attached, thus unavailable
   b. If you do speak to them, and they are single, don't have sex with them. Adi was enough. In some ways
   c. Always use protection, always, even if you get carried away, which you do so often
      i. Maybe try to work out why that is
   d. No more of the dating apps, especially not on a Sunday when everyone is feeling sad and lonely and hungover and longing for a better life that they're convinced comes with a partner thus obligatory weekend activities
   e. NO MORE GUY. He hurts you physically and also overheard evidence of late suggests that he has a girlfriend. Either that or he is really very close to his housemate
6. Spend more time with family:
   a. Try to repair relationship with Mum, despite everything (though this one you can break if it gets too much)
   b. Go to see grandmother once a week, Sunday being best day as she will have roasted a chicken
   c. Reach out to your mainly estranged dad (while not expecting too much from him, thus saving yourself from inevitable rejection blues on top of Tom rejection blues)
7. Exercise. Possibly starting with something gentle like yoga, or swimming once you figure out how to protect your hair. It might help with mental health, even though you are beginning to worry that you're beyond repair
8. Try to do something creative:
   a. Writing?
   b. Poetry?

c. Weaving?

d. Knitting?

e. Art? Nor sure about this one

f. . . . you can't think of any other creative activity, which in itself suggests that creativity is not for you

9. Be less of a catastrophist. You will try to be an optimist and won't be too harsh on yourself if pessimism creeps in, which it is bound to

10. Give 50 per cent of your things to charity after you Marie Kondo your room. No use selling on eBay, it's not worth selling something you bought for £50 for £1.99 when the money could go to Cancer Research. Already a very kind suggestion, as per resolution 1

11. GO TO THERAPY??? Think about therapy, at least

I think that's enough to be getting on with. In challenging myself to do anything at all, I've already set myself up to fail. But in limiting the resolutions I can at least make the failure less disappointing.

After finishing my resolutions and inhaling a whole pizza, I took the grease-soaked box outside and shoved it into the overflowing recycling bin. I could hear cheers and church bells chiming. I'd missed the countdown. Well. Another year.

Queenie:

Happy New Year, Tom. I hope this year is better for us than the last. X

Tom:

Happy New Year, Queenie. X

Chapter Fifteen

My head hurt and I was so tired that I could see my heartbeat pulsing in my eyes. I'd finally fallen asleep at 4 a.m., and was woken up three hours later by Rupert's usual disgusting sounds echoing around the bathroom and through my walls. When did he get back?

When he'd finally expelled every fluid from his body, I went into the bathroom after him to shower and wiped offcuts of his beard from inside and around the sink, then moved his pubic hair from the toilet seat with a tissue-covered hand. I didn't have to do this with Tom. Maybe I should make a resolution to stop thinking about Tom three times a minute, and comparing him to everyone I encounter.

I left for work, and instead of putting on my normal shoes, I put my old (but sadly not faded) bright green running trainers on and started walking to work. Resolution six. I ended up getting the bus halfway but, baby steps. I was waiting until I got into the office to change into my shoes, but when I turned the corner and was walking up to the office, I felt a tap on my shoulder. I looked around and saw Gina shaking her head.

I pulled an earbud out.

'No,' she said.

'No? What do you mean, no?' I said back.

'No. Those.' Gina pointed at my trainers. 'Get those off, now.'

'Happy New Year to you, too.' I shot her a fake smile.

'Queenie, this isn't a joke. You aren't walking into the office in those.' Gina's tone got very serious. 'Are you a fifty-year-old woman who has been wearing heels every day since the age of eighteen whose ankles need some respite? Or is it some sort of fashion statement?'

'No, but New Year, New Me – are you allowed to talk to me like that? This isn't *Mad Men*,' I huffed.

'Do not try to suggest that I am sexist, Queenie. You're a good-looking girl, don't let your personal standards slip.'

Gina powered ahead in her five-inch stilettos as I leaned against a wall and changed into my flat black pumps without stepping on the floor in my tights. I got into the office and flew straight over to Darcy's desk, swooping her up in a crushing hug. Darcy squealed loudly as Jean walked past, narrowing her eyes at both of us.

'Guess what?' Darcy said, pulling me towards the kitchen. 'We're both invited to James and Fran's engagement party! The horror.'

'I don't understand this, it's like everything is on fast-forward! What is the rush?' I snapped, probably jealously. 'You have your whole life to spend with this person, why do you need to lock it down ASAP, and do this big performance? Recipe for disaster,' I preached, spilling the milk across the kitchen counter.

'Are you all right? You seem very cross.' Darcy put a hand on my shoulder.

I wasn't being very optimistic, was I?

'I'm just tired, that's all.' I took Darcy into a quiet room and read her all of my New Year's resolutions, ignoring 3d ('Work harder, which should result in promotion: less chatting with Darcy'). I started work at around lunchtime and realised that

I hadn't heard from Ted. But this was a good thing, surely, because Tom had finally replied! And with an X!

On Monday, 3 January, Jenkins, Queenie <Queenie.Jenkins@ dailyread.co.uk> wrote at 12:04:

You're quiet . . .

I waited, expecting Ted's silence to be explained with an out of office. Nothing. After lunch I checked my email. Nothing.

I don't want to be this girl. Something must really be up with my head if I was turning into this girl.

At about 4 p.m., a meeting invite from Gina popped into my inbox.

On Monday, 3 January, Jenkins, Queenie <Queenie.Jenkins@ dailyread.co.uk> wrote at 16:03:

Gina wants to meet at 5 in her office. No explanation, no anything. I'm going to be fired, this is it, it's over! I knew there was a reason she was ignoring all of my pitches. Why is she doing it now, why wouldn't she just do it before Christmas? Maybe she thought that it would ruin my Christmas. It would be too cruel to fire me before Christmas. Oh god. Will you still love me if we don't see each other every day? Will you remember me?

On Monday, 3 January, Betts, Darcy <Darcy.Betts@ dailyread.co.uk> wrote at 16:05:

You literally just read me your resolutions. Number 9: Be less of a catastrophist

Gina must know about me and Ted. I knew this would happen, I've been such a stupid, naive little idiot girl. Maybe that's why he isn't replying, because he's been asked to leave too, and they didn't want us leaving together and drawing further attention to ourselves.

Maybe he confessed because he was feeling so guilty, or maybe the cameras filmed us going on all of our "walks" together, and security picked up on it? I wonder if it's too late to pretend that we both went into the disabled toilet because one of us wasn't feeling very well?

I'll have to email him to get our story straight, but he's not checking those – oh god, of course, they can read our emails and I don't have his number.

By the time 5 p.m. came around, I was almost catatonic with fear as adrenaline propelled me to Gina's office. I knocked on the door with a trembling fist.

'Come in,' Gina barked.

As I entered, she spun around in her chair like a film villain.

'Okay, so let's talk about your career.'

I stopped breathing.

'Queenie, sit down.'

My legs just about carried the rest of me to the seat in front of Gina's desk.

'So the issue you filed after Christmas?'

'The one I had to fix?'

'Mmm, yes. You didn't quite fix it enough and I had to send it out to a freelancer.'

'Shit. Sorry. And sorry for swearing. Sorry.'

'And that, plus everything else means, and I'm *sorry* to do this, but I'm giving you an official warning.'

'Me? But I was fixing Chuck's mistakes!'

'Don't worry, Chuck's been warned too.'

'It won't matter to him, though, this isn't his job.' I threw myself back into my chair.

'But – you've been with us for how long, now?' Gina asked, looking at a piece of paper on her desk.

'Three, I think, three years. Maybe a little more?' I answered, fear stripping my voice of any real volume. What did this warning mean?

'We don't want to lose you,' Gina said, and my heart climbed down from where it had nestled in my throat.

'You're a bright girl,' Gina continued. 'You really are, and yes, you've been distracted the last six months, so I'm hoping that, by giving you specific career goals, I can bring you back from the brink. Okay?'

'Okay. So, what do I need to do?' I asked.

'One. Those pitches you're sending me. They're not tight enough, and not topical enough. Words and thoughts everywhere, and not enough hard fact. What I *want* you to do is give me something long-form that I can show the magazine writers. You're better at telling a story than you are at fast reporting, so let's see if we can get your soft activism in the mag with that.'

I nodded quickly.

'Two. Chuck is in Boston with his family until the end of this week, and when he's back on Monday, you're in charge of him. Of his tasks, of his timesheets and of his development. I want you to give him an ongoing project. You'll feed his progress into me every month. Understood?'

'Er. Yes? I can do that? Yes.'

I went back to my desk and emailed Ted, both out of curiosity and sexual frustration.

On Monday, 3 January, Jenkins, Queenie <Queenie.Jenkins@ dailyread.co.uk> wrote at 17:13:

Are you back at work? I haven't seen you around. Anyway, hope all is well. You're unusually quiet.

A week later and I hadn't heard from him, so I went up to his floor. His mixed signals were playing on my mind and I needed some sort of answer. The uncertainty was taking up too much of my brain space. Plus, if he didn't want to continue things it would be very embarrassing to see him around the office without at least speaking about it and making some sort of privacy pact. I did some *Mission Impossible*-type moving around the sports section, only stopping to look quizzically at a whiteboard that appeared to have some sort of thinly veiled staff sex conquest and ratings system scribbled onto it. When I pulled myself away from it and kept moving, I saw him in the kitchen. I looked around and, seeing nobody near us, went in.

'Hello, stranger,' I said.

Ted jumped out of his skin and dropped his mug on the floor.

'What the fuck are you doing?' he whispered, moving me out of the way so that he could look out of the door. He closed it and began to pick up shards of broken china. 'Why are you up here, Queenie?'

'Why are you so annoyed? I've only come up to say hello,' I said, heat flooding my face the way it did when he said something to catch me off guard. At least I was used to it by now.

'Yes, but people will talk. Don't be so stupid,' Ted said. He wouldn't look at me.

'No they won't, Ted!' I said, my voice catching in my throat. 'We work together. You weren't saying this at the Christmas party when you couldn't let go of me. *Or* last week.'

He didn't reply.

I felt like an idiot.

'Ted, what's going on? Have I done something wrong?'

'No,' he snapped. 'But look, I've got lots of family stuff going on so can't really do this. We'll chat another time, yeah?'

He still wouldn't look at me.

'It's fine, we don't *have* to chat.' I hit back. 'I only wanted to say that I spoke to my boyfriend and we're going to get back together.'

Ted wasn't going to make me look like a fool. My stomach tightened as I watched him drop the collected pieces of china into the bin and walk to the door.

'That's good for you,' he said, leaving the kitchen.

THE CORGIS

Queenie:
I know that I always say I feel bad, but I feel SO bad

Kyazike:
What's happened now?

Queenie:
I just went to see Tweed Glasses to figure out why he was airing me, I thought he was off sick or something, but he was standing

in the kitchen, fine as anything, and told me he had family stuff and that he'd chat to me 'another time'!

Queenie:
He wouldn't even look me in the EYE

Darcy:
What does airing mean?

Kyazike:
Like blanking. If you give someone air, you give them nothing. Does that make sense?

Cassandra:
Well, yeah? What did you think would happen? You gave him what he wanted.

Kyazike:
@Darcy you should go on a site called Urban Dictionary if you need to know what certain terms mean

Darcy:
Thanks @Kyazike

Queenie:
Please can someone take this
seriously

Kyazike:
Queenie, we all told you about
work romance. Not worth it. Take
the L and go

Darcy:
Okay, so, I've just looked that up:
'Take the L: Stands for "Take the
loss". Frequently used to describe
flunking a test, being dumped,
being stood up, being beaten up
or robbed, or losing one's money
in the stock market, gambling,
or through exploitative business
schemes'

Kyazike:
There you go

Queenie:
GUYS

*

I left the office, my two new friends Shame and Rejection
binding together before swelling in my stomach, filling my
torso. I got the bus to Brixton and sat with my head against the

window before I heard the internal voice of my grandmother asking how many dirty heads had been there before mine.

I got off the bus outside KFC and went to cross the road but stopped when I saw a familiar face sitting in an all-too-familiar black BMW at the traffic lights right next to me.

'Hello, you,' I said to Adi, leaning on the rim of the open window, not caring if he found me attractive or not but still hoping that I didn't look completely shit.

Adi looked up at me.

'Fuck,' he said, terror flashing across his face.

He faced forwards and went to drive away but a steady stream of people walked in front of the car. He looked at me and mouthed something that I didn't quite catch.

'Huh?' I asked, leaning down closer to him.

He mouthed again and I moved even closer.

'What?' I asked again.

'Say nothing.' I thought he said, before –

'AH!' I heard a woman shriek. 'This must be her, huh?'

I followed the sound of the voice and saw a tiny Pakistani woman jump out of the passenger side. Her hair was as huge as her head and her make-up was impeccable. Her thick, sharp eyebrows framed her doll-like features.

'This must be the big girl, yeah?' The woman that I made an educated guess was Adi's wife screamed.

She walked around the front of the car and over to me.

I looked at Adi for help.

'This must be the big *kala* bitch whose big size sixteen knickers were in your glovebox, yeah?' she shouted, grabbing a handful of my twists and yanking them. 'I knew it! I've seen you when you think I'm not there, throwing stones up at her window, chatting all nice things to her, thinking nobody was watching, yeah?'

I grabbed my hair back from her and rubbed my sore scalp, looking around to see if any of my twists had been pulled out.

'Leave it, baby,' Adi said, jumping out of the car. Drivers honked angrily behind him.

'You think I'm dumb, Adi?' his wife shouted, her voice shrill. 'I've seen you talking to her like you're brown south London Romeo and Juliet, and you go out late one night and then I find those big XL panties in your car? Thought I didn't see them, didn't you? And you're telling me it's not her? And now she's coming over to your car? In front of my face? Are you both crazy?'

She swiped at me and I ducked out of her reach. I guess karma was here for me; I could hardly fight back.

'I told you, I don't know where the knickers came from, baby, it must be because my friend, he borrowed my car, innit, he's the one who messes around,' Adi pleaded. 'Him and his missus, they had a beef and he must have checked some girl, baby.'

I would have laughed at his terrible lies if I hadn't almost lost a section of my scalp.

'*Which* friend?' Adi's wife asked, her nostrils flaring.

I watched, panic keeping me on the spot, as more cars lined up behind, beeping furiously. 'If these fat girls are what you like, then be my guest.' She snorted in my direction. 'You got me going gym every day and this big, bloated *kala* bitch is what you want?'

I reached down to my soft stomach defensively.

'Get back in the car, baby, come on, let's go home. I don't know her, I swear! You think I would choose her over *you*?' Adi said, grabbing his wife's hands. 'Look at her!'

I watched as they got back in the car and sped off, Adi skidding away so fast that he left tyre marks on the road. I looked around, expecting that everyone watching films in the Ritzy opposite would have come out to watch the drama, but instead, people were getting on with their commutes.

Rejection was fine, rejection was a huge part of life, but *twice* in one day I've been completely dropped by *two* men who've really put the hours in to make sure they got to fuck me. When I got on the bus, before I opened up one of my dating apps of choice to find someone anonymous to take today's pain away, I googled *kala* with unsteady fingers.

'Meaning *black* in Urdu, the official language of Pakistan. Refers to any black masculine object.'

Bit harsh.

Chapter Sixteen

January had hit me hard. I was trying to write stronger pitches for Gina, but every time I tried my head would start buzzing. Work was made worse by Leigh moving to our rival newspaper to work on their fashion magazine. I just wanted my old life back. I wanted my boyfriend, and I wanted to not be fucking up at work; I wanted to feel good about myself. I was so far from that, so far from being who I was, but I couldn't seem to stop myself from self-destructing.

Tom still didn't want to talk to me, despite his promising New Year's text, and my social life was a myth; the only people I seemed to see consistently were the steady rotation of anonymous online one-fuck boys whose houses I'd go to twice a week. I'd slipped back into my old ways, but I couldn't help it. It was so dark and cold all the time, and I needed boys for their distraction and warmth. I didn't want to leave the house unless it was for sex, and on the days I was on my period or too tired, I'd end up on Tumblr, reading piece after piece on police brutality. I was reading an article on the protests in St Paul that had followed the shooting of a black man named Philando Castile when my phone rang. I answered it, rage pulsing in my chest.

'Kyazike, are they going to kill us all?' I asked angrily. 'For doing *nothing*. Nothing at all. For just being. For being black in the wrong place, at the wrong time? I hate it.'

I was breathless. 'It's unfair, it hurts my heart. Who will police the police?'

I was getting hot and stressed. 'I can't understand it and it makes me scared, and confused, and it makes me feel like we don't belong, like we have to prove our worth just to be allowed to exist.'

'Relax, fam,' Kyazike said. 'That's why I'm calling. I'm getting ready. Black Lives Matter march. In Brixton, Windrush Square. I'll meet you outside the Ritzy at two.'

'Kyazike, you know I don't like marches,' I reminded her. 'I'm frightened of people, lots of people. I know that lots of people aren't going to do me any harm, but I feel like I can't escape from them. It's too overwhelming. Carnival I can't do, big shopping centres I can't do, Oxford Street at any time of day I can't do. That's why I can never follow you there.'

'Queenie.'

'You're right. This is bigger than me.'

'See you there.'

I tried to meet Kyazike outside the Ritzy and failed, mainly because she is a mover and a shaker and won't stay in one place. We finally fell into each other on the literal opposite side of where we were meant to meet. We didn't have any placards or any signs, but that was okay, because Kyazike has the loudest voice I've ever heard. We started off in Windrush square, Kyazike shouting 'Black Lives Matter' on repeat while I surveyed who was around us, mouthing it, not confident enough to join in. I didn't like making myself the centre of attention. Roy had seen to that.

Kyazike was forced into silence when a figure who I guessed was the organiser stood on a podium. She was a tall, lean black woman with dreadlocks wrapped in scarves that ran down her back and over her shoulders. When she lifted her hand, the crowd hushed. She waited for a time, lifted a megaphone to her mouth and spoke.

'The system is against us,' she said, her voice strong but close to breaking. 'You cannot, you must not, brutalise the black body, but that is what we are seeing. It is all we are seeing. That is the message given. And it is traumatising. Our people continue to suffer. The trauma is too heavy for us to bear.'

The crowd shouted in agreement.

'Black Lives Matter does not diminish any lives other than ours. That's not what it's about. What we're saying right now is that *we* are the ones who are suffering.'

She lowered the megaphone, and stood looking across the crowd. Pain was etched across her face, and all too visible in the way she held herself. She handed the megaphone to a woman next to her and stepped down from the podium.

The second woman climbed up and spoke.

'Do you know what they want? They want us to *riot*, they want us to cause havoc, mayhem, they want us to burn ourselves to the ground. But you know what I say? It's not a riot, it's an *uprising*. And we will continue with our uprising until we get the justice we deserve.'

After her, one by one, protesters stood up on the small stage to speak into the megaphone. We all watched, being hit by bullets of sorrow and anger as family members and friends of black men and women who had been killed unlawfully stood up on that podium one by one and recounted not just how those who had been lost had died, but how they were kind, they were loved, they had children, they were children.

Then, we marched. We all walked, in droves, towards Brixton police station, the atmosphere electric, the crowd not angry, not aggressive, but charged. Charged and wanting answers, wanting to be heard.

Cars going in the opposite direction stopped and started as protesters weaved their way around them. The drivers beeped, raised fists out of rolled-down windows.

'HANDS UP!' Kyazike shouted through a megaphone.

Where did she get that from?

'DON'T SHOOT,' the crowd replied.

'HANDS UP,' she repeated, the crowd ahead shouting, 'DON'T SHOOT'.

Eventually we stopped outside the police station, and again we listened. This time to tales of injustice, to acts the police wouldn't explain and couldn't justify. More people joined, spilling out into the streets and stopping the traffic. Police escorts walked out of the station and stood around us. Fear unsettled my stomach.

We walked away from the station, marching free-flow through Brixton, the crowd chanting, 'NO JUSTICE! NO PEACE!' We passed the back of the market. Instead of the fruit and vegetable stalls I was dragged to on a Saturday morning by my grandmother and thought I'd still recognise, more white kids spilled out holding colourful cans of beer.

The shops where she'd buy Jamaican bun and bright orange cheese for our Sunday-afternoon treat, the fabric stalls where she'd buy cloth for curtains, the pound shops where I was allowed to buy one thing and one thing only – these had all gone, making room for trendy new vegan bars and independent boutiques selling shockingly priced men's fashion. When had this happened? When had the space that I had known like the back of my hand, the only area I'd ever been to that I felt like I could be myself in, the place where so many people looked like me, talked like my family, when had it gone?

Brixton. When had she been stripped of her identity? Why hadn't I *properly* noticed?

'NO JUSTICE!' I shouted, a new brand of anger flooding my system. 'NO PEACE!'

'Do you want the megaphone?' Kyazike asked.

'I wouldn't go that far,' I said, raising my right fist above my head.

We marched, and we chanted, settling finally in Windrush Square where we'd started. A place named after the *Windrush*, a ship and a voyage where it had all begun for some of our ancestors. We sat on the floor in the streets, all lifted out of our exhaustion when a new chant, this time a statement of truth, rather than an objection to chaos, began, and echoed into the night.

'WE ARE ENOUGH.'

'WE ARE ENOUGH.'

'WE ARE ENOUGH.'

*

'Why do you keep walking past my office, Queenie? You're putting me on edge. Come in, or go and do some work,' Gina said.

Was today one of her good or bad days, I wondered.

'Sorry, it's just that I wanted to ask you something.' I stepped into her office tentatively.

'You're not getting a pay rise, not until you give me what I asked for,' she said, not looking away from her screen.

'No, it's not that. It's just – ' I sat in the chair opposite her. 'Well, you know I used to send you all of those pitches? It's just that – well, two *more* black men were shot in America this week by police. And I know that it's not here, though it does happen here, but – I was wondering if I could write something about it? It's just that nobody is really reporting it . . . It doesn't have to be for the print edition, but maybe the blog, or – '

'The thing is, Queenie,' Gina closed her laptop. 'I know what you're saying, and I understand that it's awful. *So* awful. And if I could let you all write about every terrible thing that happened, I *would*, but I'm beholden to the powers that be.'

'But surely the "powers that be" can see that this is something that needs to be out there?'

'I just think that these matters are a little too, how should I put it? *Radical* for *The Daily Read*. I appreciate you being so proactive about writing, though. How about we get some of that passion into a pitch for the magazine that's a bit more . . . palatable?' Gina opened her laptop and carried on typing.

'Well, I was thinking I could pitch something about how it would be great to see all the liberal white women who were tweeting fervently from the women's march at a Black Lives Matter march?' I said.

'I beg your pardon?' Gina asked me.

'Well, all of these white women in the office seem to bleat about going to the women's march, but I was at a Black Lives Matter march yesterday and I didn't see anyone I recognised.'

'Bit of a combative attitude, don't you think?' Gina asked, frowning. 'Rework what you're saying, and come along to the pitch meeting at four.'

'. . . so I just think that we could use that argument to shine more of a light on Black Lives Matter, and if we do this in the context of the women's march, we make it more "palatable" for our readers,' I said to the room, praying that I managed to deliver my pitch and mask the fear in my voice with what I hoped was conviction.

'All that Black Lives Matter nonsense,' an older man I recognised from the review supplement scoffed. '*All* lives matter.'

'What?' I asked him, blinking. I took a secret deep breath.

'What about the lives of Latinos, of Asians, the lives of – I'm white, does my life not matter?' he continued.

'I'm not . . . suggesting that the lives of other ethnic groups do not matter,' I explained, gobsmacked that I *had to* explain. 'I don't think that any part of Black Lives Matter even hints that other lives are disposable?'

'Well, when you put the lives of *some* and not *all* on a pedestal, what else are you doing?'

'It's not putting black lives on a pedestal, I don't even know what that means,' I said, my heart beating fast. 'It's saying that black lives, at *this* point, *and* historically, do not, and have not, mattered, and that they should!'

I looked first at Gina, then around the room to see if anyone was going to back me up. Instead, I was met with what I'd been trying to pretend hadn't always been a room full of white not-quite-liberals whose opinions, like their money, had been inherited.

I left the meeting defeated, and feeling a lot more alone than I had when I'd walked in.

WE ARE ENOUGH, I tried to remind myself as I walked back to my desk.

Chapter Seventeen

At the sexual health clinic I filled the form in as usual, did a scan of the waiting room to check that nobody I knew was there as usual, went to sit in the corner by the window as usual. After an hour I was called in by a black girl who looked about five years younger than me and I answered the usual questions. This was not the activity in my life that I thought I would become most familiar with.

'So this isn't your first time here?' she asked, tapping away.

'No, it's not.'

'Okay. And what has brought you here today?'

'I had unprotected sex two weeks ago. I'm sort of getting better at using condoms but just got, er, carried away,' I answered quietly.

'Okay. Do you have any symptoms? Itching, any unusual discharge?'

'None of the above.'

'Would you like to take a pregnancy test?' the nurse offered.

'No thanks, I have a coil. I mean, I've been pregnant before,' I explained. 'But I think that was because I was having regular sex. Just the STI test, please, and I'll hope for the all-clear text in two weeks.'

I laughed nervously. The nurse did not laugh with me.

When she'd finished poking about, she told me to put my clothes back on. Instead of letting me leave, she asked me to wait a second and left the room. I got dressed and sat in the chair waiting for her to return when a pair of white-blue eyes framed by a harsh grey bowl cut made their way into the room. Elspeth.

'Queenie, you're back.'

Had that nurse grassed me up?

'Hello, Elspeth,' I said, confused, not knowing why she was here.

Elspeth took the traitor's seat at the desk and started tapping at the computer, as they're so fond of doing when they could be making eye contact and engaging with me at a human level.

'Now, this is your third visit in *quite* a short amount of time,' Elspeth informed me, like I didn't already know. 'And while I'm pleased to hear from Caroline that you aren't battered and bruised, she did say that you seemed very vacant. I know that you might not want to talk to *me*, but I think that you do need to talk to *somebody*.'

I stared at her blankly. What was I meant to say, that I wasn't my sparkiest when I was about to show my vagina to a stranger when I wasn't going to get anything out of it?

'Between me and you, I have a daughter your age, and in some strange way you remind me of her.'

'Is she black?' I cut in.

'No,' Elspeth said, firmly. 'When you left last time I made some calls, and while I hoped you wouldn't come back in, got you the number of a therapist to call in the event that you did return.'

'Can I go now?' I asked. 'I have to go back to work.'

She nodded, and handed me the piece of paper as I left the room. Without looking at what it said, I shoved it to the bottom of my rucksack.

*

I slid past Gina talking angrily on her phone in the foyer, some-thing about 'custody' and '*you* can have them then', and got back to my desk in time for my meeting with Chuck.

He was already in the breakout area, pen and paper in hand. I put the coat and rucksack down and collapsed into the beanbag opposite Chuck. He looked up as I landed.

'Careful. Don't hurt yourself,' he said cheerfully, his Boston twang grating on me. I definitely found the accent less thrilling since he was the reason I'd been given a warning.

'I'm fine. The whole point of beanbags is for relaxation and comfort,' I said sharply. 'Right. Are you ready for the big project? *The* big project that is going to change your life as you know it?'

'Yes. I think so. But how are you, how are you doing? You seem kinda, I dunno, messed up recently.'

Why did he always want to discuss my bad moods?

'I'm fine. Just some boy dramas and family stuff, and life always has a way of – Sorry, Chuck. Let's keep this strictly professional, okay?' I hurried along. 'So, the last few weeks you've shadowed me while I've used InDesign to fill in the listings?'

'Sure have. But you know, you can talk to me about anything. I'm kind of a good listener.' Chuck leaned forwards eagerly.

I ignored this. 'Okay, so, I'm thinking, for your project, you design a whole new layout for the listings. Think about utilising the space of the six pages, Chuck. That should keep you going for a while.'

'Er, I don't think that I'm that good yet?'

'Don't be so negative!' I said briskly. 'You'll be fine. Now, can you look away while I get up from this beanbag? Why did you pick these to sit on? There is nothing less dignified than getting up from one of these things. It's a system of thrusting.'

Eventually I made it back onto two legs and to my desk.

On Friday, 18 January, Jenkins, Queenie <Queenie.Jenkins@ dailyread.co.uk> wrote at 15:55:

Tea and talking, afternoon edition?

On Friday, 18 January, Betts, Darcy <Darcy.Betts@ dailyread.co.uk> wrote at 16:10:

Sorry, no, I've got loads to do, and Simon is calling at half past so that we can 'iron some things out'. Can we email? Or text? Group chat in case one of the others needs to step in when I'm on the phone?

On Friday, 18 January, Jenkins, Queenie <Queenie.Jenkins@ dailyread.co.uk> wrote at 16:12:

Darcy, is there something wrong with me? I just went to the clinic and this nurse who seems to be keeping tabs on me has basically said that I'm fucked up and gave me a counselling referral. Do I go there too often? Am I damaged beyond repair?

On Friday, 18 January, Betts, Darcy <Darcy.Betts@ dailyread.co.uk> wrote at 16:16:

I don't think there's anything wrong with you clinically, but there's no harm in talking to a professional about what's been going on. Maybe, and don't take this the wrong way, maybe change your attitude towards the way that you engage with men

On Friday, 18 January, Jenkins, Queenie <Queenie.Jenkins@ dailyread.co.uk> wrote at 16:19:

What's wrong with the way I engage with men??

My phone lit up. The question was too big for Darcy to handle alone. She'd taken it to the group text.

THE CORGIS

Darcy:
Queenie has just asked what's wrong with the way she engages with men

Kyazike:
Lol

Kyazike:
Lol I don't think any of us will ever be able to answer that one

Queenie:
Thanks, Kyazike

Kyazike:

You know what I mean though.
You're just boy mad, innit.
You've gone rebound crazy. But
for some reason it's all dickheads
you're going for

Queenie:

I don't think that's true

Cassandra:

Is that a joke? That tweed guy?
The OkCupid boys who throw you
about? The anal guy?

Darcy:

I agree with Cassandra, actually.
Look at the way you are with
Chuck: he's obsessed with
you, wants to know how you
are and actually listens when
you answer, stares at you in
meetings, hangs off of every
word you say, makes you
unlimited cups of tea (which he
won't do for anyone else), and
you just look past him

Kyazike:

What is a Chuck?

Darcy:

He's our intern

Kyazike:

Oh, Chuck is someone's NAME?
Skeen

Cassandra:

Why not open yourself up to the idea of engaging with men who are nice to you, Queenie? Not only ones who use you and make you feel terrible afterwards. Do you even like the sex you have? Sorry to be so personal, but do you even orgasm?

Queenie:

Well, no. But who does, when they're being slapped and bitten and pulled around? Anyway, I like it

Cassandra:

Sure you do.

Queenie:

And Chuck doesn't fancy me. Even if he did, he's too nice for me. I don't deserve it

Queenie:
And CRUCIALLY, he almost got me fired

Darcy:
Well, if we're being honest, you almost got yourself fired

Darcy:
@Kyazike, I know I should just go on Urban Dictionary but for the sake of brevity, what does 'skeen' mean?

Kyazike:
It means seen

Kyazike:
Like, I see

Darcy:
Right. I'm with you

Queenie:
THANKS, ALL

On Tuesday, 15 January, Betts, Darcy <Darcy.Betts@ dailyread.co.uk> wrote at 16:28:

Let's talk about this properly tomorrow. Maybe you should go home early, I think you should probably have a bit of time for yourself? I'll cover for you.

I am fine. *Fine*, I told myself on repeat as I packed my bag. I snuck back out of the office and saw Ted smoking on the wall opposite, his head bowed. My – at this point inexplicable – fondness for him made me walk over and hoist myself up on the wall next to him.

'Remember me?' I asked.

'Shit!' Ted grabbed his chest. 'You scared me.'

'Overreaction,' I said, rolling my eyes.

'You know, I probably should have come to find you sooner,' Ted said, his mouth stretched in a grimace.

'Or replied to my many emails?'

'I'm sorry. But after we – I just . . . It didn't feel right.'

'Oh, cheers for that,' I said. 'What's *wrong* with me?'

'No, nothing, nothi – '

Ted stopped abruptly when we were joined by Gordon, his desk mate who was still wearing clothes that were too tight for him.

'Have you got a lighter, Ted?' Gordon asked, shoving a hand in his jeans and pulling out a carton of cigarettes with great difficulty.

'Here ya go.' Ted handed it over.

'I keep meaning to ask,' began Gordon, who was obviously not going to acknowledge my presence, 'where was it you went on your honeymoon, again? I'm thinking about somewhere nice and sunny to take the missus in a few weeks. Neither of us can bear the winter.'

I hopped off the wall and tried my hardest not to be sick all the way home.

Chapter Eighteen

I stayed in bed tormented by nausea until I started to clean the house to try and take my mind off of it all. When the dark thoughts were at their loudest, I went for a walk to clear my head but took a wrong turn and ended up on the main road by the notoriously messy White Horse on Brixton Hill. I was seized by such sadness as I watched its revellers spilling out into the street, the noise of Friday-night fun all too recognisable. I never had fun anymore. It was all just shit. I turned to walk back up the hill.

'Oh, look who it is!' I heard, and though only marginally sure it was directed at me, turned round to see where it had come from.

'Long time. How are you?' Guy broke away from a group of boys, walked over to me and put his pint on the ground.

I seized up.

'What are you up to, dressed like this?' He pulled at my paint-splattered cleaning clothes.

'Cleaning! I needed some air, all of that bleach, you know. Anyway, what are you doing here?' I asked, crossing my arms, at that point aggressively aware that I wasn't wearing a bra.

'Pal of mine thought it would be a laugh to come here. I've heard some things, but I didn't expect it to live up to them,' he said, trying his hardest to stare through my folded arms.

'Well, I should go! I should get back to it. Have a good time!' I nodded goodbye, my arms still strapped to my chest, and walked away.

THE CORGIS

Queenie:
Ted is married

Darcy:
WHAT?

Kyazike:
Come again?

Queenie:
Yep. His desk mate dropped it. Didn't stay to find out the details

Kyazike:
Give me his surname and I can get you his wife's name, job and Twitter handle in less than a minute. I can go DIY FBI on it

Cassandra:
. . . are you surprised?

Queenie:
Er, I AM, YEAH. Are you NOT??

Cassandra:
It explains his behaviour, doesn't it. The intensity, the caginess,

the distance, the coming back
when he got bored again, the
withdrawal.

Queenie:
Okay Cassandra, if you have an
answer for everything, why did
he stop talking to me when we'd
had sex?

Cassandra:
There was no more excitement
or chase, only guilt in its place.
And he couldn't handle it. He's a
coward.

Darcy:
A BLOODY COWARD. I hate him
for this, Queenie. I'm so sorry

Queenie:
And I've just bumped into the
Welshman when I had no bra
on and was wearing an outfit
that was pretty much covered in
paint. I smell like I've showered
in bleach. Today is not going my
way. This year is not going my
way

Darcy:

Please stay away from Welshman! Your resilience against men who are bad for you is VERY LOW at the moment

Cassandra:

Queenie for the love of god, stop giving any of them your energy. We'll discuss tomorrow morning. See you at 11.

*

Sleep paralysis is a strange thing. I'd had dozens of episodes at university when I'd take naps, and when I looked into it, read that it's something about the brain being disrupted and waking up before the body, which is why you can't move when you're hallucinating that there's a faceless man climbing across the floor towards you. I'd been seeing him more often recently but I was aware that I was stuck in an episode when I started seeing the figure of a man emerging out of the pile of clothes on the corner chair.

The doorbell was ringing, but I couldn't get up to answer the door because I was stuck to the bed, staring at him as he contorted and reached out to me. But why was the doorbell ringing?

I gasped myself awake and sat up, heart pounding.

The doorbell *was* ringing. I looked at my phone. 2 a.m.

No response from Rupert or Nell – they must be out. I waited for the night caller to go away. After a few minutes, they stopped ringing the bell. I turned my pillow over and tried to go back to sleep. I was almost fully submerged when the bell started going again.

I crept out of my room and down the stairs slowly, my heart beating out of my chest. I was certainly testing its endurance tonight. Obviously weaponless, I pressed myself against the front door and looked through the peephole, guessing that my plan of attack would be to scream as loud as I could if they kicked the door down. Nobody was there.

As if in a horror film, a face flashed up.

Fucking *Guy*.

I opened the front door. 'What are you *doing*?' I hissed, blocking him from entering.

'You ain't go' any time for me anymore an' I'on like it,' he slurred, putting his hand on my shoulder. 'You don't wan' sex anymore an' thas crap for me because our sex is absolutely cracking.'

He moved his hand across my face and I pulled myself out of his reach.

'You see? You used to love my touch.'

His head lolled forwards and he leaned against the doorframe. I saw a porch light go on across the road as the angry Turkish woman who lived opposite opened her front door.

'Go away, Guy!' I hissed.

'Where'm I goin' away to?'

'To your house? Where you live?'

'I'on know my postcode. I'on know where my keys are. So I've come to see you!' he shouted. 'I'll tell you what – I'll sleep on the doorstep, shall I?'

'Hey, you!' the woman across the road shouted back. 'Stop making the noise!'

'Sorry!' I whispered as loudly as possible. 'Fine, come inside,' I growled, pulling Guy in and closing the door behind him.

I walked to the kitchen and he stumbled after me, throwing himself into a dining chair as I poured him a glass of water. I handed it to him and watched him down it and slam the empty glass on the table.

'Guy!' I said, smacking at his clumsy hands as he tried to grab at my bottom. 'You need to sleep.' I stood behind him and guided him into the living room. He flopped onto the sofa and lay on his back.

'Member when we fucked here? You loved it. Your big black arse was bouncin' up an' down an' up – hey, hey, where you going?' Guy made one final grab for me as I dropped a blanket on him and turned to walk out of the room.

'I'm going to bed,' I said, ignoring his comment.

'Shhh babe, don't be cranky. You're so gorgeous even in your headwrap thing. Why'on I come up with you? You missed me, surely? Missed this, yeah?' He gestured at his lap sloppily.

I turned the light off.

'I'm getting up early, my friend Cassandra is coming round for breakfast. Besides, no. No more sex.'

'No Cassandra. I don't want Cassandra.'

'Goodnight, Guy. DO NOT come up.'

I went back to the kitchen, filled Guy's empty glass and crept into the living room. He'd already started to snore. I put the glass on the table by his head, then started worrying that he'd fall off the sofa and crack his head on the table, so tried to drag it across the room silently. I dropped it on its side and froze. I looked over. He continued to snore.

I had almost got off to sleep at 3.30 a.m. when my bedroom door opened.

'It's too cold down there, I can't sleep.'

Guy, almost naked but for his boxers, climbed into my bed.

'Are you joking?' I hissed at him. '*You* can't sleep? I've been hearing your snoring through the floor!'

He moved closer and pressed himself into me. He slid my T-shirt sleeve up and kissed my neck.

'And when did you take your clothes off? Why are all your clothes off?' I hissed at him, sliding away.

'Shhh, stop talking,' he said in response.

'Guy. No.' I turned to face him. The moonlight shone on his face. 'If you have to stay in here, please can you just go to sleep? I'm up early. I don't want to have sex with you,' I said in my most stern voice. '*That* is my final word. If you push it again, I'll order you an Uber home. And I'll go through your phone and find your postcode.'

'Fine. Spoilsport,' he hiccuped, turned away from me and began to snore 0.3 seconds later.

I've no idea how I got to sleep but I woke up teetering off the edge of my bed to the sound of the doorbell. Again. I looked over at the sleeper who had taken over most of my bed. Guy was still out cold. I pulled a jumper on and went downstairs.

'Sorry, I'm not prepared for you at *all*,' I said as Cassandra stepped into the hallway and shook rain off her umbrella and onto my legs.

'Shall we go out instead?' Cassandra suggested, looking me up and down. 'I don't like the smell of this place. Plus it'll be nice for you to get fresh air. You look knackered. Those bags!' She reached out and patted the area under my eyes.

'Thanks, Cassandra. Always thinking of me, aren't you?' I smiled, wiping water from my shins. I'm sure she *used* to say some nice things to me.

'I am, actually. I transferred another £100 to you yesterday because I knew that if we went out to eat you'd ask me for money.'

'I will pay you back, and soon,' I promised.

'It's my dad's money, really. He wouldn't mind if he knew.'

'Thanks, Cassandra,' I said, wondering why I wasn't lucky enough to have a father like Jacob. 'I've got company,' I said quietly, leading her down the hallway. 'Come into the kitchen, I don't want to wake him up.'

'Oh my god, another one? How many is it now?' Cassandra snorted.

It was too early for this.

'There you go with the judgement again!' I sighed. 'That's not a very feminist question. Besides, it's not like that.' I poured Cassandra a glass of water. 'It's this inconsequential man that I used to sleep with loads, the Welsh one. I must have mentioned him.'

I shrugged. 'I actually got bored of sleeping with him because the sex was so rough, and unconnected. I mean, it was quite good, but just making me feel bad. Like everything else at the moment,' I confessed, hopeful that she'd pick up on it and ask what was wrong.

She didn't.

'Anyway, last night he turned up off his face at two in the morning. He'd been at the White Horse and was so battered he didn't know where he lived.'

'That's a coincidence – ' Cassandra started.

'Hold on, let me just run upstairs and get ready. I can't stop thinking about croissants.'

I got dressed silently as Guy continued to sleep soundly, a gigantic human starfish stretched to all four corners of my entire bed now that I wasn't occupying a slither of it. I left him a note telling him to let himself out the minute he woke up, then Cassandra and I made our way to BE/AN, another of Brixton's newest and more minimalist coffee shops. When we got there and I saw how full it was of white, middle-class, young people with Apple Macs, I asked that we went to somewhere that was run by Brixton locals.

'You mean black people, don't you?' Cassandra asked flatly.

'I do, yes,' I said, leading her to the market.

As we walked, she talked and I listened as she told me that she'd applied to do a masters in psychiatry. I wondered if she'd use me as a case study. We found a coffee and cake stall run by an old Jamaican woman in a black, green and yellow bandana.

'Black enough for you?' Cassandra asked.

'Yes.' I flashed a mocking smile. 'It is.'

When we sat down, Cassandra spoke through the academic and financial pros and cons of her new career at me for half an hour, then before I could try and talk to her about Ted, she announced that she had to head back north because she had plans with her 'gorgeous guy'.

I wondered how gorgeous he could actually be; nobody ever describes their partner as gorgeous unless they're trying to convince themselves of it. We left the coffee shop, hugged goodbye and I headed home. I pulled my headphones on and started listening to the latest instalment of my favourite podcast, *The Read*, in some attempt to lift my mood slightly, hoping that Guy wouldn't be there when I got back. Being alone probably wasn't the best thing for me, but I didn't feel like I could face anyone.

I was almost home when I felt a hand on my elbow. I pulled my headphones off and turned around.

'Didn't you hear me? I've been shouting after you for ages.' Cassandra bent over and clutched her side as she caught her breath. 'I didn't realise how fast I could run in heels!'

'Why didn't you just call me?'

'Why weren't you just listening?'

'Cassandra, why have you followed me home?'

'My umbrella, it's in your hallway,' she huffed. 'I was at the bus stop and saw that it was going to rain again!'

We reached the front door and I opened it.

Silence. No Guy.

I pulled Cassandra's umbrella from the coat stand and handed it to her.

'Anyway, now I really will go. I must get back to my guy, he was having a lads night yesterday and I said I'd make him a hangover breakfast.'

'Yes, Cassandra, it must be so *nice* having a *nice* man around! How wonderful for you to have someone actually *care* where you are and *how* you are,' I half-snapped as I heard stirrings from my bedroom.

I looked up the stairs.

'You don't need to be jealous, Queenie. When you're good and ready, you'll find someone like my – '

Guy began to walk down the stairs, his eyes half-open.

'Well, we can't all be as lucky as you,' I said. 'Morning, Guy. I trust you slept well?' I added sarcastically

He stared at Cassandra.

'Sorry, I should introduce you. Cassandra, this is Guy.' I gestured quickly at Guy, hoping that he'd nod a hello and then make a swift exit.

'Guy, what the fuck?' Cassandra's olive skin flushed red and her eyes darkened. She looked like she was summoning a demon.

'What?' I asked, bemused. 'Cassandra, this is . . . Guy,' I said, looking at Guy, then to Cassandra. Guy sat on the steps and lowered his head into his hands.

'No, Queenie, this is my *boyfriend* Guy,' Cassandra spat, pushing me on the shoulder. I am sturdy so didn't fall over, but the impact was felt.

'I'm sorry, Cass,' Guy said, muffled, his head still in his hands.

'You're *sorry*?' Cassandra shrieked. 'We barely have sex and it's because you've been fucking my best friend, Guy?' She charged towards him but tripped on the first step and fell, landing on her knee.

I rushed over to help her up.

'Don't *touch* me. You *slut*.'

I felt like the floor was whipped away from under my feet.

'What?' I said, not *really* grasping what was happening. I went to close the front door. As I did, I saw the woman opposite standing on her front step. She must think that I'm running some sort of twenty-four-hour dramatic workshop from the house.

The hallway was silent but for the sounds of three people's varied breathing. I felt my stomach toss and turn. I looked at Cassandra, then at Guy.

'Cassandra, I didn't know! How could I? You've only been together a couple of months!' I said, defending myself. 'I didn't ever meet him!'

Cassandra pulled herself up, rubbing her knee. 'And why do you think that is, Queenie? I knew that if you met him, you'd want to fuck him, like you fuck literally all men that look your way these days! Single, attached, married, anything!'

I walked back over to the stairs and held onto the banister out of fear that my legs were going to go.

'For hours I listen to you tell me about the pointless, horrific *users* you go and spread your legs for, the ones you've just met in bars, the ones you trawl on those disgusting, sad, lonely dating apps for and pick like you're choosing from a box of chocolates. And don't think that's a slight about your weight, I know how sensitive you are about *everything*. I'm talking purely about the men you select, the ones you either have here that you kick out after they've given you what you *need*, or those ones whose houses you turn up at in the middle of the night and let do god knows what to you. Oh – and *obviously* this must be one of them! Clearly! My *boyfriend* must be one of them, one of those faceless dating app guys that you don't even *name* when you tell me about them. Let me guess where he comes in the sequence? First, second, thirtieth? I hope you've been using protection!'

'All right, Cassandra,' Guy said, finally emerging from the sand in which he'd buried his head. 'Stop shouting at her. My head's killing me.'

'What the fuck is *wrong* with you?' I shouted at Guy. 'You must have known!' I stared at him.

'That's it, you two talk to each other like I'm not here!' Cassandra roared, and stamped her foot. From the stairs we both turned to look at her, briefly connected by the disbelief that an adult person could be acting so like a child.

'Cassandra, I didn't *know*, how many more times can I say? I met him at a party and he didn't tell me anything about himself! You're one of my best friends, why would I do this to you? What sense would that make?' I pleaded with her.

'Because you're fucking miserable, and you're pathetic, and since you broke up with Tom all you can do is fuck, fuck, fuck, to fill a fucking void,' Cassandra shouted hysterically. 'And of course you've done it with my fucking boyfriend. And a *million* others. You make me sick. I'm leaving, I can't look at either of you. Stay here and carry on fucking each other.'

Cassandra opened the front door and slammed it on the way out.

Guy looked at me and held his hands up. 'I'm really sorry, I didn't mean for this to happ – '

'My *god*, get the fuck out, Guy. You're the fucking worst!' I was so overwhelmed by disgust and regret and upset that I could barely see.

'I didn't mean for it to go on as long as it did, and I really do like her, but the sex is so . . . You know, she's not like you. And I know that your name is uncommon but I didn't think that the Queenie Cass spoke about could be you – '

As Guy rambled, I charged into the living room and gathered up his clothes and trainers.

'Are you really standing here telling me about your fucking motives, like I'll give a shit? Get the fuck out!' I threw it all at him with force and watched as he got dressed slowly.

'Fucking faster!' I shouted as he gathered up what was left to put on and walked out of the door without looking back at me.

I paced the living room, my head throbbing. My legs started to shake, so I sat down and the room started to spin, so I stood back up. What was happening? How and why was my world spinning off its axis at such an alarming rate? I couldn't breathe in. I left the house and walked towards the main road. I could see Cassandra walking ahead and ran to catch up with her. When I was close enough to touch her I reached out and grabbed her hand. She turned to look at me, mascara and snot running down her face, and sped up.

'We don't have sex, Queenie. We don't have sex because he says he's too tired from *shifts* and we don't *talk* about not having sex because he gets cagey, and look! I break my back to please him, and all you need to do to get his attention is suck his dick.'

I speed-walked beside her, trying to catch my breath. 'But Cassandra . . . it's not my fault . . . I didn't know – *please* can you stop or slow down?'

She sped up.

'Why are you trying so *hard* to please him?' I asked her. 'Look what he's been doing.'

'Do you know what? I love him, Queenie, not that you know what that is. I try to work things out, not push away.' Cassandra twisted the knife with her words. 'And not all of us want to act like teenagers. Some of us want to move forward with someone, Queenie. Some of us want to grow up.'

Cassandra stopped and turned to look at me. She was shaking.

'And unlike *you*, some of us don't let the past dictate the way we live our adult lives.' She carried on down the road and I stood and watched her walk away. When I got back home, my phone lit up.

THE CORGIS
CASSANDRA HAS LEFT THE CORGIS

Darcy:
Where's Cassandra gone?

Queenie:
Turns out the Welshman is CASSANDRA'S ACTUAL BOYFRIEND. WHEN SHE WOULD SAY 'MY GORGEOUS GUY' IT'S BECAUSE HE IS LITERALLY CALLED GUY AS IN THE GUY I WAS BANGING

Kyazike:
Raaaaah

Queenie:
The whole time we were sleeping together

Darcy:
Shit. Small world, isn't it?

Queenie:
I actually did some quick maths and I think I started sleeping with him before they met

Queenie:
Don't ever tell her that though

Kyazike:
Lol we ain't telling her nothing

Kyazike:

And don't worry fam I'll back
you if she comes to fight you

Darcy:

Don't worry, it won't come to
that! She'll realise that it's his
fault, not yours

Queenie:

Oh god oh god oh god oh god

Chapter Nineteen

Queenie:

It's been three weeks and you still aren't speaking to me, Cassandra. I don't know what to do. You know how sorry I am. XXXX

I rolled over in bed and pressed send, holding my breath as I watched as the blue iMessage bubble turn green. Either her phone was still off, or she'd blocked my number.

I couldn't lose anyone else in my life. I'd tried reaching out to her via every form of communication bar fax and telegram, but nothing. Kyazike suggested she go round there to 'talk to her on a level', which I'd tried to figure out was a threat or not, and Darcy thought that I should give her space and time to process everything.

Did I do something wrong? *I'm* the one who was a side chick, *I'm* the one who was nothing but some sort of sex person to yet another man who didn't think I was deserving of anything but hard sex.

I guess I don't matter. Not to Cassandra, not to Guy, not to anyone. My mum, my dad, Ted. Tom. Nobody has ever wanted me, not properly.

I rolled out of bed and pulled the nearest outfit on without looking at what it was, but obviously checking that it was long enough to cover my bum. I walked down the stairs, passing Nell in the hallway who stared at me, asking if I was okay just as I got to the front door.

I mumbled that I was fine and left the house, striding purposefully to the bus stop until I realised that I wasn't wearing a bra, so slowed down. Why did I always forget this crucial item when getting dressed? As the bus moved along, I drafted a monologue in my head, jotting very key points down in my phone.

As the bus approached my stop, I looked out of the window and saw rain hitting the glass. Deciding that I needed to get on with what I went to do rather than just go round on the bus until the weather got better, I stepped off as it started to pour, then did some sort of shuffle-running, arriving on the doorstep of mine and Tom's old building drenched through to my bones.

I took some deep breaths and rang the doorbell, wiping rain off my face and observing my reflection in the glass pane. I realised that my headscarf was still on, soaked through. I whipped it off just as a petite blonde girl I thought I recognised opened the door. She must have been a neighbour I'd seen in the short time I'd lived here. Her hair was up in a loose bun and she was wearing nothing but a black T-shirt that reached her knees. As she stepped back from the door her pert breasts shook with the motion, her nipples almost pointing to the sky. I crossed my arms in order to cover my comparatively heavy bosom.

'Hi,' I huffed, blinking water out of my eyes, 'I think I must have pressed the wrong buzzer. I was meant to press flat B, sorry.'

The girl squinted at me through small blue eyes, and her face dropped.

'Er,' she started, 'let me just . . .' Then she turned and ran up the main stairs. I stepped into the communal hallway and wiped rain off my arms and legs with wet hands, splattering the ceramic tiles. The smell of the building was soothingly familiar, and with each deep breath I felt the tension in my stomach loosen.

'What are you doing?'

I looked up and saw Tom standing on the stairs outside our old door in nothing but a pair of jogging bottoms. As he closed the door behind him, my mouth dried up as my stomach lurched half with fear and half with desire. It had been so long that I'd forgotten what he looked like topless. I thought about turning to leave, but I'd gone all that way in the rain so was going to say what I'd gone there to say. Plus, it was still pouring.

'Tom! Hello stranger.' My voice trembled. 'How are you?'

Tom didn't reply, he didn't move, he didn't show any sign that he was pleased to see me. He just carried on looking down at me.

'So,' I started, 'I know that you might not be ready to talk to me, but I just need to say something. I – '

'Queenie, this isn't fair,' Tom cut me off firmly. 'You can't just show up here.'

'Okay, and yes, you're right and I know that I should be respecting your space, but, like, I used to live here, plus you've been ignoring my messages for *five and a half months* and I didn't know what else to do,' I said in a small voice. 'I don't need to come up, but let me say what I need to.'

Tom opened his mouth to protest, probably, but closed it again. I took that as my cue to begin.

'I don't know how it's been for you, but the last few months have been fucking terrible for me,' I confessed. 'I'm so far away from where I was when I was with you. We used to speak about marriage, and babies, and at the time I didn't think I could do it, and I was scared, but now I'm even more scared that I've lost you, and lost the marriage and the babies – ' I took a deep breath. 'I'm having all of these random one-night stands with men who treat my body like it's a sex aid, and there was this one guy who I was sleeping with and the sex was, on reflection, pretty brutal, but then Cassandra came round and turns out it's her boyfriend, which is mad, and so she called me a slut,' I paused to take in a deep breath, 'and there's also this guy from my office who I knew I shouldn't get involved with but I've been so lonely and I was just waiting for you to get in touch, and he turned out to be married so I *really* shouldn't have got involved . . .'

It was like I couldn't stop it from coming out. Tom wasn't looking at me but I could see from how red his face was getting that he was angry. I carried on anyway.

'So I'm sensing that I'm probably oversharing, but the point is that I miss you and I'm scared of the person I'm becoming,' I finished speaking and took a deep breath. 'I'm not me without you. This break is killing me.'

I took another deep breath. 'I'm sorry. For everything.'

I listened to Tom breathing heavily through his nose. I opened my mouth to ask what I could do to get him to talk to me again, when he finally spoke.

'You know that's the first time you've apologised?' he laughed softly. 'The first time you've actually said sorry. After everything. The pushing away, the lashing out, the mood swings. The first time you've apologised.'

'It can't be,' I said, before realising that he was probably right. 'Well. I am.'

I started to walk up the stairs towards Tom, but he put a hand out to stop me.

'It's too late, Queenie,' he said quietly. 'It was too late months ago, I thought you got that.'

I stumbled backwards down the wooden steps and grabbed onto the handrail to stop myself from falling and cracking my head open on the tiled floor.

'But we love each other!' I said, trying to convince him.

'All this time, I thought we loved each other,' I said, trying to convince myself. 'And the text, at New Year's, I said I wanted us to have a good year, and you replied with a kiss?'

'Yeah, sorry about that, I was hammered. I should have realised you'd read too much into it.' His words were like a punch to the gut.

The door to the flat opened and the girl from before stepped out.

'Sorry to break this up.' She looked down at me apologetically. 'Tom, are you coming back in?' she asked, putting her hand on his waist.

'Yeah, give us a sec, Anna,' Tom said, turning round to her. 'I'm just saying goodbye.'

She closed the door behind her but Tom continued to face where she'd been standing. 'You should go.'

'Who's that? I thought she was a neighbour.' I told him.

No response.

'It's okay if you're sleeping with other people, I don't mind that, it's not like I hav – '

'I – uh.' Tom swallowed loudly. 'Anna's my girlfriend, Queenie. Has been for a while now.' He wouldn't look at me.

'But,' I gasped, 'I said we should revisit where we were in three months?'

'I thought you meant we'd see how the other was,' Tom offered weakly. 'I didn't think you meant we'd kick things off again.'

I, at that point, felt like I was going to keel over and die.

'So we're really done?' I asked. 'Forever?'

'We're really done.' Tom shrugged.

I opened my mouth to tell him about the miscarriage. Surely then he'd care, surely he'd be forced to think about what that actually meant, how heavy that was.

'Tom.'

'What? What?' he asked me, annoyed.

At that point I realised that I'd rather keep it to myself. He wouldn't care. I'd rather have him not know than have his apathy.

I walked home in the rain listening to 'Losing You' by Solange and 'When You Were Mine' by Prince, on rotation. By the time I got back, I was shivering so visibly that Rupert actually made me a cup of tea.

'Where did you go?' he asked as we sat in the kitchen, me still in my sopping-wet clothes, rainwater dripping onto the lino.

'Just for a walk,' I lied. My breath caught in my throat. 'I should go and . . .' I stood up and the kitchen seemed to warp. I pulled myself up the stairs while everything spun around me, and flopped onto my bed. My breathing was getting shallow. I tried to call out, but it felt like a giant was standing on my chest. I could hear a ringing in my ears, and then everything went black.

I came to on the floor next to my bed. I tried to get up but my limbs felt heavy, so I knocked my phone from my bedside table to the floor. I couldn't call any of my friends; I didn't want them to see me like this. I couldn't call my grandmother, she was too old to deal with this. Maggie! She'd probably try to sprinkle holy water on me, but at least she was good at staying pragmatic in the face of illness. I dialled her number and curled into a ball on the floor.

'Hello, Queenie, what's happening?' Maggie answered, cheerily.

'Aunt Maggie?' I rasped. 'I don't feel well.'

'Oh dear, you sound off. What's wrong?'

'I don't . . . know.'

'What do you mean, you don't know? Is it your women's troubles again?' she asked suspiciously. 'I've been praying for your recovery so it can't be.'

'No, I can't . . . breathe.' It was getting harder to talk.

'What do you mean, you can't breathe? You wouldn't be able to talk to me if you couldn't breathe, sweetheart.'

'Can you . . . come here? Sorry to, ask, I just, can't – '

'Okay. I'll get a cab over,' Maggie said. 'I'll have to bring Diana. Her dad *forgot* that he was meant to take her this weekend. Honestly, that man, he alw – '

' – Maggie, please . . . come.'

I managed to stagger down the stairs to the kitchen for a glass of water and lay on the sofa as my stomach churned. I tried to take big gulps of air down but whenever I breathed in, something stopped me. I eventually gave way to hyperventilation. After a lifetime of waiting, the doorbell rang and I hoisted myself up from the sofa. When I opened the door, Diana charged past me and Maggie bustled in after her.

'See, Mum, I told you it smells weird!' Diana wrinkled her nose in disgust, her tucked-up septum piercing catching the light from the upstairs hallway.

'Diana's right, Queenie, it smells like the whole place is damp. I didn't know you were living like this.'

I sat on the stairs and put my head between my legs.

'Diana, you go and sit down, find the front room. Don't take your shoes off, the floor isn't clean.' Maggie stood over me and bent down, looking into my eyes.

'You're shaking! Am I going to have to get an old priest and a young priest in here?' Maggie joked, putting her hand on my shoulder. 'No wonder you're shaking, you're soaking wet!'

'Can't breathe,' I told my aunt. 'And my head is swimming. My hands are shaking . . . and my stomach doesn't hurt, but it just feels like it's flipping over.'

I stopped talking so that I could try and take some deep breaths.

'Do you feel sick?' Maggie asked, rubbing my back.

I shook my head.

'Let me know if you're going to be sick,' Maggie said.

'I'm not going to be sick.'

'Diana, can you find a bucket, please?' Maggie called out. 'Queenie is going to be sick.'

'Maggie! I don't feel nauseous or anything but I feel like something is going to come up out of my mouth,' I said, flapping my hands frantically. 'I don't know how to explain it. I feel like something really bad is going to happen, I feel like I'll never feel better.'

I closed my eyes to stop my aunt's face blurring in front of me.

'Panic attack.' Diana walked into the hallway and said knowingly.

'When did you turn doctor?' Maggie asked through tightened lips.

'It is a panic attack, though.' Diana crossed her arms and leaned against the wall, smug with her diagnosis. 'Some girl in my class had them when we first started school. She used to feel like that before every class, so she had to take lessons in a room on her own.'

'Are you under a lot of stress?' Maggie asked, the sentence getting quieter so that by the time she said 'stress' she was mouthing it. Jamaicans don't typically believe in mental health issues. 'And have you been praying?'

'What do you mean by stress?' I ignored the latter part of her question. 'I've never had a panic attack,' I gasped, a wave of what was, I immediately recognised, acute panic hit me.

'Doesn't matter, Henny hadn't. They just started,' Diana said, picking at bits of the peeling wallpaper.

'Okay,' Maggie said, composing herself by smoothing down her bright orange kaftan and adjusting her wig. '*Diana*, stop touching, please. Queenie, get out of those wet clothes and grab your overnight things. Let's go to Mum's. Can we try and get the bus, or should I call a cab?'

'I don't want to go out,' I whimpered.

'You're not turning agoraphobic on me, come on, let's go. I'll call a cab.' Maggie clapped her hands as Diana helped me to stand up.

I looked at my little cousin. 'Sorry about this.'

'Don't be sorry,' she said, helping me up the stairs.

I shoved my headscarf and my laptop into my rucksack. As soon as we got into the cab, Maggie was on the phone to my grandmother, speaking in what I think she thought were hushed tones.

'. . . I don't know, Mum. She doesn't have a fever, she doesn't have a stomach ache. I don't know if she's eaten . . . Should I call Sylvie? . . . She's her mum, she'd want to know! . . . Okay. Well, we'll be there in twenty minutes.'

'Wake up. Queenie. Wake up.'

I opened my eyes to see Diana's face looming over mine. 'We're here. Do you need me to help you in?'

'No, I'm fine,' I said, swatting my cousin away. 'Why are you being so helpful this evening? It's not like you.'

I stepped out of the car and struggled up the gravel path with Maggie and Diana towards my grandmother. She was standing with her hands on her hips. I stepped through the porch door and she pulled me in by the arm and looked at me.

'Wha' wrong wid yu?' she asked as Diana sat on the stairs and got her phone out of her pocket.

'I don't know,' I shrugged, looking at the floor.

My grandmother put her hands on my cheeks and lifted my face so that my eyes met hers.

'Tell me, nuh?' she insisted.

'I don't know. I feel weird.' I moved her hands from my face.

'Have you eaten?' she asked, pursing her lips.

'I'm not hungry,' I told her, moving from the porch into the house.

'I didn't say are you hungry, I said *have you eaten?*' My grandmother's lips were tighter but still she managed to speak.

'No, I can't. Can I just go to sleep?' I said, going to walk up the stairs.

'Food first. I put some fish fingers on for you,' my grandmother told me, pointing towards the kitchen. 'Food is love' is my family's unofficial motto. Pity the motto is also 'Have you put on weight?'

My grandmother and I sat in the kitchen, Diana and Maggie's chattering in the living room occasionally broken up by my grandad begging that they 'Stop being so loud. Please!'

and my grandmother barking, 'Stop being miserable, let them live!' through the wall.

As I forced fish fingers and soggy toast down, I wondered if I should tell her about what had happened with Tom. I couldn't bring myself to offer the information, so decided to wait until she brought it up. I was surprised she hadn't asked already.

Diana came in to rummage for food, which prompted my grandmother to jump up and start preparing her a three-course meal, so I took the opportunity to sneak upstairs. I needed to watch something for distraction so pulled my laptop out of my rucksack and swore as the contents of the bag came out with it.

'Do. Not. Swear. Me teach you fi swear?' My grandmother had crept up the stairs.

'No, sorry. Sorry for making a mess,' I said, sitting on the edge of the bed.

'Get into bed. Here's a hot-water bottle, and here's your nightie. I washed it for you.' She handed me a white calf-length nightgown speckled with lavender flowers. Lace frills overwhelmed the bust and sleeves.

I removed my clothes shakily and put it on as she picked up the various bits of crap that I carry around daily from the floor.

'What's this?' she asked, unfolding a piece of paper.

I leapt over to her and grabbed it out of her hand.

'Nothing.'

She looked at me and pursed her lips.

'Get some rest. You'll feel better in the morning.' She turned the light off and left me standing in the dark.

'I won't sleep, it's 9 p.m.!' I called out after her, getting into bed and hugging the hot water bottle to my stomach.

It's over, I thought, Tom's words bouncing around my brain. How can it be over?

I fell asleep almost immediately.

As always at my grandmother's house, I woke up not knowing where I was, but immediately recognised my surroundings when I saw the moonlight shining onto a painting of the Virgin Mary on the wall opposite the bed.

THE CORGIS

Queenie:
It's more bad news, corgis

Queenie:
Tom has a new girlfriend

Queenie:
Turns out he thought we were over all along

Queenie:
He said 'When you said we should revisit things in three months I guess I thought you meant we should see how the other is'

Queenie:
????

Queenie:
And I've just been here waiting for NOTHING while he's been moving on

Queenie:
I don't know how much more of this I can take, you know. What next?

I slid out of bed and wedged my feet into my childhood slippers. I went over to the door and turned the doorknob almost imperceptibly slowly so as to make as little noise as possible.

'Queenie? What's wrong?' my grandmother shouted, and I jumped out of my skin.

'Nothing, I'm just going for a wee,' I whispered, creeping through the hallway.

'Mind the stairs!' she shouted.

'I'm going in the opposite direction to the stairs!' I whispered.

'But it's *dark*,' she replied.

I wonder how much sleep my grandad gets, on average? I sat on the toilet, feeling for the loo roll in the dark.

'Do you feel better?' My grandmother turned the light on.

I squinted and covered my eyes.

'I don't know, it's the middle of the night. Go back to sleep, Grandma!'

'Do you think I sleep, with all of you to worry about? I don't think I've put my head on the pillow and slept a full night since 1950.'

I got back into bed, my grandmother shuffling downstairs to get me some water. She came back up and put a glass onto the bedside table.

'Move over.'

She climbed in next to me and I turned to face her, putting my head on her chest. She wasn't as plump as she used to be. She felt smaller, frail, underneath the weight of my head so I lifted it and slightly hovered it above, letting my neck take the strain.

'You think I can't take your weight? I carried you when you were a baby and I could carry you now. Try to sleep, Queenie.'

Chapter Twenty

THE CORGIS

Kyazike:

What do you mean, he's got a girlfriend?

Queenie:

I mean I went back to our old flat and he was there with his new girlfriend, he was topless, and she's so small she was drowning in nothing but one of his T-shirts

Queenie:

And he literally said the words 'I have a girlfriend' to me

Kyazike:

Excuse me? How has he already got a whole girlfriend with official labels? It ain't been that long?

Darcy:

Oh Queenie, I'm so sorry xxxx

Darcy:
Why didn't he tell you before you
went there and found out?

Queenie:
I've been trying to recall our last
conversation? I'm sure it wasn't
clear that we'd broken up? I'm
SURE of it

Queenie:
What if I just heard what I
wanted to?

Kyazike:
Nah, he should have made it
clear, fam. BUT at least this
means you haven't been
cheating on him these last few
months

Queenie:
I mean, I guess? Thanks, Kyazike

Kyazike:
What's she like? She a mzungu?

Darcy:
Sorry Kyazike; I looked that up
on Urban Dictionary but it's not
there . . .

Kyazike:

Lol, mzungu is my language. It
means white girl

Darcy:

Thanks! I should have been able
to figure that one out

Queenie:

Course it's a white girl. But we
knew it was going to be, didn't
we

Kyazike:

Fam. We knew.

As Darcy and I stood in the kitchen, the fridge beeped angrily, louder than ever, and the neon light flickered dramatically.

'I looked her up on the way home,' I said, showing Darcy pictures of Anna on my phone. 'I knew I recognised her. Look, she works in his office.'

I navigated the girl's profile, showing Darcy bits of information I'd seen so much that I'd memorised.

'I fucking told him he needed a white girlfriend. Just never thought he'd get one WHEN WE WERE ON A BREAK.'

'I've just had a thought. Do you think, that they were – ' Darcy said, her hand flying up to her mouth.

'If you're going to suggest that they were seeing each other before we broke up, then please don't.' I swallowed down

255

rising dread. 'I think you know that I can't handle that in my current state.'

'Well, I guess at least if that were the case it would mean that you could start properly hating him. And hating someone is a vital stage when it comes to getting over them.'

Seriously, there was nothing Darcy couldn't find a solution for.

'Whatever,' I said, putting my phone away. I'd looked at enough pictures of Anna to paint her from memory. 'I need to suppress that for now. Got a meeting with Chuck.'

I left the kitchen and went over to Chuck's desk, feeling very managerial when I asked him to show me his progress.

'Okay, so, this new layout,' he started eagerly. 'I've printed all of the examples that you've sent me and thought we could talk them through? Right, so – '

My phone buzzed, and when I pulled it out to look I saw the beginning of a message from Cassandra flash up on the screen.

Cassandra:

If I say we can talk about it this
evening will you st

I walked back to my desk, sat down and opened the text.

Cassandra:

If I say we can talk about it this
evening will you stop sending me
messages? It's getting tiresome,
you chasing me.

'Sorry, Chuck, can we postpone?' I shouted across the office. 'I'll look over those and we can talk about it tomorrow.'

The knot in my stomach tightened as I crossed the office and slipped into an empty breakout room. I called Cassandra. She didn't answer. I tried again, and got a text.

Cassandra:
Just come round later.

I had tiny sips of tomato soup as I unpacked Cassandra's messages over lunch with Darcy.

'I don't understand why she's being so cold, though,' I said, grimacing as the soup started to churn in my stomach.

'Isn't she quite cold anyway?' Darcy said. 'You know, like a sort of Duchess "I'm better than everyone because I've psycho-analysed you all to death and I know you better than you'll ever know yourselves" way?'

'You'd noticed?' I asked, relieved that I wasn't the only one who realised that Cassandra was hard work.

'Are you joking?' Darcy laughed. 'That's exactly the vibe she gives off. Poor you, you must be used to it. Do you want some bread with your soup?'

I shook my head. 'She's not that bad, look how much money she's given me. If it weren't for her I wouldn't have been able to afford dinner most nights. Either way, silent treatment for a month and now she wants to see me? Why doesn't she just call me? I'm too scared to see her face to face.'

I put my spoon down. I couldn't eat any more.

'Unless she's going to apologise for cutting me out of her life for something that was in no way my fault.'

'I'm actually quite relived she left the Corgis. She's so anal that she'd put full stops at the end of *all* her messages. It drove me mad. Can you at least try to eat a bit more? Here, try my

257

burger.' Darcy thrust her food towards me and I jerked my head away. 'If you stop eating properly you'll feel worse, Queenie.'

'Eating *makes* me feel worse,' I couldn't stop myself from moaning. 'Every single thing I eat or drink, I can feel its route through my digestive system the minute it passes my lips.'

'Are you in pain?' Darcy leaned closer to me.

'No, it's more discomfort. And churning.' I rubbed my stomach, pressing my hand into it roughly.

'Don't do that!' Darcy pulled my hand away and towards her. 'Are you . . . pregnant?'

'No, no way. It might be panic, or anxiety or something.' I lowered my voice. 'Remember, I have my referral letter from stern Elspeth.'

'Yes, that's a brilliant idea!' Darcy's face lit up, a possible solution in sight.

'Is it?' I tried another sip of soup. 'Isn't that just *admitting* that something is wrong with me?'

'So what if something is wrong with you? There's something wrong with all of us,' Darcy said, gently.

'There is *nothing* wrong with you.' I sighed, throwing the spoon down and leaning back in my chair. 'There's too much wrong with me, Darcy. I don't think I'll ever know what it's like not to worry. About everything.'

'Well there you go, that's what you need to talk about. I think you should do it. What have you got to lose?'

*

I sat on the bus to Cassandra's. My stomach was still turning and my skin felt like it was on fire. I tried counting to ten repeatedly to stop myself from having to run off the bus screaming. My breathing was getting shallower and I couldn't regulate it. What was *wrong* with me? I'd done this journey a million times.

I stopped at the florist on the corner of Cassandra's street and picked up a bunch of irises. I went to the counter to pay and emptied all of my pockets and rucksack onto the counter before accepting that I'd forgotten my purse at work, so walked to Cassandra's house without a peace offering.

As I got closer, I leaned on the wall and bent over, taking some deep breaths as I summoned the courage to walk up the path and ring the doorbell.

'Are you okay, Queenie?'

I looked up at Cassandra's dad, who had opened the door.

'Yes! Sorry, Jacob, just a little . . . out of breath. I ran here,' I lied. 'Is Cassandra in? Please.'

'Yes, go up, she's in her room. Exciting times ahead!' he said sadly, his tone not matching his words. What did he mean?

'Now, can I get you a drink?' Jacob asked, guiding me into the house. 'I know you like my hot chocolate!'

Did he know about Guy? He wasn't talking to me like he knew. Though parents were meant to stay adult and impartial throughout these things, weren't they?

I tripped over a box as I made my way through the hallway. I fell over another as I got to the top of the stairs. I stood outside Cassandra's door, my fist poised to knock, and looked at the brass 'C' screwed into the wood. My stomach rolled over. I wasn't ready for conflict.

'Come in,' I heard Cassandra say.

My hands were so sweaty that after two failed attempts at turning the doorknob I eventually managed it with my sleeve over my hand.

I stepped into the room and stood in the doorway, puzzled by more boxes seemingly containing the contents of Cassandra's room.

'Where are you off to?' I asked.

'Leaving,' she snorted. 'Moving. With Guy.'

'Are you joking? To – to where?' My legs started to shake, so I lowered myself onto the stool by Cassandra's dressing table before I remembered that it was only decorative and could break under my weight, so stood up again. Breaking family heirlooms was not the way to forgiveness.

'To Winchester.' Cassandra smirked, like she'd just told me she'd won something I'd really wanted.

'What? Where's *Winchester*?' I furrowed my brow.

'Of course, you're terrible at geography.' She snickered. 'Hampshire.'

'Okay, but *why* are you moving to *Winchester* with *Guy*, Cassandra?' I pressed. Why was she saying this like it was the most natural thing in the world?

'Well, you'll know he's a junior doctor, I'm sure.' Cassandra flipped her golden brown hair viciously. 'His next placement is at a hospital there. Didn't he tell you that when you were fucking?'

'No.' Little spikes of anger pulsed through me.

Why was I still being blamed?

'I didn't know that,' I said, my voice calmer than my disposition.

Cassandra crossed me and shut the bedroom door. It closed with a quiet click. I felt trapped.

'Really? You were lying on your back for him all that time. Did you never actually talk to each other?'

She narrowed her eyes at me and crossed her arms tightly.

'Oh come on, that's not fair,' I groaned.

Cassandra cocked her head at me, demanding a response.

'Well maybe, but I wasn't ever listening. We weren't having a relationship!' I tried to explain. 'It was just about the sex. And remember, I stopped doing i – '

She lifted a hand to cut me off.

' – anyway, I've decided that I'm going to be adult about this. He loves me, and he made a mistake. And you know, you *were* just sex. An outlet to release tension when he was having a wobble about his career,' she said, sounding like she truly believed that. 'We've looked into it, there are psychiatry courses I can do at a university not far away. The houses there are cheap compared to London and my dad has agreed to help us get on the ladder.'

She smiled and went back to her spot, removing books from her shelves and placing them into one of the twenty cardboard boxes in the room.

'Do they, your parents, do they know what happened?' I asked breathlessly, hoping that I could call them in to help put a stop to this madness. 'Surely if they did, they'd tell you that you were mad.'

'No, and they don't need to,' Cassandra said viciously enough to make me pull back. 'Guy's said that we can start having a good life together, and I believe him.'

'Cassandra, let me get this straight.' I was trying to make sense of the nonsensical. 'You hear me talk about some boy for months. Like, the duration of the time you've been with him. *You* aren't sleeping with him, then you come to my house and watch him walk out of my bedroom with your own two eyes and your next step is to cut *me* out and leave London with him? I came here because I thought you were going to apologise, but instead you're telling me that you're making a choice, and you've chosen him? You don't even know him!' I pleaded with her.

I got up, crossed the room and placed a hand on hers to stop her from packing her life away.

'Don't.'

She pulled her hand away from mine as if mine were made of fire. 'This isn't a choice between you and him, don't be so self-centred,' she said. 'It's about me. I've found someone that I want to be with. He gives me stability. I can't carry on with the only consistent thing in my life being *your* problems.'

She let those words hang in the air. 'I've met someone that I love, he loves me and we're starting a life together.'

'But he was *cheating* on you the whole time,' I said. 'This wasn't a drunken kiss in a club! Don't you think you deserve better than that?'

Cassandra picked up a roll of brown tape and turned it around in her hands, looking closely at it for the edge.

'Do you know the thing about you, Queenie?' She found the edge and picked at it. 'You're damaged goods.'

Her words hit me like Anthony Joshua had punched me in the chest. I sat on the edge of the bed.

'You're damaged goods, so you self-destruct,' Cassandra repeated, calmly.

A good thing she repeated it, too, because I couldn't believe what I'd heard the first time.

'No wonder Tom escaped when he did. He was too good for you.'

As her words continued to strike me, I could feel my heart fragment a little bit more.

'You're so closed off that actual love is out of your reach, so you settle for sex. With anyone who'll fuck you. Your self-esteem is a joke.' She placed the edge of the tape on the cardboard and extended it, sealing the box. 'With a mum like yours, it's no surprise.'

She smoothed the tape down on the box. 'So. Take care.'
She lifted the box and put it on a pile with the others.

'Cassandra, we've been friends for so long,' I said, my voice
breaking. 'Why are you saying this? *How* can you say this?'

'It's all true, isn't it? ' She shrugged. 'You're always saying I
psychoanalyse you too much. Think of it as my final diagnosis.
You can let yourself out.'

I stood up. What was the point in trying to change her mind?

'Good luck with everything, Queenie,' Cassandra said as I
walked out of her room. 'Oh, and you have my bank account
details. I'll send you your tab.'

Chapter Twenty-One

'She's a bitch for that, don't you *dare* listen to her. She's more of a prick than that Welsh ting and he's a *major* dickhead.'

Kyazike and I stood on her balcony, smoking. She had one eye gazing out on a sparse and wintry London, the other looking through the window at the living room door in case her mum came home and caught us.

'Why don't you save yourself this drama, fam? Why don't you just date black guys?' Kyazike asked.

'Why do you think?' I asked, shutting her down.

'Sorry, no, I know. I should have thought before I said,' Kyazike said, flustered.

'Sorry, I didn't mean to snap.' I put a hand on her shoulder. 'Remember the first family party you took me to?'

'The one where my cousin Elias tried to move to you?'

'Yeah,' I nodded. 'And I was so stressed by it that I started crying?'

'Yeah and we had to pretend it was because you had period pains.'

'I just can't do it, Kyazike. I'm scared of black guys. I'll always, always think they hate me.'

'I get you, I get that,' Kyazike said, reassuringly. 'But that's pure nonsense, my strong, beautiful, black queen,' she added in a thick Ugandan accent, the one she borrowed from her mum when she wanted to hammer the point home.

'Maybe Cassandra is right. Maybe I *am* damaged goods, that's why all of that stuff with Tom, and Ted, and all the others,' I said, ignoring her compliment. 'And the king of it all, Roy. He made sure that any self-esteem I had was crushed into nothing.'

'*Nah*, I'm not having that!' Kyazike shouted so loudly that her voice echoed around the estate. 'These men, they ain't worth all this. And Cassandra?' Kyazike kissed her teeth. 'She's just vex because her man found good sex somewhere else. She's taking it out on you, fam. All of that psychology nonsense she chats and she can't even do it on herself. You think that relationship is gonna last?' She kissed her teeth again. 'She's lucky I don't spin her jaw, how can she talk about your mum like that? The stuff with you and your mu – '

'Kyazike, don't,' I warned her, then screamed and ducked as a pigeon that had nested on the balcony flew over my head.

'Sorry. Anyway, I give it two months, she'll be belling your phone telling you how she needs help moving home and how she's sorry she didn't listen and takes back everything she said. So don't think about it for now. Put it out your head, fam. Come, we go inside, it's blitz.'

We went back inside and rubbed our hands together. It was a cold February afternoon, and the air held a harsh chill.

I threw myself down on the sofa, yelping as my skin touched the cold leather. Kyazike handed me the razor blade and lowered herself to the floor.

'Beg you hand me that blanket?' she said, holding her hand out.

'Can we at least turn that fan heater on?' I pleaded. 'My fingers are shaking so much that I might scalp you.'

'Are *you* going to pay the electric bill?' Kyazike asked, turning to look at me.

'It's *your* head, Kyazike.'

She crawled across the room and turned the heater on. We both sighed with relief as the hot blast of air hit us.

'Are you going to get rid of that pigeon's nest? It can't be hygienic to have them living there like that.' I gestured to another bird as it landed on her balcony.

'I've tried to poke it with the broom but it's stuck firm. Those pigeons are crafty, they've built it on a corner we can't reach. But I'm going to get closer. I just need a white suit.'

'What? Like a white trouser suit?'

'Nah, not my Sunday best, Queenie, one of those CSI suits they wear when there's been a murder. Trust me, I will have those pigeons up.'

'Sorry, yeah,' I said, my head all muddled. 'CSI suit.'

I took a deep breath.

'Kyazike. What do you think about counselling?'

'The pigeons aren't stressing me that much, fam.' She laughed.

'No, I mean, like, when people are having a bad time. Do you know anyone who has ever been?'

'Queenie. I'm Ugandan. You think anyone in my family is allowed to say they need help? You bury that shit and you move on. If I told my mum I need counselling she'd ship me over to Kampala in a cargo barrel.'

'I'm thinking about getting it,' I said. 'I don't know. I feel, like, awful, all the time. It's not shifting. This frosty woman at the clinic wants to sign me up because she thought I was going mad. Well, first she thought I was being pimped out, but then she realised that I was just having sex for fun,' I rambled. 'But that I probably wasn't having that much fun.'

'Well, do it if you need to, innit. I don't think I'm the best person to talk about all this feelings therapy fluff with.'

*

I carried on with Kyazike's hair while she told me about a guy that kept taking her on dates and then promising her shoes or similar. I couldn't keep track of what she was saying, because I kept getting snatches of panic that would rise and fall in my chest and had to concentrate on quelling them while trying to pick up key words from the story.

'Are you listening?'

'Sorry, yes! The shoes?'

'Yeah, so eventually I was like, stop dropping hints, why do you wanna know my shoe size? He says he's in Selfridges buying me shoes as a late Christmas present, so I rushed there in case he was gonna get me a pair that I *don't* like, like the guy who bought me the nude Louboutins that were *nude*, but for a white girl.'

Kyazike shook her head in disappointment.

'Anyway, I get there, I'm trying on the shoes, I hand them to him, fine. Two two's, we're at the till and he's trying to haggle with the store girl, then he tried to pay with four cards, none of which were in his name!'

Kyazike turned to look at me.

I looked back at her flatly.

'Are you all right, fam? You usually love my stories,' she said, disappointment and worry etched across her face.

'I'm fine, just sleepy,' I said. 'Sorry.'

'All right. Anyway, I'm locking it off, fam. He's some wheeler-dealer! I'm not asking for much from my Mr Right, you know, but believe, employment is essential. Plus, this guy's phone only seems to be on when he wants to link me, and the dates are all spontaneous. Like he'll call me and say come out for dinner like I'm constantly sitting at home ready with my eyebrows drawn on. Like make-up isn't expensive.' She kissed her teeth. 'Maybe I should try white guys, like you. They'd treat me better.'

'You think?' I asked her, the last few months of gross mistreatment flashing before my eyes.

'Yeah. They wouldn't like me, though.' Kyazike shrugged. 'I'm too black for them. They don't want a dark black girl.'

'Don't be stupid. I'm proof that they don't want us, whatever shade.' I sighed heavily. 'Why can't I just have a happy ending, Kyazike?'

'You joking, fam?' Kyazike laughed. 'You think life is a film? Even if it was, fam, we're black. "Whatever shade",' she said, mimicking my voice. 'We'd be first to die.'

I finished Kyazike's hair and she went to start cooking, brave enough to endure the cold kitchen flooring. I wrapped the blanket around me and felt myself drifting off, but didn't try very hard to fight it.

I slept, but I could hear everything that was happening at Kyazike's. I heard when she finished cooking, waking up just enough to say no when she offered me dinner; I heard when she ate and watched *EastEnders*; I heard the squeeze of washing-up liquid and the clatter of dishes and splashing of water when she did the washing-up. I heard her go on the balcony when the shoe guy called, I heard her tell him that she wasn't leaving the flat because 'Your whole essence is too short notice, and I can't be going out with no fraud boy!'

I heard Kyazike's mum come home, I heard the argument they had about having the fan heater on, I heard her mum get in the bath to get ready for her second shift of the day.

At midnight, Kyazike shook me gently and handed me a

headscarf and nightie. I put them on and lay on the sofa. It was warmer now.

'Here's a quilt,' she said. 'See you in the morning.'

When I woke up Kyazike had already gone to work. When I got to the office, I had several emails from Gina asking me to see her in her office immediately. I knocked on the open door.

'Come in,' she barked. 'Oh, Queenie, are you *seriously* wearing the same thing you wore yesterday? And close the door behind you.'

'Yes, sorry,' I said. 'It's only because I stayed at a friend's house.'

I shut the door and walked over to the chair that faced Gina.

'Now. I've got some bad news for you,' she told me.

'What?' I asked, my heart beginning to pound in my ears.

'You're being suspended.'

'What?' I blinked. '*What?*'

'This extreme crush that you've had on Ted, well . . . it's not appropriate. He's filed an official complaint to HR and everyone thinks it's best that you're not in the office while it's investigated.' Gina lowered her voice, embarrassed for me.

'An extreme crush?' I asked, bewildered. 'On Ted?'

'He's spoken about it to HR confidentially, and says that you've been paying him a lot of attention, saying suggestive and inappropriate things, following him around, and that it's making him entirely uncomfortable and stressed in his place of work,' Gina explained.

What was going on?

'Suspended for that? But he, no, he's the one who – I have the emails, and the messages, he's the one – ' I stuttered, desperate for her to understand that I wasn't the one at fault.

'We have to take that sort of complaint seriously.' She paused briefly. 'Plus, you already had an official warning on your file.'

'But it's not true, Gina! Can't you tell them that it's not true?' I begged her. 'And that I just come in and do my *job*?'

'Queenie, how can I prove to them that there's a role here that you're actually fulfilling? You don't come in on time. When you do get here, you spend every second distracting Darcy, who has managed to do her job alongside the chatting, by the way. You aren't focused, you aren't committed, and when I asked you to contribute to the paper, which you wanted all along, you didn't do it, and when I give you that tiny responsibility, to look after an intern, you can't even do that. Word gets round, Queenie, and Chuck's father is head of the US edition, come on!'

'I'm sorry, Gina, it's just that there's been a lot going on. I am sorry, I just let it get away from me and I've been distracted but I will do better, I promise,' I pleaded with her as panic started to rear its ugly head.

'Queenie, we all have things going on,' Gina started. 'Between me and you, my ex-husband refuses to look after our children, my lover has been telling me he's going to leave his wife for the last six years, my mother has been moved into a hospice and my father doesn't remember who I am, but still I have to keep going. What is it I told you all those months ago? You've got to keep one foot on the ground! You focus! But you haven't, even though I've been giving you chance after chance.'

'I'm so sorry,' I whispered. 'I can't believe I've let this happen.'

'So here's what you're going to do.' Gina crossed her arms. 'You're going to leave the office at the end of the week. I've managed to swing it that you're going to be on paid leave for two weeks, as you haven't taken any of your holiday, which brings you to the end of the month. Then after that, no pay, and we wait to see what happens. I'll keep you posted on the investigation.' Gina paused. She surely knew that this was my only source of income. 'Chuck will be filling in for you, Queenie. He's done some brilliant work. He did a redesign of the culture pages, and everyone is very impressed.'

'But I told him to do that,' I said, bitterly. 'Is this because *my* dad isn't the head of a paper? This isn't fair!'

'Queenie, not much is!' Gina said heavily. 'Yes, people like Chuck have it easier than you, but instead of accepting it and complaining about it, you've got to do better!'

'I understand, Gina,' I cut in. 'Twice as hard to get half as much, right? I grew up hearing this but never thought I'd hear it from you.'

'This isn't because you're black, or because your family are poor!' Gina pointed a finger at me. 'He's got it easier than most of us here, for god's sake. Frankly, if you'd kept your eyes on the ball then you wouldn't be in this position. I am so sorry, kid.'

I started to shake violently.

Gina uncrossed her legs and jumped up from her seat. She put a hand on my shoulder and asked if I was okay. I couldn't respond. She left the office and came back in seconds later with Darcy.

'Queenie? Queenie, are you okay?'

I could see and hear my friend, but I still couldn't open my mouth to speak.

'Darcy, who is her next of kin?' Gina panicked, picking up her phone. 'Boyfriend? Shit, she doesn't live with her boyfriend anymore, does she?'

'No, it'll be a family member.'

'Do you know her mum's number?' Gina asked, her hand hovering over the phone keypad.

'Not her mum,' Darcy said. 'Don't call her mum. Her next of kin is probably her aunt Maggie. The number will be in her phone. Queenie, where's your phone?'

I stared ahead, still shaking.

Darcy left and came back in a few seconds later, my phone to her ear.

'I don't know what's wrong with her, but she's shaking a lot . . . Okay, I'll ask her. Queenie, you aunt says have you eaten? . . . she's not saying anything. But she didn't eat anything at lunch yesterday . . . I don't think she's just hungry, she looks like she's in shock or something . . . Okay . . . Queenie, Maggie asks if it's the panic attacks this time, or the women's troubles? . . . She still won't say anything . . . Shall I get her stuff ready and bring her down to the foyer? . . . Yep, I'll wait with her until you get here . . . No, it's no bother at all, I'll see you soon.'

Chapter Twenty-Two

With everything in Eardley's van, I walked down the steps of the damp, crumbling Brixton house and left the key on the kitchen table. I wouldn't miss it. Not much could surprise me anymore, but I was shocked that I'd lasted as long as I had in that house.

I ate my words and *did* miss the house days later when the reality of living with my grandparents kicked in. I thought I'd be able to spend my days recovering through sleep, rest, quiet and food.

The first night, I was tossing and turning until dawn because I was worrying that my life was over. Who moves in with their grandparents when they're almost twenty-six?

*

We sat in silence around the dinner table as the dim light flickered overhead. I looked down at my dinner, my stomach beginning to churn. I could never eat in Roy's presence, but he insisted on these weekly meals. Ultimately, they gave him the opportunity to belittle either me or my mum for an extended period of time while he had both of us in one place.

'You know what I've been thinking?' Roy said, breaking the silence.

I wondered which one of us he was going to come for first. Yesterday it was me, so today it was surely going to be my mum.

'Your daughter won't amount to nuttin',' Roy laughed, throwing his stocky frame back in his chair and chucking his fork onto the dinner table. 'Eedyats, the pair of you.'

My guess was wrong. I looked down at my plate as he laughed again. I felt like I was going to be sick.

'This girl won't amount to nuttin' at all.'

I looked over at my mum, willing her to say something.

She looked down at her hands. Why was she always letting him do this?

'Lord *God*, what did I do to end up with two fool women under my roof?' Roy growled, picking up his fork and shovelling rice into his mouth. 'I take this stupid woman in, big mistake, and me tink say her pickney ah go be better? I mus' ah been mad.'

'I'm not hungry anymore,' I said, pushing my chair away from the table.

'Where yuh tink yuh going?' Roy asked, taking a sip of his Dragon Stout. The dark liquid almost escaped his mouth as he belched loudly.

'I'm going to do my homework,' I said, desperate to run out of the dining room and out of the house.

'Finish. Yuh. Food,' he said, banging the bottle down. 'Yuh not leaving my table until you eat everyting on your plate.'

'I don't feel good,' I whispered.

'Wha yuh mean, "I don't feel good"? ' Roy copied my voice. 'Eat yuh food and stop talking like a white girl.'

'But I don't want it,' I said, pushing the plate away.

My mum finally opened her mouth. 'Queenie, please, just eat the food.'

'I never should have let you bring this ungrateful pickney in my yard, Sylvie!' Roy roared, reaching across and grabbing my plate. 'There. You eat it for her,' he barked at my mum, throwing it in front of her. 'Someone ah go eat it today.'

'I'm not hungry, Roy. Besides, Queenie might have it later,' my mum said, in a feeble attempt to normalise the situation.

'So nobody hungry? We all ah sit down to dinner, and I'm the only ah eat?' Roy shouted. 'Eat with me, nuh, Sylvie?' he yelled, grabbing my mum by the back of her head and pushing her face into the plate.

'Roy!' my mum cried out, her voice muffled by the food. She lifted her head and, with food in her eyes, reached out for a napkin with shaking hands.

'See what you've done?' Roy sneered at me. 'Look at your poor muddah. You've ruined dinner, Queenie. Jus' like yuh ruin *everyting*.'

*

I finally drifted off at around five in the morning, only comforted by the knowledge that my alarm wouldn't be going off hours later.

'Morning.' My grandmother burst into the room. 'Up you get, this isn't a huh-tel!'

Who needs an alarm when you have Jamaican grandparents?

'And when you're up, don't forget to make the bed. Come on, quick, there's porridge on the stove. You need to dish it out for all t'ree of we!'

I jumped out of bed not knowing where to turn first, despite the military instructions.

My grandmother bustled down the stairs as I made the bed, my head pounding with exhaustion.

'The porridge is getting *cold*!' she shouted from downstairs.

'Okay, I'm coming, I'm coming.' I flew down the stairs and into the kitchen.

'Your grandfather takes his with a small spoon of brown sugar and a large spoon of honey, I want mine with a large spoon of brown sugar, a handful of raisins and no honey, and you can have it how you want it but not too much sugar because you'll get diabetes.'

I started to spoon various servings of porridge and toppings into bowls and sat eating it with my grandparents.

'I'm turning the hot water off in fifteen minutes so you need to get in the bath before it runs out,' my grandmother said.

'I haven't even finished my porridge.' I showed her my bowl.

'The water rates, Queenie,' Grandad sighed.

'Then when you've finished in the bath, you're going to run the hoover and I need you to take some sheets to the launderette for a service wash. They're already in the trolley in the porch. On the way back, you can use the trolley to pick up some bits from Brixton market. I'll give you the list.'

My grandmother wasn't taking my being ill very seriously.

'I'm not Cinderella! I've come here to have some rest, not to – '

'Queenie, you've got two arms and two legs that work. Nuttin' wrong wid' you. And if you ah go' stay here, you ah go' *help.*'

'But there is something wrong with me. I – '

My grandmother looked at me from across the table, daring me to continue.

'Well if I'm going to do all of that housework, there's no point in me having a bath first.' I decided to pick another battle.

'You tink we ever sent any ah' you out without cleaning your skin? What if you walk on the road and get hit by a car, they tek you to 'ospital and cut you out yo' clothes and yo' skin dirty? You know what kind of shame dat would bring?' My grandmother kissed her teeth. 'Time is ticking. The hot water is going off in ten minutes.'

'Fine,' I said. 'I'll do what you want. But I draw the line at going to church with you on Sundays.' I stomped upstairs, a spoonful of porridge still in my mouth, and jumped back into bed while I ran a bath until my grandmother shouted, 'And do *nat* get back into bed!' from the kitchen where she was already seasoning chicken for tomorrow's dinner.

I undressed and sat on the edge of the bath watching the water tumble in, climbing in when it was almost full. I lay back carefully so that my headscarf didn't get wet, and tried to relax into the water. I closed my eyes and tried to imagine that none of this was happening, that I was only here for a night and that tomorrow I'd be getting up, going back to work and carrying on with my life.

I sat up suddenly, panic propelling me upright. Unease spread from the top of my head and down my body. I went to stand up but my legs wouldn't follow the command of my brain. My heart started to pound, and my vision blurred at the edges.

'Help!' I tried to call out, but couldn't pull enough air into my lungs to get the word out. Instead, I sat hyperventilating until the water turned cold.

'Queenie?' my grandmother screeched. 'Stop pussyfooting *around*, those sheets need to go!'

Although I could now move my legs, I couldn't stand for the shaking. I didn't know if it was the cold or the adrenaline.

'What, you still in here?' She burst into the bathroom and I pulled the shower curtain around me.

'Queenie, you must be mad. You think I'm looking? You should have seen my form when I was your age, I put *all* ah yu to shame.'

'I feel really weird, I think I should go back to bed. I'm shaking, look.' I held my hands out.

'You think I haven't shaken worse in my life? After I had your mother I shook for a year. Come out the bath.'

*

Two weeks passed. A fortnight of chores, of feeling so ill, of refusing phone calls and ignoring messages, of panicking silently so as not to make my grandparents aware of my weakness.

On Tuesday morning, somewhere between my first bath of the day and taking the recycling out, my phone buzzed with a number that I didn't know. I answered it cautiously with the hand that wasn't balancing milk cartons and empty porridge boxes.

'Hello, am I speaking to Queenie Jenkins?' a droll woman's voice said on the other end of the phone.

'Yes. Who is this?' I asked, walking down the front path.

'My name is Amanda, I'm calling from SLAM. We received your referral letter,' the woman said, her tone exactly the same as before.

'SLAM?'

'South London and Maudsley?' she said. 'We received your referral for talking therapy.'

I dropped the recycling in its box and turned to look at the house to check that nobody was watching. The coast seemed to be clear but my grandparents had supersonic hearing so I let myself out of the gate and walked towards the main road.

'Oh. That was quick,' I told her. 'I thought it would take months, if you'd get back to me at all.'

'It usually does, yes, but we had an opening. Would you be able to come in for an initial assessment?' Amanda from SLAM pushed on. 'It'll just be a chat, it shouldn't take more than an hour.'

'Er, sure. Maybe. Can I think about it?' This was all a bit of a shock. 'Where are you based?'

'Camberwell, just opposite King's Hospital and behind Denmark Hill station,' she recited. 'Once we've got your assessment booked in, we'll send a letter out to you and it'll have all the information you need. You don't need to worry about addresses now.'

The next opening they had was in a week's time, which seemed soon, but I agreed to it quickly before I could um and ah and talk myself out of it. I walked back to the house and saw my grandmother standing in the porch, arms folded.

'Who were you on the phone to?' she asked, lips suitably tight again.

'Nobody!' I said.

'So why yuh look so worried?'

'No reason. It was nobody. I'm going upstairs.' I kept my head down, concentrating on taking my shoes off.

'Hm. You think I need to look into your eyes to know that you're lying to me?' she said, before kissing her teeth and walking into the kitchen.

THE CORGIS

Darcy:
How's it going, Queenie?
Missing you! Xxx

Kyazike:
Yeah fam, it's not like you to be
quiet

Queenie:
Hi both

Queenie:
I'm not good

Queenie:
But I'll be fine

Darcy:
Take your time! There's no rush!

Queenie:
Of course there's a rush. I've felt
bad for so long. I just want to be
better. I want to be normal

Darcy:
A lot has happened to you,
Queenie. It's a huge amount to
process. But you'll get there!

Queenie:
I guess

Kyazike:
Ah, fam. I know it's mad, still,
but you'll be back to yourself
in no time. Trust me. In the
meantime, you ain't missing out
on anything. I haven't even been
on any dates I can entertain you
with

Queenie:
Ha

Queenie:
I think I'm going to go off grid
for a bit, if that's all right.
Talking to you just reminds me
that I'm a shell of the Queenie
you were friends with

Darcy:
You're Queenie! You don't have
to be one way or another for us to
love you. But you take your time.
We'll always be here. Xxxxxx

Kyazike:
Exactly. What Darcy said. Love,
fam

That night, and the night after, I lay awake, thinking about how best to approach the introduction of counselling to my grand-parents. I didn't entertain the idea of lying to them; since I'd been staying here every second of my time was accounted for, logged and discussed.

On Friday morning, after our porridge, I'd decided that after I'd taken a letter to the postbox for my grandad would be the time first to tell my grandmother about it, then, judging from her reaction, navigate how to tell my grandad.

*

'I heard you fall out of bed last night,' my grandmother shouted from the kitchen as I walked down the stairs.

'Sorry,' I shouted back. 'Second time that's happened this week. Maybe I should put some pillows on the floor!'

'You're not putting *anyting* from the bed on the floor,' came the expected response. 'And what's this?'

'What's what?' I said, walking into the kitchen. She was sat at the table, arms folded like a mob boss.

'Close your dressing gown when grandad is around,' she tutted, unfolding her arms and sliding a letter across the table towards me.

I picked it up and saw the NHS header. An apology left my lips before I could read any further.

'You trying to shame all ah we?' she asked. Her eyes burned like hot coals.

'No, but I need help, don't I?' I half-asked her. 'And a, a nurse referred me, and I didn't want to do it because I know that we should just be strong and try to get through these things bu – '

This one wasn't going to go well.

'You know how much pain me carry?' My grandmother slammed her hand on the table. 'You know how much pain I have to tek tru' my yout' and my twenties and beyond? You know what my madda, your grandmadda, woulda said if me did tell her me ah go seek *psychotherapy*? You mus' be MAD.'

'I don't know what to say,' I said. 'I need to go and speak to someone, Grandma. I feel ill, I have this weight, on my chest, I lost my job, I'm not well.'

'None ah we *well*. Look at yo' mudda, livin in hostel after that man bruk up her life and beat 'er an tek 'er money. Yuh tink *she* ah go *psychotherapy*? Ah *you* mek yourself lose your job becah *you* nah hold it together. You are *nat* going.' My grandmother was shaking.

'Maybe I should leave here, then, and go – '

'*Where* you ah go stay? Cyaan stay wid yo' mudda, yo' fadda swannin' around in Jamaica wid young gyal, Maggie cyaan tek you in. Das why you're wid *us*, under our *roof*.'

My grandmother's accent had become so thick I had to work hard to keep up with what she was saying.

'I'll go and stay with friends, then,' I said. 'Grandma, I never ask anything of you, I never do anything to bring shame on anyone!' I tried to say this calmly, to not anger her any further. 'I was the first person in this family to finish school, to go to college, to get a degree, to get a full-time job – '

'Yes! And di firs' person to go to *psychotherapy*!' My grandmother hit the table again. 'I am telling you. You are *nat* going.'

She folded her arms. 'And dat is dat.'

The conversation was over.

'What's going on, Veronica?' My grandad shuffled into the kitchen, trailing his walking stick across the linoleum. 'What coulda 'appen to make you speak such *strong* patois and bruk up di table?'

'Let yo' granddaughta tell you,' my grandmother said, kissing her teeth and pushing herself up from the table. She went over to the sink and started to wash up so furiously that suds splashed onto the ceiling.

'Well?' my grandad said, looking down at me. I gulped and handed him the letter. He took it from me and surveyed it, slowly. My heart was going to beat out of my chest.

'I don't have my glasses, Queenie, what it say?'

He handed it back.

'It's an appointment,' I said, wincing.

He stared at me. I'd never known him to pay this much attention to anything but the news, and this turn of events was terrifying.

'Appointment? Fi what?' he finally asked.

'To go and get some counselling. Like, talking therapy. Because – '

He lifted his hand and I stopped talking, my breath catching in my throat.

'Let her go, nuh?' he said to my grandmother. She stopped washing up immediately, but carried on looking into the sink. 'Maybe if all ah we had learned to talk about our troubles we wouldn't carry so much on our shoulders all the way to the grave.'

He turned to walk out, his stick hitting the floor with purpose.

'Maybe we haffi learn from this new generation, Veronica.'

Chapter Twenty-Three

'. . . and so what brings you here today? If you could explain the events that have led you to seek talking therapy?'

I looked around the room I was sat in with a woman I'd never met before but was expected to tell all of my secrets to.

'Take your time.'

The room was cold, clinical. It didn't have the smell that hospitals had, the smell of illness and of disinfectant. Instead it smelt of darkness, sadness. It smelt like the sort of space that doesn't see light or air, candles, flowers, anything that gives a room the sense that somebody cares for the person inside it.

'Well. I didn't seek it,' I said, finally.

'Well, your file says that you were referred from a sexual health clinic, is that right?'

'This nurse, Elspeth. She thought I was being pimped out but then realised that I was just having sex with basically everyone.' I rolled my eyes and threw myself back into my chair. 'Stupid.'

'Okay, well, we can come back to that later. For now, could you tell me why you understand that you need therapy?'

'I don't really know how to describe it,' I said, biting the inside of my cheek and pointlessly looking out of the window that had been frosted for privacy. 'Er. I don't know. I feel a bit like things are falling apart? Well, they've already fallen apart.'

'Okay. And in what way do you think that things have fallen apart?' the woman asked softly.

'I had a job. I lost that. And . . . I lived in a house which was kind of rubbish but at least I could pay my rent, but now that I don't have a job, I've lost that, so I'm living with my grandparents, so I've lost any independence. I had a relationship with a guy who was probably the love of my life. But that fell apart, and that was my fault.'

I stopped speaking, remembering the way Anna had tenderly put her hand on Tom's naked waist. I took a deep breath.

*

'Could you not touch me?' I groaned, rolling over onto my side and away from Tom. 'I feel sick.'

'Oh shit. Do you want me to get you anything?' he asked, putting a hand on my shoulder.

'No, get off me.' I wriggled away.

'Will you be all right for Saturday?' Tom asked.

'What's Saturday?'

'My mum's birthday, remember? We're meant to be staying there for the weekend?'

'I don't know, do I?'

'Queenie,' Tom started, 'are you sure everything is all right? You've been . . . off for a while now.'

'I've felt like shit for a few days, all sick and light-headed. Maybe it's a bug or something,' I said, pulling the covers closer to me. 'I'm going to try and sleep it off.'

'Yeah, must be one of those bugs that makes you angry and withdrawn, too,' Tom huffed, leaving the room.

I lay on my back and closed my eyes but it made me feel worse. I took some deep breaths through my nose.

'Here you go.' I opened my eyes and saw Tom standing over me with a cup of tea in the T mug.

'No thanks.' I shook my head.

'I've just gone to make it for you!' Tom snapped. 'Don't be so ungrateful.'

'But I didn't ask for it, did I?' I said. 'When I feel like I'm going to throw up, why would I want anything, let alone a cup of milky tea?'

'Oh right, so I'm a bad boyfriend for not being able to read your mind?' Tom slammed the mug down on the bedside table and crossed his arms. 'You're impossible lately!'

'I didn't say you were a bad boyfriend, did I? Why are you overreacting?'

'Me, overreact?' Tom asked, wide-eyed. '*Me*? *You* feel a bit nauseous and you're acting like you've been to war!'

'You do realise that you're having a go at me because I feel sick?' I narrowed my eyes. 'Do you know how stupid you're being?'

'Oh, so I'm stupid for trying to be nice?' Tom threw his hands in the air dramatically.

'You're not trying to be nice, though, you're trying to fix things immediately,' I told him. 'Just go away, let me sleep.'

'This wouldn't have happened if you'd just taken the fucking tea.'

'Don't swear at me!' I yelped, 'I'm very fragile!'

'You just told me to go away!'

'Yes, fucking go away!' I shouted. 'Get the fuck away from me!'

'Fine, Queenie, if that's what you want, that's what you'll get.'

Tom slammed out of the bedroom door and out of the flat.

*

'Why was it your fault?'

'I pushed him away. I didn't know why I felt so bad, I didn't know how to talk to him about how I felt, and by the time I knew what was wrong, it was too late,' I said. 'I'd had a miscarriage. And yeah, even though I didn't want a baby, I still lost one. So maybe that doesn't count, in my theme of loss,' I tried to joke.

'And my friends, I think they're just bored of my problems. It's not the same with them. I seem to piss them all off, or just burden them, and one of my best friends, Cassandra, she's moved to the countryside with her boyfriend, some guy that I slept with without knowing – sorry, this probably all sounds really silly, doesn't it. Like playground drama.'

I tried to wrap it up, not yet understanding the limits of what you should say to a therapist and what you should write in your Dear Diary.

'Queenie, none of this is silly at all,' Janet said, smiling.

She was plump and small, and had a kind face puckered with dimples and her slightly tanned skin was dotted with tiny moles. She spoke slowly and chuckled often, her voice deep and precise, with a lilt that told me she was from up North but had been living in London a while.

Her short hair curled around her face, auburn mainly but grey at the temples. I started off calling her Dr Cosima as the letter had said, but she'd asked me not to, telling me that she didn't want me to feel as though I was being examined.

Janet continued. 'Try to remember that we all encounter many issues, big and small, and that they're all relative to us. They impact us all, in different ways. There's nothing too trivial. It also sounds like you are dealing with some quite big losses, in a concentrated period of time. Could you tell me a little bit about how these things have made you feel?'

'I don't know. I feel like I can't breathe a lot of the time. Sorry, I don't know how best to say these things, like I should know technical terms, or something.'

'It isn't for you to know technical terms, that's my job. Just try to relax, and tell me, in your own time, how you feel. Even if it's physical pain, discomfort, if it's tiredness, sadness, anything at all.'

'Okay? Well, yeah, I feel tired a lot. Like, exhausted. I feel like I'm always trying to concentrate on being normal again. And I don't really sleep that well. I feel worried, like something really bad is about to happen, but I can't pinpoint what, and then I feel even more worried because I can't work out why I feel the way I do. I feel frightened, like, properly scared. Especially at night. I have these nightmares, this sleep paralysis. I end up physically fighting everyone I share a bed with in my sleep, which is *not* cool.'

I stopped to catch up with myself.

'I feel nervous about really small things that I used to be able to do without even *thinking* about them, like going to the shop, or eating – and I used to really like eating. I don't feel sick, but my stomach is always flipping over and over, and when I get really upset sometimes it feels like my stomach is like, closed off. So I don't have an appetite, is what I'm trying to say. Sometimes I feel frantic? And I feel like everything has just spun out of control, out of my hands? I don't know. Like, I feel a bit like for a while I've been carrying ten balls of wool. And one ball fell, so I dropped another to catch it, but *still* didn't catch it. Then two more started to unravel, and in trying to save those I lost another one. Do you know what I mean? Sorry.'

'Don't apologise, Queenie. I understand what you mean. You used a term that I don't really like to be used here – '

'Oh, sorry. What was it?'

'You're apologising again.' Janet laughed. 'Normal. What is normal to you?'

'Oh, sorry. Sorry. Sorry for apologi – you know what I mean.' I shook my head quickly as if to reset myself. 'Well, you know, normal is normal. Like being happy, and being able to get up and go to work without worrying about everything, and being able to have a nice time with your friends without thinking something bad was going to happen, and being able to eat without feeling shit, you know, just normal.'

'I think that we all need to scrap this idea that normality is something to strive towards. I personally cannot pinpoint or prescribe what it is to be normal,' Janet explained. 'I think it's a lot of pressure to put on yourself.'

'Maybe,' I tried to concede.

'Try to bear that in mind as we go along,' she said. 'I'd like to ask you something, Queenie.'

'Go for it,' I said, trying to make myself comfortable.

'What do you think about yourself?'

I froze. I hadn't realised the question would be such a hard one to even approach answering.

'That I'm insane, mainly.' I quickly threw an answer at her before I could start getting in my head about it.

Janet chuckled. 'Well you aren't insane, I can tell you that now. I mean, what do you see when you look in the mirror, when you think about yourself as a person?'

'I try not to look in the mirror. I don't know, I'm just me, I guess. I'm nothing special. I'm not pretty, I'm not ugly. I just get on with it. I don't know.'

I looked at the frosted window again. 'This is a hard question.'

Janet nodded slowly. 'I notice that you haven't mentioned

your parents at all. Do you have a good relationship with your mother and father?'

That question was even *worse*. What was she going to ask next?

'Ha.' A bitter laugh burst out of me. 'No. Ha. My dad isn't here. He's in Jamaica, I think? Nobody really knows where he is or what he's up to.' I shrugged.

'And my mum – ' I cleared my throat, feeling something familiar rise from my stomach. 'I don't – is it okay if I don't talk about her?'

Janet pushed a glass of water towards me. 'I think that it would be good if we could touch on your mum at some point, if that's okay? We don't have to do it today.'

When I walked out of the door after doing some breathing exercises to stop me from panicking that only served to make me feel stupid, I decided firmly that I wasn't going to go back.

*

Can it truly be called 'living' when you're sharing a house with your grandparents?

Pros of living with grandparents:
1. I can honestly say that my surroundings have never been cleaner
2. Nor my body
3. Quiet night times – eight hours a night at least. I might not be able to sleep, but it's better than the sound of Rupert being sick or Nell crying and listening to the same sad song on repeat
4. Haven't had to spend money on food

5. Even though explaining it took a hundred years and they're still suspicious about it, I made them get broadband so I can watch Netflix (even though I have to watch everything with my headphones in)

6. Seeing Diana more, communicating with 'the youth' and so being able to understand newly emerging memes and slang. Bonus pro: she doesn't seem to be fazed by my temporary breakdown

Cons of living with grandparents:

1. I myself have to clean the surroundings

2. My bathing is timed by my grandad who, after two months, still lectures me about the water rates every time I run a bath. What *are* water rates?

3. I get sent to bed at 10 p.m. and live in fear of my night terrors scaring either of them

4. I have to eat the food my grandmother makes, most of which is too spicy for me, and then endure the 'we should send you to Jamaica to toughen up your mouth' line EVERY TIME I CHOKE

5. I also have to go and buy the shopping and pull it home in a nan-trolley

6. My grandad turns the 'internet box' off every night before he goes to bed and I have to sneak out of the room to turn it back on and wake up before them to turn it off again

7. Defending myself to my grandparents and Maggie about not going to church on a Sunday

8. My grandmother keeps trying to force surprise interventions between me and my mum. I've manage to avoid them by sneaking out of the house, but I can't imagine that I'll continue to get away with it

Two weeks after my session with Janet, I was called down from the attic where I'd been instructed to 'organise' the net curtains. I climbed down the ladder and went into the kitchen.

'Letter for you.'

My grandmother gestured to the white envelope on the table while wiping down the surfaces with a J-cloth that was on its last legs.

'Was that urgent enough for you to call me down from the attic?' I said.

'Excuse me?' she asked. 'Who are you talking to?'

I mumbled an apology and went to take the letter into the front-front room but my grandad followed me in and shooed me out before I could sit down.

'Who is it from?' my grandmother shouted from the kitchen.

I took it up to my room.

Dear Queenie,

I really do think that, with proper care and attention given, I can help you to overcome your issues. It will take time, and it won't be easy, but it's a journey that we can make together. Now, having worked with many patients in my time, I know that many factors can affect how the patient feels about treatment. If it's that you don't like the office, we can find a place that you find safe, a coffee shop, or I have a registered studio in my house in Golders Green.

What was in this for her? She was being like Miss Honey from *Matilda*, or something.

When you walked into my office, I saw both the person that you are currently, and the person that you could be. You've experienced a lot of loss, and a lot of grief, in a very concentrated amount of time. It's no wonder you've had to take some time out of your life.

With me, you can get your life back. I don't usually make promises, but I can promise you that if we work hard, we will get you to a place where you can be you again. And not just you, but the best version of yourself. I'll let you think about that.

Please call me.

Janet

I took a deep breath and sensed that I would have a very trying few weeks ahead.

*

Time really goes slowly when you're doing nothing. After all of the chores for the day have been done, and as per the rules, I'm bathed and in bed by 10 p.m. At least now I'm sleeping again, which is helpful as I'm still expected to be up at seven every morning. Today was Monday, counselling day and my fifth session with Janet.

My recovery wasn't going as miraculously as I thought it would. Thank god for the NHS, because if I had to pay for these sessions myself I wouldn't get close to halfway to recovery before bankrupting myself. In our sessions in Janet's tiny flat in Golders Green, once I've endured the journey there, we've battled over antidepressants (I am *against* because I think I'll turn into a zombie, Janet is *for* because apparently they'll calm me down enough for the therapy to take), we've touched on my relationships with friends (I am dependent on them to validate my thoughts and actions), the casual sex (I am dependent on it, to validate my body and my control), Tom (how dependent I was on him and how much that frightened me, leading to self-sabotage), my dad (I was absolutely not dependent on him, which is why I treat men as throwaway – not sure how keen I am on this Freud-type linking of the father to the sex). We've worked out that the reason I don't like holding hands and hugging is because I'm not comfortable with loving and tender physicality; I'm scared it'll be taken away from me and leave me feeling abandoned. I did *not* realise just how much I had going on in this little head of mine. This week, though I thought I had successfully avoided it, we had to talk about my mum.

'So. You grew up with your mother?' Janet asked, putting her notepad and pen down.

'Yes.' I nodded. 'We lived with my grandparents until I was six. Then we moved to a little house of our own. Then she met someone, and we moved.'

'And by someone, you mean a partner?'

'Roy. Yeah, Roy,' I said, and took a sip of water to coat my sandpaper throat.

'And this Roy. Did you get on, you and him?' Janet shifted in her chair.

'No,' I said swiftly.

'Go on?' Janet asked me, her brow dipping slightly.

'When he wasn't screaming at me, he ignored me,' I said, taking a deep breath. 'I don't know, maybe this isn't important. His house, it was clean, there was a garden, he was a good cook – '

'Well, you being either screamed at or ignored when you

were growing up is hugely important to your development, so try not to minimise that,' Janet said. 'Can I ask, Queenie, what was his relationship with your mother like?'

'Why?' I could feel panic rising. As always.

'Well, any trauma in childhood will present itself in adult-hood,' Janet told me, shifting herself in the chair again.

'But I'm not my mum,' I replied.

'If you had to witness your mother's pain, that will of course have an effect on you,' Janet explained. 'And I've allowed you to skirt around the issue up until now, but we need to get into it.'

'Is it going to make me feel better, to talk about this?' I asked.

'Not immediately,' Janet replied. 'But it needs to come out.'

My head was swimming. I waited for it to be still before I started to speak.

'My mum, she's always been nice,' I began. 'She's mild-mannered, she's very kind. She's naive. She's not very sharp, and she's too trusting.'

I listed all of the positive characteristics that I could mine from memories of my early childhood.

'And when she met Roy, she'd been single since my dad. Not that you can call that a relationship.' I paused and took another sip of water. 'We lived together, me and my mum, in a tiny little house in Mitcham. We were obsessed with each other, I remember. I couldn't go anywhere without her, and she couldn't go anywhere without me. We had our own world, me and my mum.'

I felt my skin prickle. These were memories I hadn't unearthed for a long time.

'Then Roy moved in. He was *mean*. Really mean.' I dug my nails into my palm involuntarily. 'He had this thick Jamaican accent. It was so strong that I couldn't always understand it, and he used to laugh at me. Call me a bounty – '

'A bounty?' Janet interrupted.

'Like the chocolate. White on the inside,' I told her. 'Brown on the outside.'

Janet shook her head sadly. 'I'm sorry to hear it. Go on.'

'I stopped talking to him, hoping that if I didn't say anything he'd stop picking on my voice, but he just did other things to upset me. He'd break my things, tell my mum I'd said rude things about him, or stolen from her, he'd make me sleep in the car.'

I reeled off some of the things I never thought I'd tell anyone.

'Eventually she stopped speaking to me about anything but getting up for school and going to bed. They only spoke to each other.' I croaked. I took another sip of water and carried on. 'After a few years, I can't remember how old I was, he made her sell our little house. He took the money and bought somewhere new. We all moved there – that's the house with the garden, the one that had to be kept spotless – anyway, we moved there. Sorry.' I paused. 'Am I talking too much?'

Janet shook her head.

'Okay. Well, he started to cheat on her. She knew it, even *I* picked up on it. He'd disappear for weekends, and when he'd come back my mum would never say anything, because she didn't want to rock the boat, and I guess it was more important for her to be in a relationship. One day she *did* say something, though, and when she came to the flat she had a black eye and a split lip.'

I looked down at my palm. My nails had pierced the skin.

'I'm sorry to hear that, Queenie. But what do you mean, she came back to the flat?' Janet frowned, confused.

'For a bit, I was living in a flat,' I told her. No turning back now. 'With myself, mainly. She popped back, from time to time. I wasn't there for long, just a few months. I could take care of myself. It was fine.' I tried to convince her, and myself.

'How old were you?' Janet asked quietly.

'Eleven, I think? I started my period while I was there, so I must have been eleven.'

'They rented a flat for you to live in when you were eleven?'

'No, it was for me and my mum, initially, he wanted us out. But after not very long it just ended up being for me. She stayed with him.'

'That's illegal, you do know that? You were a very vulnerable young person, and put in a *very* dangerous situation.' Janet's voice hardened.

'I was fine. And it was better than the alternative. I couldn't live with him anymore. I didn't fit in with his *warped* idea of the home he wanted. He hated me. He made her hate me. It was destroying me.'

I sat on the tube home picking dried blood from my palms. When I got back to south London and out of the station, my phone pinged with a text from Darcy. We hadn't spoken for weeks.

Darcy:

Hello, just checking in! How's it all going? How's the therapy going? Xxxxxx

Queenie:

Hi Darcy, nice to hear from you!
Yeah, it's a lot, but think I'm
getting some – pretty horrific
– stuff out. I've been told to go
swimming as a 'form of physical
release'. I pointed at my hair and
my therapist told me to get a
cap, if you can believe it. X

I went back to my grandparents' and was so exhausted that I crawled up the stairs and into bed. I barely slept, Janet's voice in my head asking if I spoke out when Roy had hurt my mum.

'I did,' I replied. 'Every time, I said something! When he pulled chunks out of her hair, when he pushed her down the stairs, when he broke her jaw, I said something!'

I woke up and saw my grandmother at the end of the bed.

'Me never know you suffer so bad,' she croaked, patting my foot. 'Try an' go sleep.'

I slept again, eventually, for hours. I would have slept longer if I were allowed to miss meals.

*

Darcy:

Morning! Sorry I didn't reply
last night. Simon hid my
phone because I was being
'uncommunicative'. Swimming
is a great idea! Maybe Brockwell
lido? It's a scorcher today.

Queenie:

I'm on my way there! Had to buy an ugly but functional swimming costume from Sports Direct. Wish me luck.

I stood on the concrete steps up to the lido café and took some deep breaths. I was wearing my costume under my clothes and I could feel sweat pooling in the space between my boobs and my stomach.

I fanned the neck of my dress and blew down into my cleavage. My eyes were blurring, so I concentrated on the peeling white paint flaking off the handrails.

'Are you all right?'

I followed the high-pitched, scratchy voice and looked up and into the face of a waitress with enough thick, dark blonde hair piled high on her head to give her neck strain. She pulled a carton of cigarettes from her apron and lit one.

'Yes, sorry, just loitering.' I laughed awkwardly. 'Going to swim but putting it off! Feel a bit weird.'

Why was I telling her this?

'Yeah, I know what you mean,' the girl said, taking a giant drag. 'I'd never get in there, it's too cold. You must be completely mad.'

'Ah, thanks. Really looking forward to it now!' I said, making my way in.

I squeezed my way through the changing room, the air thick with the smell of chlorine. It was full of women of varying shapes and sizes but, as with work, parties, university, *anywhere*, saw nobody like me. Nobody black. You wouldn't know I was round the corner from Brixton.

I breathed slowly through the anxiety and took my dress off. I whipped it over my head quickly and looked around to see who was staring at my big thighs. Nobody seemed to be looking.

Predicting that everyone would turn in horror when I walked out to the pool, I wrapped my towel around my waist and held my arms close to my sides so that I minimised their jiggling.

I navigated my way around dozens of trim sunbathers presenting their flat white bellies to the sun, their bodies void of hair. Should I have had a wax? The quick shave I had might not be enough. I looked closely at my legs and saw dark, wiry patches of hair, Guy's voice telling me to shave popping into my head. I very rarely compare myself to other women but in situations like this, how could I not?

I wrapped myself in my towel and found a slither of space next to the pool. I lay my towel on the ground and got down quickly, covering my lap and legs with my bag.

'And do you know what I said to him, Stella? I said, "Cosmo, we're going to have to sell the second flat! The Brixton one! Because we just *can't* be dealing with these tenants anymore!" Honestly Stella, if it's not one thing, it's another.'

I looked over at the woman next to me whose sharp, clipped voice was almost physically grating slices from my skin. I could only see the back of her brown bob but could guess what her face was like.

'The ones we have in at the moment sent us an email saying that they had *mould,* of all things. Is that our problem? Honestly!' she scoffed.

'Well actually, I think it is, Tanya,' her blonde-bobbed companion said.

'Oh. Is it?' Tanya asked, shocked.

'Well, you know the little rental we have in Peckham?' Stella began. 'The three-bed that Damon's father gave us?'

I saw the brown-bobbed one nod.

'There was *such* terrible mould in there that the walls were *black*. The tenants kept threatening us, saying they were going to call Environmental Health or something, so we had to sort it. Honestly, T, it was awful,' she said, and I was pleased that she had some empathy. 'We lost so much money.'

I put my headphones in and settled back, putting my foray into the water off by telling myself that I'd listen to *The Read* before I braved it in the pool. The second I closed my eyes to settle into it, they shot open when I felt a dripping on my leg.

I sat up and saw a little redhead staring at me, water falling from her long hair straight onto my knees.

'Hello?' I said, trying to smile in a non-aggressive way. 'Are you lost?' I moved my leg out of the water's path.

'No! I'm a sea creature!' she shouted, shaking her head so that freezing water flashed across my face.

'Tabitha, come *here!*'

My eyes followed the voice and settled on Tanya, who turned round to look at me. Her face was exactly as I'd predicted. Soft, puckered, red from too many glasses of wine when the kids had gone to bed. I looked at her, water dripping from my chin.

'Can she say sorry, please?' I asked the woman.

'Tabitha darling, can you please come to Mummy, get dry please.' Tanya ignored me, standing up and wrapping her daughter in a towel.

'Did you hear me?' I asked, looking from her over to the blonde-bobbed Stella, her friend with the same face.

'I'm a sea monster!' Tabitha yelled, reaching over and pulling my hair. 'And so are you!'

'Are you just going to let your child behave like this?' I raised my voice to hide its trembling.

'I think we'd better go, Stella, I'm not going to be *attacked* at my local pool!'

'Don't worry, I'll go!' I said, standing up. 'I don't fit here, anyway.'

I stood up to go and locked eyes with another family who were all looking at me. I looked around the pool and into the eyes of strangers who were staring. They all hated me. I could tell. None of them wanted me to be there. I felt dread rise from my feet and into my stomach, where it started to lurch painfully.

'So aggressive!' I heard Tanya whisper as I stumbled out of the turnstiles.

Everyone's voices grew louder, so loud that I had to cover my ears with my hands. I half-collapsed, half-sat on a patch of grass, intrusive thoughts in my head growing as loud as the sounds around me. I couldn't bat them away. I put my head between my knees and stayed that way, the sun beating down on my back. I don't know how long I sat there, but eventually I found my phone and called Janet.

'Hello?' she answered.

'I didn't fit, I'll never fit,' I said. 'Roy didn't want me in his house – nobody wants me at the fucking *lido* – Tom didn't want me, my own mum . . . she didn't – ' The words forced their way out, the sentence broken by my jagged breaths.

'Queenie? Where are you?'

'There's no place for me, Janet,' I said.

'Queenie, remember your breathing. Can you tell me where you are?' Janet said in her most measured voice.

'I've tried swimming, it all went wrong,' I said, trying to calm down.

'Okay. I'm going to stay here on the phone until you can breathe again.'

I kept the phone by my ear as I counted to three, then to eleven repeatedly. After a few seconds I heard someone walk over to me.

'Are you okay?'

Was I now destined to live my life with people asking about my well-being at every juncture?

'Yeah, thanks,' I said, my head still between my knees.

'You're okay?' Janet asked from the phone.

'Sorry, no, someone is – ' I tried to explain.

'Do you want these?'

I looked up and the blonde waitress with all of the hair handed me my towel and my dress.

'I saw you run out in your swimming costume, thought I should bring your clothes to you. There are children around, so . . .' she said awkwardly.

'Oh, god, did I – ' I reached out and took the dress. 'Sorry. Thanks.'

'Queenie?' Janet's voice again.

'Sorry, I'm here. I think I'm okay,' I said, my breathing returning to normal. 'I don't know. I've been thinking about her.'

'Thinking about your mother?' Janet guessed.

'I've been thinking about why this all started. Why it all started to come back and why I stopped caring about my life and started to fuck up.' I took some deep breaths. 'Is it because I could have been a mum? Did me being pregnant throw up all of my mum issues?'

'Mmm, that may well be it. Pregnancy, whatever you choose to do – that sort of life event won't just pass you by without having an effect,' Janet told me. 'And does this make you feel differently about your mother?'

'Well, yeah. I guess I never thought of her as a person, I just saw her as someone who should protect me. And in a way she did, in the end. It's my mum who took the pain. No house, living in a hostel on her own, not many friends, she alienated them all while she was with Roy. Court case to try and get her money back, so fucking fragile now that she can't work, she doesn't have a life anymore. She was such a mess when Roy kicked us out that she couldn't make it through a day of work, but look! I've followed in her footsteps. Like mother, like daughter. Except this time I'm the one to blame. Not Roy. I've done all this to myself.'

I trailed off. 'Sorry for babbling, I think I've got heatstroke. I should go and put my clothes on.'

I put the phone down, feeling unease shifting in my chest. The dark thoughts had quietened.

Queenie:
Darcy, I think I just had a breakthrough at the lido. I'd always assumed it would feel good, was obviously wrong, still feel quite bad

Queenie:
Also I could have been put on some sort of sex offenders register for indecent exposure

Maybe I should try yoga for relaxation? Swimming was obviously not my thing, and I hadn't even made it into the pool.

Chapter Twenty-Four

'How old are you today?' my grandmother asked, sliding an envelope that she hadn't bothered sealing across the kitchen table.

'Twenty-six,' I replied, my mouth full of porridge. I picked it up and turned it over in my hands.

'Are you sure? I thought you were younger,' she said, watching me as I opened the envelope. 'I didn't write in the card, you get the point,' she added impatiently. 'But there's twenty pounds in there. Maybe you could go to the high street and get yourself a nice top?'

I got up from my seat and walked over to her, bending down and putting my arms around her neck.

'Time flies. Are you sure you're not twenty-two?' my grandmother said, wistfully. 'I remember when you were born! Nobody had seen as much hair on a baby's head. There still hasn't been one in our family with as much you.' She sighed. 'You were born worried, I remember that, too.'

She paused. 'Anyway. Better go and clean your skin, then you can start the day. I'm turning the hot water off in an hour.'

'I was thinking, Grandma,' I said, before I left the kitchen. 'I was wondering if you'd invited my mum?'

'Queenie, listen. I did, and I am not taking the invite back,' my grandma snapped. 'Whatever mistakes she's made, she is my daughter, and your mother. So she is coming to celebrate the birth of her child.'

'No, that's fine. I think she should be here,' I said.

*

As I ran the bath and asked my grandad if he would give his sighs a rest for this one day, I replied to birthday messages from people I hadn't seen for years and probably wouldn't see again on Facebook. Nothing from Tom.

*

'How does it feel to be twenty-three?' Tom asked, handing me a cup of tea.

'Rough,' I smiled weakly, putting it on the bedside table. 'I think I'm too fragile to ingest at the moment.'

'Nobody told you to have a fourth glass of wine.' Tom laughed, climbing into bed next to me.

'Oh, Mum and Dad's present to you is being delivered today, and they're calling us at midday. They want to wish you a Happy Birthday themselves.'

'Why and *how* are your parents so nice?' I asked. 'Oh – you've given me the wrong mug.' I showed him the Q.

'I'm surprised you can even see which one you've got.' He laughed again, swapping with me.

'This is entirely your fault,' I rasped, my mouth dry. 'You know by now what my limits are, and you are wholly irresponsible for not jumping across the pub and knocking that last glass out of my hand.'

'I know, but you're so sweet when you're drunk,' Tom said. 'No arguing at all, all you want to do is cuddle and thank me for looking after you.'

'I lose my need to be defensive when drunk!' I told Tom. 'You're taking advantage.'

'Trust me, nobody can take advantage of you, drunk or not. Did you have fun?'

'I think so. That was my first birthday with people and presents for a long time. I haven't wanted to celebrate it in ages,' I realised. 'Thanks for organising everything.'

'It's the least I could do for you,' Tom said, grabbing my hand. 'Right. If you're twenty-three now, how long until I get you down the aisle and get a bun in your oven? Twenty-nine and thirty-two respectively?'

'That's a long way away,' I said, burying my face in his chest. 'You might not love me by then.'

'Rubbish. I'll always love you.'

*

I shook my head, trying to dislodge a pointless memory. My phone started to vibrate violently in my hand.

THE CORGIS

Darcy:
Happy birthday

Kyazike:
To you

Darcy:
Happy birthday to you

Kyazike:
HAPPY BIRTHDAYYYYY

Darcy:
Dear Queeeeenieeeee

Kyazike:
Happy birthday

Darcy:
To you!

Kyazike:
Ayyyyyyyyyyyyyyy!

Kyazike:
We want to see you one of these days, you know!

Queenie:
You just want your hair done, Kyazike. I'll be up to it soon

Kyazike:
Nah, fam. Just want my Queenie back

I sat in the bath feeling strong enough to reinstall Instagram and remind myself how HAPPY everyone was when I heard the doorbell ring. I listened closely to the shuffle of footsteps and the dull thud of cane on carpet to the front door.

'Hi Grandad!' I heard Diana squeal. 'Where is she?'

'She's where she always is. In the bath.' My grandad sighed his reply.

I heard a flurry of footsteps and pulled the shower curtain across the area of the bath that my body occupied just in time for Diana to come running in.

'Happy Birthday!' she shouted, thrusting a small envelope in my face. 'It's nothing big. Just a gift card for H&M. Only for £10, but still, you can buy some accessories or something.'

I reached through the plastic curtain and took it from her.

'Thank you! You didn't have to do that.' I put the card on the bath rack.

'Aren't you going to open it?' Diana asked me as though I wasn't in the middle of washing.

'Should I see you downstairs?' I suggested.

'No, it's okay, I'll keep you company,' Diana said, lowering the lid of the toilet and putting her feet up on the radiator. 'I was gonna go out with my friends today because Kadija got us half-price tickets to go Thorpe Park, but I felt bad if you were just going to be here with Grandma and Grandad on your birthday. How old are you today?'

'Twenty-six. And it's not so bad. I don't like birthdays that much anyway.'

'Oh my god, are you *joking*?' Diana laughed. 'Birthdays are the best! On my fifteenth me and my friends went to some Clapham rave, it was wavey. And they all put money in so that we could have a table in the VIP area – '

' – VIP? How did you afford that? You're all babies,' I pointed out.

'Um excuse me, fifteen means I am almost an *adult*. Anyway, the night was *sickening*, I was the centre of attention *and* Mum extended my curfew. *That* is why birthdays are so good.'

'I've never had a birthday like that, and I'm much older than you.'

'Well maybe that's why you're depressed?' Diana asked as though she'd hit a eureka moment. 'Sorry, I didn't mean it like that. No offence. I just mean, maybe if you had more fun times you wouldn't think about bad stuff, maybe? I dunno. Sorry,' Diana shrugged, backing out of the bathroom.

I finished my bath, got dressed in a calf-length floral dress that used to be my grandmother's and went downstairs. Diana was standing in the hallway with her trainers on.

'We're going out,' she said, looking me up and down. 'But get changed first.'

'But Diana, I'm ready. This is vintage,' I said, standing in front of her, allowing her to take the full outfit in.

*

A change of clothes later, Diana and I were on the high street, me in the changing room of a charity shop. Not the one that our grandmother works in; we're not allowed to go in there. She says it's mixing business with pleasure.

I was struggling into an orange and turquoise Paul Smith shirt. Being out of the house for this long was taking its toll on my anxiety levels. When I did finally get it on, having had to negotiate the fabric over my sweating arms and back, it would pop open at the bust every time I took a deep breath in.

Diana opened the changing room curtain and looked at me.

'No.' She closed it again. 'Do you wanna go Morley's? I want four wings and chips,' her voice asked from the other side of the curtain.

'No.'

'I should have known you're too stuck-up for that. Let's get a milkshake then,' Diana said, steering me by the elbow towards one of those weird urban-designed modern ice cream parlours.

We sat opposite one another in a booth in the corner by the toilets and peeled the sticky menus apart.

'What do you want?' Diana said from behind the menu. 'I know what I'm getting. Oreo waffle, I always get it.' Diana held up her phone and scanned the room with it. 'Hold on, just snapchatting our settings! I've captioned it *Cuz is 26*.' She showed me a picture of myself looking at the menu, bewildered by the choice.

'Twenty-six, and this is my life,' I thought, looking around at the teenagers leaning on tackily decorated walls, all staring at their phones. Three years from now and I was meant to be getting married. I was meant to be stable and loved and – I looked back down and the words on the page started to blur. I looked over at the toilet door. If I ran in there and had a panic attack, I could at least not let Diana see me fall apart again. I was meant to be getting better, and if she saw me having a panic attack she'd tell my grandmother, and then there'd be a whole *thing* about me going to therapy and it not working, so bringing shame on the family for no reason.

'You all right?' Diana asked, locking her phone and putting it on the table.

I must have looked really bad if she was stepping away from her phone.

'Set an example,' I thought, breathing in slowly and counting to three, hoping that my nostrils weren't flaring too obviously.

'All fine, just looking for a waiter,' I said.

'You've got to go up and order, obviously,' Diana said, looking at me suspiciously. She slipped out of the booth. 'You sure you're all right?'

'Sorry. I'm fine!' I said, my heart rate slowing. 'Just get me the same thing as you.'

I handed her the twenty-pound note from our grandmother and watched her walk to the counter. When she was there, I put my head in my hands and closed my eyes. *Just breathe, Queenie. Breathe, imagine you're* – what is it Janet said, why can't you remember? – *That's it, the safe space, find your safe space. Where is it? That's it, it's the attic room in Grandma and Grandad's first house. The room that they said was haunted, but you didn't mind, you used to love the creak of the floorboards, and the way that the temperature of the air dropped when you stepped into the ro* –

'Are you sure you're okay? We can go back if you're feeling weird?' Diana threw herself back into the booth.

'No, I'm fine,' I said, surprising myself by meaning it. 'It's all good. So, what's this Oreo waffle, then? How exactly does it work?'

*

We walked back to the house, the sugar from our 'treat' coursing through my veins like a shot of adrenaline. Diana was telling me, and the street, exactly how annoying it was to have a mum as religious as Maggie.

'She makes me pray before every meal, Queenie,' she moaned. 'Even snacks! Have you ever had a packet of crisps smacked out of your hand because you didn't thank Jesus for them first?'

That topic lasted all the way back to my grandparents' house. We walked through the door and I saw three extra sets of shoes in the hallway. I could hear voices coming from the front-front room. I stepped out of my trainers.

'Hello!' Darcy said, walking out of the room holding a bright pink helium balloon with BIRTHDAY WISHES emblazoned on both sides in blue bubble writing.

'Happy Birthday, Queenie!' Maggie jumped out after Darcy, holding a small gift bag.

I looked for the owner of the third pair of shoes, and saw my mum trail out nervously, trembling arms holding a birthday cake studded with candles, only half of them lit. My stomach tightened and I had to force myself to get back into my grandparents' old attic, my safe place. What I *actually* wanted was to climb into my grandparents' current attic to escape all of this attention.

Maggie handed the bag to me and swept me up in a hug.

'Maggie!' I protested, easing away from her.

'Hi, Mum,' I said quietly to my mother, who was still standing behind her sister, the weight of the cake testing her strength.

'Oh, come on, birthday girl! Cheer up!' Maggie said, rolling her eyes. 'Diana, was she this miserable when you were out?'

'Mum, you know she doesn't like hugs. It's all right not to want people to touch you, you know.' Diana walked over to Darcy. 'You must be Darcy, yeah? I'm Diana, Queenie's cousin. Nice to meet you properly.'

My grandmother stepped out of the front-front room.

'Can we all go inside one room and stop congesting the hallway *please*?' she barked, herding everyone except for Darcy in. She looked at me knowingly. 'You have some time to say hello to your fren,' she said, walking into the room and closing the door behind her.

'What happened to the candles, Mum?' I heard Diana moan. 'I tried to plan all of this properly.'

Darcy and I stood for a moment in the hallway, looking at each other. She'd put on weight, and her blue eyes stood out against her unusually tanned skin.

'Been on holiday?' I asked, suddenly unreasonably feeling very awkward about standing with her when I was such a shit version of the me I used to be.

'Yeah, Simon and I went to France a couple of weeks ago. It was a nightmare. He didn't want to leave the villa. Said that we needed to spend the whole holiday working on "us".'

She stepped towards me and handed the balloon over. 'Happy Birthday, friend.'

I put Maggie's mysterious gift bag down, took the balloon and patted her on the shoulder.

'Thank you. This is nice. Why are you here? How did you know the address?'

'Your cousin is very wily . . .' Darcy smiled. 'We've been in contact for a while now. She tweeted me a few weeks ago. We've been "DM-ing".' Darcy raised her eyebrows, smug about using lingo she wasn't used to. 'And I was going to invite Kyazike but thought that might be too much for you right now.'

'Yeah, you might be right,' I said, realising how much I really, really missed Kyazike. 'I'll be back to my usual text self soon, sorry for being so rubbish.'

'You don't need to apologise,' Darcy said softly. 'I guessed you needed to switch off from it all. I feel horrid, though. I should have handled it properly, helped you more.'

'You didn't need to handle anything!' I protested, horrified that she thought she had any responsibility where my mental health was concerned. 'It wasn't for you to sort. I put a lot on you. Wasn't fair of me. I'm sorry.'

I was getting good at this apologising business.

'I bet you get more work done without me, though.'

'So much more, you wouldn't believe it. But it's not as fun.'

'I wasn't much fun those last few months. It must have been like watching someone on self-destruct.' I laughed awkwardly. But felt less awkward.

'I'm not your friend because you entertain me,' Darcy said.

I moved towards her and hugged her tightly, surprising her and myself.

'I've missed this,' she said into my shoulder, her voice muffled by my hair. For the first time in ages, I felt like me.

'Thank you for being my friend,' I said. 'Even though I didn't make it easy.'

I pulled away after a while, and pointed up at the balloon. 'So. Where'd you get this classy gift from?'

Darcy didn't reply, and when I looked at her for some sort of response, I saw that her face was wet with tears.

'What's wrong?' I asked.

'What's happening?' my grandmother asked, throwing the door to the front-front room open. She looked at Darcy in horror.

'I just – I've just missed her!' Darcy sobbed.

'Oh, there there, dear!' my grandmother said, pulling Darcy into her bosom and patting her on the back gently.

I wish she'd consistently extend the same comfort to me when I was upset.

'Come on, let's all go in here,' I said, and we walked into the front-front room, my balloon blithering along the doorframe as I pulled it in behind me.

'Okay, please can we do the candles *now*? I had to blow them out once already,' Diana snapped, pulling a lighter out of her pocket and lighting the candles.

'And why do you have that?' Maggie asked, cocking her head, her wig going left as her head went right.

'It's, er, Kadija's, she left it in my bag, Haaaaaappy Birthdaaaaay . . .' Diana began to sing, nervous eyes on her mum, who stared back at her, neither of them dropping a note.

I looked down at the cake and blew the candles out.

'Did you make a wish?' my mum said quietly, her voice cracking halfway through the question.

'No. No point,' I said, continuing to look at the cake. 'I haven't believed in wishes since I was a child.'

My grandmother bustled into the kitchen for her best china plates ('it's because we have a white visitor,' Maggie had sighed) and Diana started to cut the cake up into huge slices.

'Shall we say grace?' Maggie asked, gesturing to the cake. Diana looked at me.

'Oh, aren't you going to open your present?' Maggie asked, pointing at the gift bag. I picked it up and pulled a little wrapped present out.

'It's nothing big, just a little lavender oil that I bought from Holland and Barrett. I thought you could drop some around your room, help you to relax,' she said, smiling.

'Thanks,' I said, putting the wrapped object back in the bag.

'Should we maybe go for a walk, or sit in the garden or something?' I asked Darcy, tying the balloon's ribbon to my wrist.

'I haven't had a chance to talk to you,' my mum interjected quietly. 'Or to meet your friend properly.'

She looked at Darcy and smiled, then looked back at the floor.

'I'm Darcy! Queenie and I have worked together for three years now, I think? She does the listings, I'm picture editor.'

'Oh, that's lovely. And what does a picture editor do?'

'Basically, when we're running an article in the magazine or online, I have to find the right picture, make sure we're allowed to use it, that sort of thing.'

'That sounds very hard! I couldn't do that!' My mum cooed.

'Sure you could, Mum,' I said, trying out my new-found forgiveness. 'You could do anything.'

'That's not true, Queenie,' my mum said, looking down at her hands and smiling. 'I'm not like you.'

'I've got a question for you, Sylvie.' Darcy jumped up. 'Why did you name Queenie, Queenie?'

'That's an easy question, Darcy.' My mum looked up at us and settled back into the armchair. She was so small that it almost swallowed her whole. 'When I was growing up, I always used to wish I could be a princess. It sounds silly, but because Maggie was in the room next to my mum and dad, so they could keep an eye on her, my bedroom was almost at the very top of the house, underneath the attic. It was a huge, beautiful Victorian house that my dad bought when he first came over.'

'The haunted attic room,' I told Darcy.

'The only thing it was haunted by was my dad, moaning at me about the water rates.' My mum laughed. 'We were the first black people on our street, you know? My dad literally worked night and day to afford it. Anyway, I'm drifting away from what I was saying, sorry!'

My mum looked back down at her hands. 'I used to stare out of the window and pretend that someone was going to come and rescue me.' She paused and looked up again, her eyes bright. 'I grew out of that, the looking out of the window thing, when I was a teenager, but I was still obsessed with princesses. In all of the stories I used to read, they were so beautiful and perfect, and so delicate, and, well, when I met Queenie's dad, he was my prince.'

'Mum,' I cut in, 'he was married.'

'Well I didn't know that, at the time. And, well, to me, he'd come to rescue me. He was so handsome, this man with *beautiful* dark skin. I thought he was so cool! He was in the music scene, he had a house full of records, he used to take me to all these concerts! And he had this gold tooth that flashed whenever he'd smile. He was so charming.'

'FYI Darcy, he really isn't charming.'

They both ignored my remark, lost in the story.

'. . . and when I was pregnant I thought, this is it, this is it, she's here. The princess I'd been dreaming about was here. That was going to be her name, I'd decided. I didn't mind that it might have been tacky.'

'I would have minded,' I said.

'At least you weren't called Diana!' my cousin shouted from the hallway as she walked past the front-front room.

'Ah, yes. Queenie's grandmother gave Diana her name. She was obsessed with the royal family.' My mum laughed gently. 'Still is. Anyway, when *my* little girl was born, I put my finger in her tiny hand and she opened her eyes and squeezed it so tightly. And I looked at her, and I realised that she was more powerful than any delicate princess I'd read about. I'd just given birth to a queen. A girl who would grow up to be strong and brave. So I called her Queenie.'

How could I have been so selfish, how couldn't I have seen? This tiny, meek woman being swallowed by an armchair was the same woman who started to raise me, the woman who'd been so obsessed with me that we wore matching outfits until I was eight, who always told me that I was strong enough to be a queen. She'd been so mentally and physically battered by men that she couldn't find her voice anymore. But she was still my mum.

I looked over at Darcy, whose eyes were wet with tears.

'Oh, come on, no more crying,' I said, pulling her up, knowing that if she started crying I'd be next.

I led her through the kitchen, where Maggie was quizzing '*Diana*' about the lighter, and out into the garden.

We sat on the grass for about three seconds before my grandmother practically sprinted out with a blanket, shrieking about Darcy's white skirt getting dirty.

'How are you doing, though?' Darcy asked, letting her bare legs stray from the blanket so that she could scrunch blades of grass between her toes.

'It's up and down. That's the only way I can put it.' I shrugged. 'No day is ever all good, or all bad. I don't feel quite myself, yet. I know I'm not doing a very good job of explaining myself. Sorry.'

'You don't need to explain anything to me. We can talk about something else if you like,' Darcy said brightly. 'Have you read anything good lately?'

'I think I need to explain it to myself, if anything,' I said. 'You know how someone might be like, how are you, on a scale of one to ten, one being the worst, and ten being absolutely elated? Well at the moment I'm operating on a "How are you out of five?" flex. I feel like I'm living a half-life at the moment.'

I fiddled with the knot of the balloon ribbon on my wrist as I spoke. 'I live here, sleeping in a room full of crucifixes and Bibles. I don't see anyone but my family because seeing my friends reminds me that I'm not how I used to be. I haven't had sex for ages – '

'Which is a good thing, I think, Queenie.'

'The counselling is tiresome. I always have to drag myself on my face to the bus stop afterwards. Then sit for ages staring at nothing in particular out of the window. I almost always miss my stop, just because my brain can't engage with what's going on until the next day.'

'Do you feel better every week, though? Like you're crying all of the sadness out? It must be cathartic.'

'What's the point in crying?' I asked.

'Do you know, that might be the most psychopathic thing I've ever heard anyone say.'

'Strong black women don't cry,' I said to myself.

The balloon ribbon slipped from my wrist and a gust of wind took it up out of my reach.

Diana walked out into the garden with a piece of sponge cake on a paper plate in each hand. The best china was obviously not allowed outside.

'That's a waste of your friend's money,' she said, watching the balloon drift away.

She passed us one plate each and stood with a hand on her hip, lifting the other to shield her eyes from the sun. 'Grandad has told me to make myself useful and water the plants. You can never just come here and relax, can you,' she huffed, walking over to the outside tap.

She turned it on and went to look for the watering can.

'*Don't* waste watah!' Grandad croaked from the conservatory.

Diana looked at us and closed her eyes in frustration.

'I should go,' Darcy said, standing up. 'I've got a big day at work tomorrow.' She smoothed her skirt down.

'Oh yeah? What's happening?' I asked, holding my hands out so that she could lift me up. 'Anything to do with my Ted investigation? Are you being called as a character witness? Tell them I'm a virgin.'

We both laughed. It felt unfamiliar to laugh. The way you might feel starting a car when you haven't driven in years and had also forgotten that cars even existed.

'Nothing's been said about that, if that helps,' Darcy said, putting on her shoes by the front door. 'It was nice to see you. And to meet your mum, finally.'

I opened the door and hugged her goodbye.

'You're better than you think,' she said, then turned to walk down the path.

I went back into the kitchen and found my grandmother peering into the oven, Diana's confiscated lighter in hand.

'What are you doing?' I asked.

'It won't light. I'm not paying to fix it,' she said, getting on her knees and moving her head further in.

'Your mother had to go when you were in the garden. She left a card for you.' My grandmother gestured to the table, head still hidden.

I looked to the table and saw a pink envelope with my name written on it in writing practically the same as mine.

I poured myself a glass of water and took the card upstairs. I opened it. The card had the words, 'To my darling daughter on her birthday' on the front in pink writing. A bright yellow 99p sticker she'd forgotten to remove sat in the corner.

To my dear daughter Queenie Veronica Jenkins, Happy 26th Birthday! I am proud of you every day. Even on the days that you think are bad. I am always here for you. Continue to be stronger than I could have been for you.

Love, your mum Sylvie. XX

P.s. I hear you are in therapy. That is a good thing.

I climbed into bed and reread my mum's card. I could hear tinny music playing from Diana's phone as she moved around the garden watering the plants.

Queenie:
Thanks for my card mum. It was nice to see you today. X

I pressed send on my phone and looked out of the window. I watched the balloon from Darcy float further away into the distance.

Chapter Twenty-Five

'Now, I think we need to talk about your phone call.'

I blinked at Janet, pretending not to know what she was talking about.

She looked at me and sighed. Isn't that the exact reaction that therapists weren't meant to have?

'From the pool,' she reminded me.

'Yeah, what about it?' I asked, in a tone that I knew I was too old to have taken.

'Your upbringing was not one you should have had, Queenie,' Janet said. 'You witnessed some traumatic things, you should have had love and care, and I'm sorry that you didn't.'

'It's all right, it's not your fault,' I snapped. 'These things happen. It happens a lot in my culture. Us black girls, we're always meant to know our place.'

'And do you think that you've trapped yourself in this message to the present day? Do you think this is how you see yourself? As having to stay mute, to know your place? It certainly sounds this way,' Janet said sympathetically. 'Perhaps that's why, sexually, you go along with these acts, so as not to rock the boat, and – '

' – how could I not be trapped in it?' I interrupted. I was on one today, apparently.

'Well, Queenie, I think that you're taking on a burden that isn't yours. You can't carry the pain of a whole race.'

'It's not a burden I'm taking on, it's one that's just here.' I could feel anger building in my chest. 'I can't pick it up and drop it!'

'Is that how you see it?' Janet asked as calmly as she could in an attempt to counter my distress.

'That's how it is.' I started to get louder. 'I can't wake up and not be a black woman, Janet. I can't walk into a room and not be a black woman, *Janet*. On the bus, on the tube, at work, in the canteen. Loud, brash, sassy, angry, mouthy, confrontational, bitchy.'

I listed off all of my usual descriptors on my fingers.

'There are ones people think are nice, though: well spoken, surprisingly intelligent, exotic. My favourite is 'sexy', I think. I guess I should be grateful for any attention at all.'

My voice was getting hoarse.

'You know, when we go out, my friends get chatted up by guys who say, "I'd love to take you for dinner", and in the same *breath* they come over to *me*, put their hands on my bum and tell me they want to take me back to theirs and fuck me over the arm of the sofa. This past year has shown me that I can't have a boyfriend who loves me, who can stop and think about what I might be going through.'

I dug my nails into the arms of the chair. 'I can't have any love in my life that isn't completely fucked by my fear that I'll be rejected just for being born *me*. Do you know how that feels, Janet?'

'No, Queenie, I don't.'

'Exactly. With respect, Janet, you aren't best placed to tell me how to deal with this "burden".'

'Okay, try to calm down, Queenie. Remember your breathing.' Janet poured me a glass of water.

'Why should I calm down? This is what you wanted, for me to stop holding things in! My best friend, Cassandra? The one who moved away with a man that fucked me for months but actually cared about someone else? You remember? I used to do this thing with him – I knew it was pathetic, but I couldn't stop it. Even though I hate any *meaningful* closeness, when he stayed over, I used to try and tuck myself into his back while he slept. I just wanted some comfort, I wanted someone to like me after they'd had sex with me. Isn't that pathetic? Do you know what he used to do? Push me off him, every time. But that's me. I'm an option for a man to fuck, but not an option to love.'

My hands were shaking.

'And if you're going to fuck me, then at least it's going to be in my control,' I shouted. I couldn't stop myself. 'And do you know why? It's because I'm so damaged, Janet. Years of being told I was nothing, years of being ignored! I'll take any attention, even if it is being fucked!'

The room started to warp. I couldn't breathe. I stood up and started flapping my hands as if to cool myself down or push the air into my mouth, I wasn't sure which. I looked at Janet and opened and closed my mouth.

Even if I knew what I wanted to say, it wasn't coming out. She was saying something. I couldn't hear what. I tried to do my breathing, tried to focus on her face, to count to ten, to think of that safe space, it was all so overwhelming and –

I felt my surroundings before I opened my eyes and saw them. I was on a bed, I knew that much. I'd been in a lot of beds that weren't mine in the past year, so I wasn't as frightened as I might have otherwise been.

I was lying on my side, and quite possibly in the recovery position, as my limbs weren't in a position that they might have organically and comfortably fallen in to.

My head was throbbing. I opened my eyes and squinted as the low light from a lamp next to the bed hit them.

'Hello?' I whispered, looking around the room. The room was small, lilac, with only the single bed that I occupied in one corner and the bedside table and lamp next to it. No posters, no pictures, no clue that the room belonged to any person. I lowered my legs off the bed slowly and put my feet on the floor.

I tried to stand up, but fell back down onto the bed.

'Queenie?'

My eyes followed the voice that had called my name and I saw Janet rush over, mug in hand.

'How are you feeling? Here, drink this. Let it cool for a couple of minutes.'

She went to hand me the mug, then placed it on the bedside table. 'Don't want you to burn your hands on top of everything else.'

Janet perched at the end of the bed.

'What happened?' I asked. I was shaking.

'Let me give you a blanket.'

Janet opened a drawer and pulled out a knitted patchwork blanket from it. She covered me and sat back down.

'I'm not cold, just shaking,' I said.

'That will be the adrenaline leaving your system. Just let it pass. Nothing bad is happening to you,' she said, taking a sip of her tea. 'You fainted, Queenie.'

'That happened before, when I lived in Brixton,' I told Janet. 'It was horrible, that floor was so dirty. But why is it happening *now* – shouldn't I be better? What's wrong with me? Is something seriously wrong? Am I getting worse?' I asked, sitting up straight for Janet's question time.

'No. It doesn't mean that at all,' Janet reassured me. 'The road to recovery is not linear. It's not straight. It's a bumpy path, with lots of twists and turns. But you're on the right track.'

'Lots of therapy buzzwords there, Janet,' I said, reaching for the cup of tea and propping myself up on one elbow to take a sip. 'Jesus, this is sweet!'

'How much sugar have you had today?' Janet asked.

'I don't think any. I've only had toast. I didn't have much of an appetite,' I said, lying back down.

'Well there you go. Finish it. Your grandmother is on her way.'

'Excuse me? My grandmother is leaving south London? To come here?' I launched myself up and put the mug down. 'She hasn't left south London since she came here in the fifties, and she has family in north. Oh, god.'

'She's down as your next of kin,' Janet said. 'There is nothing to worry about. You must try to be aware when you're catastrophising, Queenie.'

'I'm going to be in so much trouble,' I groaned.

'Let's lay it out as it is,' Janet said, looking me dead in the eye. 'Queenie, you are an adult woman. And you have made an adult choice to come to therapy. Your family have accepted that, it seems. There is no trouble to get in. Today you have had a funny turn, and your grandmother is coming to collect you. I spoke to a cab driver and gave them the full address, so she won't have to negotiate public transport. You will get the cab back, and then I suggest that you rest and think little more of it. Okay?'

Janet stood up and went to leave the room.

'Okay,' I said. 'Dammit, Janet.'

Janet turned and looked at me.

'My daughter used to say that to me. Is that in reference to *The Rocky Horror Picture Show*?'

'Yeah! I didn't know you had a daughter. I'm sorry, was this her room? Did she . . . pass away?' I said, horrified.

'Queenie. You must stop thinking the worst. She's very much alive. She works in Hong Kong. She flew out a year ago, after her twenty-fifth birthday. Very accomplished, my daughter. Now. Have your tea and rest until your grandmother gets here.'

I must have fallen asleep, because I woke up to my grand-mother's bony fingers shaking me by the shoulder.

'Come on, the cab is outside, the meter ah run.'

We rode home in the back of the cab, me in forced silence as my grandmother listed all of the reasons why she was never leaving south London again. Points three to seven were all variations of how she didn't trust the buildings. Points eight to fifteen were all about smells. Though I felt exhausted, probably from the fainting, I also felt as though some weight had been lifted from my shoulders. I didn't feel brighter. Just lighter.

Chapter Twenty-Six

'Hello, Mum,' I heard my mother say breathlessly as she walked in through the front door. 'Where's Queenie?'

I rolled my eyes.

'In the front-front room. If you two *haffi* to sit in there, don't stay long. This isn't a special occasion,' my grandmother said, walking off into the kitchen.

'How are you?' my mum said, perching on the edge of the armchair opposite.

'I'm all right,' I replied. 'You're still not eating.'

'God, you're as bad as Mum. Anyway, thanks for saying you'll have a chat,' she said. 'I know you're probably busy.'

I watched her clench and unclench her fists nervously, her brittle fingers trembling.

'I'm not that busy, I'm almost always here,' I told her. 'I'm usually cleaning or taking things to and from the launderette, but I'm not busy.'

'Mum's got you cleaning to pay your keep here?' my mum asked. 'I should have known. It's why we've all got cleanliness OCD.'

I laughed. I hadn't heard her make a joke in years. Not that what she said wasn't true.

My mum continued quietly. 'It's about the court case. You remember, the one against Roy?'

I nodded slowly, hoping she wasn't going to ask me to testify.

'I've had a bit of good news. After almost three years, we won!' she said, wrapping her arms around her small frame. 'I didn't think it would ever end! And I can't get the house back, or most of the money because he's spent the majority of it. But I've been given what was left.'

'Well, that's good!' I said, hiding my disappointment that I didn't feel instant relief. 'And him?'

'He's not going to prison or anything like that,' my mum explained. 'I wasn't really listening, if I'm honest, just happy that it was all over and done with. Anyway, I wanted to give you this.' She rummaged in her handbag, eventually pulling out a cheque that was folded in half.

She stood up and handed it to me. 'It's a fair bit of what I got. Not a lot, but I thought you could use it as a deposit to rent somewhere for yourself, and pay a few months' rent. That way you won't have to keep paying your way here in manual labour.'

My mum went to pat me on the shoulder but pulled her hand away and whispered another apology.

She smiled at the floor and walked noiselessly out of the room into the kitchen, where I heard my grandmother immediately berate her for her weight loss.

I unfolded the cheque. I'd never seen so much money in my life, and my mum had handed it over like it was nothing.

'You don't need to do this,' I said, walking into the kitchen and putting the cheque on the table. '*You* actually need the money. You're the one living in a hovel.'

'The hostel is not a hovel, Queenie. It's actually quite nice, you should come and see it. I've got friends there, and I feel safe. It was my little port in the storm.' She put her fork down and sat on her hands.

'Why don't you eat your dinner, Mum?' I said, sitting opposite her.

I watched my grandmother unload the washing machine and slink into the garden to shake each item three hundred times before she hung it out.

'Sorry that I never ask how you are,' I said, angry with myself for not being a better daughter. 'I think children forget that their parents are people too.'

'I'll be okay. Once I get this eating sorted,' she said, moving chicken around the plate. 'It's horrible, I get this lump in my throat whenever I put anything to my lips. Then I have to concentrate on forcing it down. It's just not worth it. And these last few months, having to see Roy throughout this whole thing, it's been so drawn out. Well, I haven't bothered to even try eating. I've been living on tea.'

'Maybe you can try what I do,' I started. 'When it's really bad, I imagine that there's a bird in my stomach, and that the butterflies and the churning is the bird flapping, asking for food. And when I eat, and feed the bird, the flapping will stop.'

'I don't like birds, Queenie,' my mum said fearfully. 'Especially pigeons, they're horrible.'

'I don't like birds either, but you know what I mean, Mum.'

She put a forkful of food into her mouth and chewed slowly.

'Feed the bird,' I encouraged her.

She swallowed, her face contorting with discomfort. I poured her a glass of water.

'Thank you. You're so caring, you know. I don't know where you got that from.' She took a sip of water and ate another forkful.

'You're caring, Mum,' I said. 'I must get it from you.'

She smiled and loaded more food onto her fork than before.

'Do you think you'll go back to work?' she asked.

I shrugged in response, really not wanting to go into it.

We sat quietly together while she ate. She put down her fork and looked at me.

'Do you know what?' my mum said. 'I think you've changed history in this family. You're the first person to go to counselling and not get disowned by Mum and Dad. That's bigger than being the first Jenkins to go to university.'

'But I also might be the first person in the family to be fired.'

'Queenie, we've all been fired from every job we've ever had. Have you ever spoken to your grandmother about her career history? And you should *definitely* talk to Maggie about the time she got fired from Blockbuster for recording over the videos. Ask her what she did to the manager to get revenge,' my mum said, picking up her fork again and taking another bite of dinner. 'What happened at work?'

'It's a long story that I'm not going to go into,' I said, 'but what I will tell you is that I had a great job and I'm pretty sure I've thrown it, and my whole life, away.'

'No such thing,' my mum said. 'You've just turned twenty-six, your life hasn't even begun. I had *you* just after I turned twenty-six. Best year of my life.'

She chewed another forkful of food, smiling.

*

'It's nearly my last session, Grandad. Only one left.' I couldn't think what else I could say to break the silence in the dining room, so took a chance on engaging in some therapy chat.

'That's good,' he said sternly. 'And wha' yuh going to learn today?'

'Well,' I began, bewildered that he'd asked me a question about it, 'I'm not sure. One of the most helpful techniques I had to learn was safe spaces, so maybe we'll revist tha –'

'Wha' dat?'

'A safe space is sort of like a mental place you go to cope with things,' I explained. 'It's all in the mind.'

'Mi' shed used to be mi' safe space until you put all of yuh tings in deh,' he said, getting up from the table.

'Queenie, your phone is going off!' my grandmother shouted from the kitchen. I followed the sound of my phone and by the time I located it, it had rung off. I had a voicemail, annoyingly.

'Queenie, hi, it's Gina. I hope things are better. Right, I'll make this quick because I know that voicemails are awful and that everybody hates them. Take some time to think about this, but not too much time, obviously. The investigation fell apart when one of the security guards said that he'd seen Ted leading you into the disabled loos – I don't want or need to know what you did in there, but ultimately his actions don't seem like those of a person being coerced, so everyone thinks it's best that we drop it. Nobody wants a scandal, let alone a newspaper. You'll have to sign a weekly timesheet for the first month or whatever because you'll be back on a trial basis but don't be too scared of that, it's just protocol. Give me a call by the end of the week. In fact, can you just give me a call in the next hour so that we can just wrap this all up and move on, thanks.'

'Who was that? You look like you've just seen a *duppy*,' my grandmother said.

'Nobody,' I croaked, sitting down in the nearest chair.

'Lie you ah' tell.'

'No, it's fine,' I said, standing up on shaking legs. 'I'm going to therapy now.'

'Are you sure you're in a state to cross London?' my grand-mother asked as I grabbed my bag and walked out of the front door. 'I'm not coming to get you again. I've just put the pot on.'

*

'I know that you want to do some final techniques today, but something very shocking has come up,' I said to Janet as soon as she opened the front door an inch. 'My boss has asked me to go back to work.'

'Well, that's wonderful news!' Janet smiled.

'Is it? Is it, *Janet*?' I asked, my head swimming.

'Yes, Queenie. This day was always going to come, and I think we can agree that it's going to be less demanding going back into a job you already know than having to search for a new one. Sit down, please.'

I threw myself into the chair opposite Janet.

'But I am not *ready*, Janet,' I said, gripping the arms of the chair.

'Says who?'

'Do you, a trained professional, think that I'm ready?'

'I don't see why not. We'll have to adjust this session to work on some coping methods, but all in all, I think that this can only be a good thing. It's a real positive. And even though our run is over, I'll always be here. You aren't as alone you think.'

Chapter Twenty-Seven

If I could remember how I felt on the first day of secondary school, I imagine it was exactly like this. My rucksack is packed, my shoes have been shined (metaphorically, but I think that my grandmother might have actually polished them in the night), and I ironed a dress for the first time in ten years, hung it up for tomorrow and went and found my grandmother giving it a going-over ten minutes later.

Darcy insisted she'd meet me in the square outside the office to quite literally ease me back in, which was one less thing to worry about. If I couldn't walk, I could be carried.

I had a bath at 8 p.m., said goodnight to my grandparents and got into bed. I was feeling very wholesome. I set my alarm for 7.30 a.m. and settled into bed. Sleep came easily. Success. Maybe I was a changed person.

I woke up and checked my phone. 2 a.m. I was wide awake. Why had I never felt this alert when it was time to go to work?

'Come on, come on,' I sighed, turning over in bed.

'Queenie? What's wrong?' my grandmother shouted from her bedroom.

'Nothing!' I whispered. 'Just talking to myself.'

'Guh ah yuh bed. Yah 'av work ina di' marnin'.'

At 4 a.m. I was still awake. At 5 a.m. I was even more awake. At 6 a.m. dawn started to break and the birds in the garden began to sing. There was no point in trying to go back to sleep.

At 7 a.m., I heard my grandmother stirring. She shuffled into my room.

'Are you sleeping?' she asked, full volume.

'Even if I had been, that would have woken me up. Morning,' I said, stretching to full length and simultaneously burying my head in the pillows.

'I'm putting the hot water on. Come down for your porridge and wait for it to warm,' my grandmother said as she trotted down the stairs gently, her dressing gown trailing behind her.

'I'm not hungry,' I whispered after her so as not to wake my grandad.

'You think she's letting you leave here without breakfast?' he yelled from their bedroom.

When it was time to go, I stood by the front door looking in the mirror. I looked like a version of me that was only slightly familiar to myself. Thinner. Less colour in my face. The bags under my eyes were maybe here to stay.

'You look nice. Smart.' My grandmother walked out of the kitchen and fixed the lapel of my coat that had tucked itself in. 'Like my mother when she first came over to visit me. She was a proud woman. Go, go mek me proud.'

'That's a lot of pressure. I'm only going back to work,' I said. 'Not stepping off the *Windrush*, Grandma.'

My grandmother turned me by the shoulders and pushed me out of the door gently.

'Don't overthink things. What's the word the therapy woman say? Catastrophise. Nah badda catastrophise.'

The journey was unbearable. But, I remembered, mainly unbearable because it's commuting, and everyone finds public transport oppressive and horrific. It wasn't just because I was weak.

At times of acute anxiety, I did some deep breathing and tried to count all of the blue things in my eyeline. When that didn't work, all of the green things. By the time I'd gone through all of the colours of the rainbow, I was off the train and walking towards *The Daily Read* office.

I felt my stomach drop to my knees and I stopped in my tracks. I held onto a nearby wall.

'Morning! Welcome back!' Darcy beamed, launching herself onto me.

'Hello!' My voice gave me away.

'Right,' she said, very seriously. Solutions-driven Darcy was back in her element. 'I have a list of reasons why you're going to be okay. One: I am here for you, always. Even when I am in the toilet. Two: we have all of your ways of coping written down. The deep breathing, the safe space, the colour-counting. So even if you forget them, I can go into the quiet room and remind you. Three: nothing can harm you here. Four: you've made it this far, and once you make it to lunchtime, it's basically the end of the day, and we can go and get a treat. Okay?'

I nodded and let Darcy take my hand. We got just outside the building and she let go.

'You can do this.'

We stepped into the building and I closed my eyes as I took in its familiar smell.

'You okay?' Darcy asked, grabbing me by the shoulders.

'I'm fine. Just smelling,' I said as we walked across the foyer, our steps echoing around the space.

'Phew,' Darcy said, pushing the button to call the elevator.

My eyes darted around as others queued for the lift. Now was not the best time for me to see Ted.

My heart climbed my chest with every level we ascended, and by the time we got up to our floor it was about to flop out of my mouth. We stepped out of the elevator and I stood, waiting for all eyes to be on me. Instead, though, everyone was just . . . getting on with their work.

'Wait until I cross the floor,' I thought. 'That's when they'll all stop and stare.'

I made my way over to my desk, Darcy behind me guiding me gently. We attracted no interest at all. I lowered myself onto my chair slowly and turned my computer on.

'You're okay,' Darcy smiled. 'I think Gina is going to come over and say hello, and then we can probably sneak to the kitchen for tea.'

Darcy left me and I got back into the rhythm of things. The morning was mainly fine. Only minor wobbles when I forgot how to do the simplest things that I used to be able to do with my eyes rolled to the back of my head. I flirted with the idea of going back home, but very quickly realised that the alternative to work was going back to my grandmother and trying to explain that I couldn't do it.

After Gina had come to say a sheepish hello, and Darcy and I had made a very swift tea, I sat back down as an email popped into my inbox.

On Monday, 7 November, Lief, Jean <Jean.Lief@dailyread. co.uk> wrote at 11:55:

Dear Queenie,

It's good to see you back. I knew that scumbag was lying. You can never trust a man wearing that much tweed. Just keep your head down.

With warmest wishes,

Jean

P.S. It's not my place to say this, but you don't look as good having lost that weight. You used to look so cheerful.

On Monday, 7 November, Jenkins, Queenie <Queenie. Jenkins@dailyread.co.uk> wrote at 12:02:

Dear Jean,

Thanks for your email. You know, apart from Darcy, you're the only person to welcome me back, even though I annoy you so much by hovering by yours and Darcy's desks saying things not suitable for the office. I promise there'll be none of that this time around.

Queenie X

P.S. I don't much like myself having lost all this weight, either. I don't think it suits me, really

On Monday, 7 November, Lief, Jean <Jean.Lief@dailyread. co.uk> wrote at 12:07:

Oh, don't worry about the chatter, Queenie. I'm 72 and I've been working at the newspapers for longer than I can remember. Nothing can shock me. I've heard all there is to hear.

Jean

On Monday, 7 November, Jenkins, Queenie <Queenie. Jenkins@dailyread.co.uk> wrote at 12:10:

Darcy, does everyone know?

On Monday, 7 November, Betts, Darcy <Darcy.Betts@ dailyread.co.uk> wrote at 12:10:

Yes. But nobody is *judging* you. XXXX

Eating food at lunchtime wasn't the ordeal I'd predicted, and by the time it got to five and Gina had signed my timesheet, even though I felt exhausted, also like I could maybe be all right again.

At five thirty I packed up my bag and walked over to Darcy, who was waiting by the lift as agreed. We went down and when we left the building, a familiar face was waiting outside.

'Kyazike! What are you doing here?'

I rushed over to my friend and hugged her, happy to see her, also relieved to be out of work.

'What do you meeeaaan, fam? I'm here to congratulate you. Back to the job and that. Working girl. You look *tiny* fam!'

She smiled, holding me at arm's length. 'I need to feed you up, we're not meant to be skin and bone.'

'Okay, so Kyazike, as discussed, Queenie isn't drinking, so we're going to go to a café for a little cake and a hot drink,' Darcy said cautiously.

'That's cool. As long as the cakes aren't them little ones that you pick up with two fingers and inhale. I want value for my money.'

Kyazike put her arm through mine as we all walked. 'Did you see that dickhead today?' she asked.

'Which one? There are lots of dickheads in my building. You need to be more specific.'

'That married one. The *biggest* one,' Kyazike sneered. 'The one you need to not let even look at you.'

'No,' I said, quietly, hoping that what I was saying wasn't a lie. 'I won't.'

And for the next two hours, I remembered what it was like to be normal again. *Then* remembered Janet saying that there was no such thing as normal, and was finally grateful that she hadn't let me walk away after one session.

As the week went on, I grew more exhausted. I was coping, but I had never been so tired in my *life*. Halfway through the week I emailed Janet to let her know that I was probably on the edge of a relapse, but she replied saying, 'The more tired you are, the more likely your defences are to be down. Doesn't mean relapse, means you're adjusting to working again. Rest at the weekend.'

I was determined to fill in my timesheet for the week, so battled through the intrusive thoughts that popped into my head every other second. By Friday I was hanging on by a thread. My stomach's movements were incredibly dramatic and my head refused to stop buzzing. I had to work slower than I did when I first started, and when Gina sent me an email asking me to go into her office at four, by 3 p.m. the contents of my desk were in my rucksack.

'I understand,' I said, walking into the office.

'You understand what?' Gina said, putting a pair of glasses on.

'Didn't know you wore glasses.' I sat down in the chair opposite her.

'They're new. Contacts getting a bit too fiddly for me. Nice, though, aren't they?' She looked up at me and smiled.

'Yeah, they're nice,' I said. 'Where are they – '

' – we're not here to talk eyewear,' Gina said. 'Well done.'

'Pardon?'

'For this week, Queenie,' Gina explained. 'It must have been hard, but you did it. And you did it well.'

'I was slow, though.'

'Well, it's not a race. You've only just got back, and you'll get quicker. You were at your desk, doing the work, and that's what I want from you.' Gina turned back to her computer.

'Okay?' I said, suspicious. 'Thanks, Gina.'

'Word of warning,' Gina said, standing up. 'Ted is back from holiday on Monday. Avoid.'

'You don't need to tell me twice.'

'I've signed your timesheet off for the week and sent it to HR. You can go home now. You look absolutely shattered. See you on Monday.'

*

Two full weeks of work passed. Two weeks of completed timesheets, two weeks of to-the-brink-of-death exhaustion, two weeks of deep breathing in the toilet and two weeks of avoiding Ted.

The less I thought of him the better, but still, I was doing a lot of ducking and diving around the office in an attempt not to bump into him. I could cross that bridge when I came to it, even though I was doing everything in my power to ensure that I was taking every alternative route that I could in order to avoid bridges.

It was a Friday night and I was bored of my grandmother asking when I was going to get a pay rise as we watched the news.

In an attempt to actively move myself away from married men, and from men who just want to have sex with my body as and when it suits them (admittedly the two are not mutually exclusive), this time when I go on OkCupid, I am going to talk to somebody who is normal and nice-looking, and who talks to me in a normal and nice way.

As I brushed my teeth, I thought about the men I would avoid even messaging, let alone meeting on OkCupid this time around:

1. The ones who mention my 'black curves' as though I'll be flattered by the suggestion that curves are in this case only acceptable because I'm non-white
2. The ones who completely bypass any of the varied film, TV and music I have listed on my profile. Not acknowledging that I might have interests beyond your dick is a real red flag
3. The ones who want to migrate to WhatsApp a little *too* soon after starting to chat. It's *obviously* because you want to send and receive x-rated pictures
4. The ones who I can *tell* are using pictures from at least three years ago. Unless you can send me a picture of you

344

holding a newspaper from the day we chat, I'm going to assume that the ones you've posted are from Fresher's Week

5. The ones with x's in their profile. Cutesy doesn't tend to equal somebody who is going to want to have a discussion about intersectional feminism
6. The couples that want someone for a threesome. Obviously. Though I'm not ruling that out for the future when I'm a bit more stable. Life should be about experiences, after all

I washed my face, put my headscarf on, the usual ritual, and got into bed. It was 7 p.m.

I reinstalled the app and logged in, lying on my back in the reclining butterfly pose (knees apart, feet together), a yoga move I'd seen on the internet that guaranteed opening some sort of chakras. I woke up an hour later, phone in hand and hips as stiff as boards. I turned the lamp off and crawled under the duvet. Three hours later I was still awake.

Courtney84:

Hello, how are you? My name is Courtney, nice to meet you. Having a good night?

NJ234:

You've got a really nice smile. Hope you're having a good evening.

Maybe God has been listening to me even though I haven't attempted prayer since Midnight Mass? Maybe she sees that

I am on the path to recovery and am ready for a nice person who'll treat me like I'm more than an orifice.

I replied to both, being very well behaved and not saying anything remotely sexy to either of them. Maybe I am a changed woman? It was hard to be so restrained, yes, but the smut can come later once they've proved that they're able to talk to me for a day without telling me that they're wanking over the pictures on my profile.

Two days later and many messages from NJ234 telling me that his 'cock's big enough to split a girl's cunt in two', I blocked him and arranged to go on an actual date with Courtney84 (aptly named as he is called Courtney and was born in 1984). I so desperately wanted to feel like a normal girl again, and it was worth it even though I had to do lots of seeding with my grandmother by telling her that I'd be working a bit late on a new project and that Darcy would be with me in case I had some sort of episode.

I was nervous about this date because we hadn't spoken about anything rude *at all*. I'm trying to move away from the belief that my only conversational currency with men is sexting, is why.

So far, Courtney84 is unlike anyone I've ever experienced before in that he's thirty-two, owns two houses, is bald and has a beard but, crucially, asks normal questions about normal things.

He seems polite, and quite possibly somebody that I could spend non-sexual time with. He's passed the Darcy test, who was at first apprehensive because he was bald, but when Leigh came to meet us for lunch and referred to him as a 'Balding Alpha', she laughed so much that she came round to the idea.

Come Thursday, I was toying with the idea of cancelling because surely an actual adult handsome man with two houses wouldn't want to spend any time with me, a weird flailing baby who has basically just had a nervous breakdown. I went to a quiet area of the canteen and called Kyazike for some help and support.

'Help me. What if he's one of those white guys who likes black girls who are properly put together, and not ones like me who are a bit "alternative"?'

'What?' Kyazike asked. 'What do you mean, fam?'

'You know, like what if he expects me to turn up wearing Louboutins and a bodycon dress and have, like, contour on my face? And fake eyelashes? And a lace front wig?'

'You don't need to go, you know,' Kyazike said. 'You're stressing about this when you could just go home after work.'

'I know! But I need to prove to myself that I can do this. That I can be a normal girl and go on a normal date, and maybe that normal date will help to cancel out all of the very, very bad dates.'

'There are ways of being normal that aren't dating,' Kyazike told me.

'Please can we get back on to the topic of me not being black enough, please?'

'Fine.' Kyazike refocused. 'So you started chatting on OkCupid, yeah?'

'Yes,' I confirmed.

'And on this app, you have pictures of yourself?'

'Yes. Five of them.'

'And in these pictures, are you standing on one leg showing off the red sole of your Louboutins and wearing a bodycon dress the way I do on Snapchat?' Kyazike continued with her line of questioning.

'No.'

'And in any of these pictures do you have contour on your face, or fake eyelashes?'

'No. And no.'

'Are you rocking a lace front wig?'

'I'm not, no.'

'So you see my point, yeah? Or do I have to keep on?'

'I do. You don't.'

'And *you* don't have to dress like the black girls you see on Insta to be bla – '

I looked up from my seat and saw Ted standing in front of me. As we locked eyes, guilt settled on his face. In direct response, my throat seized up and I dropped the phone on the floor. It clattered by my feet and he walked over, reaching down to pick it up.

I grabbed at it and looked at him, shaking my head. I put the phone back to my ear and walked away, my legs working very hard to carry me off in a straight line.

'. . . wear what makes you comfortable, innit. Just do *you*,' Kyazike said. 'Remember that time in the playground in Year Nine, when Tia asked me in front of everyone why I was friends with you when you were white on the inside and black on the outside like a coconut?'

'Why are you bringing that up, Kyazike?' I asked, letting myself into the first aid room and sitting on a pile of blankets in the corner.

'What did I say to Tia then?'

'You said that I could be any type of black girl that I wanted to be.'

By the time Friday came around, I was so nervous that all I could eat were two tiny fruits for breakfast and slowly sip at half a carton of soup at lunch.

Although Balding Alpha and I were meant to go to dinner, I panicked at 4 p.m. and asked if we could go for a drink instead. I still wasn't great at eating and a first date didn't seem like the setting to accommodate that.

Darcy had to escort me to Brixton after work and sit with me in the pub opposite the bar he'd suggested until it was time for the date.

'But why are you so nervous? Balding Alpha seems like a nice guy!' she said, sitting down at the table.

'Exactly that, Darcy,' I said. 'This one is nice. Plus it's been a long time since I went on a date! Don't forget that since Tom, despite me wanting them to be *nice* and *romantic*, all of my dates have been sex appointments. What if my chat is all rubbish, and so he hates me and just thinks I'm annoying?'

'I'm not going to dignify that with a response,' Darcy said, opening a bag of crisps.

'No, please don't do this! I'm not fishing, my self-esteem is legitimately so low that I actually feel like he's going to walk in, take one look at me and then walk out.'

'Queenie,' she said sternly, offering me a crisp.

'No. I don't know how you can eat at a time like this.' I pushed the bag away. 'Anyway, just as importantly, in the unlikely event that he *does* fancy me, I'm not going to have sex with him.'

'I think that's wise,' Darcy said, chewing carefully. 'You've been through a lot, and I think that if you are going to have sex again, it should possibly be with someone who is *not an arsehole*.'

'I'm not, I mean it,' I promised. 'I'm trying to turn over a new leaf with this sort of thing.'

'Okay, good.'

'One question, though. If by some fluke he is blind and so is attracted to my personality, can I go home with hi – '

'No.' Darcy shook her head quickly, her dark hair flashing across her face.

'But just to kiss him?' I asked.

'Do you want to go back to how you were before?'

'What do you mean?' I asked.

'Put bluntly, when you were just going along with what men did or didn't want from you.'

'Alright, alrig –' I started.

'Queenie.' Darcy interrupted, impatient. 'If you're serious about prolonging anything then, and I absolutely hate to say this, but you should at least wait until date two. Women should be free to have sex on date one, two, fifteen, without being judged or cast aside, but sadly, men aren't as evolved as women.'

'Okay. Fine. Anyway, all pointless, and yes I'm being repetitive, but it won't even come to that,' I predicted.

'Let me look at the messages?' Darcy asked, reaching for my phone. 'There's one in particular that proves that he isn't going to see you and recoil, and also suggests that *you* are the one that won't like *him*. It made me cringe so much, Queenie.'

I watched my hands tremble slightly as I slid the phone over. Darcy opened WhatsApp and scrolled up through the dozens of messages we'd exchanged in the last few days.

She paused, furrowing her brow as she skimmed volumes of getting-to-know-you chat.

'This.'

She pushed the phone back towards me and spun it around.

> I have always felt grateful that I never wanted to pigeonhole myself into having 'a type'. I never felt that way. I think any kind of woman can be attractive, but I do not find all women attractive.

For example, and I hope this comes across well, but I've got white mates who are honest and say that they don't find non-white women attractive. They aren't racist, I wouldn't be friends with them if they were, it's just a preference for them I guess. I have a black mate who says the same about white women. I got a mate who only likes big women. Some of them only seem to go out with petite women. Or some tall and thin women (we'll come to the size zero thing, I have a bit of a problem with that) and some only like blondes. You hear this all the time from men and women: having a type.

I just think it's a shame to be made that way. Not their fault or even anything they can do about it. I'm just grateful that I can see beauty and in any variety.

'What's wrong with that? I thought that it's literally the most normal thing a man has said to me in the last year?'

'Firstly, Queenie, he obviously likes the sound of his own voice a lot, so you'll have to get on board with that tonight. You don't need to know all of that stuff.' Darcy said. 'Nobody does. You didn't even ask what his type was but he's written a small thesis on it.'

'I think it's quite nice, it's just him explaining that he doesn't always like traditionally good-looking girls, and that he can see beyond that, and fancy girls like me,' I said, trying to bat off years of negative reinforcement and failing.

'But you *are* traditionally good-looking!' Darcy spluttered. 'I don't know why you have it in your head that you aren't! It makes me so sad that you can't see what I do.'

I looked down at the table and moved so that I sat on my shaking hands.

'Anyway, look, you've got two minutes until he gets here. You'll be fine. And you can leave any time you want to.'

I left the pub and crossed the road, shifting my weight from one foot to the other as I waited.

I could see Darcy watching me through the pub window and laughed when I saw her giving me a thumbs up.

'What's so funny? Come here, give us a kiss, then.'

A man that I hoped was Balding Alpha in real life descended upon me from nowhere, kissed me on both cheeks and slipped a hand down so that it rested on my bum. I hadn't expected him to be this forward; *big* disconnect between his messages and his actions.

I stepped back and took him in. He looked like his pictures. Slightly older, but it was definitely him, even though he was wearing a flat cap to cover his bald head.

'Hello!' I hugged him and did a thumbs up behind his back for Darcy's benefit.

'Shall we?' he said, holding open the door of the busy bar I'd been looking at nervously for the last hour. Balding Alpha ordered a bottle of wine and we drank it quickly, speaking non-stop.

*

We laughed about our families, moaned about living in London, compared dream holidays, our hands occasionally touching and our legs constantly pressed together under the table. He ordered another bottle, and before I could realise how much I was drinking, we'd made our way through a glass of it each when he leaned over the table and said, 'How about I ask them to cork this and we walk back to mine?'

'Maybe,' I said, standing up to go to the toilet. I had to hold onto a stool to steady myself as it hit me how much I'd had to drink and in such a short amount of time. I made it to the toilet and opened my bag, retrieving my phone with unusually clumsy hands.

I called Darcy with some difficulty, looking in the mirror above the sink, staring at myself in some weak attempt to sober up purely through focusing my eyes on my own reflection.

'Are you okay? Are you safe? Is he a psycho? Are you having a wobble? Do you need me to come and get you?' Darcy asked, her voice high. 'Simon, get my coat!'

'No! But shall I go home with him, Darc? I've, I've had I think the equivalent of like a bottle of wine and so, Darcyyy, I am feeling quite loose and free!'

I leaned on the sink to balance myself. 'Fuck it. Did you see that he snogged me when he saw me? He is so confident. It's 'mazin'. And his bald head is *quite* sexy.'

'No. You aren't doing it. Think of your grandmother,' Darcy warned. 'Be careful, please, I don't want you to jump back into a pattern that made you ill in the first place. Remember why you're going on a date and not just meeting him at his house, because you want something long-last – '

'Darcy! He is an adult, I am an adult. Sort of. Yes! I am less of an adult than him but he is an adult grown man and I'm a grown woman like Beyoncé sings and he surely will respect me enough to continue things if he so wants to. Both adults – '

I stopped talking when a man walked into the toilet.

"Scuse me, sir!' I slurred, looking around the toilet for another woman to back me up and chase this pervert out. I only saw urinals.

'Sssorry.' I walked out of the men's toilets and put my phone back in my bag, managing to get back to the table in one piece.

Balding Alpha was tapping on his phone. He looked up as I sat back down, placing it face down on the table.

'Ready?' he smiled, standing up and grabbing the bottle of wine.

We left the bar and crossed the road. Balding Alpha slipped his hand in mine and I wondered if it took me more than five seconds to pull my hand out of his because I was drunk, or because the counselling had worked.

As we walked back to his house he spoke, at length, about himself. I didn't mind, because I wasn't entirely sure that anything that came out of my mouth was going to make any sense.

'Here we are!' he said, as we got to one of those ex-council houses that have in recent years either been bought by property developers, or young people whose parents are happy to 'help with the deposit'.

'Come in.'

A wall of heat hit me as I stumbled in. I looked around and familiarised myself with his house; if I knew where everything was I'd be able to keep my anxiety at bay.

'I'm going to hang my suit up, but let me just . . .' He bent down and kissed me, me having to crane my neck 90 degrees to work with his height.

He left the kitchen so swiftly that I was left standing there, pouting as though kissing the invisible man. I was thirsty and thought it might be weird to look for a cup so stuck my head under the tap and turned on the cold faucet.

'You could have asked for a glass,' Courtney said, walking back into the kitchen in nothing but a pair of tracksuit bottoms.

'But you might have laced all of your glasses with drugs,' I said, wiping water from my mouth with the back of my hand.

'What?' he said, going to the cupboard and retrieving two wine glasses.

I watched his body, open-mouthed.

'Nothing,' I gulped as I took in the muscles that rippled down his back. 'Do you go to the gym a lot?'

'Ju-jitsu. The torso ain't what it was ten years ago, though.' He turned to face me and patted his six-pack.

'What was it ten years ago?' I marvelled. 'Are you sure you'd want to see me naked? I don't go to the gym at all and the thing I eat most is chocolate. I mean it. Like, family-sized bars.'

'Don't be silly,' Balding Alpha said, leading me into the living room. 'You have a beautiful face. Wait here, I'm just gonna go and get a condom.' He stood up and turned to look at me.

Wait, at what point had he decided that we were going to have sex?

He bent down and pulled the shoulder of my dress down, licking the skin that was underneath.

'Tastes like chocolate,' he said as he left the living room.

Why was I surprised?

When he came back in to the room, I was getting my coat on.

'Where are you going so soon?' he asked, flopping onto the sofa and pulling me down with him.

'Ah, I think I should go. I'm not feeling so good.'

'Nah, you're fine, sit down,' he said, stroking my thigh. That did actually make me feel not so good.

I opened my mouth to say, 'Sorry, I just feel like I shouldn't do this. I don't think I have a very good relationship with sex, and I thought I was getting better, and this is the worst idea and also what you said was racist, whether you know it or not, so I'm going to take myself home.'

But instead I said, 'The chocolate thing. Why?'

'The chocolate thing?' He laughed nastily. 'I knew you were one of those.'

'One of what?'

'One of those Black Lives Matter girls.'

'Of course I am. It says it really high up on my dating profile.'

At least I no longer had to worry about how I was going to sober up. I was halfway to stone-cold sober in a second.

'Don't you think it's just a stupid movement?' he asked me, quite seriously. 'Look, don't get me wrong, I'm not racist or anything' – always good to say it! – 'but don't you think it causes more problems than it solves?'

'Yeah, I really need to go,' I sighed, bored of the discussion before we even got into it. 'This is a bit much for a first date, Courtney.'

'Really? I thought you'd want to be challenged, strong black woman like you?' he said, arrogance flashing across his face. 'We can sit and talk about music, about films, about all that nonsense, but don't you want proper conversation, proper stimulation?'

'Well, not when it's about this. I expected to go for a drink with a nice man and talk about everything *but* this. I shouldn't have to defend myself and my beliefs.'

'Sorry, no, come on, I don't want to upset you. Let's talk about something else.' He poured himself more wine as I looked at him, knowing exactly what would come out of his mouth next. 'I bet you think that you can't be racist to white people, too.'

Two hours. We debated, non-stop, for two hours. I kept my coat on. One hundred and twenty minutes of me having to explain why the *Oxford English Dictionary* definition of 'racism' that he kept waving in my face was tired, how racism is systematic, how reverse racism was NOT a real thing, why it wasn't okay to refer to his Senegalese friend Toby as 'black as the ace of spades', while he tried to counter and manipulate all of my points and say, at the end of every other sentence, 'but don't listen to me, I just like to provoke'.

'That's the thing about people who love to play devil's advocate!' I shouted. 'There's no emotional involvement in it for you, there's nothing at stake!'

I made my way to the front door.

'It must be nice to be so detached from a life that someone like me actually has to live.' I slammed the door behind me. Unbelievable.

THE CORGIS

Darcy:

Queenie, you've never put the phone down on me before. Can you let us know you're okay?

Kyazike:
What happened?

Darcy:
She called me from the pub, I was trying to tell her not to go home with this guy, she said something about being like Beyoncé, and the line went dead. She was really drunk

Kyazike:
Do you know where they were?

Darcy:
A bar in Brixton, I don't know the name I can meet you at the station and I can find it on foot

Kyazike:
Aight cool, let's wait until 11. If she hasn't replied by then I'll come meet you

Queenie:
I'M FINE

Queenie:
Sorry

Queenie:
SORRY

Kyazike:
KMT

Darcy:
KMT indeed

Queenie:
Sorry both. I bet you didn't miss how much of a liability I was! Anyway, my battery died, I just got home. Will explain all tomorrow

Queenie:
I just snuck back into my grandparents' and I think my grandmother has just woken up, so actually you might never hear from me again

Queenie:
You must have been REALLY annoyed to say kiss my teeth Darcy, sorry again

I popped into Kyazike's bank the next day and stood in line until I was close enough for her to look up and make eye contact with me. She left the woman she was serving and came over to me.

'Hello, madam, I am so glad that you could come in for your appointment.'

Why was she talking to me like a robot?

'If I can just lead you to the consultation room? I'll be with you shortly.' Kyazike whisked me into a frosted glass compartment in the corner of the bank and closed the door behind me.

Five minutes of me playing with the pen chained to the desk later, Kyazike walked in carrying various folders and shut the door.

'You might be the only bank in the country with these pens attached to the desk,' I said, yanking it. 'Is the stationery that valuable?'

'Fam, did you hear how I have to switch up my voice out there? The new manager, some prissy white woman, has told me that I need to speak "*better*". Doesn't want me to "intimidate customers". Can you believe that? The only person I'm intimidating is her, fam.' Kyazike kissed her teeth and sat opposite me. 'This shit gets on my nerves. Anyway, what's good?'

'Hanging,' I groaned. 'For the first time in ages.'

'That'll teach you,' Kyazike laughed. 'So how was it then? Was the beating from your grandma worth it?'

I winced at her volume and at the memory.

'My date with Balding Alpha? *Proper* racist. He said some very questionable things last night.'

'Huh?' Kyazike furrowed her brow. 'Like what?'

'At one point he asked if I agreed that young black women got pregnant just so they could get council houses, to which I obviously asked if he'd taken something.'

'Tell me you're joking, fam.'

'I wish I was. He also dropped a slavery whipping joke that made me want to set his house on fire!'

Kyazike clenched her fist.

'And do you know what, this all began when he accused me of being a "Black Lives Matter girl".'

'This is making me so fucking mad – do you want me to get some black boys to run up in his house, raid the ting?' Kyazike offered.

'No, no!'

'Cause then he'll know that black lives matter, *trust* me.'

'No, that'll give him justification to keep on thinking that we're all aggressive. But thank you.' I patted her on the hand. 'I just don't know where it came from. All of his texts were so tame!'

'I fucking hate chiefs like him. He knew what he was doing, you know, it's calculated. I've heard about guys like him. White guys who like to bait black girls, use them for what they want, then humiliate them. I bet he waited until getting you drunk and back to his house to start with his Jim Crow nonsense. He did, innit?'

I nodded, and she shook her head.

'I'm sorry, fam. I know you thought this one was a good one.'

'I did, I did,' I sighed, rubbing my temples. 'But if anyone was going to get back on the dating horse and end up in the house of a neo-Nazi, it was going to be me.'

'Queenie. He might have been a neo-Nazi but all men are trash, innit.' Kyazike shrugged. 'At least this might finally stop you from dating white guys.'

Chapter Twenty-Eight

After trying and failing to convince my grandmother that my hangover was a mysterious illness, I've been on some sort of adult grounding for the last three weeks. I've been allowed to go to work and come home, and do my usual million chores at the weekend. As a new and exciting development that hasn't actually benefited me at all, my grandparents are converts to believing that actual mental health illnesses exist, and have thrown the term 'relapse' at me a million times.

Today, though, I am free, and to celebrate, I am going to go to the cinema on my own after work.

The working day is getting easier. Not in the way of a Karate Kid wax on, wax off style improving by the hour montage or anything, only that I don't want to run screaming from the building now. And, if I keep this up, with the money from my mum, I can think about renting somewhere. I can live on my own, which will obviously come with huge adjustment hurdles, but, crucially, those issues can be overcome.

The perks of behaving properly at my job and actually doing the work meant that I was having to do more stuff because my colleagues and bosses were seeing me as a responsible professional human. Determined to get to the 6pm showing after work, I battled through and left only an hour late. The lift doors opened for me to go down and I stepped in, and looked up.

'Queenie!'

Ted looked frightened to see me.

'Have a nice evening,' he said, his voice catching in his throat. He ran his hands through his hair agitatedly.

I turned to step out but the doors closed before I could. I kept my mouth shut and stood as far away from him as I could, practically becoming one with the metal walls. I could hear him breathing loudly, rapidly. I looked over quickly. He was sweating. We got to the ground floor and I shot out, throwing my security pass at the barriers and crossing the foyer at the speed of light.

I escaped from the building and when I was sure that he couldn't see me, sat on a bit of wall. I could feel my chest tighten, and the first swoops of panic. I closed my eyes and breathed in for three seconds, then out for eleven. Panic was coming at me in choppy waves. My legs began to shake so I leaned onto them with my elbows to keep them still. I squeezed my eyes closed tighter and tried to remember my safe space. My arms started to shake so much that my elbows slipped off my thighs.

I sat up and opened my eyes. Why wasn't this working?

I looked ahead. Ted was in front of me. Far away, but close enough for us to see each other. Next to him, a woman. She was turned away from me, so all that I could see was that she was blonde, and wide-set. Ted turned on his heel so that I was looking at both of their backs. I couldn't look away. He put his arm around the blonde woman and tried to steer her away.

'Where are we going?' I heard her ask.

'We need to go this way!' he said.

'But the tube station is this way!' she said, turning around and looking past me. I was hardly anything of significance. What was of significance to me, though, was that her stomach swelled outwards and her hands lovingly caressed a very sizeable bump.

*

THE CORGIS

Kyazike:
I'd wanna know, if I was her

Kyazike:
Rather be single than married to
a cheat who was fucking about
when I was pregnant

Darcy:
I feel sorry for her, but imagine
how bad Queenie would feel if
the revelation sent his wife into
premature labour?

Kyazike:
Can you at least get him fired?

Queenie:
But that would mean throwing
myself under the bus with him

'Queenie.'

My chair was turned around and I came eye to eye with Gina.

'Eyes on the computer, not the phone,' she said, spinning my chair back around so that I was facing my screen.

'Don't let me down. Please.'

'Sorry, Gina, no, I'm not. I wouldn't,' I whispered after her.

I did actual work for the rest of the day with only one very small break to arrange a house viewing, asking for one of the women estate agents to show me round this time and bringing Kyazike with me. Is this what growing into an adult woman is, having to predict and accordingly arrange for the avoidance of sexual harassment?

I started to pack my bag at five, ready to meet Kyazike before the house viewing as soon as it hit five thirty. By now I was well versed in estate agents showing you the house with ten other people waiting to go in after you, and I was determined to get there first.

On my way back from the toilet pre-leaving, I saw Ted lurking by the kitchen and sped up to get to my desk. By 5.31 p.m., I was in the lift. I walked out of the building and smack-bang into him, his eyes red-rimmed and his usually pristine every-strand-has-a-place hair a mess. He took a sharp drag of his cigarette and pulled it from his mouth.

'Please, let me speak to you,' he said, his voice wavering. He snatched at my arm with a free hand.

'Fuck off,' I growled, trying to pull my arm out of his grip. He was stronger than he looked.

'Let me talk to you. I need to explain, please. I need to do this.'

'Exactly! *You* need to do this for *you*, it's not about me.' I said, panic rising again. 'It's always about you. I've only ever been a need for you to fulfil, I realise that now. Please leave me alone. If you don't let go of me, I'll scream.'

'Sorry.' He let go of my arm. 'Don't you see, this is what you do to me!'

'No, it's not me doing anything. It's you, you get fixated on things and you're *consumed* by the latest source of excitement until you get what you want from it, Ted.' I was so frustrated that I could have burst into tears on the spot. 'Fuck off!'

'I need you to forgive me.'

'What, why?' I shouted. I didn't care who was looking.

'Can we go to our place, to the park?'

'No, Ted, we can't. If there's something you need to say, please say it here and now, and then I'm going. I mean it.' I started my calming breathing.

'Fine,' he said, dropping his voice. 'I've had two major break-ups in my life, Queenie. And after each of them, I . . .' He paused for dramatic effect. 'I tried to take my own life. Nobody knows this. Just my family, obviously, because they had to pick up the pieces, and . . . my wife.'

He paused again.

'I just – I couldn't deal with the thought of being alone. So when my wife came along, well, before she was my wife, I knew that because she was older and wanted children soon, *she* wouldn't leave me. So we got married. And everything since has all been so quick, and I should have thought about it, I know, but I didn't, because I was just so relieved not to have to be alone anymore, but then I met you, and you turned my life upside down.'

Another pause.

'You said it yourself. You're young, and you're so appealing, with your beautiful big lips, that skin and those *curves.*'

He stopped talking to light another cigarette.

'Do you have anything to say?' he asked after taking an aggressive drag. 'Don't you care about what I've just told you?'

'I don't!' I said, though internally *obviously* I did care about the suicide part. If it were true. Who knew anymore?

'I guess I deserve that,' Ted said, running his hands through his hair, his trademark move. 'I should have told you about the bab – '

'For the hundredth time, you should have just left me alone!' I screamed.

I was sure everyone in the square looked over.

'I hate you!' I screamed again, shaking. 'You trying to kill yourself has nothing to do with me, everyone has problems, Ted, and it doesn't excuse what you've done. Leave me alone!'

'You're a *prick*,' Kyazike ran into my eyeline and swung her Longchamp handbag into Ted's face.

When did she get here?

'Get the fuck away from her *now*,' she barked, swinging the bag again and catching him on the shoulder. He put his hands up to protect himself, his cigarette still lit.

'Guys like you make me fucking *sick*. You're married, bruv, you've got a baby on the way, go home to your fucking wife. From when I was walking over, I could hear Queenie telling you to back off,' Kyazike stood firm and pulled her arm back, ready to strike again. 'What's wrong with you, bro?'

A guy that looked liked Ted came running over to protect his fellow man. 'Are you all right, mate? Do you need me to call the police?' he asked, making sure he kept well clear of a handbagging.

'Nah, bruv, the only police I'm calling is on this dickhead here. He's harassing my friend,' Kyazike shouted. 'From over there I could hear her asking to be left alone and nobody wanted to help, but you want to come running when the man is being troubled? You've got it all wrong.'

'Okay, fine, sorry.' The man backed away, his hands in the air. 'As you were.'

'You heard what I said,' Kyazike turned her attention back to Ted. 'You wanna come round the corner, fam?'

She stared dead into his eyes until he looked at the floor.

'Didn't think so. If you come near her again I will *done* you, I swear. No emails, no chats, no waiting outside the building, no looking at her, no *nothing.*'

Kyazike smoothed her shirt down and pulled me away.

The next day, a letter appeared in my pigeonhole.

Dear Queenie,

I just wanted to say thank you for letting me speak to you.

> *I understand how hard this has all been and I know it is all my fault.*
> *For what it's worth I wish I'd done that much sooner.*
> *You're such a sweet and sensitive person and I should have seen that beneath the steel.*
> *Yesterday, I told you things I never thought I'd tell you. I know they don't make up for anything but I hope they at least made you understand me better.*
> *Nothing can ever make up for what's happened, or the things I've done. But I hope you know I want to be a better person.*
> *I also want you to be happy and know that I have been an impediment to that.*
> *Above all, I'm sorry.*
> *And, yes, I hope you can find it in your heart **<u>not to tell my wife about us</u>**. I know I have no right to demand that, but I do at least believe that no good can come of it for anyone.*
> *I wish you nothing but happiness and love and decent people*

368

in your life. I hope that, if things don't work out with my marriage, you might welcome me back into your life.
Love, Ted

Xxx

P.s. Your friend has some swing on her

Before I left work, I put his letter on Gina's desk. I didn't care what happened to me. There was no way I could carry on with this if I wanted to get better.

On Friday, 5 December, Row, Gina <Gina.Row@dailyread. co.uk> wrote at 11:34:

I'm guessing this is a little late, but thanks for the letter all the same. I should have listened to you. He'll be gone by Monday.

Chapter Twenty-Nine

'I've got a task for you,' Gina said, standing over my desk. 'We need a piece written for the gigs page, and Josey is off. Can you step in?'

'Er, what do I need to do?' I asked, the weight of responsibility crashing over me like a wave.

'There's this hot young thing everyone's talking about, a singer called, I don't know how to pronounce it, big hair, started her own record label, high-pitched voice.'

'I . . . think I know who you mean?' I said.

'She's playing at Heaven and we need someone to do a write-up. You're urban, aren't you, you probably know about this sort of thing.'

'Am I *that* urban, Gina?' I asked her.

'Anyway, gig is tomorrow, the PR gave us two tickets. Five hundred words from you, please. You won't get paid more, but good for the CV. File by Tuesday.'

*

'I don't think I've ever been described as urban before,' I said to Kyazike, looking around the club.

'Fam, you're not urban,' Kyazike shouted over the noise of the crowd who were talking over the support act, a young black guy with a high-top on the stage with a looping machine.

'I think that guy thinks he's urban with that hairstyle, though.' She laughed, her whitened teeth lit blue by the club lights. 'Hold this, I wanna go toilet before she starts.'

Kyazike handed me her glass and walked off in search of the loo.

'Please don't leave me, I'm still not okay with crowds,' I whined in the direction of her back as she pushed through.

I took some deep breaths and looked at my shaking hands.

'Careful!' I yelped as a blond boy wearing what he probably typed 'African-print dashiki shirt' into eBay for fell into me and spilled Kyazike's drink down my arm. He stood up straight and sniffed, handing a little bag of powder to his friend.

'Do you mind?' I shouted, staring at the boy and his friend, a short brunette with a piercing that went through her bottom lip.

'What? We're not *doing* anything,' she snapped, staring at me and putting the bag in her pocket. I turned back to the stage. Seconds later, the boy fell on me again, this time staying where he landed.

'Fine,' I huffed, squeezing through sweaty bodies until I got to an open space. I looked around for Kyazike as panic began to rise up from my feet.

I found some room to breathe at the bar and leaned against it, steadying myself.

'Have I met you before?' A good-looking sandy-haired man me leaned over and shouted into my ear.

'I don't know, have you?' I asked him, leaning away.

'Who knows?' He smiled. 'Maybe you've just got a familiar face.'

'Maybe!' I said, turning back to the stage.

The man leaned into me again. 'Is this the first time seeing NAO play?'

'No, and I've actually got to review her, so I'm going to pay attention if you don't mind,' I said, not wanting to be rude but mainly not wanting to talk to anyone but Kyazike who was *still* not back from the toilet.

'It's just the support act, you've got time until she comes on,' he mansplained. 'Can I get you a drink? Yours looks like it's almost done.'

'No thanks, I'm not drinking,' I said, stern. 'This is my friend's.'

'I usually drum for her.' The man leaned against the bar, pleased with himself.

'That's nice,' I said, my eyes still on the stage.

'Can I get you a soft drink at least?'

I looked around for Kyazike again.

'*There* you are! The toilets are full of druggies, fam, I watched about ten pairs of girls go into the cubicles giggling and come out sniffing when I was standing there, needing a piss.' Kyazike looked at the man. 'Who's your friend, Queenie?'

'Sid,' he said. 'I was just asking your friend here if she wanted a drink but she seems to be too into this guy.' He gestured to the stage.

'Fam, let him get you a drink, he's *buff*,' Kyazike said into my ear. 'Bit older, too. *Nice.*'

'You have him, then,' I said, handing her drink back.

'If I liked white guys I'd be all over him,' she said, winking at him.

He smiled back fearfully.

'We should get closer to the stage, come on. Nice to meet you!' I pulled Kyazike by the arm. 'You shouldn't encourage me, you know I'm trying to be better at this stuff, Kyazike,' I said when we found somewhere to stand that allowed me to see the stage.

'I wasn't telling you to *sleep* with the guy, Queenie,' Kyazike shouted behind me. 'Nothing wrong with a little flirt. Besides, no wedding ring.'

'Too soon,' I said. 'Besides, rings can always be taken off . . . Look, she's coming on!'

*

'It was *so* good, Darcy, she was amazing!' I chattered. 'She had this transfixing neon light show in the middle of the stage that pulsed with the bass, and the *band* were amazing, and the *songs* – '

'So you had fun then? That's good!' Darcy said encouragingly.

'Yes. I did. For the first time in a million years. And no men, if you can believe it. In fact, you'll be so proud of me. This guy, this drummer, and drummers are obviously the best band members. You know. Because of the arms . . . and the rhythm, well he asked to buy me a drink, but I very firmly said *no*.'

'Oh, well done.'

'Thanks. He was one of those mainstream millennials, which wasn't so appealing, but I wouldn't have let him buy me a drink even if he wasn't. He didn't try to bang me on sight, though, so that's something, I guess.'

'What's a mainstream millennial?' Darcy asked.

'Have I made this term up?' I questioned myself. 'I'm sure I've seen it on the internet. You know those men: bike-riding, knitted jumper, loves Jeremy Corbyn? Pretends Facebook isn't important to them but it really is?'

I was met with a blank stare, so carried on. 'Craft beer, start-ups, sense of entitlement? Reads books by Alain de Botton, needs a girlfriend who doesn't threaten their mediocrity?'

'Oh, right,' Darcy said, not as mediocre-man-hating as me. 'Anyway, well done you! One of these days we'll go a week of conversation where we can pass the Bechdel test!'

'Wouldn't go that far. Right, as much as I love tea and talking, I need to go and write this gig up for Gina.'

*

Four weeks, three thousand fucking pounds to useless estate agents and one phone call to Eardley later, I was packing to move into a very, very tiny studio flat that I would have trouble swinging a kitten in, if I were that way inclined. My grandparents had sat me down to talk about how renting was for fools and that I should use the money from my mum as a deposit for a house, but they were forced to open their eyes to the fact that times had very much changed when I went on RightMove and showed them what a deposit of ten times that couldn't even get me. I had to listen to the, 'In our day you could buy a house in Brixton for £3' thing for the next hour, but at least I'd won the first round.

Despite his bad hips, my grandad was practically jumping for joy at the prospect of having all of my grandmother's attention back, while she was pretending to be totally unbothered by my leaving.

The doorbell rang and I heard Diana's voice fill the house.

'This is going to be long, I swear,' Diana said loudly enough for me to hear her.

'*Diana*. Come on, your cousin needs help,' was Maggie's equally loud pantomime-like response. 'My back is too bad to do much, though, so I'll just be sat here.'

I walked into the kitchen to get another box. 'Hello both,' I smiled.

'Today's the big day!' Maggie beamed. 'We're very proud of you, you know. You've come a long way. Aren't we proud, Diana?'

'Yeah,' Diana said, opening the fridge.

'I don't think she's ready to live alone,' my grandmother said, moving Diana out of the way and taking a raw chicken from the fridge.

'Mum, she's not moving far away,' Maggie defended me, before changing her tune. 'But who knows what could happen. She might have one of her attacks, and fall and hit her head.'

'Everybaddy always so *cautious*.' My grandad shuffled into the kitchen. 'You can't see how *sturdy* Queenie is?' He grabbed my shoulders and shook me to make his point. 'She'll be fine. And even if she's not, she's not coming back here.'

'You too dyam wicked,' my grandmother shouted at him.

'Me jus ah joke!' My grandad laughed loudly. 'Queenie, start by getting the stuff out of my shed,' he said, and stopped laughing instantly.

My grandmother removed the chicken from its plastic packaging and threw it into the sink. She turned the tap on and Diana watched the events unfolding, horrified.

'Grandma, they're saying on the news that you shouldn't wash chicken before you cook it! Bacteria can splash around the sink,' she squealed.

'Has my food or my food preparation killed you before now?' My grandmother kissed her teeth. 'No. Go and find suttin' to do.'

She put on a pair of rubber gloves, tackling the chicken and listing to Maggie further reasons why living alone was going to kill me. I left the kitchen when Maggie offered to come round and bless my new flat with holy water.

I walked through the garden to the shed and stepped in, bending my head to avoid collecting all of the cobwebs from the ceiling with my hair. I was stacking boxes by the rickety wooden door when I heard my grandad coming up the path.

'That cane is a dead giveaway, you can't sneak up on anyone,' I said, wiping sweat from my forehead. 'Come to make sure I get everything out?'

'I know we never really talk,' my grandad began quietly, leaning against the shed wall.

'I don't take it personally, you don't talk to anyone.'

'Queenie, just listen, nuh?' my grandad said, knocking his cane on the floor.

'Sorry, Gandalf.'

'Who?'

'Nobody.'

'As I was saying,' my grandad started again, 'I know we never really talk. But, as you say, that's just my way.'

He paused to readjust his position on the wall, wincing. 'But because I don't talk nah mean I don't *feel*. When you came to stay those months ago, I felt bad.' He sighed. 'I felt so bad that you were going to end up like your mother. I could see it in you, in your eyes.' He stopped. 'I could see the fear, and the resignation. I thought you'd given up. And I felt like I did, in my chest, when she turned up here after Roy hit her so hard she almost didn't get up.' He paused again. 'But you didn't let it take you.' He paused and lifted his glasses to wipe his wet eyes. 'You're full of fight, Queenie. Full of fight.'

He turned away and ambled back down the garden path, leaving me standing there unable to process anything he'd said.

Diana bounded up past him to join me. She watched me blow the light layer of dust off boxes of belongings that hadn't seen the light of day for months.

'We are proud of you, you know,' Diana said awkwardly. 'My mum wasn't just saying that.'

'Are you joking?' I asked.

'No? What's funny?' Diana said, lifting one box and being pulled back down by its weight. 'You weren't well, but you got better, and you went back to work and now you're moving into your own place. That's good. That's progress,' she said, wisely.

'I wouldn't say I'm better,' I told her, wiping sweat from my forehead with the back of my hand. 'Be careful. You don't need to lift the heavy ones.'

'Jeez, take the compliment,' Diana said, scraping a cobweb from her hand onto the wall of the shed.

'Let me tell you something,' I said to my cousin. 'You're going to go through a lot, in your life. Us black women, we don't have it easy. The family, they come with their own stuff –'

'You don't have to tell me about *that*,' Diana cut in.

'And school, university, *work*, it's all going to come with its stuff. You'll meet people who "don't see race" and are "colourblind", but that's a lie. They do see it,' I explained. I knew how my cousin's attention span waned when being taught anything, so I tried not to sound like I was lecturing her. 'And people *should* see it. We're different, and they need to accept our difference,' I continued, and Diana nodded along. I kept going while I had her. 'We aren't here for an easy ride. People are going to try and put you in a mould, they're going to tell you who you should be and how you should act. You're going to have to work hard to carve out your own identity, but you can do it. I'm not going to tell you about the men until you're older but that's a discussion we're going to *have* to have,' I told Diana. '*Or* women. Whoever, whatever, it's your choice.'

'You think with Grandma I'd have a choice?' Diana pursed her lips at me.

'Anyway,' I said. 'I'm here with you. Remember that.'

'I know, cuz.' Diana smiled. 'I hope I can grow up to be as strong as you are.'

I clambered over boxes and hugged Diana.

'Queenie,' she said.

'Yes, Diana?'

'Can I come and stay with you when Mum gets on my nerves and I need somewhere to just kick back and relax?'

'No.'

Chapter Thirty

'We are gathered here today – ' Kyazike began, standing to address those of us sat around the large circular table.

'It's not a wedding!' Diana shouted, cutting her off.

'Hello? I know that, Little Miss *Attitude*,' Kyazike said, raising an eyebrow.

I looked around the quiet Italian restaurant to see who else's dinner my family was disrupting.

'As I was saying, we are gathered here to celebrate the well health and recovery of your girl and mine, our warrior, our badboy, Queenie Jenkins,' Kyazike said, surveying everyone around the table to make sure they were paying attention. 'This year has been a madness, but she's pulled through it. Even if I had to swing for man.'

'Hear, hear!' Darcy shouted, putting her arm around me.

'Swing for which man?' Diana asked Kyazike.

Everyone turned to look at me.

'You'll find out when you're old enough,' Kyazike told her.

'Er, I'm her cousin and I'm fifteen, you can tell me.' Diana looked at me.

'It's nobody. Nothing,' I said, glaring at Kyazike.

'And if she can get through this year, she can get through anything,' Kyazike continued.

What else was she going to say? I looked around again as my face got hot.

'Dassit. I'm done. Let's eat,' Kyazike said, sitting back down.

'I'd like to say something,' Darcy said, standing. She patted her floral dress down and opened her mouth to speak.

'Please,' I said, covering my face with my hands.

'Now, I haven't known Queenie for as long as you guys, but when I met her I knew that she was grea – '

I yanked Darcy back down into her seat. 'That's enough, thanks.'

'Well, I wanna say something,' Diana said, standing on her seat.

'*Di*ana. Get. Off. The chair,' my grandmother and Maggie said, staccato and in unison.

'I think that Queenie is very brave and I'm very proud that she's my cousin,' she said quickly, stepping down.

'Yes, we're all proud of you, Queenie,' Maggie said. 'In fact, before we say grace, I'd like to say a few words, in Jesus' name – '

'No grace today, Maggie, your father needs to eat,' my grandmother cut in.

'Thanks everyone, that's enough,' I said, taking a sip of water. The lump in my throat was rising.

'She's *my* daughter,' my mum said, looking at Maggie pointedly. 'So I'm going to say something.'

Everyone turned to look at my mum.

'Go ahead, Sylvie,' said my grandad, trying to hang his cane on the back of the chair.

'Next year is going to be better,' my mum said, picking up her wine glass. 'To Queenie.'

'To Queenie,' the table said.

'Everything okay?' Darcy asked quietly, knowing how little I liked being the focus of attention.

'Yes, all fine.' I looked down at my pizza and began to cut into it slowly. Trust my appetite to start waning at the dinner to benchmark my getting better.

*

'Oh, hello you!' I heard my mum squeak, my eyes still fixed on a piece of mushroom that looked particularly challenging. 'Don't you look well, Cassandra? You've really blossomed since I last saw you.'

I looked up and saw Cassandra standing behind Diana's chair, biting her lip aggressively. She flipped her hair over her shoulder and smiled as our eyes met.

'Why are you here?' I asked, turning to look at Darcy, who shrugged and smiled at me as if to say, 'Sorry for majorly fucking up but I thought it would be okay, though now I realise that I was totally wrong about that.'

'Have you come for your money?' I asked drily. 'I can't pay you back yet, but I will.'

'No, no, don't worry about that.'

'Okay,' I said, with no choice but to accept her presence. 'I'll tell the waiter that we need another chair and menu.'

I stood up to find someone and Kyazike stood up too.

'Want me to handle it?' she asked.

I shook my head and walked away from the table. Cassandra followed me and we stood by the waiter's station, both staring ahead.

'Go on, then.' Cassandra broke the silence. 'Have a go at me, tell me I told you so.'

I looked at her and caught the tail end of her rolling her eyes.

'Why would I do that?' I asked her. 'I've never done that.'

'Because I went running off to the middle of nowhere with a guy who started sleeping with a new colleague after two weeks of us being there.'

'I didn't know that,' I said, completely unsurprised. 'And even if I did, I wouldn't say I told you so.'

'I thought Darcy would have told you. I messaged her a few weeks ago and asked if you hated me.'

'Nope. I had a lot going on, Cassandra. Too much to waste time hating you. Though I'm guessing you knew that?' I asked her. 'Things were falling apart before you left.'

'Darcy filled me in. But I didn't want to text you, I thought it might be too, I don't know, whimsical.' Cassandra shrugged. 'When I caught Guy cheating, which he did in our bed, by the way, I packed my stuff up, but he did his usual "transitional weakness" spiel and I forgave him, again. But when he did it *again* I left him.'

I looked around to see if a waiter was coming. I'd have to build a chair for her at this rate.

'Cassandra,' I turned to her, 'you haven't even said sorry.'

'Well I am sorry, obviously.' She rolled her eyes again and flipped her hair over her shoulder.

'It's not in any way obvious.' For the first time ever, I was actually standing up to her and not feeling terrified.

'I'm sorry,' she said quickly. 'Okay?'

'Cool.' I put my arm around her stiffly. I was a stronger person now, and one that wasn't going to be petty even if it killed me. 'Let's put it all behind us and move on.'

'That's very adult of you!' she exclaimed. 'Did you have a lobotomy?'

'Well, I'm trying to be better at letting things go. What is it you said to me?' I snorted. '"Some of us don't let the past dictate the way we live our adult lives"?' I mimicked her voice so perfectly that she looked shocked.

A waiter finally made himself known, and I asked him to seat Cassandra. It would be one of Maggie's blessings if I were able to eat anything at this meal. We sat down and tried our best to hold independent conversations despite being distracted by Maggie lecturing our table (and all surrounding tables) on how Brexit would fuck us all over but how, ultimately, faith in Jesus would save us, with my grandad being uncharacteristically vocal in his support.

'This sparkling drink is nice,' my grandmother said to the table. 'What do you think, Wilfred?' She was trying to get him off Maggie's line of fire before he had a heart attack.

'Very nice,' my grandad said, finishing what was in his glass and pouring some more. 'I've had three now.'

'You know that's alcohol?' I said to my grandmother across the table.

'No it's not, it's a sparkling soft drink.' She picked up the bottle and passed it to me. 'Look.'

'No, it's literally alcohol. Look here,' I said, tapping the sticker on the bottle, '5.5 per cent.'

'Jesus Christ,' my grandmother said, terror in her voice. 'Get that wine away from Grandad,' she said to Diana, who immediately started to prise the glass from his hand.

'Maggie, we've poisoned ourselves! Get us some water!' my grandmother shrieked. 'Sylvie, you call the ambulance.'

'Nobody is calling an ambulance,' I said, standing up.

'You're right, a cab to the hospital will be quicker,' my grandmother said, snatching the bottle of water from Maggie and pouring a glass for my grandad. 'What's that thing you use? H'uba? The H'uba, call the H'uba!'

'Just drink water, you'll be fine!' I said. 'I'm not getting you an Uber!'

'We're on so much medication, Queenie, we don't know how the alcohol will mix with it,' my grandmother barked at me.

Panic had taken over. This was obviously where I got it from.

'Is anyone in here a doctor?' she shouted across the restaurant.

'Cassandra, your boyfriend's a doctor, innit, shall we call him?' Kyazike grinned.

Cassandra pretended not to hear her.

'I need to go,' I said to Darcy.

'To go where?' she asked. 'They'll honestly be fine if they stop flapp – '

'I'll be back in a sec.'

I walked to the toilet and turned back to see if anyone had noticed me leave. Kyazike was pouring glasses of water for my grandmother, while my grandad drank from his glass with one hand and flapped himself with his flat cap with the other; my grandmother was rooting around in her handbag and handing Cassandra various boxes of pills and asking her to read what happens when each tablet was mixed with alcohol; my mum was trying to explain what was happening to the restaurant manager while Diana filmed it all on her phone and Maggie told her off for not taking it seriously.

I pushed the toilet door open with my foot and stepped inside, taking deep breaths as I stood in front of the sink and looked in the murky mirror. It was quiet in here. The only noise I could hear was the steady drip of a tap. My grandparents would be fine, that wasn't the issue.

Despite everything, I wanted to call Tom, to tell him that my life was back on track, that I was celebrating being *mostly* better in more ways than I knew I could be. I took my phone out of my pocket and scrolled through my phonebook. I found Tom's contact page and stared at it. My finger hovered over the call button.

'Are you ill?' Darcy walked into the toilet.

'No. Not physically, anyway,' I replied, putting my phone into my pocket. 'What's going on out there now?'

'They've calmed down. Turns out the manager used to be a doctor, and as soon as he told your grandparents the alcohol was too weak to make a difference to their medication they went back to normal. It was weird. Like someone turned their hysteria switches off.'

'They're Jamaican, Darcy. Doctors are the only people they trust. If he'd told them the alcohol was going to kill them they'd have jumped in a cab to the cemetery.'

'What's wrong?' Darcy said, squeezing next to me and putting an arm around my shoulders. I rested my cheek on her hand.

'When all of that commotion was happening, I saw everyone in the restaurant looking at us, and it made my head feel funny, and when my head felt funny, my stomach dropped, and I felt a bit like I did before. And I know it sounds stupid, but just for a second, I wanted Tom to make it right. After everything, he – '

'Yes, Queenie, that sounds *incredibly* stupid,' Darcy said, interrupting me. 'After everything that's happened this year, that is honestly the maddest thing I have ever heard. Take a few deep breaths, have a *think* about why it's the maddest thing I've ever heard, and when you've finished, come back out to the restaurant. We, all of the people who love you, who have been there for you, will be behind that door.'

'Firm words. Are you channelling Cassandra?' I asked her as she left the toilet.

'I'm not a therapist,' Darcy turned to look at me. 'Nor do I need to train to be one to tell you that you love what Tom represented more than you love him. We both know that he's incredibly basic.'

'Okay,' I said to myself, after I'd checked that there wasn't anyone in either of the toilet stalls. 'Even though things aren't tip-top, they are definitely better, and here's why.'

I stared at my reflection.

'One. In a shock twist, Gina told you that after your "surprisingly great" gig reviews, *The Daily Read* is going to give you a regular music writing slot. Scary, yes, and not quite as political as you wanted, but you can get there. So you're doing great things at work, even though you were almost fired for sexual assault earlier in the year. Talk about a comeback! Two. Ted's been fired for misconduct and lying by omission and you never have to see him again. Three. You've deleted those bleak-as-fuck dating apps that only really served to make you forget that beneath the big boobs and bum you are a human person who is easily damaged. Plus now, you don't want to *look* at men, never mind have sex with them.'

I tensed up as the men of the last year flashed before my eyes. Mouths and hands biting and pulling and smacking and scratching and –

I took some deep breaths to stop myself from getting all het up again. Darcy might be right, but I still missed Tom. I missed him so much. Maybe if I apologised to him again, with a bit more space between us, maybe he'd soften? I should have been able to tell him what I was going through. I won't make that mistake again, I promised myself, if someone – non-married (times two), not sexually aggressive or with a girlfriend, manipulative or a secret neo-Nazi – ever wanted to be with me.

I took some more deep breaths. I was feeling better.

'Four. As for the anxiety, and the head feeling weird and then the stomach following, even if you *do* go back to how things were, you made it out before, you'll make it out again. You have tools to cope this time, and even though deep breathing and safe spaces don't sound like they'll help, they *do*.

'Five, the night terrors have eased off. Maybe not forever but at least you haven't punched your grandmother in the night or fallen out of bed for a significant amount of time. Six, when you go back into that restaurant, look. Look at all of those people, who *love* you. You are worthy of love, and they prove that. They'll always be there for you like they have been when you needed it most.' I paused. 'Possibly not Cassandra, she is definitely a variable. And seven. As for Tom,' I said, pulling my phone back out, 'you know what you need to do.'

I unlocked it and looked at Tom's contact page again. Something shifted. His picture was the one I'd taken on our one-year anniversary, on Clapham Common where we first met, just after he promised that whatever happened between us, he'd never abandon me. Time to let it go, I accepted.

Delete.

I walked back into the restaurant and with the heat that hit me, a different type of warmth filled my chest. I sat down at the table and looked around at my family. Kyazike was showing Diana a video on her phone that taught her how to blend her make-up, my grandmother was very loudly listing to Doctor Manager all of the medication she was on while my grandad eyed up the sparkling drink, ready to risk it all again. Maggie was talking loudly, obviously, and slicing up her pizza, putting bits on my mum's plate for her to taste. Cassandra and Darcy were locked in an intense conversation that I had no plans to get involved in; Cassandra was clearly being made to feel *very* bad.

I looked over at my mum as she picked up a slice of pizza with her hands and bit off a huge mouthful. She threw her head back, laughing so hard at something Maggie said to her that she put the pizza down and slapped her thighs with both hands. I stood up to pour myself a glass of water and we looked at each other as she turned in my direction. She smiled at me and I smiled back.

'My queen,' she mouthed, lifting her glass.

Acknowledgements

To the main matriarch, my nan Elaine, thank you for loving me more than you love anyone else (and admitting to the favouritism), and for being my #1. Thanks to my mum Yvonne, and my sister Esther. Gang gang gang. The two funniest people in my life, you've not just always managed to make me laugh, but also to navigate my extreme moods. Well done both.

To my Ugandan sister Isabel Mulinde, forever in my heart and forever making me laugh. There is nobody like you on this earth. To Claude Hylton, the brother I picked up aged 6 and stuck to, thank you. To Selena Carty, thank you, and to the rest of my siblings (7 and counting), we don't talk but I know you're out there, and that's enough. Aunty Su, Aunty Dor and the rest of the Forrester/Browns, and the Petgraves, love to you all.

To my godmother Heidi Safia Mirza, I wouldn't be who I am without your unrivalled love, guidance, kindness and uniquely undefeatable approach to life.

Lettice Franklin, I could fill hundreds of pages thanking you for too many things, for being my personal problem solver, for keeping so many of my secrets, and for never judging me. Tom Killingbeck, you are still the only person to make me laugh so much that I've fallen on the floor, you are also still the only person to have unironically sung 'Cool' by Gwen Stefani at me when I was going through a break up. You are 10/10.

To my first readers with whom I would trust my life: Hayley Camis, Lettice Franklin (obviously), Sharmaine Lovegrove, Harriet Poland, Susannah Otter and Jessie Burton, you saw Queenie when she was in bits and pieces (in all senses), and you gave me important, funny, loving and critical feedback. I am very lucky to have had your eyes.

Jo Unwin – I love you for so many things, but mainly for offering me representation before I'd even sat down. I knew you were a real one from that point onwards. Milly and Donna, I love you both too.

To Katie Espiner (whom I forced out of editorial retirement) thank you for understanding *Queenie*, for understanding me, and pushing me to make this novel its best self. I am so lucky to have you as my editor. To the rest of my Orion corgis Katie Brown, Rebecca Gray, Cait Davies, Sarah Benton and Sophie Wilson; I will never be able to thank you enough for your brilliance and for your 24-hour cross-platform championing.

To my personal corgis! Morwenna Finn, Cicely Hadman, Lydia Samuels, Hayley Camis (so good you're acknowledged twice), Daniellé Scott-Haughton (wife), Anya Courtman and family, Patrick 'it will happen' Hargadon, Selcan Tesgel, Selina Thompson, Afua Hirsch, Ella Cheney, Hazel Metcalfe, Hannah Howard, Hattie Collins, Keso Kendall, Nikesh Shukla, Julian Obubo, Indira Birnie, Will Smith, Will White; your love and your phone calls and texts and voice notes and songs and inspirational playlists have sustained me. Special shout out to Lydia for forgiving me after I crashed her car.

Michael Cragg. Babes. The only person I could wish to be stuck in an office in Dalston with whilst a riot rages outside. Thank you for lots of things, but most notably for the £200 you lent me. And thank you for lending it to me when I needed it again after I paid it back. And then again. I'm not sure where we are with it now; please let me know.

Thank you to Kid Fury and Crissles of The Read podcast; your voices kept me company, and kept me laughing, when I was sat in front of a laptop in the dead of night and everyone else was asleep.

And finally, thank you to Jojo Moyes and Charles Arthur. No matter how much you protest, this book probably wouldn't have been started if it weren't for your kindness.

#BlackLivesMatter

Credits

Trapeze would like to thank everyone at Orion who worked on the publication of *Queenie* in the UK.

Editorial
Katie Espiner
Katie Brown
Charlie Panayiotou
Jane Hughes
Alice Davis

Copy editor
Sophie Wilson

Proof reader
Jenny Page

Audio
Paul Stark
Amber Bates

Contracts
Anne Goddard
Paul Bulos
Ellen Harber

Design
Lucie Stericker
Joanna Ridley
Nick May
Clare Sivell
Helen Ewing
Jan Bielecki

Finance
Naomi Mercer
Jasdip Nandra
Afeera Ahmed
Elizabeth Beaumont
Sue Baker
Victor Falola

Marketing
Sarah Benton
Cait Davies
Amy Davies

Production
Claire Keep
Fiona Macintosh
Katie Horrocks

Publicity
Rebecca Gray
Leanne Oliver
Maura Wilding

Sales
Jen Wilson
Esther Waters
Rachael Hum
Ellie Kyrke-Smith
Viki Cheung
Ben Goddard
Mark Stay
Georgina Cutler
Jo Carpenter
Tal Hart

Andrew Taylor
Barbara Ronan
Andrew Hally
Dominic Smith
Maggy Park
Elizabeth Bond
Linda McGregor

Rights
Susan Howe
Richard King
Krystyna Kujawinska
Jessica Purdue
Hannah Stokes

Operations
Jo Jacobs
Sharon Willis
Lucy Tucker
Lisa Pryde